UNRAVEL

ALSO BY IMOGEN HOWSON: LINKED

UNRAVEL

IMOGEN HOWSON

SIMON & SCHUSTER BFYR

NEW YORK · LONDON · TORONTO · SYDNEY · NEW DELHI

SIMON & SCHUSTER BFYR

An imprint of Simon & Schuster Children's Publishing Division
1230 Avenue of the Americas, New York, New York 10020

SIMON & SCHUSTER BFYR

is a trademark of Simon & Schuster, Inc.
For information about special discounts for bulk purchases, please contact
Simon & Schuster Special Sales at 1-866-506-1949 or business@simonandschuster.com.
The Simon & Schuster Speakers Bureau can bring authors to your live event. For more
information or to book an event, contact the Simon & Schuster Speakers Bureau
at 1-866-248-3049 or visit our website at www.simonspeakers.com.
Also available in a SIMON & SCHUSTER BFYR hardcover edition
Book design by Lizzy Bromley and Alicia Mikles
The text for this book is set in Garamond and Sevigne.
Manufactured in the United States of America
First SIMON & SCHUSTER BFYR paperback edition July 2015
10 9 8 7 6 5 4 3 2 1

The Library of Congress has cataloged the hardcover edition as follows:
Howson, Imogen.
Unravel / Imogen Howson.
pages cm
Sequel to: Linked.
Summary: When Lissa and Lin return to Sekoia to help remedy the chaos caused
by their revelation of the government's secret experiments, they find conditions
far worse than they imagined and an unexpected threat to Spares is lying in wait.
ISBN 978-1-4424-4658-8 (hc)
[1. Science fiction. 2. Sisters—Fiction. 3. Twins—Fiction. 4. Love—Fiction.] I. Title.
PZ7.H849Unr 2014
[Fic]—dc23
2013002032
ISBN 978-1-4424-4661-8 (pbk)
ISBN 978-1-4424-4659-5 (eBook)

TO ELINOR,
who would enjoy playing
Zombie Uprising and who,
unlike Elissa, would probably
complain that *Parasite Invasion*
wasn't scary enough. With apologies
from her mother for failing to
give her a twin of her own.

ACKNOWLEDGMENTS

Hugs, kisses, and smiley-face emoticons are due to the following people:

My agent, Mandy Hubbard, who always knows how to make books better. And who has a cow.

Everyone at Simon & Schuster who has been involved in the production of this book, especially my editor, Navah Wolfe, who made the (*very*) rough original version into the book I wanted it to be; Lizzy Bromley, who designed the beautiful cover *and* thought of its new name; managing editor, Katrina Groover; production manager, Chava Wolin; copy editor, Valerie Shea; and proofreader, Alexandra Alexo, who, again, saved me from much embarrassment.

For a whole range of things, including cake, entertainment, texts and tweets, bringing congratulatory alcohol and/or flowers, receiving emergency phone calls, asking the right questions, hand-selling of *Linked* over neighbors' garden hedges, and a *great deal* of emotional support: Becky Hancock, Dayna Hart, Jane Blatherwick, Jasper and Netti South, Jay Williams, and Michelle Puffer. Also my sister Jossy and brother-in-law Hywel; my cousin and family, Mark, Jemma, and the amazing Jack; and my mother-in-law, Mary.

Plus everyone who dressed up as fictional characters and came to celebrate with me at my combined book/birthday party.

For being their wonderful selves: the Society for the Prevention of Being Bored, aka SPOBB.

And finally, to my favorite daughters, Philippa and Elinor, who put up with me pulling weird faces at my laptop, staring vaguely at them while they're talking, and for occasionally trying to feed them such disasters as the tzatziki soup.

And to Phil. Of course.

# ONE

IT DIDN'T feel like coming home.

The *Phoenix* broke into the upper atmosphere of Sekoia, flying nose down, and for a moment the desert plateau flashed into view through the glass windscreen of the pilot's cabin, dizzyingly far below, patched with tan and ocher and the bleached yellow of dead grass.

The pull of the ship's artificial gravity, of what felt like *down*, didn't correspond with the actual ground, and Elissa, harnessed into her seat in the front passenger row, just behind the copilot's seat, had one of the moments she didn't think she'd ever get used to, when ears and eyes and mind all disagreed, creating the momentary illusion that the ground they were going to land on was rising up like a wall in front of them.

The *Phoenix*'s wings had swung out the moment they breached the atmosphere, and now Cadan adjusted the flight angle so they were flying parallel to the desert plateau. Sunlit sky blazed through the glass above Elissa's head, a wash of color that seemed, after the darkness of space, impossibly bright. A long way off, a line, a joining of land and sky, of dusty ocher and flawless blue, showed her the horizon.

Some hours before they entered Sekoia's orbit, Cadan had set the *Phoenix* into what he called amphibious mode, able to go seamlessly from traveling through space to flying within the atmosphere of a planet. The main flight deck and most of the body of the ship had been sealed off, and Cadan was piloting it from a secondary cabin tucked in the side of the ship beneath the flight-deck floor.

The first time Elissa had seen the ship, it had looked like a giant silver squid, head pointing toward the sky it would launch itself into, the impression strengthened by the surrounding tentacle-like landing gear. Now she thought that with the ship's wings out, flying belly-down, it would seem more like a wide-finned fish, the little pilot's cabin a bulging eye on its smooth silver head.

Cadan set them on a course toward the Central Canyon City spaceport while he called ahead to initiate landing protocol. Between the ship and the far-off horizon, the upper levels of the city glinted, the sunlight bouncing off what, much closer, would reveal itself to be an eye-wateringly bright tangle of steel walkways and glass-domed roofs.

Elissa had lived there her whole life, traveling the slide-walks, using the beetle-cars, walking under the shining expanse of roofs that kept the city's precious water from evaporating into the baked-dry desert air.

And now she found herself looking at it with alien eyes.

It wasn't like she'd never descended toward the city from the upper atmosphere before; she'd done so twice, once returning from a school outing and once from a family vacation, and both times this view had come with a rush of familiarity, a feeling of being back where she belonged. Not this time.

But then, I don't belong here anymore.

She'd known that, really, six weeks ago, standing on this same ship, surrounded by black, endless space, watching Sekoia dwindle to a silvery sphere of cloud and ocean. Back then, though, she'd thought she was leaving for good. That she'd never see it again.

Now, descending toward the city where she'd lived her whole life, and yet somehow looking at it as if she'd been away, not for a few weeks, but for a lifetime, she was realizing that, whatever Sekoia was to her, it was no longer home.

Elissa gave her head a little shake, refusing to be morbid. Sekoia was a whole different place than it had been some weeks ago, even for the people who still lived there. The *Phoenix* was Elissa's home now. And if it was a little weird to think of a spaceship that way, well, what over the last few weeks *hadn't* been weird?

Finding out three years' worth of hallucinations were actually her telepathic link with the identical twin—Lin—she'd never known she had, discovering that Lin had escaped from the secret government-run facility where she'd been brought up, then turning fugitive with her to prevent the authorities from taking Lin back to imprisonment and torture . . . it would take a whole lot of weird to top that.

Cadan eased the *Phoenix* into a lower speed, angling the ship down to skirt the city itself, bringing them into a careful descent toward the spaceport.

The secondary cabin was set up, like the bridge, with a

copilot's seat next to the pilot's, and two short rows of passenger seats behind them. Now Lin began to lean sideways from the copilot's seat to get a better view of the main screen, then caught herself and sat back upright with a look of such conscious virtue that Elissa had to stop herself laughing out loud.

Lin was endlessly fascinated by spaceflight and determined to learn everything Cadan could teach her, but it had taken weeks of him snapping at her for Lin to finally grasp how *very* much he didn't appreciate her craning over his shoulder.

Elissa thought he wouldn't have snapped if it hadn't been supremely obvious that Lin was only a slow learner with the things that didn't interest her. Everything to do with actually *flying* the ship, she'd picked up so fast it didn't seem possible.

Even after all these weeks, Elissa sometimes found herself taken aback by how easily her twin could work out anything technological—and how difficult she found it to remember the social norms that came instinctively to everyone else on the crew.

But then, when you'd grown up in a secret government-run facility, when you'd been taught that you weren't even human, but a "nonhuman human-sourced entity"—a *Spare*—how could you end up like a normal person?

The *Phoenix* banked, sharply, as Cadan pulled her out of her glide.

"What are you doing?" said Lin, still—just—managing not to lean over, sitting determinedly upright in her seat. "I thought we were going down to the spaceport."

Cadan pulled the *Phoenix* away from even the perimeter of the city, the desert plateau swooping below them. "They've made it a no-fly zone."

"You mean because there's no space to land?" Lin said.

Cadan shook his head. "No. That wouldn't warrant a no-fly order." He made a noise of irritation at his own mistake, pulling up an info-screen. "I *thought* air-traffic control was slow in responding. Turns out it's because they're not intending to respond. They've closed off airspace over the whole city. The spaceport's shut down."

"We saw no orbital patrols on the way in," Markus, the head—and now the only—technician, said quietly from his seat next to Elissa. He was one of the three crew members who'd remained when Cadan had discovered that Elissa and Lin were fugitives from the Sekoian authorities, when he'd made the decision to help them escape his own government, when he'd given the whole crew the opportunity to leave.

Cadan didn't look around, but his head came up a little, alert. "You think that's why?"

"We could already guess they were overstretched. It makes sense, don't you think?"

"Unfortunately, yes."

No orbital patrols. Something inside Elissa tightened. When she and Lin had fled Sekoia, the authorities had pursued them, forcing them eventually to seek refuge on the planet Sanctuary, the headquarters of the Interplanetary League. There, Lin had been given full human status, and the Sekoian government's treatment of her—and of the other Spares—had been judged illegal under interplanetary law. The Interplanetary League had deposed the Sekoian government and instituted a planetary takeover.

Elissa had already known they were coming back to a planet with a disrupted social order, a planet with military law imposed on it. A planet that, when it had lost the ability to use the Spares' psychokinetic powers, had also lost the top secret superfuel that had powered its ships into hyperspeed. A planet that no longer had a long-distance spaceflight industry of its own. It was why she and Lin were returning, to offer Lin's electrokinesis, enhanced by their telepathic link, to support the spaceflight industry, to try to stem the slide toward planetary disaster.

But no orbital patrols? All her life had been lived in the safety that orbital patrols brought to the planet, the defense measure that meant people could go about their business without the threat of attack or abduction by space pirates. You heard awful stories sometimes, of isolated settlements on unguarded planets. . . .

Now Sekoia was one of those unguarded planets, able to institute only such protections as closing off airspace, so that any unauthorized craft could be instantly identified and repelled.

The idea of space pirates descending into Sekoia's residential canyons made her go cold all over. If shutting down air travel would prevent that, she understood why the IPL authorities had done it, it made sense. But all the same . . .

She'd grown up within earshot of that spaceport, built on the plateau at the top of the canyon, above the residential shelf where her family's house stood. She'd only needed to look out of her bedroom window to see the fiery streaks of ships, night and day, rising or descending against the sky.

Sekoia's whole society had been built on their spaceflight industry. She already knew that, she *knew* that was why it was so catastrophic that it had been shut down. But she hadn't expected to feel it like this, to feel the knowledge of catastrophe like a physical blow, so strongly she couldn't speak.

"But we've come to *help*," said Lin. "They'll be IPL people, won't they? They'll know who we are." There was a slightly arrogant tilt to her head. Interplanetary League personnel would indeed know who she was: the fugitive Spare who'd precipitated a whole-planet takeover. "Why don't you just land, and then we can explain?"

In the seat next to Elissa, Felicia, the forty-two-year-old light-skinned woman who'd been part of the security team on the *Phoenix*'s original crew, smothered a laugh. Cadan slanted a half-exasperated look toward Lin. "Because no-fly zones are enforced. I don't know about you, but I've had enough of being shot at for the moment. But if I can land just outside the perimeter—" He tapped the screen. "Ah. Damn it."

"*What?*"

Elissa and Lin spoke at the same time, but while Elissa's voice came out sharp with sudden fright, Lin's was full of nothing but curiosity.

Cadan spared a quick smile over his shoulder to Elissa. "The no-fly zone extends a lot farther than I thought it would, that's all."

"We can't land near the city? Not at all?"

"That's right." His hand moved on the controls and, with a roar of its engines, the *Phoenix* swung right away from the city, out over the desert.

"But then where are we going to go?" Elissa asked.

"We'll have to land outside the no-fly zone."

"But how will we get back to the city?" She was trying to hold her voice steady, but couldn't keep it free of an edge of anxiety. "If it's a no-fly zone, we won't be able to even use the shuttlebug, will we? But we can't walk for hours across the desert—people die trying to do that!" Memories of news stories flashed across her brain—drunken college boys, schoolkids taking dares.

"Not necessarily," said Cadan calmly. "But it's okay, I don't think it'll come to that."

"But then what are we going to do? You and Felicia have to find your families, Lin and I have to find some kind of central IPL command so we can find out where we can offer help—"

"It's okay. We will."

His voice was still calm, but now she could hear that it was deliberately so. She stopped, her cheeks heating.

Weeks ago she'd gone to Cadan Greythorn to get her and Lin off Sekoia. She had gone unwillingly, driven by desperation, hating to have to be indebted to her older brother's arrogant best friend and fellow high-flying Space Flight Initiative trainee pilot.

And she'd lied to him, and cheated him, paying him with a stolen credit card, with phantom credit that didn't really exist. Drawn danger—although she hadn't meant to—after him and his ship and his crew. The Sekoian government had sent bounty hunters, intending to recapture Lin and destroy the link between her brain and Elissa's. Because of her, Cadan's ship had been damaged, most of his crew had resigned, and they'd all come closer to death than she liked to think about.

It had been the most terrifying time of her life. And probably his as well. And yet through it all, they'd come to know each other as something other than Bruce's arrogant best friend and Bruce's spoiled little sister. And despite all the trouble she'd brought after him, he'd fallen in love with her.

And she . . . Well, she'd found out what she should have realized ages ago, that she'd been in love with him since she was thirteen years old.

Knowing that he loved her should mean she no longer felt like a little girl around him, ignorant and inferior, without any of the intense work and training that had made him able to command a spaceship, fight off pirates, have knowledge of things like the Humane Treatment Act that had eventually helped save Lin. It should mean that. But somehow it didn't. And she no longer had the defense of pretending she didn't care.

"There's a training base we used to use," he said now, in possession, as always, of all the most useful information. "SFI owned it, of course, although I'm guessing it's technically IPL property now. I can't imagine IPL will have commandeered all the land vehicles we used to keep there. We might even be able to use the facilities there to refuel the *Phoenix*."

"For free?" Lin said, eager and interested.

Cadan laughed. "Wouldn't that be nice? Let's see when we get there. Do me a quick scan of this route, okay, Lin? Let's just check that there aren't any other unexpected blocks."

Lin bounced into action, throwing open a screen and tapping in a line of commands.

Knowing the best thing she could do was not distract either of them, Elissa sat still, a well-behaved passenger, watching while Cadan dealt with everything and Lin did everything else. He'd been teaching Elissa some of what it took to fly the *Phoenix* over the last few weeks, but she couldn't hope to match Lin's lightning speed at picking up all the skills required, and it would be a long time before she'd be able to act as copilot for him—or as anything else useful.

Weeks ago she'd joined with Lin in saving them all, linking telepathically with her twin and using their joined minds to throw the ship into hyperspeed, escaping that last attack by SFI ships. If it hadn't been for her, her link with Lin providing the extra power and steadiness that Lin needed, they wouldn't have made it. Lin would have killed herself trying to do it by herself, and the rest of them—herself and Cadan and the three crew members—would have been blasted to pieces under the bombardment from the SFI ship.

But all she'd done was *helped*. It had been Lin's power—and Lin's willingness to sacrifice herself—that had really saved them.

Elissa bit the edge of her thumbnail as Cadan took the *Phoenix* out over the desert.

She had paid for half the refueling of the ship, too. And—*obviously*—if she hadn't helped her twin in the first place, Lin would never have escaped Sekoia.

Elissa shifted in her seat, feeling as if the straps were digging into her. It wasn't like she'd done *nothing* over the last few weeks, it was just that, compared to everything Lin and Cadan had done, that was how it seemed.

It was weird. She'd spent so much of the last few years just surviving, wanting to fit in, to be ordinary. Now, compared to the others she was sharing the ship with, she was *too* ordinary.

The three crew members were all specialists in several different fields—you didn't get a place on an SFI ship without attaining excellence in a whole bunch of disciplines. Cadan had aced every test he'd ever taken and had been fast-tracked to captain duty even before he'd graduated. Lin was the superpowered version of Elissa. Among them all, Elissa was the most normal, the most ordinary.

It didn't feel as good as she'd thought it would.

After all, when you're with a guy like Cadan . . .

Having your big brother's best friend, the person you'd adored since you were seven years old, fall in love with you—it still felt too amazing to be real. Amazing in a good way, obviously, but also, sometimes . . .

It wasn't so much that she was younger than him, but that she was so far behind in terms of everything else. Going on the run with Lin meant that she hadn't quite completed high school. But even if she had, it would have been with a bare handful of passing grades, scraped together during those years made a nightmare by attacks of pain and disorienting flashes of a life that wasn't hers. And before that, back when her life had been flawless, easy—well, he'd said himself he'd thought she was . . . The word still hurt, and she tried not to think it, but all the same it came floating inexorably into her mind. *Shallow.* She'd thought he was amazing, had hero-worshipped him, glowed whenever he spoke to her. And he'd thought she was shallow.

"All clear," said Lin, calm and competent at the controls. Cadan turned his head a little to smile at her, and something stabbed through Elissa. Something she tried to push away before she needed to acknowledge what it was.

Lin was her *sister.* Her *twin*, who over the time since they'd met had become more important than anything, more important than Elissa's home or family. She might be struggling with jab after nasty jab of insecurity, but she was *not* going to start feeling jealous of her own sister.

"And we're there," said Cadan.

Elissa dragged her thoughts back under control as the *Phoenix* banked again. The straps tightened against her body. They'd been in Sekoia's atmosphere long enough for the ship's gravity to switch off; it was Sekoia's own gravitational field she was feeling now.

The *Phoenix* skimmed downward, circling as she lost height, and under them the desert floor swooped and slid away. Then a complex of buildings rose up beneath them: stone-built, squat and utilitarian, connected by steel tunnels.

"Hang tight for landing," said Cadan, and, as sand rose in clouds and rocket-fuel smoke billowed up around the ship, enveloping the glass and filling, for a moment, the viewscreens with a blur of yellow-tinged smog, the *Phoenix* touched down on Sekoian soil.

Lin turned slightly in her chair. The lit-up look she got whenever she did anything to do with flying the ship had dimmed. She was biting her lip, her face tight, and Elissa instantly forgot all other preoccupations.

If it was weird for her to return to Sekoia, what must it be like for Lin, being back on the planet where she'd been trapped and tortured?

Elissa unsnapped her harness, wriggled out from the tangle of straps and leaned forward to put her hand on Lin's shoulder. Lin reached her own hand up to clasp Elissa's.

"They're gone," said Elissa. "The facility staff, the people who ordered what they did to you—they'll be in prison by now."

Lin's head moved a tiny bit. "Not all of them."

"Yeah, okay, not all. But most. And any of them who haven't been arrested yet—they'll be keeping a completely low profile. They're not going to want to come *near* us."

Behind them, Ivan the chef, huge and gorilla armed, added, "And they'd be sorry if they did. No one's going to be touching you girls without your permission, not anymore."

Markus laughed, a wordless acknowledgment of what they'd seen Lin do, of what they knew her electrokinesis could accomplish.

Under Elissa's hand, Lin's fingers relaxed a little.

The sand and smoke cleared. Blue sky and brilliant sun blazed once again through the glass. Cadan ran a quick hand over the controls, turning everything down to maintenance level, a standby setting that would save fuel without shutting the ship down entirely. They'd all learned over the last few weeks not to make any premature assumptions about safety.

Which was just as well, because when they'd gone through the dilating door that led from the cabin, climbed down the narrow staircase, then through two more safety doors and an external air lock, and emerged into bright, dusty sunlight, they found themselves surrounded by an armed crowd.

TWO

CADAN'S, MARKUS'S, and Felicia's hands flashed to their own weapons, but the crowd's leader was quicker. There was a gun in his hand, a real gun, steel-loaded, not the short-range blasters spaceship crews carried. He held it leveled at Cadan's face.

"Drop your weapons."

The crew obeyed. Next to Elissa, Lin went tense. Elissa didn't dare make any movement that could be construed as a move for a weapon—like *she'd* have one—or she'd have stretched out a hand to clasp her twin's. *How did they get here so fast?* The crowd must have come from the buildings, of course, but she would never have expected them to move so quickly—or to react like *this*.

"We're not a threat," said Cadan steadily, straightening from laying his blaster on the sand. "Look at the ship. It's one of SFI's. You can see we're not pirates."

The man gave a bark of laughter. "Like pirates are all we've got to worry about? Do you even *know* what planet you've landed on?"

Cadan kept his hands up and open, an unthreatening posture. "I can see it's not the same planet I left a few weeks ago."

"A few weeks? And you've chosen to come back now?" The man's lips curled into what was nearly a smile, although the gun stayed pointed at them. He was about Elissa's father's age. He looked rough edged, unshaven and not altogether clean, like she'd always imagined criminals, illegal immigrants, but he couldn't be either—his accent was that of the upper sections of Sekoian society, and his manner seemed one accustomed to authority. "This must be quite the homecoming."

Cadan grinned a little. "You could say that."

"Do they know, out there? Do they know anything of what's going on in our world?" Grim lines drew themselves into his face.

"They did about a month ago," said Cadan. "I have no way of knowing what the coverage is like now."

A stir, a low-level angry mutter, came from the crowd. Elissa caught scraps of speech. ". . . betting they don't." ". . . think that's all? *I'm* betting they know and they just don't care."

"So what are you doing here?" the man asked. "Your ship's SFI, and you've got the SFI look so I'm inclined to believe it—what the hell are you doing coming back here?"

"My family's here," said Cadan. It was the truth, but only part of the truth, and he made sure not to look at either of the twins as he said it. Tension hummed within Elissa. These people—they were armed, and pretty hostile so far. If they found out who she and Lin were, that they were the twins who'd precipitated the whole situation, what would their reaction be? Elissa's family had accepted IPL's offer of relocation within days of

the takeover, getting them out of the reach of possible repri-
sals from a furious population. And they'd been at risk just
for being *related* to her and Lin. If discovered, she and Lin
would be at a whole lot more of a risk.

They'd talked about it—she and Lin, Cadan and the crew—
before they made the final decision to return. If the twins'
names or faces had ever actually appeared on the newcasts
that had gone out all over the star system, Elissa wasn't sure
she'd have dared to come back.

Given the supersensitive nature of the situation, though,
as well as Elissa and Lin's underage status, interplanetary
protection agreements had come into effect, agreements
that had extended to the whole of the crew. In all the newscasts Elissa had seen before they left Sanctuary, the *Phoenix*
had been referred to only as an "SFI-owned ship," and Cadan
as a "young SFI pilot." Sometimes, depending on the channel, "a young maverick pilot"—and once, "a young *heroic*
pilot."

Elissa knew she couldn't count on their identities staying
secret forever—at *some* point there was bound to be an information leak—but at least they weren't returning to Sekoia as
instant celebrities. And they'd taken their own precautions.
Lin had kept her fake tan and had rebleached her hair, continuing to wear it swinging sleek and straightened around
her face, a contrast to Elissa's tumble of dark waves. It was
impossible to conceal all the things that made them identical, but they'd done their best to ensure they didn't betray
themselves by being mirror images.

"Your family? So you've come to get them out?" the man
asked Cadan.

Elissa sensed Cadan stiffen, and as his tension reached her, she saw the *Phoenix* how this crowd must see it—as an escape route from a world tearing itself apart. If they forced Cadan to take them on board, forced him off the planet, and if in the meantime the authorities shut off airspace over the whole of Sekoia, then they might never get back. They might never find out what was happening to Cadan's family, they might never be able to help avert their world unraveling into chaos.

"Not exactly," said Cadan.

"Then what? No—forget it." The man made a gesture so impatient it hovered on the edge of anger. "I'm done playing Twenty Questions. Where's your ID?"

Cadan hesitated—only for a moment, but the man's grip shifted very slightly on his gun, a silent message.

"Inner jacket pocket," said Cadan. Elissa's throat tightened. They hadn't planned on this, hadn't planned on having to give up their identities to anyone other than the IPL authorities.

"Fine," said the man. "Undo your jacket and pull it fully open before you reach in, all right? And don't think we won't shoot."

"I don't." Cadan's voice was dry as he reached for the zip on his dark blue SFI jacket. It crossed Elissa's mind to wonder why he still wore his uniform, now that SFI was no more. Was it just for situations like this, to give an immediate indication that he wasn't a pirate? Or was it because, despite everything, despite what SFI had done, he could not yet let go of them, did not know how to see himself as someone other than an SFI employee? *He has to. He can't hold on to something that was false, wrong; he can't keep feeling he owes them for his training, for his job—not after what they did to Lin.*

But when you'd defined yourself as part of SFI since you

were eleven, how long would it take you to let go?

Cadan flipped the jacket open.

The man nodded toward him. "Okay, Bryn. Get his ID." His eyes focused, unblinking, on Cadan's. "Try anything and I'll—"

"Shoot," said Cadan with a snap. "Yes, I know."

Another man—Bryn—stepped forward, keeping to the side, out of the way of the gun, slid two fingers into Cadan's pocket and pulled out his ID card, then stepped carefully back.

The first man took it, flipped it over. His eyebrows shot up. He tilted the card away from himself, then sideways, checking the tiny holograms that appeared at different angles, tokens that the card wasn't a fake, then held it up, shutting one eye to check the glinting edge of the tissue-thin metal sheet within it.

He gave a sharp look back at Cadan, eyebrows slanting into a frown. "Seriously? Bright young cadet, with the luck to have sole command of a ship *and* to be safely off-planet for the whole of this crisis? You decided to come *back*?"

Cadan watched him, still tense, wary. "Like I said, my family's here."

"You didn't have strings to pull to get them out?"

Cadan's mouth twisted. "You'll find that off-planet, SFI strings don't work as well as they used to."

The man gave a short laugh. "*You'll* find they don't work too well on Sekoia, either. We have ex-SFI people here, Captain, taking refuge from a city that used to damn well worship them. Here." He flipped the card back to Cadan, who caught it. The man holstered his gun and threw a glance toward the crowd. "No danger. He's SFI, all right. Rising star among the cadets, if you can believe it."

There was nothing but some wry amusement in his tone. But the other man, Bryn, jerked his head up, staring at Cadan. "*Which* rising star?"

"Greythorn," the first man said, shrugging.

"*Cadan* Greythorn? The pilot who went off-grid forty-five days ago? The information-blackout one?"

The first man frowned. "Yeah, you're right, that's the one, isn't it? Bryn, what—"

But Bryn's eyes had left Cadan and swept straight to Elissa and Lin. Elissa saw the second it happened, the second the realization hit him. His gaze flicked from her to her twin, taking in all the similarities that their different hairstyles and clothes had obscured to start with, then he turned to the other man. "It's him. He's *that* pilot. No wonder SFI wanted a blackout on him! He didn't just go off-grid, he *went to IPL*. And those two—Miguel, for God's sake, *no danger?*"

For a moment Miguel stared at him. Then his expression changed too, going from realization to shock, and then to horror. He looked back at Cadan. "Tell me you haven't," he said.

"What?" In contrast to the horror in the faces of the other men, Cadan's expression remained blank. But Elissa knew it was deliberate, a mask over his own emotions.

Anyone else, if we'd met anyone else, *they'd have had no idea which pilot Cadan was. We had to run into SFI people, people who heard about Cadan taking the ship off-grid, people who'd be able to put two and two together. . . .*

"Tell me you haven't brought them back to Sekoia," said Miguel. "That runaway girl and her clone. Tell me you haven't brought them to *my camp*."

Anger scalded through Elissa, eclipsing—for an instant—everything else. *Don't call her a clone!*

"I did bring them," said Cadan, his voice flat and calm. "Tell me the problem."

That stir came again, a ripple of anger, of tension, running through the crowd.

"The *problem*?" Miguel made an exasperated sound almost like a laugh. "God, you have no idea, do you?"

"Like I said, deep space for about a month." This time a slight snap came though Cadan's words. "The last newscasts we got were back on Sanctuary. So tell me. We've come back to help–tell me what's been going on."

"Help?" Miguel gave that laugh that wasn't a laugh. "I'd say we're pretty much beyond help at this point–and when I say 'we,' I mean you as well. The best chance you have is to get back on your ship and get back into space. Unless that one ship is the forerunner of a fully functioning fleet, you don't have anything to offer that's going to help anyone."

"You'd be surprised," Cadan said. Apprehension prickled up Elissa's spine. He was talking about her and Lin. Which made sense–that was why they'd returned, to offer their combined power to Sekoia's space force, to help stop Sekoia sliding into poverty and chaos. But she'd never expected to be offering it under these circumstances, to someone who seemed so sure that by coming back they'd done everything wrong. And although their combined power had saved them before . . . *we still don't understand it. Not properly. We've tried to practice, but we didn't dare do much on board the ship, and the link still comes and goes–it's not there all the time, and it doesn't always seem to work the same way. . . .*

"Surprised? Really? You sure it's not you who's going to be surprised?" Miguel jabbed his finger toward Elissa and Lin. "You think you're going to be able to help us? You don't get back on your ship, you'll have enough to do trying to keep those kids alive for the next twenty-four hours."

Elissa's stomach dropped. She reached for Lin's hand and felt her twin's fingers close tightly around her own.

"So tell me," repeated Cadan. His voice had flattened back to calmness. If Elissa hadn't heard that note in his voice before, if she hadn't known it was a deliberate closing off of his emotions, she'd have thought he hadn't heard what the other man had said. He flicked a look toward Elissa and Lin. "They're in danger? Who from? Most people don't have SFI inside knowledge—they're not going to work out their identity as quickly as you did."

"She's a Spare, isn't she?" Miguel said. "Who *isn't* she in danger from?"

All over Elissa's back, her skin tightened.

"There are at least three groups who've made it their stated mission to wipe out all Spares," Miguel continued. "And if the Spares hadn't been rushed into safe houses, they'd be well on their way there."

Cadan made as if to ask something else, but Elissa was ahead of him. The man hadn't said specifically that anything had happened to Spares yet, but those words—*they'd be well on their way there*—clanged, a warning bell, in her head.

"Have they managed it?" she said. "Have they managed to kill any Spares?"

Cadan took a step closer to her, and his hand settled, warm and steady, on her back.

Miguel's expression flickered, suddenly uncertain, as if he were deciding how—or whether—to answer her. Her throat closed, and for a few long, horrible seconds all she could do was wait, speechless, hoping he'd tell her the truth straight out and she wouldn't have to argue and demand with this awful weight of dread inside her.

"Some," Miguel said.

"How?" Her throat was still frozen shut. The question came out as scarcely more than a silent movement of her lips.

"Some were shot. By snipers, we assume, when the Spares were on their way out of the facility where they'd been kept. And some of the flyers taking them to the safe houses have been attacked. Not all of them went down, but . . ." He lifted a shoulder, a gesture that would have looked careless if it hadn't been for the grim cast of his mouth.

Falling, trapped, safety programming and parachutes and defenses all useless, all of them going down with you. For a moment Elissa had to screw her eyes shut, concentrate on just breathing. It didn't do any good to let herself think about it.

"In—" She had to stop, swallow, start again. "Here? In this city?"

Miguel shook his head. "Attacks, yes. No deaths." Then, heavily, "Not so far."

Not so far. Oh God, and I agreed to Lin coming back. I agreed to her coming back here, where there are people who want to kill her. They'd known there could be danger, they'd *known* it, but there was a difference between knowing it as a possibility and hearing—*oh God*—that people were dying.

"Why?" came Lin's voice from beside her, her voice holding all the calm Elissa had tried for and hadn't been able to manage. "Why are people killing Spares? And who are they?"

Still cold with shock, Elissa turned her head to look at her sister. Lin looked straight-backed and alert, as if she'd just asked a question to which there was sure to be an interesting answer. *How does she do that? She's just heard that people like*

*her are being murdered, and you'd think she'd found out only that
they're being—oh, given, like, haircuts.*

Out of place though Lin's reaction seemed, the fact that
she, at least, didn't seem frightened had its effect on Elissa,
too. The tightness in her throat eased.

It was Bryn who answered her. "God knows who they are.
Well, God and IPL, we guess, but no one's telling us. And
as for why . . ." He shrugged. "If it weren't for Spares, we
wouldn't be in this mess, would we?"

"If it wasn't for *SFI*, you wouldn't be in this mess!" Elissa
burst out, but Miguel interrupted. "There's no time for this
now. We have to get underground. Even if you"—he nodded toward Cadan—"get away immediately, if you've been
tracked, if someone thinks you've left the clones with us,
thinks we're harboring them, we're dead ourselves."

His voice was urgent, and something close to panic
showed in his face. In that one moment, Elissa saw clearly
what she hadn't picked up on before. She'd gotten it wrong:
Miguel wasn't accustomed to exercising authority. He'd *taken*
authority, maybe because he was the most competent, but
he had no practice in it. And now he was trying to handle a
situation for which he not only had no experience, but also
no skills that had prepared him for dealing with it.

*But he said they had SFI people here. If there are other SFI person-
nel around, then how come it's him acting as leader? Okay, so SFI
doesn't exist anymore, but still—where are the officers? Where's the
structure all gone to? If any of these people are SFI, they'll have been
working there for years—all that organization can't just melt into
chaos like that, not this quickly. They need to take responsibility for
what's been done to Spares—they need to make sure it doesn't happen
again!*

Cadan's voice remained calm. "Okay, so there're groups—several groups—targeting Spares? Because they blame them for the current situation. And those sheltering them too?"

Bryn gave him a bitter look. "Should have stayed off-planet, right?"

When Cadan glanced at him, his eyes were like blue steel. "Cut the posturing. You're saying we're in danger here—and we've put you in danger too?" His gaze swept the crowd. "Then what are they doing standing here? This is an SFI base—it's equipped with underground shelters. Get these people into them!"

As if that was all it took, Miguel jerked into action. He snapped an order to Bryn, who swung away to relay instructions to a handful of official-looking people—mostly the ones, Elissa realized, who were holding weapons.

Had been holding weapons. They weren't bothering now, tucking guns back into belt holsters and inside jackets, focusing instead on shepherding sections of the crowds in different directions, back inside the buildings.

Miguel looked back at Cadan. "You need to go," he said. "They'll have clocked the ship entering the atmosphere—it's likely they'll have tracked it here. You could come in the shelters with us, but if they break through this time . . ." There was despair in his face. "Captain, listen to me. I have to keep these people alive. If they break into our shelter but neither you nor the clones are with us, at least—"

Cadan interrupted him. "This time? The base has been attacked before? How many times?"

"Since I got here? Six. Not all from the same group, though, as far as we can work out."

"You can tell? How?"

Miguel shrugged. "Firepower. Some of them are using SFI craft. Some of them have nothing more than target-practice guns strapped to souped-up beetle-cars."

Markus gave an unexpected choke of laughter. "Seriously?"

Miguel looked at him, bleak. "It's funny when you're not living it. We've got the shelters, and the aboveground buildings are pretty well fortified, but if they get a direct hit on our solar cells, or the purifier . . ." He nodded toward the familiar shape of the half-buried water-recycling station.

Up until this point Elissa hadn't thought about that—she was still struggling to deal with the impact of finding out that people were killing Spares—but of course. This far out in the desert, the base would have to operate independently of the city's resources: power, water, medical supplies. When things had been running normally, they'd have been able to rely on deliveries, but now, out here, more than a day's walk from the city, if they ran out of water, or the power that kept their perishable food and medicines refrigerated—how long would they last?

And then, selfishly: *If we end up stuck out here, how long will we last? I knew we were taking a risk coming back to Sekoia, but I didn't plan on not surviving my first day back!*

"Why are they attacking you, though?" Cadan was saying. "If you think they're after Spares, why have you come under attack anyway?"

"We've got ex-SFI personnel with us," said Miguel. "And some government officials who swear they never knew what was going on but who got chased from their homes anyway, and a few immigrant families—legal ones, but people are saying if we'd closed to immigration years ago, Sekoia would never have come under so much pressure that the government was forced into using clones—"

"*Spares,*" snapped Elissa, shock and fear making her careless, almost before she was aware she'd opened her mouth to speak. "They're not clones, they're *Spares.*"

Miguel shrugged without looking at her. "Whatever. The mood in the city . . . it's not a good place to stay for anyone who could take any of the blame. A connection with SFI, or the government, or Spares . . . People are here because they were afraid to stay, Captain. And if we can manage to go even farther away, we'll take it. Right now we're stuck within easy attack range. We haven't come under serious fire, not so far. It's more of a harassment—angry people looking for scapegoats. I don't think anyone is intent on actually destroying our camp— no one here is *liked*, but we're not hated like the clones."

"*Spares.*" Heat rose behind Elissa's eyes, momentarily erasing the fear.

This time Miguel did throw her a glance. "Do I look like I have time to argue semantics? Whatever you and she are, you're hated. And you're in danger."

Calling them clones isn't just semantics! If everyone keeps calling them clones then everyone keeps seeing them as nonhuman and when people attack them it won't be a big deal because it won't matter like the way an attack against ordinary people matters. It does matter. It matters what you call them.

"You must have some SFI craft here, though?" Cadan said. "When I was last here, we had flyers, and small amphibious craft for practicing air/space maneuvers. They weren't cleared out at the takeover?"

"No. IPL requisitioned most of the pilots, but only to fly large craft, not the little two-mans. They're still here."

"Fueled?"

"Yes."

"IPL took the pilots. Do you have anyone who can pilot them, then?"

"Ten qualified pilots—they arrived well after the takeover, and IPL haven't come back yet to recruit more. And yes, Captain, we're not completely inept. We've been using them to defend the base as best we can. They'll be suiting up now."

"Any cadets? Once they're past their first year, they'll be good enough to defend the base. I can vouch for that, if you need—"

"No." Miguel's voice sounded wry. "Trust me, we can't afford to fetishize rank right now—we'd use them if we had them. All the SFI personnel here are mostly maintenance—it's pure luck we've ended up with any pilots at all." His mouth twisted. "We have a hundred people who can fix the ships, just hardly anyone who can fly them."

"The ships, are they armed? Last time we were using blanks."

"We fixed that, first thing. We've got real firepower."

"Okay. I can take one ship. If you'd introduce me to the pilot in charge, he can get me up to speed on his defense plan?"

Miguel stared at Cadan. "You're staying? You're joining our defense crew?"

"Well, not permanently. But yes. We brought this trouble on you. I can't offer to evacuate you all—well, at least not until I've spoken to IPL—but I can help you defend against any attack that follows us."

Miguel stared at him a moment longer. "Okay. I get you. I'll take you to the docking bays."

"Thanks."

"*You're* thanking *me*?" There was dry amusement in Miguel's voice. "And what about those kids? Was getting them caught up in this part of your plan?"

Next to Elissa, Lin quivered, indignant. "We're not kids. And we can *help*—"

"No," said Cadan.

"I can! I don't *want* to go in the shelters—"

"You're not. The base shelters are good, but I defy any air- or ground-based attack to get through the *Phoenix*'s defenses." His glance swept from Lin over Elissa and the rest of the crew. "You—all of you—you're getting back on board now."

It was his crisis-management voice, one of automatic command, and Elissa responded to it, turning back toward the *Phoenix*, fear making her cold all over again, a little clumsy, her feet numb enough that they didn't seem to be quite connecting with the ground.

All around her, the crew were doing the same, albeit a whole lot more smoothly. *If I end up staying with the ship as long as some of them have trained, will I ever learn to be that calm in the face of danger*—more *danger, yet again?*

She forced her breathing to slow down. A million years ago, at school, she'd been taught yoga, and Felicia had encouraged her and Lin to join in her daily routine on board ship, but right now Elissa had no hope of gaining the steady, focused breathing she should be able to achieve in any situation. The best she could do was to not completely freak out and hyperventilate.

If they're not freaking out, I don't need to. The Phoenix *is super-safe. And Cadan's in charge. . . .*

She didn't want to be feeble enough to reach for his hand,

to need him to reassure her before she left him out here. She'd done without it before they were dating, for goodness' sake; she wasn't going to collapse into a stupid needy girl-friend now. But all the same, she couldn't help wishing he'd, just quickly, give her a look that wasn't the look of a captain speaking to his crew.

Of course he didn't. She was looking at Cadan in full crisis-management mode, triaging the whole situation in his head. Irrelevantly, she wondered if it was pure SFI training coming to the fore. Faced with this, would Bruce, too, react with the same steel-cold efficiency?

As if in proof that this version of Cadan could scan all the complications before they entered anyone else's thoughts, he glanced toward Markus. "I won't be there to activate the *Phoenix*'s shields. You and Lin know how to run the codes. The moment you're on board, get them up to full strength."

"Yes sir."

Ivan was already standing by the open door of the ship, waiting for the others to go through, and even as Markus answered Cadan, he turned too, to go on board.

Felicia held back for a second. "Captain?" she said. "Am I best used on the *Phoenix*? Do you want me to stay on the ground?"

Cadan hesitated. "No. I need you on the *Phoenix* too. If you're left without anyone who can fly her, you'll need to find a way of getting the girls to the city. They'll have to seek sanctuary from IPL, and they'll need your protection to get them there."

Cold sank through Elissa. He hadn't said it in so many words, but she'd have to be stupid not to know what *if you're left without anyone who can fly her* meant. Cadan was making contingency plans. *Plans for* . . . She'd known he was staying out here, known he was going to fly one of the defense ships, but now all at once it washed through her, a multitude of horrible images flashing into her brain. The little ship he was planning to fly coming under fire, the windscreen cracking to pieces, the ship falling in a ball of flames. *Cadan* . . .

Don't. Don't do it. Come to safety. Don't make me leave you out here.

But she couldn't say it. He was right: By coming here, they had unknowingly brought danger—even *more* danger—on the refugees living in the base. They owed them anything they could offer in terms of protection.

Unbidden, her hand went out to him, a movement as if she would hold on to his arm. A stupid movement, given that he was out of reach, and that she'd already told herself she couldn't expect anything from him.

But he saw, and looked at her. Their eyes met. For a moment there was no one else there. "I know," he said. "But I have to."

"Yes." Surprisingly, her voice stayed steady. She let her arm drop. "We're going."

He smiled at her, the moment stretching out, holding them both.

Then Elissa set her teeth and walked past him to where Ivan waited. Her legs felt numb now as well, as if her body were shrinking in on itself, trying to avoid awareness of the approaching danger.

Behind her, Cadan said, "Markus, I'll keep in touch." He twisted the little com-unit on his wrist. "Keep my channel open, okay?"

"Got you, Captain. Lin, you coming?"

Elissa was at the door, a step behind Markus, before she realized Lin hadn't followed her.

She turned. Lin wasn't moving. She stood still, arms folded, eyes fixed on Cadan.

"Lin," said Elissa, "we have to go."

Lin didn't glance at her. "What am *I* supposed to be doing?" she said to Cadan. "You know I can be useful. You know I can do stuff. You don't mean for me to go sit in the *Phoenix* as well?"

"Lin, there's nothing for you to do out here. Go in the *Phoenix*, get the shields up—"

"Markus can do that. You already said so. I could do a million better things."

"No." Cadan's voice had a no-argument tone in it. But Lin had never been good at picking up that sort of cue.

"Why *not*? We came back to help, didn't we? You know what I can do. I can fly ships too—"

"Not by yourself. Not safely. Not yet. Lin, no one has time for this. Get on board."

"I don't need to do it by myself! I can come as your copilot. You know I can do that! You *know* I can."

"*Lin.*" The word came out with a snap like the crack of a whip. "I'm not using a copilot. I don't need you." Lin opened her mouth and he cut across her, not letting her get a word in. "And I don't want you. You're not up to this kind of fight, if that's what it comes to, and I don't need the distraction. What I need"—she started to speak and he raised his voice, speaking over her—"*what I need* is for you to keep out of the way and keep your sister safe. Now go and do it instead of delaying me and keeping her here in danger."

Lin shut her mouth, then marched over to where Elissa

waited. Her face was flushed, her eyes glinting and narrowed. When she unfolded her arms to shove her hands into her pockets, Elissa saw her hands were balled into fists.

But at least she wasn't resisting, or arguing. She followed Elissa through the door and into the coolness of the air lock in silence, then up the stairs and into the flight cabin.

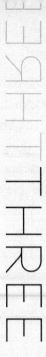

THREE

ELISSA FLICKERED a look at Lin as the door snapped shut behind them. Her twin's face was still flushed, her jaw set. Despite the terror flaring in her mind whenever she thought of Lin being caught, hurt . . . imprisoned again, impatience prickled at Elissa. *Oh, for God's sake. All those people we're leaving in danger, and you're angry because you want to be in danger too? It's not like we came back to Sekoia to fight off attacks—that's not the help we wanted to offer.*

Was that what it was, just Lin wanting to be involved, or was there something else going on? Elissa's shoulders slumped. Just as there were so many finer points of normal social interaction that Lin didn't get, there were probably a whole bunch of things about *Lin* that Elissa didn't get. Sometimes you got tired of trying to work them out.

"Lin," said Markus, in the pilot's seat, flipping up switches one after another. "We're getting the shields up, okay?"

Lin marched across to the front seats. "You don't need me for that. You can do it yourself."

Lights sprang awake along the control panel. Screens woke, flashing code. Markus's voice remained steady. "I can, but I'm not as conversant with the code as the captain is. If you double-check it for me—"

Lin flung herself into the seat next to him. "You don't need to call him the captain when he's not even here."

Elissa's chest clenched. That wasn't just anger in Lin's voice, it sounded like . . . but no, it couldn't be hatred, not for *Cadan*.

"You're right." Markus tapped out a sequence on the keyboard, hesitated, backspaced, then tapped out the rest. He nodded toward one of the screens. "Check that for me, would you?" Then, in the same steady tone, "I don't need to call him that. But nonetheless, we do."

Lin scrolled through the code. "It's fine. First shield ready." The words were bland, but her voice was still dark with anger. "I don't see *why*. It was one thing when he was in charge, when you were all being paid to do what he said. . . ."

"Second sequence coming through. He's still in charge. The SFI going down—it doesn't affect anything. This is his ship."

"Oh it's so *not*. He was only put in charge of it temporarily—"

"It is. He was given charge of it. That makes it his. That's not a pleasant fiction to make the pilots feel good, Lin, it's legal fact. It was meant to be a fixed-term ownership, sure, but now SFI's gone, and it's only IPL who has the authority to terminate his ownership. If they do . . . well, they do. But unless—and until—that happens, it's Cadan's word that matters on board the *Phoenix*. And the crew—either we obey his orders or we resign." He nodded at the screen again. "And that's why he gets called *captain* whether he's present or not."

"Code's fine." Now Lin's voice sounded more sulky than anything. "Second shield ready."

"Third sequence."

"I just . . ." She shot a sideways look at Markus. "He's been teaching me how to be his copilot. He *knows* I can do more than this, and he's all rules and 'you're not up to it' and 'look after your sister.' Like I need *him* to tell me to look after Lissa!"

"There's more to being a pilot than flying," Markus said mildly. "Lin? Are you checking that code for me?"

"*Yes*. It's *fine*."

Markus's eyes went to the screen. He waited. After a second Lin followed the direction of his gaze. "What are you doing? I— *Oh*."

From where Elissa stood she couldn't see which bit they were looking at, nor could she understand the code that Lin had picked up so easily, but the arrested tone in Lin's voice told her all she needed to know.

Markus tapped out a correction. Lin scrolled through it, slowly, then back. "It's fine," she said again, her voice filled with resentment.

"Thank you." Markus activated the sequences, and around them the *Phoenix* seemed to come alive, humming awake as the shields—the enhanced force fields that, in space, protected them from meteorites and other space debris as well as from attack—built themselves around the ship.

Markus leaned away from the controls, angling screens to get the best view of outside. His voice kept exactly the same quiet tone as he said, "And that's why you're not ready to fly a ship."

Elissa saw Lin's head snap back as if he'd hit her. "That's not fair. You did that on purpose—"

"And *you* didn't pick it up. Because you were angry, and you let it distract you."

"Yeah, well, it's not like *Cadan* never gets angry." There was that tone in her voice again, an edge like the edge of an electro-whip. Not just anger, but something more like resentment.

"But he doesn't let it interfere with how he flies the *Phoenix*."

Lin didn't answer. She got up with an irritated, jerky movement and went over to grab a chocograin bar from the little nutri-machine set on the back wall of the cabin. Markus turned enough in his seat to meet Elissa's eyes. He gave her the merest flicker of a smile.

She was smiling back before she knew it, grateful that he'd had the argument with Lin so Elissa didn't have to. Then guilt needled her. *It's not fair. She only wants to help—and she has so much ability, so much power, it must be driving her crazy not being able to do anything with it.*

Outside the *Phoenix*, it had felt like they were on the very brink of being attacked. Even now that they were safe, tension seemed to hang, buzzing in the air, and Elissa, all nerves, chewed the edge of her thumbnail until it was sore. But when the first twenty minutes had passed and nothing happened, the atmosphere relaxed a little.

Over the next twenty minutes, outside the ship, the sun dropped lower, sinking toward the horizon, staining the sand red. Inside the ship, they waited.

There was no reason, really, why at least some of them couldn't leave the cabin to go find something to do in another part of the ship, but, as if none of them wanted to leave the view of the base afforded by the cabin windscreen, no one made a move.

Lin ate a second chocograin bar leaning against the wall next to the windscreen, looking up and out at the empty sky. At the controls, Ivan, sitting sideways on the copilot's seat, told Markus the best ways to thicken soup, and Markus at least appeared to listen, and Felicia lowered herself to sit cross-legged on the floor and reached both arms over her head in what Elissa recognized as the start of one of her many yoga routines.

Elissa sat still, clasping her knees, her gaze on the darkening sky. She'd taken her thumbnail away from her mouth and tucked her thumb safely inside her folded hand, but her insides remained knotted. Her thoughts knotted too. Back on Sanctuary, everything had seemed so clear. But now, within hours of landing on Sekoia, she was swamped with anxieties and fears.

People were *still* referring to Spares as clones. Oh, she could see why. Before Spares had become public knowledge, most people on Sekoia hadn't known it was even possible for them to exist. The birth of identical babies, born from a single fertilized egg, had ceased thousands of years ago—even the term *twin*, an archaic word meaning "double," had fallen out of existence. She remembered Lin explaining it to her, saying that some kind of spontaneous mutation had caused the phenomenon to re-emerge forty or so years ago.

That's impossible, Elissa had said at the time. She'd known, of course, that sometimes a pregnancy produced two babies—it was the only way couples ended up with a second child without applying for a license—but she'd known, or thought she'd known, that it only happened when *two* eggs were simultaneously fertilized, and that the babies might be alike, in the way siblings often were, but they wouldn't be identical.

When she'd first met Lin, one of the first things she'd thought of was cloning; she couldn't blame other people for initially thinking the same, even though science had not yet developed a full-body clone. *But they've been* told *now. They know what she is, they know she's her own person, not just a copy of me. If they still keep insisting that she's a clone, how are they ever going to let her fit into society, lead a normal life?*

Except—everything Miguel had told them came back into her mind, overwhelming her—was life on Sekoia ever going to be normal again? And was Lin—*oh God please no*—going to get killed before they even had a chance to find out?

And now Cadan's out there, putting himself in danger. And it's selfish to even be thinking it, but I'm still scared he thinks more of Lin than he does of me. And our identity isn't anywhere near as safe as we thought it was going to be. And . . .

Elissa let her forehead drop onto her knees.

Lin pushed away from the windscreen. "Nothing's *happening.* There isn't any attack. We don't even need to *be* here. We could be at the city already, actually doing something useful."

"Cool your jets, would you?" Ivan interrupted what he was saying about bread crumbs and glanced over at her. "You'll get there. Dig deep. Find some patience."

"But why can't we go there *now*? We have room for lots of those people. It would only take a few trips to take them to somewhere else on Sekoia. There must be other places they could use. And then we could stop worrying about the base being attacked, and we could stop hanging around here."

Felicia had finished her exercises. Now she lay, stretched and supine, on the floor, her eyes shut and her breathing relaxed.

"Where would you take them?" she said. "This is their home—the only home left to them. If they don't defend it, what will they end up with?"

Lin narrowed her eyes at Felicia. "We took *weeks* just getting back to Sekoia. I want to *do* something—"

She broke off. Her eyes went suddenly blank, as if she were looking at something not physically in front of her. "There are engines," she said. "Two . . . three . . . coming really fast."

Elissa jerked her head up to scan the sky she could see through the windscreen. Empty. She couldn't hear anything either. Aside from the gentle hum of the instruments on the control panel, the far-off buzz of the shields, the world seemed to lie silent, waiting.

"Lin, are you sure?" Lin's ability to understand the ship's controls was one of the most impressive things Elissa had ever seen, and before, she'd seemed to pick up when the hyperdrive was malfunctioning. But Elissa had thought that was mostly to do with sensing the imprisoned Spare powering it—did Lin really sense electronics? And had her abilities developed to such a point that she could pick up approaching aircraft?

Lin gave a tiny, half-distracted nod.

"Then where are they coming from? Which direction?" Elissa looked back and forth, checking the empty sky for any signs of movement, for the glints that would be the last light of the setting sun reflecting from metal wings.

"I don't . . . I can't tell. Above us . . ." Lin shook her head as if trying to clear water from her ears.

Markus, hand already on the communications unit, looked past Lin to Elissa. "Is she right?"

Elissa stared at him.

"*Lissa.* I'm running a scan, but if she's right, I'll alert Cadan now—"

"I don't *know*." Harassed, she looked at her sister. Lin's hand had gone to her head, cupping her temple as if trying to shut something out. She turned her head to meet Elissa's eyes, and her own were wide with panic.

"Lissa, I can't tell where they're coming from. They're so fast, and if they don't slow down they'll—"

Elissa scrambled to her feet, hurried across to clasp her twin's hands. They curled around hers, a tight, desperate grip. "It's okay. We're safe. We're safe here."

"*Lissa,*" said Markus, behind her.

She didn't turn her head, all at once sure beyond all doubt. "Yes, she's right. Call him. Lin, it's okay. It's okay."

Lin dropped Elissa's fingers and clamped both hands over her head. "They're here. They're here. I feel them—"

And as she cowered, shaking, the sky was torn apart.

Flyers exploded out of nowhere, screaming down over the desert, hurtling so low over the *Phoenix* that the roar of their engines killed every sound. Three of them, sleek silver craft flashing the color of fire in the dying light.

Then real fire, as flames spat from their engines, as they whipped around to come screaming down again. And then the sound of gunfire, pounding onto the desert floor in clouds of dust, sweeping across the roofs of the base, spitting sparks and chips of broken masonry.

Bullets thundered across the *Phoenix*'s shields in a glittering rain, then a blast of fire came, sliding like water off the impenetrable surface of the force field. Elissa's hands shot to her ears. They'd weathered other attacks in the *Phoenix*, but that had been in space. Nothing had prepared her for the noise of an on-planet attack: the shrieking rattling roar of engines and weapons that seemed to get inside her brain, vibrating in her bones, thumping nausea into the pit of her stomach.

Outside, shots screamed through the air, up rather than down. Flames burst against the shields of the attacking ships. Then, almost faster than her eyes could see, faster than her brain could register, flyers shot up from the base. They looked tiny against the attacking ships, a little swarm of two-man crafts. Cadan and Bruce had trained in ships like them. Cadan was in one now. That one, racing up to what seemed like the zenith of the sky, boosters flaring? Or that one, diving between two of the attack ships, blasting them as it went? Or one of the ones that shot straight over to the *Phoenix*?

Cadan. Fighting to keep her and Lin safe. Risking his life. And both things not for the first time.

Something shrieked overhead, so loud that the sound stabbed Elissa's ears. She shrank, hands pressing harder against her ears, wanting to shut her eyes but not being able to, not while Cadan was out there, not while if she stopped looking, if she lost concentration, somehow he might lose concentration too, make the mistake that would send him plummeting out of the sky, craft in flames, escape hatch fused shut, trapped and—

Oh God. Bullets sprayed across one of the little ships. If it had possessed a shield at all, it was gone now, blown to nothing by the relentless onslaught. Elissa saw the dark holes pierced all over its flank, saw the attacking ship rake it with another blast, saw the flames swell, a fireburst of igniting fuel. It fell, tumbling from the sky, tracing a fiery trail in the dark air behind it, over and over, out of control, a fireball falling to earth.

Cadan! Then, as her mind refused to accept it: *No. It's not Cadan. It must be someone else, it must be.*

It was a terrible thing to think. She didn't care. *As long as it's not Cadan, as long as I don't lose him.*

Beside her, Lin lifted her head. "They're going to *win*." Her voice was raised to a shriek to battle with the noise, but it had gone from outright panic to nothing more than indignation.

"*No. Don't* say that. We have more ships. They can't win. They can't." Thoughts jumbled in her head. *And win what? Who are they? What do they want? To wipe out the whole camp? Because they think we're in there? How can people be like this?*

And then, again, shot with terror, with a feeling like the bottom falling out of the world: *Cadan. He can't be dead. He can't.*

"Their weapons are way better," shouted Lin over the noise pounding against the ship. "Those little ships—their shields are no good against this! Cadan should have used the *Phoenix*."

All at once that was worse than anything, that Lin should criticize Cadan—*again*—when it might have been him in that—*No, I won't think it. I won't.*

"He *can't*," she shouted back. "You *know* he can't. It won't maneuver fast enough. He explained that to you weeks ago—"

"But she has tons of firepower." All the fear had cleared from Lin's face. Her eyes were bright with a look Elissa had come to dread. "Lissa, *I* could use her."

"You can't fly! Cadan said you're nowhere near ready!"

"I don't need to fly! All I need is to get her high enough to use the weapons. Cadan should have done it himself—"

"No. *No.* You can't do takeoff by yourself. You've *never* done that. If you were ready to try Cadan would have told you. You'll get everyone killed! And you don't know what you're talking about—if Cadan had thought that would work, *he'd* have done it. You can't—"

"Then what *am* I going to do?" Lin flung a hand up toward the Armageddon of fire above them. "Because your *boyfriend* says I'm not ready, I just wait here and let them all die? Is that what we came back to Sekoia for?"

The words hit Elissa as hard as the rain of bullets against the ship's shields. She felt herself recoil, body tightening as if that would protect her from what Lin was saying. "Stop it. Don't. If there was anything you could do, you know I'd—"

She broke off. Lin was all at once not even listening. The bright look had spread all over her face. It was hard, blazing with sudden triumphant realization. "There is." She grinned. "I should have thought of it hours ago. I can. I *can.*"

She tilted her face toward the curve of glass above them, her teeth clenching so hard Elissa saw her jaw lock.

Fear swept Elissa. She'd seen that look on her sister's face before. Back when she'd been terrified she was helping a sociopath escape, someone who needed to be shut away, imprisoned. She hadn't thought she'd see it again.

"Lin, what are you—"

Lin didn't answer. Her eyes widened, dark and blank.

"*Lin.*"

"What's going on over here?" Ivan was on his feet, striding toward them. "What's she doing?"

"She says she's helping. I don't know. I don't *know*." Elissa flung a frantic look at the control panel, watching for more lights to jump awake, for the throttle to move by itself. If Lin really did decide to take them into the air, it was too late to stop her, too late to do anything.

"Lin." Ivan put a hand out. "You do something weird, you're going to hinder, not help. If you distract the pilots defending the—"

In the sky above them, with an ear-shattering thunder-crash, something exploded. Fire rained down all over the *Phoenix*, enveloping the ship momentarily in sheets of flame. Elissa felt her throat open in a scream she couldn't hear, saw Ivan duck, arms instinctively going up to protect his head.

The flames cleared, sliding down the shields. But smoke followed, smoke everywhere, oily and black, swirling and thick with sparks. Elissa couldn't see beyond the walls of the *Phoenix*, couldn't see what had happened, whether any craft were left in the sky, whether anyone was still alive out there.

Lin's mouth moved, saying something. There was no chance of hearing her—Elissa's ears had gone dead—but after a few seconds she managed to make sense of the movement of her sister's lips. *One down.*

The attacking ships. Lin had used her electrokinetic power—the ability to control electrical currents—to explode one of the attacking ships.

She'd threatened to do something like that once before, when they were on the run from Sekoia's security forces, but it had just been a threat to get Elissa moving—she hadn't actually intended to do it.

This time—this time she had.

It was as if Elissa's mind, as well as her ears, had stopped functioning. She couldn't think further than the realization of what Lin had done, couldn't produce a reaction to it.

Around the *Phoenix*, the smoke thinned enough to reveal the continuing battle outside. Another of the defending crafts was down, burning in blackened wreckage on the desert floor. It was impossible to tell if the pilot had managed to escape, or if there'd been no time. Impossible, too, to tell if Cadan . . .

Way above them, one of the attacking craft seemed to judder, its trajectory checked for a half second. As if a connection had ceased momentarily to work—

Lin.

Elissa's head whipped back toward her twin. Lin's hands and teeth had clenched again. Her eyes were screwed shut, and her whole body was shaking as if she were under a weight too heavy to bear. *One down,* she'd said. *Two to go?*

But she can't. The power it must have taken to do that to one ship—she can't do it to all of them.

As if she'd had the same thought at the exact same time, Lin's eyes shot open. Her gaze went straight to Elissa. She put out a hand.

She can't do it by herself. It's too much. But linked, we moved a spaceship. If I help her, if I do what we did before, we can do this, too.

All she needed to do was take Lin's hand, let the physical touch strengthen the link that was always there between them, give herself—as she had before—to act as combined anchor and catalyst for Lin's electrokinetic power.

She didn't move. The explosion sounded again in her head, flames filled her vision. What Lin had just done wasn't just moving a spaceship, it wasn't just getting them out of danger. Whoever had been in that craft—Lin had killed them.

They came here to kill us. They've shot down two of the pilots already. They wouldn't hesitate to shoot Cadan down too, or kill me and Lin, or take us both away for experiments that are no better than torture.

She should reach out to take Lin's hand. She could help save them all. Could help save Cadan, and the other pilots, and maybe all the refugees.

I can't. I can't kill people. I can't help her do that.

Lin shook her hand impatiently toward Elissa. Her face was tight with strain, she couldn't waste energy speaking, but it was more than obvious what she was asking, what she needed from Elissa.

She was willing to die to save my life. To save all our lives. I owe her forever. And I love her. There shouldn't be anything you wouldn't do for someone you owe your life to, for someone you love.

"I can't," said Elissa, knowing Lin couldn't hear her, hoping she could read her lips, her gestures. She shook her head, stepping back. "I can't. I'm sorry."

Incredulity swept over Lin's face. Then a look of such betrayal Elissa felt it go through her like an electrical shock. Lin's lips moved. *You have to.*

Elissa backed farther away. "I'm sorry. I'm *sorry.*"

Lin opened her hands, staring at Elissa, a gesture of helplessness and blame. Then her fingers curled into her palms, and she lifted her face back to the fiery slashes of the ships dogfighting above them.

One of the attacking ships jerked, its flight path disrupted. It dipped, seemed to pull back. Within it, was the pilot fighting to keep hold of it, not knowing why his instruments were going mad, why the controls were no longer responding to his touch? Was the control panel smoking as Lin overloaded the circuits? Was fire licking out from beneath it? Was he already snatching his hands away, terrified, panicking, not knowing what was going on?

They came to kill us. They don't deserve mercy.

It didn't make any difference. Elissa realized her face was wet; she could taste salt on her lips. At some point in the last few minutes she'd started crying.

Lin staggered. Her legs shook, and she grabbed at a seat to support herself. When her eyes met Elissa's, they were bloodshot. Elissa had seen that before: When Lin was at the end of her stamina, when she'd expended too much energy, blood vessels began to burst in her skin, her eyes. *If she keeps trying, if I don't help her, what else will happen to her? What else will I let happen?*

Elissa's nose was running. She wiped her sleeve across it. "I'm *sorry*," she repeated, wretched and helpless, knowing she could take the burden away from her sister but unable to bring herself to do it.

Lin's lips moved again, so slightly that it took Elissa a couple of seconds to read what she'd said. *So am I.*

What? It made no sense. What was Lin sorry for?

Then, as Lin made a lunge toward her and grabbed her hand in a death grip, Elissa knew.

"No! I said *no*!" She tried to wrench her hand away, but Lin had hold of it with more strength than Elissa would have thought she could spare. She swung around, pulling Elissa with her, to look back up at the sky, to find the ship.

No. I won't let it happen. I won't make the link. I won't—

A jerk. Too late. Just like before, the link clicked into place. She was looking through Lin's eyes, experiencing the world in Lin's body.

She was shaking, her legs trembling beneath her, her lungs burning as they tried to pull in more air than they could manage. She was looking at the sky through a haze of red. Her hand—*Lin's hand*—clenched tight around her sister's, grasping it with every last reserve of the strength left in her body. Her thoughts—*Lin's thoughts*—burned in her mind as her breath burned in her chest. *She has to do this with me. She has to.*

She scanned the sky, then focused on the ship that had nearly—twice—escaped her. Sent her mind along the electrical connections, forcing the power up, up, up, feeling the circuits heat and heat and break like tiny explosions.

And then another explosion, a huge explosion, like fireworks in her brain, behind her eyes.

Flames in the sky. Falling metal. Smoke and dust and gouts of liquid fire—the fuel burning as it fell.

Elissa snapped back to herself, a scream bursting against the inside of her head, her throat throbbing with the silent sound. Once again there were flames and smoke all around the *Phoenix*. But this time *she'd* done it. This time she'd *felt*, not just seen, it happen. Felt, too, that firework burst of triumph. Lin's emotions, not hers, but it didn't matter. She'd *felt* it. Felt triumph, delight, in doing something that had killed someone.

Lin, white with exhaustion, crumpled to her knees in front of her. Blood was smeared across her face—her nose was bleeding. For the first time Elissa saw her sister looking hurt, vulnerable, and her immediate instinct wasn't to help or comfort.

You did that to me. I can't believe you did that to me.

She didn't know if the thoughts showed in her expression, but she could see when Lin's eyes dropped from her own.

Ivan's face, immobile with shock, turned from one of them to the other.

Then, as if from far away, only just penetrating through the feeling of cotton wool in her ears, Elissa heard the beep of the com-unit. And Cadan's voice—alive, unhurt, for that moment the only good thing in the whole world—saying, "Attention, *Phoenix*. It's over. Two attackers down, and one in retreat. It's done. It's over."

FOUR

"I HAD to," said Lin.

They were standing outside the *Phoenix*, amid a nightmare jumble of blackened, twisted metal, of still-burning fuel puddles. The reek of rocket fuel and smoke and dust coated the inside of Elissa's nose, bitter at the back of her throat.

Not far away, metal against metal whined and screeched as the hull of a third downed craft was cut open. It had been hit, and had crashed, but miraculously, unlike the first two, hadn't burst into flames, so there was a chance the pilot was still alive. Cadan was over there, and Markus. Felicia had joined a small extinguisher-wielding ground crew, and Ivan had disappeared the moment they exited the *Phoenix*.

"Lissa, please. Look at me."

Elissa turned her head. Something even bitterer than rocket-fuel fumes dried the inside of her mouth, made her throat and chest and stomach tighten as if there weren't enough oxygen in the dirty air around her.

"I *had* to," said Lin again. "Lissa, please, say you understand."

"I don't." The words came out in a thread of sound, as if her throat could only open enough to let just that much of her voice out. "I don't understand."

"Lissa . . ."

Once she'd said those words, she could manage to follow them with more. "I don't understand how you could do that to me. I said *no* and you did it anyway. I don't understand, Lin. You *didn't* have to, and I *don't* understand."

A flush climbed into Lin's face, dyeing just the skin under her eyes. "Then why was it okay when I did it before?"

"Before? *When* before?"

"When we were being attacked on the *Phoenix*! Cadan let me, he let me take the controls and fire at the SFI ships! You didn't give me that look back then. Is it only okay to kill people when *he* says it is? Am I supposed to have some kind of license in that, too?"

"I'm not talking about it being okay to kill people!"

Lin threw her hands out. "Yes you are! That's the thing you've always said, the thing I'm not supposed to do—"

"*No*, Lin! Jeez, we were being attacked—"

"When?"

"*Both* times. Of course I don't blame you—or Cadan, or anyone—for firing back. It's not that you probably killed people—"

"*Probably?*" Lin gave a furious laugh. "Probably, *nothing*. Didn't you see what I did to those ships?"

"*Yes*, I saw! Yes, I know what you did! It's not *about* that, Lin. It's not about *you* killing people." Somewhere, very faint on the screen of her mind, a word flickered, uninvited, unwelcome. *Hypocrite.* She refused to acknowledge it. She wasn't being a hypocrite, she *wasn't—*

"Then *what?*" said Lin.

"It's about you making *me* kill them!" She'd thought she was mostly just angry, but the words came out on a sob, and when she tried to say something else tears choked her and she had to stop.

"Lissa—"

Elissa shook her head, putting her hands up to her face, trying to get control of herself. She was furious, and beyond furious, but she couldn't afford to let herself fall to pieces now. The attack was over, but God knew when there'd be another one, and they still needed to get themselves safely— somehow—to the city, to the closest IPL command. But if they couldn't fly, and couldn't use the *Phoenix*, there was no way of *getting* safely to the city.

Thinking of all the reasons why she couldn't fall apart wasn't exactly helping her *not* fall apart. She tried to shut them out, tried to just breathe, tried to think of the fact that Cadan was alive and unharmed, that the people in the base hadn't been killed. . . . But that was it. She'd run, for the moment, out of good thoughts.

"Lissa . . ."

Elissa shook her head again, not looking at her sister. "Not now. I can't talk about it right now."

"But I—" Tears thickened Lin's voice. "Lissa, don't be angry. I can't bear it when you're angry with me."

Then stop making me angry!

The words were on her tongue, but she refused to say them. She wasn't going to *have* this conversation. Lin might not be capable of respecting her—oh my *God*—her right not to *kill* people, but she could damn well respect her right not to talk if she didn't want to.

She didn't answer Lin. She didn't look at her. There was, God knew, nowhere she could really go to get away from her. Partly because they were in the middle of the desert and partly because of—*oh yeah*, the telepathic link that bound them. But she could walk away. And she did. Through the patches of blackened smoking sand, through the twisted lumps of wreckage, out to just beyond the end of the buildings, past where the light reached, into the very edge of the night that had fallen across the world.

Behind her, metal still screeched, people called to one another, fire extinguishers hissed onto flames. Her hands still tingled with the memory of the power—Lin's power—rushing through her. But as she stepped out of the light, she felt as if she were stepping away from the noise, too. From the noise, from the memories, and from the awareness of how, in the space of five minutes, everything had changed.

When the wrecked flyer was cut open, it turned out the pilot wasn't dead. But judging by the rush of frantic activity going on as she was lifted out, she was badly hurt. Standing at the edge of the light, arms crossed over her chest, Elissa watched as the limp, uniformed figure was stretchered into one of the buildings. *She's not dead. She's hurt, but they'll have medical facilities—she could survive, she could. And Cadan's not even hurt. And I didn't kill anyone, not really. It was Lin's mind overriding mine, it was the link. It wasn't me.*

Which was all true, but somehow didn't help at all.

Some half hour later, when the wounded had been taken away for patching up and the burning fuel reduced to smoking, oily inkblots on the sand, Cadan came over to her.

"Lissa? How're you doing?"

Really not good. But something held her lips closed. Loyalty—despite everything—to Lin? Or shame, for what Lin had forced her to do? *I've gone through this already! It wasn't me, it's not my fault.* But the thought had no force to it. It felt like a fiction, like an excuse.

"I'm okay."

He smiled at her. "As much as you can be, huh? Miguel's offered us dinner in the base, and Ivan's been carting a bunch of our prepacks across to their nutri-machines, so we needn't feel guilty about sharing their food. They've had to institute rationing, of course. But, so Miguel says, that's no different from the city."

"There's rationing in the *city*?"

Cadan had put his arm around her, and now he turned, bringing her with him as he moved toward the buildings. "Yeah. IPL declared official rationing in place two weeks ago."

"But that's *crazy*. It's hardly been longer than a month!"

"Yeah, I'm with you. When I think of the city as it was when we left, I can't believe they're anywhere near running out of food yet. I guess it's like Miguel says, the panic buying got out of control. Apparently, the public nutri-machines all got raided to restock people's private ones. So IPL instituted rationing, and now people are lining up for the sort of stuff our families used to get auto-delivered. Milk, you know? And dry mixes, and those curly-grain-vitamin things Bruce and I used to kick up such a stink about being made to eat?"

His tone was light, but Elissa couldn't get past what he was telling her. *Rationing.*

It made sense, sort of, if the panic buying had been really

crazy. But all the same, IPL doing that so soon . . . it was like forcing Sekoia fifty years into its past, making people relive the time when faulty terraforming had left their planet on the brink of environmental disaster.

People don't panic-buy unless they're frightened. So they were frightened to start with . . . and then IPL hit them with food rationing. Food *rationing, on Sekoia, with our history* . . . Hadn't IPL seen that doing that would make people even *more* frightened?

By the time they reached the entrance to the building, most other people, including the crew and—thank God—Lin, had disappeared inside it. Cadan slid open the first door they reached, using the emergency handle to drag the metal panel across rather than passing his hand over the sensor at its side. Elissa blinked at him, surprised, before she realized the tiny light that normally glowed above the sensor panel was dark. The sensor had been turned off.

As they went in through the door, Elissa instinctively braced herself against the usual blast of air-conditioning, but it didn't come. They walked into a corridor scarcely cooler than outside, and lit to a gray dimness by low-energy strip lights.

Cadan pushed through another door and they entered a dining area, all shiny steel and smooth white-surfaced tables. It looked like every dining area in every public-funded facility Elissa had ever seen, but at the same time there was something a little alien about it, as if the drink machines and nutri-machines were props, set dressing rather than part of a real room that people used.

Here, although the room was nearly as dim as the corridor, and was already filling with people, no electric lights had blinked on. *Aren't their sensors picking up that the room is occu-pied?* A scatter of sand fell from Cadan's boots and Elissa's shoes onto the floor, but no quick blast of suction from the vents at the base of the walls vacuumed it hygienically away. The room's auto-settings—light, hygiene, temperature con-trol—had been turned off.

And now Elissa caught on to the reason that, even before she'd noticed those things, it hadn't felt like a real room. The constant low-level hum she'd subconsciously expected to hear wasn't there. Tiny lights shone steadily from each of the nutri-machines ranged around the room, showing that the power wasn't off entirely, but the room settings—the set-tings of the whole building?—had been turned to their most economical. The refugee population was rationing energy as well as food. It made sense, of course, but it seemed so . . . drastic, a decision made in a world Elissa had never lived in and that she didn't recognize.

The crew of the *Phoenix* was sharing a table with Lin, Miguel, and some other people Elissa didn't know. There were a few places left free—one of them next to Lin. On Sanc-tuary, and on the flight back to Sekoia, that was something the crew had seemed to do without conscious thought—always leaving a space for Elissa and Lin to sit together. It was an allowance no one seemed to make for Cadan and Elissa, even though the whole crew knew they were dating—just for Elissa and Lin.

And even though, when she thought about it, it seemed weird that it even mattered, Elissa was usually glad to take the seat next to Lin. Doing so felt . . . right, as if it were somehow making up for the years they'd spent apart, when she hadn't even known Lin was real.

Right now, though, Elissa didn't want to so much as look at her sister. She went toward one of the places at the far end of the table, then realized abruptly she didn't want to sit at the same table, either. Not yet, not until her vision had stopped blurring with furious hurt at just the awareness that Lin was *there*.

She should be hungry. The rest of the crew was eating, and Cadan had gone straight to one of the nutri-machines. And when Elissa thought about it, she knew she *was* kind of hungry, but it was a vague sensation, like hearing a far-off noise. She didn't want to sit at the table, but nor could she face getting herself anything to eat just yet. She went to the nearest drinks machine instead of the nutri-machine where Cadan stood, and dialed herself a hot chocolate. When it was there, sugary-sweet, curling steam up into her face, she didn't want that, either. But the heat of the cup felt good in her hands, and at least it gave her something to focus on, something to stop her gaze sliding to where Lin sat. *How could you do that to me? How could you do that when I said no?*

Her fingers tightened on the cup. She looked past the table to where Cadan still stood at the nutri-machine, waiting for the dinner he'd dialed. She couldn't even *think* about Lin, not yet. And anyway, having gone through those horrible ten minutes of refusing to consider the possibility that Cadan might be dead, she could really do with a few minutes of being close to him instead. Close enough to remind herself he was alive. Safe, and alive, and in love with her.

She left the drinks machine and went toward him. She had to go past where Lin sat, eating her food—a bowl of long noodles and crispy protein. The scent of soy sauce, chili, and ginger, sticky-salt-and-sweet, came up to Elissa, and she couldn't help but be aware that as she went behind Lin's chair, Lin looked around at her, appeal and hurt showing in the way her head moved, the hunch of her shoulders. But Elissa still couldn't respond. Lin was doing better than she was, for God's sake. At least she could bring herself to *eat*.

Elissa went to stand beside Cadan. He glanced down and put his arm around her.

The machine hummed, tomato soup pouring into the cup waiting on the dispenser ledge. She leaned against him, smelling dust and burned rocket fuel, and, almost hidden underneath, the scent that was Cadan. When he tipped his head so his cheek brushed the side of her forehead, stubble scraped against her skin.

"I'm glad you're not dead," she said.

She felt him smile. "Trust me, me too." He took the full cup of soup from the dispenser and set it on top of the machine. The display blinked to let him know its next item was on its way: Baked Potato Cheese Meal. "Lissa?"

Even with her nose trying to close itself off from the burned scent that clung to him, there was a ton of comfort just being here with his arm around her. "Mm?"

"Thanks for not freaking out when I sent you all back to the ship. If you'd made a scene . . ."

"You'd have been completely distracted. And you might have ended up dead."

He laughed a little, quietly, into her hair. "I do most sincerely hope I'd have avoided being quite *that* distracted. But yeah, pretty much."

The platter containing Baked Potato Cheese Meal—a steaming, bland white mound that probably, Elissa thought, didn't retain even a cellular memory of being a real potato—slid out of the machine. Cadan disengaged his arm from Elissa and was digging a fork through it almost before he'd taken it off the tray. She had a sudden memory of him and Bruce as constantly starving fourteen-year-olds, hacking into the programming of the stove in her mother's kitchen so they could get it to produce unlimited amounts of pancakes. She hadn't seen Cadan eat like that since he'd finished growing a couple of years ago, but she guessed a high-stress fight like the one he'd just gone through burned a whole lot of extra calories, in fear and adrenaline if not actual physical work.

"Lis? You having anything?"

She screwed up her face. "I'm not trying to, like, *diet* or something. I just . . ." she reached over to scroll up and down the menu, her throat sticking at the idea of actually eating any of the options on it. "I keep thinking I'll be sick if I try. Although I guess, like you said once, electrokinesis does use up energy fast, so I really need to . . ."

Cadan swallowed a mouthful of potato so big Elissa had been vaguely surprised he could fit it on the fork. "That *was* you, then? Both of you?"

She scrolled back to the top of the menu before speaking. She'd assumed he knew. Somehow, having to tell him, having to admit to it, was worse than if he'd already guessed. "Yes."

"Okay." His voice didn't betray anything. He picked up his soup with his free hand, blew on it, and took a gulp.

Her insides cramped. She hadn't looked up at him and couldn't hear any emotion in his voice. But if he were feeling the same horror at what she'd done as she was . . . *If Lin has made Cadan look at me differently I will never forgive her, never, never, never. . . .* "You didn't know?"

"Well, I wasn't certain. It made sense, sure, but I've seen Lin do some pretty impressive things by herself, too. And . . . I guess . . . it seemed more like her style than yours?"

Elissa opened her mouth to reply, and realized that she was right on the edge of tears. She clamped her mouth shut, clenching her teeth so hard her jaw twitched. Hell. Hell and hell and *hell*. She had to get control of herself or she was going to cry. And she was *damned* if she was going to cry in front of everyone—in front of Lin, who'd done this to her. She lifted her cup to take a sip, needing to do something to distract herself, but her hand was shaking enough that a little of the hot liquid slopped over the edge, sploshing onto the floor.

"Lissa." Cadan put down his own cup and plate, and both his arms came around her, one hand steadying hers. "What is it? What's wrong?"

"I can't . . . ," she said, her voice a whisper, a thread holding back the tears. "I can't *talk* . . . not here . . ."

"That's no problem," said Cadan, and then somehow he'd gathered up her drink and his own food and, arm still around her, he was turning her away from the table, turning her so they wouldn't get a glimpse at her face, steering her toward the nearest door. "Markus," he threw over his shoulder, "Lissa and I need some fresh air. We'll be back in thirty minutes, okay?"

Over at the other side of the table, Ivan chuckled. "Fresh air is what you kids call it nowadays, is it?"

Cadan laughed, as if everything were normal, as if the worst thing going on was Ivan trying to embarrass him. "Keep your comments to yourself, would you? You've surely seen me go get some fresh air before Lissa came along?"

"Actually, Captain, that's something I'm glad I always managed to avoid," said Ivan, a world of suggestion in his tone, and Elissa heard several people break into laughter too as she and Cadan reached the door and he let go of her to slide it open.

"Jeez," he said, as it snapped shut behind them, and now there was embarrassment in his voice, "I should have known I was opening myself up to that one, huh?"

They went along another of the dim corridors, then out of the building to where floodlights poured over the sand, colorless, and so bright that Elissa's eyes stung momentarily.

Cadan set their sort-of meal down on the sand and dropped to sit beside it, picking his fork up from where it had been standing upright in his potato plate. He patted the ground beside him, and Elissa sat. She picked up her cup, then put it back on the sand and hugged her knees to her chest.

"Tell me," Cadan said.

Where she'd moved the cup, the edge of spilled chocolate on the bottom of it had left a semicircle of damp stickiness in the sand. She ran her finger along it, pushing the sand up to cover the sticky line. "It *was* both of us," she said.

"Yes."

"But I didn't want to. Lin"—she spread her hand, digging each fingertip under the sand, still warm from the heat of the day—"Lin made me."

She heard hesitation in Cadan's voice. "You mean, like when they were doing the procedures on her and she dragged you into going through them with her?"

"No." What Cadan was talking about—that had happened, and it had caused the pain and blackouts that had wrecked three years of Elissa's life. But she'd never blamed Lin for it—it had been involuntary, a terrified, automatic reaction to pain that the human body wasn't meant to bear.

"No, not like that. She . . ." Elissa swallowed. It should feel like a relief to be telling someone, but it didn't. It felt like revealing an awful, shameful secret. "She exploded that first ship herself, and then she was trying to do the same with the next one. But she couldn't, she was running out of strength. She asked me to help her. I mean, no, she didn't really ask, she put her hand out—I knew what she needed me to do."

She stopped, turned the cup around and around, screwing it into the sand. "I said no. I *couldn't*. I know they were attacking us, and I know it was pretty much self-defense, but I—I just . . ."

"It's okay," came Cadan's voice above her bent head. "It's not a little thing, to kill someone, even if it is self-defense."

She hadn't known if he'd understand. Tears burned in her eyes and she blinked them away. "So I couldn't. I said no. I said sorry. And she"—all at once, it was as if a huge fist closed on her insides, making her belly burn and tighten—"she said *she* was sorry too. And then she grabbed me, she wouldn't let me go. She forced the link, and then she used me to help her explode the second ship." Within her, everything cramped, the huge fist clenching tight. "I felt it happen. I felt what she was feeling—the triumph. And now—"

She rose to her knees, shaking all over, her voice cracking. "Now it's in *my* freaking memory! Now *I* know what it's like to kill someone! Even though I wasn't the one who intended it, I wasn't the one who did it. I don't *want* that memory in my head!"

"No," said Cadan, a single syllable, very calm.

Now that the words had come, they wouldn't stop. Elissa

knelt in front of him, still shaking, words falling over one another and tangling together, gesturing with wide jerky movements, punctuation to words that by themselves would never be enough to convey what she needed him to understand.

"It's not like she doesn't know! I said, way back, I'm not *okay* with killing people. I get, I *get* how if it's self-defense, that sometimes someone might have to do it. But I said *no*. I told her I couldn't. It wasn't like she panicked and didn't realize—it wasn't like how she used to reach out to me when she was in tons of pain and she was too desperate to know what she was doing. I said *no*. I said no, and she *knew* I was saying it, she *knew*. She said sorry and then she *did it anyway!*"

She threw her hands out, fury pouring through every nerve, so fiercely that it felt as if her fingers would throw sparks as she moved. "That's not sorry! It's not sorry if you do it *anyway*! It doesn't freaking *count!*"

"I know."

"And what if she does it again? If I can't trust her, if she—" She broke off. She dropped her hands to her lap, fingers winding tight around one another. "I don't want to be scared of her, Cadan. I was, to begin with, but I haven't been for ages. I got so I was sure I could trust her—I knew she wouldn't hurt me on purpose. But this time . . . she did hurt me. On purpose. And I . . ." This time her voice trailed off before she got herself together and carried on.

"I went through everything to keep her as my sister. When I thought she was going to die, when she was going to put the *Phoenix* into hyperspeed by herself—I knew what it would be like to lose her, I knew if she died it would . . . like, leave me hollow. I knew I wouldn't be a whole person ever again.

But, oh God, if this is the sort of thing she's going to do . . . how can I live with it?"

She ran out of words, finally, and as if it had been just their energy holding her up, she felt herself fold, her head dropping so her ponytail flopped forward, brushing past the side of her face to hang into her lap.

Cadan didn't speak.

After a minute Elissa slanted a look up at him. "Say something helpful."

A smile touched his mouth. "Lis . . . God, like I have a clue how to manage this kind of thing? She . . . Lin doesn't react like ordinary people, you know that."

"Yeah. But this—it's so beyond the usual 'not ordinary' you have to get used to with her. This is *my mind*, and she just . . ."

"Reached into it. I get you." Cadan laid the fork carefully along the middle of the scraped-clean plate, then began to roll the plate up around it, activating the process that made the cellular structure of both plate and fork collapse, pushing the air out from between each cell so that it became a pencil-slim cylinder, ready for disposal.

"Do you think she sees it like that, though? Like your mind and hers, totally separate?" He glanced down at the quill of compressed material in his hand. "I mean, if she sees it as one structure, and you see it as still a plate and a fork, all separate . . ."

His eyes met hers, and a trace of self-consciousness slid over his expression. "Okay, so that's not the neatest analogy."

"It makes sense, though. Kind of. But she *did* know it was wrong—she said *sorry*."

"Well, it's not like I think she didn't *know* it would piss you off. But, you know, if you and I were living in a halfway normal world, if we were dating like normal people, I'd say *sorry* if I knew I was going to break a date. But it wouldn't be the same sort of sorry I'd say if I was—" He broke off. "Okay, this is definitely not a good analogy. I was going to say if I was going to cheat on you, but I wouldn't cheat on you, so I wouldn't need to say sorry in the first place." A flush spread across his face. "Yeah, I'm saying this all wrong. I think I'll stop."

Elissa's stomach did a little flip. It wasn't often that Cadan looked vulnerable—he was pretty good at being Mr. Calm-and-in-Charge whatever the situation. "I get your point," she said, the corners of her mouth curling upward as her eyes met his.

"Jeez, well, I'm glad *you* do."

The sand was becoming cold as the heat of the day withdrew from it. Elissa shifted position, moving to her knees, pulling her hoodie around her so she could zip it up. "So, to Lin, doing that might have been breaking-a-date sorry, but to *me* it was saying sorry and then . . ."

She dragged the hoodie closer still, tugged the zipper right up to her neck. "And all the same . . . Cadan, it's still kind of terrifying. If she really thinks of us—me and her—as, like, one mind that's just sort of split into two halves . . . it gives her the right to do *anything*—"

"She's like a child, though, isn't she? In some ways, at least. She has to be taught things. I mean"—he laughed—"don't think I haven't noticed you teaching her just plain good manners."

Elissa found herself laughing too, leaning against him as he moved so he could put his arm around her again. Whereas her skin was cold, his was still warm, and under his sleeve his arm was warm too.

She's like a child. . . . If all Lin's abilities had made Cadan value her more than he did Elissa, he wouldn't talk about her like that, would he? *Okay*, so it was petty to even be thinking about that now, with so many bigger issues to worry about, but all the same . . .

"Yeah, I *do* do that," she said. "I mean, I feel like I'm nagging her or something, but I just think, if you're going to live on this planet—or on any planet where that kind of thing matters—you have to *learn*, right? Otherwise you're always going to stand out as the weird one. And if some people struggle with even seeing you as *human* . . ."

"No, I'm with you. I get it."

The crook of his neck, where his collar ended, before the roughness of evening stubble began, was warm and smooth—and *didn't* smell of burned fuel. Elissa turned her face into it, breathing him in. "You think it's just another thing she needs to learn—another thing she *will* learn, if I explain it to her?"

"I do. You're too important to her for her *not* to learn."

"Okay." For the first time in hours her chest relaxed, her hands naturally unclenched themselves. Thinking of it as Lin deliberately stamping all over Elissa's rights and feelings was so much worse than thinking of it as Lin genuinely not getting why it mattered.

"I guess we should go back," she said. "You said thirty minutes. . . ."

"And they're not up yet." She felt his cheek move as he smiled. "And see how romantic it is out here with the carcasses of flyers lying all over the place."

"Oh, completely romantic." She thought back to what he'd said, his messed-up analogy of a few minutes ago. "Cadan, if we *had* started dating when everything was normal, where would we have gone out to? Like, for our first date?"

"Hm." He shifted, his arm loosening where he held her, then tightening again. "On the base, the guys with girl-friends . . . well, the ones without inherited membership of the Skyline Club, 'cause obviously if they had that, they went *there* . . . there was an entertainment complex a few minutes away. Cinemas . . . that underwater restaurant . . . oh, and those gardens that only open at night, the Starlit Park?"

"Oh, I've heard of it." She leaned against him, shutting her eyes, enjoying the idea of what they could have had, if they hadn't gotten their wires crossed a million times, if he hadn't thought she was spoiled and she hadn't thought he was arrogant. . . .

She hadn't really dated at school. The pain and visions had taken over her life, making her popularity dwindle, marking her as weird. But if Cadan had known what was going on, *he* would have understood. She'd been a whole lot weirder when she'd come on board the *Phoenix*, after all—running from the police, desperate to rescue the Spare sister neither of them had known she had. And if that hadn't put him off . . .

"Would you have taken me on your skybike?" she asked. "Or would we have borrowed one of our parents' beetle-cars?"

Cadan laughed. "Would you have *gone* on my skybike?"

"I might have."

"Oh, come on." He was still laughing, bending his head to drop a kiss on her hair. "I just can't stretch that far. Your mother would *never* have let you."

The alternate world taking shape in her mind fell apart, too insubstantial to cope with the touch of reality.

She felt her shoulders hunch, drawing her into herself,

away from him. Had he really needed to say that? Couldn't he have let them spin out the fantasy a little longer?

"Hey," he said. "I'm sorry. The thing is . . . I can't even really imagine us starting to date back then. And trying to picture the specifics . . . my brain just won't let me leap that far."

Something tightened inside Elissa. She swallowed. "You're saying . . . if it wasn't for everything that's happened, we'd never have—never gotten together at all?"

"No. I guess . . . I'm just saying I don't know. It's difficult to imagine how we would, don't you think?"

"No," she said, hearing a mulish note in the word that reminded her suddenly of Lin. "When we spent any real time together, when we got to know each other, it took hardly *any* time—why couldn't it have done the same back then?"

Reticence threaded through Cadan's voice. "Well, that's why, isn't it? We *weren't* spending any real time together. It wasn't until we saw each other out of context that we were able to get to know each other. How would we have done that with me training and you dealing with—with everything you were dealing with?"

"Okay, what if I *hadn't* been dealing with that? What if I'd never got the visions and stuff?"

"Lis . . ." He pulled her around enough so he could look into her face. "Come on. That's a whole alternate universe you're asking about. How do I know? And why does it matter? Like you said, the minute I did get to know you, I fell." A little smile curled the corner of his mouth, crept into his eyes. "So hard it took my breath away. Isn't that enough?"

Elissa flushed all over, a sudden shiver like electricity dissolving the tightness within her. "Yes," she said.

Cadan bent his head to hers, that little smile still warming his eyes. When he kissed her, she lost her own breath. And it didn't matter what would have happened in an alternate universe, or even in a universe with a slightly different order to events. What mattered was that he'd fallen for her now.

But when their thirty minutes were up, and Cadan pulled her to her feet, tucking the hair that had come loose when he ran his hand into it back behind her ears, when they went back toward the building, still the question nagged at the back of Elissa's mind.

If her life hadn't changed so catastrophically, if she and Cadan hadn't been basically forced to work together, would they have just continued as they always had, their paths only crossing enough to annoy each other?

As far as I was concerned, I was in love with him when I was thirteen. Okay, it wasn't the same as it is now, but it was still something. For him, it never happened till we were thrown together. If it hadn't been for that, would he ever have looked at me and seen what he does now? Ever? Ever?

By the door to the building, Cadan paused to look down at Elissa. "You don't have to come see everyone again. We'll be sleeping back on the ship anyway. If you want to just go there now, not deal with anything else tonight . . . ?"

The suggestion brought a wave of relief so intense she felt her shoulders slump. It wasn't kind, leaving Lin hanging on longer, wretched because Elissa was angry with her, but . . . *ugh, I just can't do any more big conversations. If I can just go get some time by myself, maybe go to bed without having to see her again tonight, I'll wake up with more patience—I'll be able to explain it properly.*

It was an excuse. She knew it really, at the back of her mind. It wasn't about explaining it properly—it was about not having to explain it *now*.

She didn't care. She shut off the thought of Lin's face the way it had looked when Elissa walked past her at the dining table, the confusion and distress in her twin's eyes, the knowledge that—as Cadan had said—Lin was in some ways like a child, and a child needed teaching.

She glanced up at Cadan. "I *could* do without Ivan's comments."

He gave a wry smile. "Yeah, I'm sorry about that." A spark of amusement lit his eyes. "Hey, we should be glad we *didn't* start dating back when life was normal. If Ivan is bad, can you imagine what Bruce would have been like?"

She managed a smile. "Oh please, I don't *want* to imagine." As he turned to walk over to where the *Phoenix* lay, she was glad he wasn't watching her expression, glad he didn't see the hastily manufactured smile fade. It was stupid to feel the words like a careless touch on sore skin, stupid to let them wake the shrill insecurity she'd managed to suppress. *He loves me* now. *What does it* matter *what would have happened if everything were different?*

She took a step after him, and again the guilt came, the drag back toward where she knew Lin waited, confused and hurt. She pushed it away. *It's not like I'm never going to deal with it. I'm just going to deal with it later.*

Behind her, metal rasped on metal as the door slid open. Lin's voice sounded from inside the corridor, shaky with tears. "Lissa?"

Oh. So, after all, she was going to have to deal with it now.

FIVE

ELISSA TURNED around. Lin stood just inside the doorway, her toes lined up where the edge of concrete met the sand, as if she couldn't step outside without Elissa's invitation. She was shivering, her arms wrapped around herself, her lips bloodless.

"I'm sorry," she said before Elissa could speak. "I'm sorry for what I did, I'm sorry I made you angry, I'm sorry I made you not want to talk to me." Her words fell over one another, shaking as much as she was shaking. "I don't know how to make it okay, I don't know what to do, but if you tell me I'll do it. I'll fix it. I'll make it better. Please stop being angry. Please tell me what I have to do."

For a minute they stared at each other. For a minute everything—the hot metallic smell of fuel residue, the gritty breath of the wind, the floodlights that cut the night into harsh-edged shadows—combined to tip Elissa into a sensation of déjà vu so intense it was like flashing back to the moment she'd first met Lin.

That had been like this too—this beyond-strange feeling of staring into a face that was at once entirely familiar and utterly alien. *I know you, but I don't. I don't understand what you are, how you think, why you're here. . . .*

There were tears in Lin's eyes, unshed, a gleam in the harsh, colorless lights.

The moment broke. Elissa wasn't looking at a weirdly alien-familiar face. She was looking at her sister, her twin, someone whom she might not understand, but whom she knew, whom she loved.

"It's okay," she said, and with the words, with the deliberate step away from anger, the remorse she'd been trying not to feel rushed over her. *I shouldn't have left her like that, not understanding why, not knowing if I'd ever speak to her again. A few minutes, while I got myself together, was okay—that was fair. But leaving her for all this time, that was just cruel. And I knew it was. I knew and I wouldn't listen.*

Lin was shaking her head, all vehemence and panic. "It's not okay. You're angry and you won't talk and I don't know how to fix it. But I will, Lissa, I *will* fix it if you tell me—"

"Lin, it is okay. I'm talking to you. I'm sorry I didn't before. I know you don't understand."

In the corner of her vision as she spoke, Cadan was moving quietly, tactfully away into the shadows along the building. A few seconds more and a farther door clunked shut.

"I won't do it again," Lin said. "I won't use my power like that, I won't make you help me—"

"Lin, listen. I was going to explain—"

Lin shook her head again. "You don't have to explain. I'll

just promise. I'll just promise not to do it—"

"Do what? What are you promising not to do?"

"Any of it. All of it. Anything that makes you angry—"

"Lin, come on. You can't promise if you don't understand exactly what it was." Elissa caught back a sigh before her sister heard it. This—Lin promising not to do something almost in the same breath as she admitted she didn't know what she'd done—it would be funny if it weren't so awful. The thought came, as it had before: *No one should matter that much to someone.*

"It was you using the link," she said. "I don't blame you for attacking the ships yourself—I'm not angry about that. It was you using the link, making me attack the ships with you, when I'd said I didn't want to. You need to not do that again. Like, ever."

"Okay. Okay. I won't." Lin's words tumbled over the end of Elissa's sentence. "I won't do it again."

"I don't know if I can even explain why it matters so much. . . ."

"You don't have to—"

"No, I'm going to, I just can't think of how right now."

Lin shook her head. "You don't need to. I won't. I won't do it again. I didn't know it would make you so angry. I know now. I won't do it again."

Elissa suppressed another sigh. It would be easier to just leave it at that, to avoid tangling herself up in explanations and analogies that would never quite fit. But she couldn't. Partly because if Lin didn't grasp *why* she shouldn't, Elissa couldn't be sure that, under stress, she wouldn't do exactly the same thing again. Partly . . . oh, it just wasn't fair to ask Lin to do things if she didn't know why. It wasn't fair to get her to obey rules that—to her—seemed arbitrary, out of nothing but fear of making Elissa angry. Lin might sometimes seem like a child, but she wasn't one, and it wasn't fair to treat her as if she were.

Elissa took a breath, thinking of how to get Lin to relate, thinking of the right words. "I *want* to explain," she said. "Listen, you know how you feel about being, like, held down—controlled?"

Every one of Lin's muscles seemed to tighten. "Yes," she said.

"That's kind of what I feel about you linking us when I said not to."

Lin's head snapped up. "No you *don't*. That's *not* how it was! You *don't* feel that!"

Anger flashed over Elissa, heating her hands, her face. *Don't you tell me how I feel!*

She set her teeth against showing it, forced it down. "I know that's not how it was. I *know* what they did to you was so much worse. I'm saying, it's—*kind of*—how it *felt*. To me."

Lin's face was uncomprehending, her eyes confused. "But it can't have. Those people—I hated them. I would never have let them touch me if I'd had the choice. You—you don't hate me." Her voice quavered suddenly.

Even through the anger she was still fighting not to show, Elissa couldn't bear to leave Lin unreassured. "Of course I don't hate you. Lin, I'm not saying you're *like* them—"

"And I've linked to you a million times, and it never made you angry before. Not even when it hurt you."

"Yeah, I know. That's why I'm saying I know it wasn't the same—you weren't acting the way they did. But it's *how I felt*."

"Even though"—Lin shook her head as if trying to shake the

words into a pattern that made sense—"it's so much *smaller*?
Even though it was just once, and it was to help us, and—"

"*Yes.*" The anger Elissa was trying to keep back escaped
into her voice, giving it a broken-glass edge. "It doesn't feel
so much smaller to me."

"Okay." Lin frowned. Her eyes met Elissa's. "I don't get it.
I'm sorry. I get that it matters to you, though, and like I said,
I don't want you to be angry. I'll try."

"No. Not *you'll try*. That's like me saying that I'll try . . . oh,
I don't know . . . that I'll try to not to drop a nutri-machine
on your head."

Their eyes met. Lin's lips curled upward at the corners
before she forced them back to a somber expression. Elissa's
own lips twitched.

"No 'trying,'" she said. "Just *no*. Just you won't do it."

"I'll—" Lin broke off, then nodded. "Okay. I won't do it."

"Promise?"

"Yes. Yes. I promise."

"Thank you," said Elissa. Inside, she was still a jumble
of residual anger and pain—and a horrible, out-of-control
feeling that nothing in her life was quite working how she
wanted it to—but, faced now with the need and vulnerability
on her twin's face, the only thing she could do was push it all
aside, let it wait for later when she could deal with it. "And
Lin, listen, I shouldn't have—"

She broke off. Lin wasn't listening. Or at least she wasn't
listening to Elissa. She'd tilted her face upward, the floodlights slicking the residue of tears on her cheekbones with a
pale gleam. "A flyer," she said.

Elissa was dragging open the door of the building before
she knew she was moving. *Not again. They can't be coming back*

so soon. Lin just promised . . . but I don't know, I can't trust that she won't crack under that pressure again. . . .

The door stuck. Elissa dug her heels into the soft sand and wrenched sideways at it, and it came free. Then she was running back down the corridor, Lin at her heels.

The door to the dining area opened more smoothly, free from drifting grains of sand creeping into its mechanism, and they shot into the room. Faces turned, the sound of conversation died.

"What is it?" The question came in several different voices, each one charged with urgency, but it was Cadan whom Elissa answered.

"A flyer." If they'd been in private, she'd have added *Lin says so*, but not within earshot of everybody, not without knowing how they'd react to hearing that someone with electrokinesis was among them.

All over the dining area, people surged to their feet, grabbing up food platters and half-full cups, making for the exits that were marked with green emergency arrows.

Cadan was halfway across the room. "The ship. Both of you, get to the ship. Felicia, Markus—"

Lin interrupted. "It's not attacking."

"How do you know?" Although Cadan spoke sharply, he dropped his voice so his words didn't reach beyond the twins. "Lin, is it armed?"

"It has firepower, but it's not . . ." Lin automatically lowered her voice to the level Cadan had used, screwing up her eyes as she tried to explain. "It's not . . . it's not active. I don't know if they use codes like us, but . . . whatever they use, they haven't."

Cadan frowned for a second, making sense of the confused

sentence. "You're saying it's not a danger to us?"

"I don't know *that*," said Lin, sounding indignant, forgetting to keep her voice low. "It might be a danger. All I know is—"

"That it's not going to be firing on us?" Cadan sounded as if he were fighting with both irritation and amusement. "That's fine, that's all I—"

But now Miguel interrupted him. He'd been one of the people—like those in pilot uniforms, Elissa noticed now—who hadn't fled the room. He'd pulled a handheld out of his pocket instead, unfolded it to four times its size, and had been scanning it, his head tipped sideways to catch the signals—messages?—coming through the earpiece he wore. But he'd obviously still picked up on what Cadan and Lin were saying.

"She's right," he said. His voice was blank, and as he raised his head from the handheld screen, his gaze rested on Lin with incredulity. "What the SFI were using them for . . . what people have been saying since . . . we knew there must be some kind of psychic energy. But . . . that? Is *that* what she can do—read electronic information?"

Cadan's eyes, full of sudden rueful amusement, met Elissa's. *One of the things she can do.* The words hovered, unspoken. "Yes," Cadan said.

Miguel gave him a sharp glance. "And the other Spares?"

"I don't know." A pause. Cadan spread his hands. "Genuinely. I don't."

After a moment Miguel nodded, accepting it . . . or choosing to let it go. "Anyway," he said, "she's right. It's okay. They're sending us their signal. It's IPL."

When Elissa and Lin got outside, the flyer was just coming

into view. The cloud cover had cleared since earlier, and the flyer was a dark shape against the stars, tipped with light at the end of its wings, its tail. It described a huge lazy circle overhead, curving down, filling the night with the sound of its engines, and, almost before Elissa had grasped that it had come—that *they* had come—it had touched neatly down on the landing space at the far end of the base. For a moment it stayed in the position in which it had landed, belly down, wings out, not much different from an airplane in miniature, then its nose lifted and the whole ship tipped up until it was angled toward the sky, ready for instant take off.

Elissa had seen official IPL craft back on Sanctuary—both the ships built for spaceflight and the flyers for use within planetary atmospheres—but she hadn't seen that particular mechanism in action before. She glimpsed Markus's approving, lifted eyebrows, and the appreciative smile curling one corner of Cadan's mouth.

She did recognize the sleek, distinctive shape, and the broad white stripe that ran over nose, wings, and tail, reflecting brilliantly in the floodlights that came from the base. IPL's aircraft had been modeled, so people said, after a type of bird, long extinct, its name forgotten, one of the species that hadn't survived the emigration from Old Earth. A bird that had, apparently, once served as a symbol of peace.

The symbol might have had more power, thought Elissa—a random, out-of-nowhere thought—if it weren't for the guns that edged each side of the ship's underbelly. But she wasn't stupid enough to think peace could come without firepower. And in the place Sekoia had become, and with people intent on hurting her and Lin and Cadan and the crew, she couldn't pretend that the sight of all that weaponry—all that *protection*—didn't send relief flooding through her.

Now the crew of the *Phoenix* could be absorbed into the larger structure of IPL. They'd share their security, be directed to the places where they could actually *help*, not just be thrown into reacting as they had today.

We're not ready to be solo heroes. At least, I'm not, and Lin can't be allowed to try.

Under the wing of the flyer, the edges of a doorway opened in what had looked like an unbroken silver-colored surface. Two armed officials—their identical white uniforms and close-fitting helmets meant that Elissa couldn't tell if they were men or women—jumped out and came to attention on either side of the doorway. A smaller—much smaller—figure followed them.

From behind Elissa, the handheld that Miguel must have brought out with him beeped, a peremptory sound. Elissa turned her head in time to see him tap it in order to accept the call.

A voice came through, very clear. "IPL flyer *Savior*, licensed for active duty on Sekoia, calling former SFI property eighteen-forty-twenty-two. Do you read me?"

"Reading you," said Miguel. His voice was flat. *What must it be like, to have been abandoned out here, fending off harassment and attack, afraid all the time that this might be the one that destroys your power or water sources, and then, the moment we arrive, IPL swoops in?*

The voice repeated a string of letters and numbers that Elissa recognized as having the pattern of a security code. "Do we have a match, eighteen-forty-twenty-two?"

Miguel took a moment to answer, his gaze moving over the handheld. He raised his head. "All matched up."

"Cadan David Greythorn, please take the handheld and step forward until you're at least three feet clear of all other persons."

Cadan obeyed, head up so he could look straight across to where the figures stood by their craft.

"Please enter the first six digits of your ID number into the handheld." A pause while Cadan did that, too. "The last six digits of your ID number will now appear briefly on the handheld. Please confirm if they're correct."

"They are correct." A whine of sudden interference obscured his words, and a series of fuzzy lines chased one another across the screen.

"Would you repeat that, please?"

Cadan said the words again.

"Confirmed. Please step back. Markus Baer, please take the handheld and step forward until you're at least three feet clear of all other persons."

They went through the procedure five more times, for the crew members and for Elissa and Lin. Lin, of course, had no ID number, but instead they requested a thumbprint and that she read a short paragraph that appeared on the screen, and the combination of the two identifiers seemed satisfactory, because as soon as they'd confirmed her identity, the six of them were invited to step across to the flyer.

Despite the two-way security checks—their ID details were no longer available to anyone but approved IPL officials, and as far as Elissa could remember, IPL security had *never* been hacked—tension climbed her spine to settle between her shoulder blades as they walked the short distance across the desert.

She had to brush past a broken sheet of metal waiting

for more thorough cleanup tomorrow, and its jagged edge caught the hem of her pants leg, making her trip as the material first caught, then tore.

Lin stopped, and Cadan put a hand out as she regained her balance. "You okay?"

"Yeah." Her face heated in embarrassment at her clumsiness. She bent and tucked the trailing edge up inside the hem of the pants. When she stood, Cadan was waiting. His eyes crinkled infinitesimally in a tiny smile meant just for her before he turned to catch up with Ivan and Felicia, who were walking ahead.

After a couple of seconds, Elissa realized something she hadn't noticed before: She and Lin were walking in time, legs moving in the same synchronized stride. *Well, it makes sense— our legs are exactly the same length, after all.* But it didn't feel as if that were all it was. It felt more as if Lin were connected to her by something invisible. As if, if she were to stumble again, Lin would stumble too.

Felicia stepped sideways to skirt a patch of slickly shining fuel, and Lin had to slow down for a moment so as not to collide with her. The rhythm broke. They weren't two weird halves of a single entity; they were just identical twin sisters with the same length legs and the same pelvic-bone shape and the same length stride.

But all the same, when they came under the shadow of the *Savior*, and Elissa heard Lin's breath catch in a little nervous sound, she automatically put out her hand and, without needing to look, took Lin's.

The three officials were waiting by the still-open door.

Now that Elissa was near enough, she could see that the two who'd gotten out first were both men. The smallest figure was a woman, a very slight woman, several years older than Elissa's parents, with gray hair cropped so short it was nearly hidden by her helmet. When she spoke, Elissa recognized the voice that had come through the handheld—and realized with a slight shock that the command in it had taken all her attention, leaving her, until this moment, not even registering the gender of the person speaking.

The voice had been cool, and the woman's eyes were cool too, her jaw a little set.

"Captain Greythorn?" She held out a hand. "IPL Commander Dacre."

As Cadan shook her hand, her gaze flicked past his shoulder, took in the crew—and stopped at Elissa and Lin. Cadan was starting to say something, but she spoke over him.

"I thought we'd find out we were mistaken."

Cadan broke off. "Mistaken?" He followed her gaze, and as he realized who she was looking at, his face went a little stiff. "Commander—"

She didn't let him finish. "Perhaps it would be more accurate to say I *hoped* we'd find out we were mistaken. But no, the case is exactly what, when we picked up your ship entering the atmosphere, we hoped it would not be. You have returned to Sekoia with one of the former Spares we're fighting to relocate—with the one, moreover, who precipitated the whole situation."

From where Elissa stood, her hand clamped in Lin's, she could see Cadan's back stiffen. "Commander Dacre, Lin has been given full human status. This is her home planet—she's free to—"

"Free to return? Yes, thank you, Captain, I'm aware of the legal situation." The commander's eyes flicked over Lin again.

"She's also free to visit any number of planets that do not adhere to the Interplanetary Charter, that have no laws on human rights or where slavery and forced prostitution are legal and unchecked. She would, however, be well advised not to take her life in her hands by doing so." The commander looked back at Cadan. "As she—and her sister—have done by coming here. And as you have permitted by bringing them."

Next to Elissa, Lin gave an indignant quiver. Elissa dug her nails into her twin's hand—*Lin, don't, you'll just make it worse*—but she'd reacted too late.

"He didn't *permit* us!" Lin said. "We *chose* to come."

The commander glanced at her. "Unless you can fly a spaceship, he most assuredly did permit you."

Lin let go of Elissa's hand and folded her arms, defiance in every angle of her body. "Well, I *nearly* can. If he hadn't taken us, I'd have just had to wait a bit longer till I learned myself—"

"Lin," said Cadan, his voice exasperated, "for the hundredth *time*—"

But the commander's attention had already snapped back to him. "You've been *teaching her to fly your ship?*"

There was a world of condemnation in her tone. Cadan flushed. "Yes. Commander, she's preternaturally fast at picking up that kind of thing. And I've been strictly supervising her—it hasn't been a risk to the safety of the crew at all—"

"Good God." Commander Dacre sounded as if she hadn't heard him, as if she were speaking to herself. "And to think we were given to believe that SFI pilots were well trained."

Cadan's flush deepened. He didn't say anything else.

Sympathy, and outrage at how the commander was treating him, prickled all over Elissa's body. She'd thought anyone with IPL would be . . . respectful, kind, in the way the officials back on Sanctuary had been when she and Lin turned up, exhausted fugitives from their own planet's authorities.

"Are you aware that they're being killed here?" The commander directed the question to Cadan. "Spares and their twins?"

Elissa's back stiffened. Her chin went up. *She's trying to scare us—or trying to make Cadan feel bad. And, yeah, she's succeeding, but she doesn't need to know that she is.* "Yes," she said before Cadan could. "We heard about the attacks."

The commander eyed her, her expression chilly. "Did you also hear about the abduction attempts?"

Abduction attempts? For a second the world stopped turning. There was nothing except those words hanging in the air.

"What?" Elissa said.

What might have been a glimmer of satisfaction showed in the commander's eyes. "Not all the citizens of your planet want Spares to be relocated or wiped out. Some of them appear to feel that Sekoia's space force was the only thing standing between Sekoia and chaos. So, declared-legal humans or not, Spares are a resource they can't afford not to"—a tiny hesitation before she said the word—"use."

A blaze of shock and fury like fire shook Elissa from her knees to the top of her head. "*Use?* What the hell does that mean? What do they mean, *use?*"

The commander met her eyes. "You've lost your space force. What do you think they mean?"

"It's been ruled *illegal!* Doing that—what SFI did—it's what's made IPL take over the government! They can't be trying to do it all over again!"

"It has been ruled illegal, yes. But according to our sources, there's at least one group who'd like to challenge that ruling."

Cold swept over Elissa, as swift as the fire. Her knees went weak, and she took a step back as if the ground had given way beneath her. "No," she said, and all the strength was gone from her voice. "No. They said it was *illegal*. They said she'd be safe. We have *compensation money*."

Next to her, Lin had gone rigid. *"No,"* Elissa said again, speaking this time to her sister. "They can't change it, Lin. They gave you refugee status. They said you were human. They *can't—*"

"Lissa." Cadan's voice was steady, and it seemed to hold her, as if it were keeping her from falling apart. "People challenge rulings all the time. It doesn't mean anything. It won't get them anywhere."

She looked up at him, aware she was having to force herself to move, as if every cell in her body had frozen with shock. "But how *can* they? How can anyone know what SFI did to the Spares and think it's okay? How can they think about doing it again? And if they're abducting them . . ." *If they're trying to do that now, and I brought Lin back here . . .* She reached out without looking, without needing to look, and her hand met Lin's, cold fingers against cold fingers.

"Trying to abduct them," said Cadan. "Abduction *attempts*, that's all. They haven't succeeded. And people who've formed a pressure group are very different from people who are willing to act so far outside the law that they're making abduction attempts. It doesn't mean they're all working with the same agenda, Lis."

His eyes were as steady as his voice.

"You're making a bit of an assumption there, Captain," said Commander Dacre.

Cadan turned his head to meet her eyes. "So, it seems, is IPL."

For a second, silence hung between them, then the commander moved away, back toward her ship. "You'll need to come to the nearest IPL command center so we can do what we can to sort this out."

"Look, Commander"—although Cadan's voice remained steady, Elissa could hear an undercurrent that meant he was having to make an effort to keep it so—"this base, it's full of refugees. It's been attacked seven times already. I know IPL has a list of priorities, but these people are still in danger—"

The commander gave him the briefest of looks over her shoulder. "Thank you, Captain, I'm well aware of the situation. How fast can you prepare one of your shuttlecraft to follow us to the city?"

For a moment Elissa thought Cadan would try arguing further, but he said only, "It can be ready in ten minutes."

"And your ship can be left secure?"

"Yes."

"Go and do it, then. I'll send you the flight coordinates. You'll be required to follow them precisely so you can shadow us from takeoff to landing." She stepped into the ship, using a grab handle to pull herself briskly up into the doorway.

Her voice had assumed automatic compliance; she didn't even look around to check that Cadan was moving to obey.

He cleared his throat. "Commander, the *Phoenix*—my ship—it's a lot more useful than the shuttlebug. If it's possible to bring that instead—"

Now she did look around, her face coldly disapproving. "Captain Greythorn, I'd like nothing more than to send you *and* your ship immediately off-planet. However, I'm constrained by strict IPL policy. You've brought two under-age passengers with you—one of them a Spare—and whatever *you* intend to do with them, right now they have to come to the nearest command center. Which is in Central Canyon City. You may have noticed there's a citywide no-fly order, from which only IPL craft are exempt. Your shuttlecraft is small enough that I can get clearance for it as long as it accompanies the *Savior*. If you don't use that and come with me now, you don't get there."

She turned away, again not waiting to see whether they were obeying her.

SIXTY-SIX

THEY WENT on board the *Phoenix* and made their way to the dock where *Shuttlebug Two* waited.

In Elissa's hand, Lin's was still like ice. And there seemed to be ice throughout Elissa's body, too. Hearing that Spares were being attacked, killed, had been bad enough, but knowing that someone, some awful, conscienceless group, wanted to put them back to being *used* was so horrific she didn't even know how to think about it.

I never thought of that. I knew we'd be coming back to danger, but not that kind of danger. I was so stupid.

Given this new threat, it seemed like a terrible mistake to be leaving the *Phoenix* behind. The reason for doing it made sense—they'd come here to work with IPL, they wouldn't gain anything from refusing to cooperate with how they wanted them to travel around the planet. But the *Phoenix* had become her and Lin's home. In this crazy new Sekoia, where people did things that showed their previous behavior had been nothing but a facade of civilization, the ship seemed like the only place of real safety, the only thing that represented—if necessary—escape.

Cadan tapped in the unlock codes at the shuttlebug dock entrance, and the doors slid back with a hush of displaced air. They filed through two independently operating air locks, then into the low-ceilinged shuttlebug. Leaving Felicia and Markus to seal the air lock that belonged to the shuttlebug itself—the *Phoenix*'s air lock was set to seal itself a certain time after it had been used—Cadan went straight up the narrow center aisle to the pilot's seat and began to activate the controls.

Elissa eased her hand from Lin's and fastened herself into one of the twenty passenger seats that stood either side of the aisle, cold hands fumbling at the straps. Next to her, Lin, as she always did, was managing better, although from the look on her face, she was operating on autopilot.

Elissa reached out to her as soon as she'd strapped herself in. "Lin, it's okay. We're with IPL now. We're safe."

Lin's face, shocked, blank, turned to hers. "We're not safe anywhere." Her voice was a whisper. "People are trying to take us back to the facilities."

"Not necessarily. Like Cadan said—"

Lin gave a little, helpless shrug. "How does Cadan know?"

"Lin . . ." But there was nothing she could say. She closed her hand tightly around her sister's, willing Lin's fingers to warm through, to relax. They'd been through much worse than this, had gotten through danger far more immediate. And now they were under IPL's protection, being taken to one of IPL's command centers, probably as safe as it was possible to be anywhere on the planet.

Oh God, though, it's not enough. We both chose to come back, we both wanted to, but was I completely wrong to agree?

The shuttlebug's engines woke with a low roar that vibrated up through the floor, tickling the soles of Elissa's feet. The shutters across the windscreen slid back onto the dark desert and the star-pierced sky, the bulk of the *Phoenix* blocking out all but an edge of the light coming from the base.

From a small com-screen at Cadan's elbow, numbers flickered, tiny sparks of bright gold. Cadan double-tapped them and they stopped flickering, freezing in place. He moved his hand to his main screen, tapped with three fingers, and the numbers appeared there, to blink red for a second before they cycled through orange, amber, gold, finally turning a steady green. Elissa couldn't read them from where she sat—she was pretty sure they'd been designed too small for anyone aside from the person in the pilot's seat to be able to decipher—but she assumed they were the coordinates the commander had said she'd send. *Because we can only get to the city—our own city— by shadowing her flyer.* Resentment flared within her. Which was silly—like Cadan had said, they risked getting shot out of the sky if they went unauthorized into a no-fly zone. But all the same: *It's our city, not hers. We came here to try to help it, and we can't even enter it without her permission.*

Metal scraped and clanged against metal as Cadan disengaged the clamps that held the shuttlebug locked close in its dock. The floor lurched a little. Then, one hand on the steering panel, Cadan eased the throttle forward. The floor took on a sudden slant toward the nose of the shuttlebug, and despite the five-point harness holding her securely in place, Elissa grabbed for the sides of her seat, needing to hold on to something as the floor tipped beneath her.

If she'd thought about it, she'd have known Cadan

wouldn't turn on the shuttle's gravity drive, not flying within the planet's own gravity, flat over the desert to the city. She'd once been used to this kind of sensation. She'd grown up on an overcrowded planet, in a city where, had traffic not made use of the full three dimensions, it would have come to a standstill long ago. She was entirely used to traveling by flyer, beetle-car, fast-moving slidewalk.

But the weeks of being on no vehicle but the *Phoenix*, with its steady, continuous gravity drive, had unacclimatized her.

The floor tipped more. For a moment, harness or not, death grip on the seat or not, it felt as if she would come out of her seat and fall helplessly toward the dark-filled windscreen.

But instead it was the shuttlebug that fell, in one smooth drop, swooping down and away from the side of the *Phoenix*.

The shuttlebug hovered for a moment, engines growling, then from overhead came the roar of the IPL flyer. Cadan took the shuttlebug up to follow it, so fast that Elissa's stomach dropped like a plummeting elevator. Her ears crackled, almost painful. They were way up in the darkness within seconds, the base a splodge of light below them, the stars suddenly extraordinarily bright.

The flyer tipped, Elissa's stomach lurched again, and then they were roaring through the night, high over the desert floor, back toward where a very distant glow was the only sign of the city in which Elissa had grown up.

The commander had left the com-channel between the two craft open. Miles before they neared the city, she initiated communication with the forces there, rattling off what was presumably a security code, a warning of their approach. *It's not a total no-fly zone. And if they can get authorization for the shuttlebug, why not for the* Phoenix?

They descended in a narrowing spiral, down toward the glow of the spaceport. The rest of the city seemed very dark in contrast. Elissa was used to seeing it laid out like a glittering spiderweb: the silver lines of the pedestrian slidewalks and the brilliant cobalt monorails the beetle-cars ran on, the lights strung sparkling from building to building, the softer amber bloom of lamps down on the city floor. But now it was as if the spiderweb had been broken, as if all but a few strands had been swept away, as if the blooms had been trampled and crushed out of existence. It was a darkened city that stretched out beneath them. Little squares of light all over the city floor and dotted up the canyon sides spoke of lit windows in houses and apartments, but it was a world away from the nighttime blaze Elissa was used to.

Why is so much of the power out? The slidewalks and streetlamps are all run on solar power—no one's taken that *away!*

"So that's what curfew looks like," said Ivan, behind her.

Felicia's response held a sharp note of surprise. "That's what it is? Who said?"

"Bryn mentioned it. You didn't hear?"

"I didn't. Seriously, Ivan, a *curfew*? They don't have the personnel to get those refugees to safety, but they have enough to enforce a curfew?"

"It's a whole-planet takeover," Ivan said. "Pretty sure a curfew's standard IPL protocol. If they get resistance, that is. Riots, terrorism . . . you can see why they'd want to clamp down."

"I can see, yes. It doesn't mean I think it's the right idea. Treating every Sekoian citizen like a criminal whether they are or not?"

"Oh, I'm with you. I know. But what're you gonna do? It's

a takeover. That's how they do it—how they've always done it before. And, you know, I don't suppose the populations of Endymion and . . . which were the others . . . ?"

"Galapagos and—"

"—Rin, yeah, I remember now. I don't suppose they liked it any more than Sekoia, but they did accept it."

"Well, if you were an Endymion citizen, anything must have seemed better! They were living with the systematic disenfranchisement of transgender people, for God's sake. And Rin was on the verge of global famine. They'd probably have accepted imprisonment if it meant they could get a guaranteed half a meal a day. Sekoia, though—Ivan, I've lived here since I was nearly as young as the twins, and if I could sum up what the average Sekoian citizen believes, it would be 'As long as I don't break the law, I'll have nothing to worry about.' I swear, most Sekoians think everyone's divided into two groups: decent people and criminals. And now IPL's treating them like they're *all* criminals? If that's not a recipe for disaster—"

Sudden pain jabbed through Elissa's eardrums, jerking her attention from the conversation. Lin flinched, putting her hands up to her ears.

"Swallow," said Elissa, remembering long-past information Bruce and Cadan had given her. "It's the air pressure. It doesn't happen in spaceships, 'cause they adjust it for you. If you keep swallowing, it won't hurt so much."

Lin screwed her eyes up, swallowing, swallowing again, fingers pressing just in front of her ears.

Elissa did the same, cupping her hands over her ears, swallowing against the pain, feeling her ears crackle as the air pressure shifted.

Then the spaceport lights rose around them, a bright, colorless ocean. The shuttlebug touched down. The pain in Elissa's ears dissipated, leaving no more than a faint ache that made her want to keep rubbing them.

Cadan touched the com-screen. "*Phoenix* to *Savior*. Permission to disembark, Commander?"

"Feel free to disembark, Captain," came the commander's oddly inflectionless voice. Now that it was once again unconnected to a physically present person, Elissa found the voice difficult to hear as something that belonged to either a female or male.

Cadan unsnapped his seat belt and got to his feet.

Made clumsy by hurry, Elissa fumbled to undo her seat belt as Cadan went to the door at the back of the shuttlebug. She and Lin joined the rest of the crew as they gathered behind him.

If things went wrong, how were they ever going to get back to the *Phoenix*? They'd given up so much control already—it seemed suddenly terribly important to stay close together, to make sure they couldn't get separated. Then, a sudden, unnerving thought: *Why are we at the spaceport? Are they just going to push us onto a ship and off-planet? And if that's what they want to do, how are we going to stop them? How will we get back?*

A little bit of her couldn't help feeling relief at the thought of being away from Sekoia, away from the people who wanted to hurt—or use—Lin. But she was kind of surprised at how strongly the rest of her rejected it. Despite the terror of finding out what was happening on Sekoia, what could happen to Lin, she didn't like the idea of running away. If it wasn't okay for Lin to be in danger, it wasn't okay for *any* Spare to be in danger. *We came back to help. If helping means*

*saving other Spares, then we're going to save other Spares. Even if it
puts us at risk.*

Cadan unsealed the air lock and went through into the
small chamber, then tapped in the codes that would open
the exit. Lights blinked from red to amber to green. Then the
shuttlebug doors whooshed open, letting in a flood of light
and a rush of hot air, full of dust and the scent of rocket fuel.

Cadan paused in the doorway, a silhouette against a wash
of brightness. He was braced, not quite tense, but alert, his
hand close to his hip, ready to go for his blaster—or, Elissa
realized, the whip she'd seen him use with such devastating
effect.

Then he froze. Clearly outlined in the spaceport floodlights,
the hand near his hip clenched. Every cell in Elissa's body
jumped, before she realized he hadn't gone for a weapon.
Whatever he'd seen out there, it wasn't a threat.

"Cadan?" said Felicia, at his shoulder. "What—?"

Like an echo from outside the flyer, another voice came. A
man's voice, one that seemed familiar but that Elissa couldn't
immediately place. "Cadan?"

Cadan's hand dropped. He swung out of the doorway, and
two strides took him from Elissa's sight.

"Who is it?" said Lin. Sudden interest seemed to have
shaken her out of her shock. "Someone who knows Cadan?
Ivan, I can't see *past* you!"

"Moving. Moving." Ivan gave her a tolerant look over his
shoulder as Felicia and Markus followed Cadan, then stepped
down after them out of the shuttlebug.

Elissa hurried after him, suppressing the urge to push past.

She got down the steps and landed on concrete, which was
warm enough that the heat came through the soles of her

shoes. For a moment the full impact of the floodlights blinded her, and she blinked, trying to see through a dazzle of tears. The crew were dark shapes in front of her, and beyond them was a confusion of more dark shapes.

She blinked again, and the shapes resolved themselves. Cadan had his arm around a tall woman who looked thirty or so years older than him, his free hand on the arm of a man who looked a similar age. They were both wearing the sort of protective jackets Elissa had seen Cadan wear to ride his sky-bike, and the woman's short fair hair was ruffled. Cadan was grinning, his whole face alight, more relaxed—*more at home*—than Elissa remembered seeing him.

As she stopped, uncertain, he turned to see her, his arm still around the woman. His grin spread, shining as brightly as the floodlights. "There she is. Mom, Dad, you remember Elissa, don't you? Lissa, you remember my parents? Can you believe, they came over on my skybike?" He looked down at his mother. "After everything you said about safety issues . . ."

Elissa went forward as the woman laughed. *It's stupid to be shy. It's stupid. Cadan said, when he had that one interplanetary call back on Sanctuary, they're not mad with him for rebelling against the government—they don't blame him for ruining his career. And they were always nice to you when they met you before.*

But before, she'd never had to meet them as Cadan's girl-friend. And . . . *I can't remember, how much did he tell them in that one phone call? Did he tell them that I lied to him to get on board the* Phoenix? *Did he tell them how much danger I put him in? That I only told him the truth after his ship had been attacked for the third time?*

Elissa pushed the thoughts aside as best she could and smiled at Cadan's mother, remembering the angular lines of the older woman's face, noticing for the first time how similar they were to Cadan's.

"Elissa." Mrs. Greythorn slipped out of her son's arm and put both hands out toward Elissa. "My dear girl, I'm surprised if you can manage to remember *anything* after the time you've had." Her hands, warm and smooth, closed around Elissa's. "You've been incredibly brave, I hope you know that? I hope *someone's*"—she gave her son a little sideways look—"made sure to tell you? We've only had the barest bones of the story so far, but what you managed to do . . ." She gave Elissa a smile, as warm as the feel of her hands. "Clement and I have been saying, if we, as a society, have managed to raise young people capable of doing what you—and Cadan—have done, then Sekoia really isn't in such dire straits as the news reports would have us believe."

All at once the tears were back in Elissa's eyes. She'd never thought to expect that Cadan's parents might not just refuse to condemn, but *approve* of the actions she'd taken. Her own mother hadn't, and although her father had been kind, had acknowledged Lin was his daughter, he hadn't told her she was brave, hadn't said he was proud of her. Until this moment she hadn't realized she'd wanted him to.

"That's really kind," she said, stumbling a little over the words. "I didn't—I mean, I didn't plan it, I didn't really mean to do it until it was happening. And I couldn't have done it without Cadan. He was amazing, Mrs. Greythorn—he saved us, like, a million times."

Mrs. Greythorn laughed. "That many?" But it was kindness, not mockery, in her tone. "Let's get you back home with us, okay? And you can fill me in."

"Home?" Her voice came out sharp with sudden panic.

"But . . . everyone's been saying the city's not safe?"

A shadow crept over Mrs. Greythorn's expression. "Everyone's right. When I say *home*, I mean the safe house whose exact location I'm not permitted to give you until you've been given security clearance." There was a wry twist to her voice. "But we are allowed to take you there."

"All of us? The crew, too?"

"All of you. I have to say"—she gave Cadan a teasing look—"my son showed great foresight in getting rid of most of his crew. I know there's room for an extra six at the safe house. We'd have struggled with an extra eighteen."

"It was entirely deliberate, of course," Cadan said drily. "Obviously I *like* flying a ship with a quarter of the crew it's supposed to have."

"Oh, please," said his mother. "It was a challenge, wasn't it? How many times have you said you wanted more challenges?"

Elissa laughed, charmed by the snapshot portrait of Cadan as seen through his mother's eyes, and Cadan gave her a wry look. "Don't go ganging up on me with my mother, now. I have enough of the female solidarity with you and Lin."

Lin. All at once Elissa realized that Lin was no longer by her side. As Elissa had gone forward to meet the Greythorns, Lin had backed away. Guilt shot through her. Enfolded in the warmth, the welcome, of Cadan's family, she hadn't remembered that Lin didn't know them at all, that to Lin they were just more people who'd had legal human status their whole lives, who might see her as a freaky full-body clone, something subhuman, something to be wiped out or gotten rid of or *used*.

They were welcoming Elissa, but it didn't mean Lin knew

they'd welcome her. And although Mrs. Greythorn was being kind enough that Elissa *thought* she would, she'd gotten it wrong before, had underestimated how people would react when faced with a Spare. The words of Cadan's former copilot, Stewart, came back to her. . . . *the freak double you stole. Your twin? It's not even a real word.*

Lin was standing near the shuttlebug entrance. Her shoulders were a little hunched, her hands locked together, the pale fingers tight against one another. She was looking at Elissa, and the expression on her face was as if she stood on some last remaining edge of rock, watching as everything around her fell away beneath her feet.

"*Lin.*" Elissa ducked out from under Cadan's mother's arm and hurried across to her sister. She'd been going to say something calm, something that would reassure Lin with its ordinariness, its assumption that of *course* no one was trying to leave her out, that she wasn't losing Elissa. But when Lin's eyes met hers, when she saw the desolation in them, all the ordinary words went out of her head.

"Don't," she said. "Don't look like that. I'm not leaving you behind. I'm not leaving you out."

Lin's hands twined tighter around each other. "I forgot . . . coming back here, I forgot. You had a whole life. You . . . fitted in."

"You know what my life was like here," Elissa said. "And anyway, Cadan's parents weren't part of that—not really. I only knew them 'cause of Bruce in the first place, and I haven't seen them properly for years. I didn't fit in with *them*."

Lin's eyes fixed on hers, huge and dark. "You fit now. I . . . I can see. It's okay—you should. You *should* fit in. I just . . . I wasn't expecting . . . I'd forgotten . . ."

"Lin." Elissa took her sister's cold hands in hers. "They're being really nice. They'll be nice to you, too. I don't know them well, they're not my family. It's just"—she hesitated, lowering her voice, not wanting anyone to hear—"it's *Cadan's* family. I thought they might be angry with me. His SFI career—they were so completely proud of him when he got in, of how well he was doing. I thought they'd blame me, maybe. So now his mother's saying she's impressed at what we managed, and she's just . . . being nice, ordinary, like we didn't—*I* didn't—turn the whole world upside down."

She looked at Lin anxiously, willing her to understand. "I thought they'd be angry," she said again. "And it's *Cadan*, and I . . ."

Lin nodded. Her fingers relaxed in Elissa's grasp. "You want them to like you?"

Elissa hesitated. It was more complicated than that, a whole mix of wanting some kind of outside sign that, despite everything, she was good enough for Cadan, that it wasn't just luck they'd ended up together. And wanting that approval and acceptance she hadn't gotten from her own family. And . . . oh, after weeks of having to be responsible for herself, *and* for Lin, of having to be an adult when she'd never even had a proper chance at being a normal teenager, it was such a relief to be with *real* adults, proper grown-up parent types who'd know all the right decisions to make so she wouldn't have to keep guessing and second-guessing.

"Yeah," she said. "I do. I want them to like me. And I want them to like you."

Lin grinned, in one of her disconcertingly sudden changes of mood. "Well, we're here to fix the world. What's not to like?"

Elissa laughed, in relief as warm as the ground beneath her feet. "I'm not sure they've a *hundred* percent grasped that's what we're here for yet. Here." A whole lot more confident this time, she tucked her hand through Lin's arm and pulled her to where Cadan's parents stood. Cadan, she noticed, had walked over to speak to the *Phoenix*'s crew.

"Mr. Greythorn, Mrs. Greythorn, this is my sister, Lin." She didn't quite mean it to, but "sister" came out with an edge of emphasis, almost defiance. *I do want them to like me, I do, but if they react to Lin the way Stewart did—the way my mother did—it doesn't matter that they're Cadan's family, I don't care, they have to treat her like a proper human. . . .*

Mrs. Greythorn's smile was as warm as the one with which she'd welcomed Elissa. "How lovely to meet you, Lin. I think Cadan said you and Elissa chose that name for you?"

As Lin nodded, half-shy, half-eager, and began to explain how they'd come up with the name, Mr. Greythorn looked across at Elissa. "The safe house isn't far," he said, and she realized that, overwhelmed by meeting Cadan's mother, she hadn't yet spoken to his father. "You look tired, all of you."

"Yes." She smiled at him, shy—*ridiculously*—all over again. "The base we were at got attacked."

"We heard." Grimness showed in his face, and frustration. "It's not as if we didn't know people's capability to resort to violence. But this . . . It's not coming from the known criminal element, or from what you'd normally think of as people who are criminally predisposed—it's not even coming from a distinct level of society. This is coming from ordinary citizens—throughout every level. All the planet had to do—*all* it had to do—was comply with IPL, and instead the riots, the attacks, plain vandalism . . . they got worse and worse until

IPL had no choice but to institute full military law."

Cadan's father was—had been?—on the city police force, Elissa remembered now. The same as her father, but whereas her father had been high up in the tech-crime unit, Mr. Greythorn had been an ordinary police officer, lower grade and unspecialized.

"*Full* military law?" Cadan said, walking back to them accompanied by the three crew members.

"Yes, believe it or not. On our planet." Mr. Greythorn gave a frustrated shake of his head. "I should be past being shocked by people, I know. But for God's sake, safe houses being needed for *teenagers*?" He looked at Felicia. "Ms. Ambra, isn't it? I have a message from your mother."

Relief relaxed every line on Felicia's face. She put out her hand for the myGadget Mr. Greythorn offered her. "Mr. Greythorn, thank you so much."

He made a courteous, dismissive gesture. "I'm only sorry none of your family were permitted to come with us. We asked, but the security forces are desperately overstretched. They did agree that the *Phoenix*'s crew members needed the same level of protection as Cadan, but that was as far as they were willing to go."

Felicia tore her gaze from the myGadget screen to look up at him. "I understand. Please—it's enough to know they're safe."

Cadan made introductions, then, and there was a wave of conversation that seemed to wash over and around Elissa without touching her. She was horribly tired, she realized. She wasn't wearing her watch, which meant she'd probably left it back on the *Phoenix*, but it couldn't be earlier than midnight—and it was probably a lot later. She must have been keeping awake on adrenaline born of tension, and now that the need for tension had gone, she was crashing fast.

Cadan came over and put an arm around her. She leaned her head against his shoulder, breathing in the familiar scent of his jacket.

Clement Greythorn glanced toward where they stood. For an instant his gaze seemed to catch, then he spoke to his wife. "Emily, we're keeping the cars waiting. Let's get these kids—and the others—home, okay?"

Emily Greythorn turned, a friendly hand on Lin's arm. "Yes indeed. Elissa, there are three IPL-approved beetle-cars just the other side of the passenger shelter—" For a moment her gaze, too, snagged on where Elissa's head rested on Cadan's shoulder, then she raised her eyes to meet Elissa's and smiled. "You poor girl, you look exhausted. Cadan, don't let her fall asleep on the way to the car, all right?"

They moved away across the concrete landing ground to the shelter Cadan's mother had pointed out. Elissa eased away from Cadan a little. The approval in his mother's face had been too welcome for her to be willing to lose it by looking like some kind of clingy-vine girlfriend.

Wait. Hang on. He did tell *them I was his girlfriend, didn't he? When he talked to them before . . . or when he introduced me just now?* She couldn't remember. The different bits of conversation were blurring together, filming over with exhaustion like the wrecked ships back at the practice base had filmed over with soot and dust.

As Emily Greythorn had said, there were three beetle-cars waiting behind the shelter, their squat shapes familiar, propeller blades folded away in the shiny domes of their roofs. Clement Greythorn motioned Elissa toward the nearest.

"Why don't you and Lin take that one? And would you like someone else with you?"

Cadan, thought Elissa, then caught back the selfish thought. His parents hadn't seen him for over a month, and they must have worried. The beetle-cars would hold only three passengers each—if Cadan should travel with anyone, it should be his parents.

She shook her head. "We're okay."

"You sure? The drivers are all with IPL, of course, and the safe house is no more than ten minutes away, but if you'd feel more secure with one of us—"

Felicia stepped forward. "I'll grab a seat, if that's okay with both of you." Her mouth curled up a little. "Secure? As long as they take us somewhere with a bed, that'll do fine as far as I'm concerned."

The glossy green sides of the car had sprung up while they talked. Lin climbed over the folded-down front passenger seat and into the back.

Cadan's arm tightened around Elissa, and he bent his head to give her a quick kiss. "I'll see you at the safe house, okay?"

She couldn't help but respond, but even as she smiled up at him, her skin prickled with the awareness that his parents' eyes were on them. *Surely he said I was his girlfriend? At some point?*

As she climbed into the beetle-car after Lin and pulled the front seat back up to make room for Felicia, she slanted a cautious look under the raised side of the car. Cadan and his father were getting into the next vehicle. Cadan was saying something, but his expression was a little self-conscious, as if he was trying to talk through an awkward moment. Elissa caught a glimpse of Clement Greythorn's face as he bent to climb after Cadan. He was looking taken aback, his eyebrows drawn together in a frown.

As he folded himself into the seat, Elissa, stomach already knotting itself in apprehension, found her gaze going toward Mrs. Greythorn's face. Cadan's mother stood by the car. Her husband and son were out of the way, and she could have moved to get in, but instead she stood still, one hand on the raised side, staring toward the vehicle where Elissa sat. Her face had the same arrested, surprised look as her husband's, but worse than that—it was filled with disappointment.

The driver of Elissa's car touched a button and the sides came down, shutting off Elissa's view. The car vibrated as its propellers woke, then buzzed up into the air, flying no more than a couple of feet above the ground.

Felicia and Lin were talking. Felicia's voice was still alight with relief. In Elissa's ears, it buzzed like the buzz of the propellers, a background distraction she wanted to shut off. She felt sick.

When they'd welcomed her, when Cadan's mother had acted like she was proud of her, they hadn't known she was Cadan's girlfriend. They hadn't known, and now that they did, they weren't pleased.

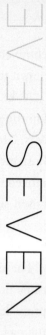

CADAN'S FATHER had been right: The ride to the safe house took scarcely ten minutes. The beetle-cars buzzed along, just clearing the ground of the spaceport plateau rather than rising farther into the air. To avoid contravening the no-fly order? For some other kind of security reason?

Lin's side of the conversation with Felicia died away within the first couple of minutes of the journey—when Elissa glanced sideways she saw her sister's eyelids drooping—and the driver was all business and, beyond his first brief greeting, didn't speak to them. For Elissa, it was a relief not to have to make polite small talk, not to have to drag her mind away from the questions she had to find answers to.

They're not pleased. It can't be because they have something against me, though—his mother was so nice to me, and his dad, too.

Was it that they didn't want Cadan to have *any* girl-friends? *I remember, my mother used to say she was glad Bruce wasn't entangling himself with girls, wasn't letting himself get dis-tracted, 'cause he needed to focus on his career. If Cadan's parents feel the same way* . . . But that didn't make sense. SFI was dead. Cadan's career with them was over. What would it matter if he got distracted now? *He has a whole new potential career with IPL, though. . . . Is it that? Is it that they still don't want him to be distracted?*

They came to the edge of the plateau, and the beetle-car dropped off the edge, sinking swiftly down past the canyon wall into the darkened city. Even when they reached the first level of the monorails, the driver didn't steer the car onto them, but continued to pilot it down through the air, keep-ing close to the canyon side.

At first Elissa thought it was another security thing—if they were afraid of being attacked, it made sense to stick close to the cover of the cliff side. But then her memory of the din-ing area back at the practice base—the absence of the familiar hum of machinery—came together with the absence of lights all over the city. Like the auto-settings every building had, that she'd taken for granted her whole life, the monorails had been turned off. In which case the driver must be confined to using only the beetle-car's built-in solar panels.

Which would be fine, except that the power for the beetle-cars was only an inexhaustible resource as long as the cells kept working. She couldn't remember what the typical life-time of a solar cell was, but she was sure it wasn't indefinite.

They dropped farther down into the canyon. More mono-rails rose past them, then the familiar steel spaghetti of pedes-trian slidewalks. This late, the slidewalks would mostly be switched to stationary, anyway, so Elissa couldn't tell whether they'd been permanently powered down too.

Was it part of the military law Cadan's father had mentioned? Had IPL shut down the monorails in order to enforce control on the city's population?

It's not fair. Everyone uses the monorails—the whole city needs them. And we're not all rioting, we don't all need to be controlled!

Felicia's voice sounded, a sharp echo in her mind. *Treating every Sekoian citizen like a criminal whether they are or not? If that's not a recipe for disaster . . .*

But Felicia's voice was followed by that of Cadan's father. . . . *this is coming from ordinary citizens. All Sekoia had to do was comply with IPL . . .*

It *wasn't* fair. But . . . like Mr. Greythorn said, people were behaving like criminals. No, people were actually *being* criminals. Ordinary people, people from all through the levels of Sekoian society, people she'd have known, people her parents might have worked with.

If you couldn't tell who was going to be a criminal next, or which level of society they were going to come from, then, despite how it might make people feel, it was *kind* of fair, wasn't it, to treat the entire population like criminals? To impose military law, curfews . . . whatever else IPL was doing, just in case? Wasn't that just making things safer for the people who *hadn't* become criminals?

All her life, whenever there'd been a proposal for enhanced surveillance—cameras in private homes, routine tests for women to check they weren't pregnant with an unlicensed second or illegal third child—the whole human-rights-and-privacy argument had blown up again. But although some people had said Sekoia already used too much surveillance, Elissa remembered other people—*plenty* of other people—arguing that you only needed to worry about surveillance if you had something to hide. And that if you weren't ashamed of what you were doing, why would you need to hide it anyway?

Wasn't that something like what IPL was doing now? After all, no one *needed* to go out at night, and if you weren't planning on breaking the law, it surely didn't really matter if that law was imposed by the IPL military.

It feels wrong, though. It still feels wrong.

Oh, but what did she know about the measures needed to protect a society in crisis? Questions kept stacking up in her brain, a frustrating list of things she didn't know the answers to and that everyone else seemed to answer in different ways. And the more she realized she didn't know, the more insane it seemed that she'd ever thought she had anything to offer the planet that had once been hers. Maybe the only thing she had was the added power she could lend Lin. Maybe, if that was all you had, it was crazy—selfish—to be squeamish about how that power was accessed or what was done with it.

Cadan's parents . . . If I sometimes wonder if I'm not good enough for him, I shouldn't be surprised that they might think that too.

The beetle-car made a sudden plunge, shooting under a tangle of spiraling stairs joining two sets of old-style, static walkways. It seemed to shake the thoughts loose in Elissa's head. She straightened in her seat, taking a breath, putting her chin up. She was being dumb. It wasn't about being "good enough." He loved her, that was all that mattered. And as to what she could offer her world—she'd never *thought* she had superpowers, or some amazing understanding of how to rebuild Sekoian society. What she did have, what she and Lin were *both* offering, was an understanding of Spares and their powers. It wasn't everything, but it was more than anyone else could offer right now.

With a whir and rattle of overstrained propellers—the beetle-cars had never been meant for such long flights, only short hops onto the monorails—the car dropped through the space made by two tall buildings and landed in the dimly lit narrow alley that ran between them. There was just space for the sides of the car to flip up.

The driver had been periodically scanning an instrument fixed to his dashboard ever since they set off, but now he jerked a fast, intent look up and around them before indicating to Elissa that she could get out of the car.

Skin prickling, she slid out to stand behind it, looking up as he had done, seeing nothing but high, blank walls. She heard Lin climb out after her, moving carefully, as if she, like Elissa, felt that any unwary movement could bring an attack down upon them.

Their feet scraped on something gritty on the floor of the alley. Sand. Weird. Sand did blow from the surrounding desert into the city, obviously, but there was a citywide automated cleaning program that kept it from ever building up to more than the merest trace. And Elissa was pretty sure it, like the slidewalks, ran on solar power, so why would anyone turn it off?

Oh, maintenance, of course. She felt silly for not thinking of it immediately. Why would she expect maintenance schedules to be running on time? Keeping the city shiny clean wasn't exactly going to be a priority right now.

The other beetle-cars settled into the alley behind the one Elissa, Lin, and Felicia had come in. Doors sprang open and the others climbed out, as quiet and tense as the twins.

"We okay?" asked Mr. Greythorn.

The driver of Elissa's car was leaning out, one foot on the

ground, the instrument from the dashboard in his hand. "As far as I can tell. Josh, Hussein, you?"

"Not picking up anything," said the driver of the car the Greythorns had ridden in, and behind him, the driver of the third car gave a brief nod, visible through his windscreen.

Mr. Greythorn already had a keycard in his hand, and now he edged past the cars to an unmarked door farther along the side of one of the buildings and drew the card through the scanner by the side of the door.

"We're going in the back," he said, directing his words at the group as a whole. He hadn't looked at Elissa since getting out of the car. Which didn't mean anything—she didn't think he'd looked at Lin either—and anyway, it didn't *matter*, because it was what *Cadan* thought that mattered. . . .

The door slid open, and within the passageway behind it, little pale lights glowed awake. Now Cadan's father did look Elissa's way, nodding to her to go past him into the building.

She did so, feeling Lin's hand slide into hers, the fingers clasping tightly.

The building was cool, but not chilled. The air-conditioning must be off here, too. And once she was in the passageway, she realized that only every other light had blinked on.

"It's fine," said Mr. Greythorn from behind them. "Go right ahead."

The passageway turned left, and then there were stairs stretching up into more half-lit dimness, leading—as they climbed them—around one corner after another. Elissa had used the gym on board the *Phoenix*, but obviously not enough. Within a few flights her calf muscles were burning, and she was far too glad of the handrail she was using to pull herself up onto the next step.

It wasn't *that* pathetic—it was totally late at night, after all—but she was terribly aware that Cadan and his parents were coming up behind her, with no hesitation at all, or at least none that she could hear.

*They'll think I'm like one of those people who have their staircases turned on all the time, who use remote or voice-activated every-*thing, *who practically forget how to walk.*

Oh, for God's sake. It doesn't matter. *Cadan doesn't think that—* Except then came, like an echo from a previous life, a world away, the memory of how he'd used to talk to her. . . . *The star system doesn't revolve around you, you know, princess. It wouldn't kill you to work for what you want . . .*

On the fifth floor, or maybe the sixth, Mr. Greythorn opened another door with his keycard and directed them along a short, low-ceilinged corridor studded with doors that were clearly entrances to living apartments. The maze of narrow, windowless corridors, the cramped spaces, spoke of low-grade housing, the only sort Central Canyon City's lowest-paid workers could afford.

Behind her, she heard Cadan's voice rise a little in a quiet question, then his father answering. "Yes, exactly. Much safer. IPL were housing all of us in a central block at first, but once the location got out, you might as well have put a bea-con on the roof. Dispersed in the normal population—and as long as they're discreet and don't show themselves in pairs—there's nothing to say we're not ordinary refugees. There are enough of those, too, God knows."

A shiver caught Elissa, a blend of anticipation and appre-hension so intense it felt like fear. . . . *as long as they don't show themselves in pairs . . .* The safe house—although it sounded as if it wasn't so much a safe house as a safe apartment—that they were being taken to wasn't just for SFI families. It was for Spares and their twins. *I'm going to see more Spares. And other people who've gone through what I've gone through. For the first time, people who I won't have to explain anything to. People who can't possibly see Lin as a clone.*

"Elissa," said Mr. Greythorn, "next door down, okay?"

She stopped at the unnumbered door. A small light patch on the gray plastic showed where the number plaque had been removed. Another security thing?

Mr. Greythorn touched his keycard to the sensor, and the door gave a soft chime as it slid open. They went through into a small, low-lit lobby, doors set in the walls around it.

Mr. Greythorn indicated a couple of the doors with a nod of his head. "Those rooms are empty. They each fit three, so there's room for all of you. Go quietly if you can. People will mostly be asleep. We don't have any of the younger Spares here, though—it's all people your age."

Emily Greythorn moved past Elissa to open a farther door. In the room beyond, lights flicked on. "This is the kitchen. If any of you want drinks, the fresh products have all run dry, but there's a reasonable amount of everything long-life."

Markus was already making for one of the rooms, but Ivan and Felicia moved toward the kitchen, and Cadan turned to Elissa for the first time since they'd gotten out of the beetle-cars. "It's like being back on the *Phoenix* already. You want a nice long-life drink, Lissa? Lin?"

Irritation spiked through her. What she *wanted* was half a minute to talk to him without a million other people around. *Did you notice your parents' reaction? Have they said anything to you?* She hesitated, wishing there was a way to ask, wishing there was a way to grab even the tiniest amount of privacy.

He smiled at her. "Lis, you look dead on your feet. Go to bed if you want. I'll see you in the morning."

There was nothing different in his expression, no new reticence that had appeared in the last half hour. Inside her, something cold and tight began to unwind. She returned his smile. "Yeah, I will. Good night." Then, with a slight effort, "Good night, Mr. Greythorn. Good night, Mrs. Greythorn."

"Good night, Elissa." Cadan's mother's voice, and the nod his father gave her, were no different from how they'd been before. But all the same she couldn't shake the impression she'd had earlier. The almost-shock on their faces, and Mrs. Greythorn staring at her with . . . She was sure she hadn't imagined it. It *had* been disappointment.

Well, she definitely couldn't ask them now—if she ever could. Lin following her, she moved away to go toward the room Markus had left free. But as she did, her foot caught in the torn hem of her pants leg and, clumsy with tiredness, she stumbled, putting out a hand to stop herself falling into the wall.

Her hand brushed the door panel next to one of the doors, and it slid open.

The room beyond was lit only by the glow of a screen—one of the cheap multifunction ones—tilting down from a far corner. The dark shapes of two couches and a scatter of beanbag chairs bulked between the screen's light and where Elissa and Lin stood. After a moment while her eyes adjusted, Elissa recognized what was playing on the screen as one of the more popular teen dramas. She'd never watched it much—the impossibly beautiful, confident, and polished actors had only seemed to accentuate the difference between her life and the life normal teenagers could lead.

The volume wasn't on high, but all the same it must have masked the swish of the door sliding open, because it was a few moments before one of the occupants of the chairs looked around.

He was a boy about Elissa's age, so dark skinned that when he smiled his teeth seemed to glow in the dimness. "Hey," he said, "new bodies!"

Blurs of other faces turned to look.

"Lights up," said the boy, and Elissa blinked as the room brightened.

Behind her, Cadan's father's voice was simultaneously exasperated and resigned. "*How* late are you people awake?"

The boy grinned, but a second boy, this one maybe a year older, with light skin and longish brown hair, looked a little guilty. "We didn't have the sound on loud."

"Yeah," said the first boy. "Ms. Thing *seriously* can't complain this time."

"But she so will, all the same," said a pretty blond girl sitting next to him on the couch. "I keep *saying*, she completely thinks we're students. If she *didn't* think we were having wild sex-and-drugs parties, she'd be disappointed." She wriggled around, rising onto her knees, and smiled at Elissa. "Hi. I'm Sofia. What's your name?"

For a moment Elissa's answer caught, unspoken, in a rush of shyness. Going through her last three years at school as the freak girl with the undiagnosed headaches and blackouts hadn't accustomed her to expect welcome, or even courtesy, from anyone her own age.

"I'm Lissa. This is my sister, Lin."

For an instant, Sofia stared at her across the back of the couch. And despite the background noise of the onscreen drama, silence seemed to fall into the room.

Elissa folded her arms, automatically defensive. "What?"

Sofia blinked, her gaze going from Elissa to Lin. "You're twins, aren't you? A Spare and a—"

"Yes, of course." It must be the most obvious thing about them, surely. Just sisters—even sisters born at the same time, from two fertilized eggs rather than from one—would never look as freakishly identical as Elissa and Lin did.

"You . . ." Sofia was staring at Lin now. "But how did you both get names?"

Oh, so *that* was what was confusing her. Defensiveness melting into relief, Elissa almost broke out laughing. Except it was kind of horrific, too, the reminder that Spares, unlike their human counterparts, had been raised with numbers, not names.

"We made it ourselves," said Lin. "When we first needed ID cards, we made up a name I liked—"

"Hang on," the long-haired boy, the one with lighter skin, interrupted. He'd been staring too, but as he spoke it became obvious it was for a whole other reason. "Wait a minute. You said— You're *Elissa*? *Elissa and Lin?*"

"No *way*," said Sofia. Her voice rose, incredulous, and at least three people automatically said, *"Shh."*

"That's who you are?" said the boy who'd spoken first. He was wearing a yellow T-shirt, bright under the lights. "Seriously?"

"Yes," Elissa said.

"Wow." He grinned at her. "We were pretty much expecting new people—but we weren't expecting them to be *you*. You're famous, didn't you know?"

"Famous?" Elissa's throat closed.

"*Absolutely* famous," the boy said cheerfully. Then he seemed to pick up the tone in which she'd spoken, and the smile slid from his face. "I mean, kind of. Not, like, *actor* famous–"

"They're *not* famous," Sofia said, interrupting him. She looked straight across the room at Elissa, her expression suddenly sober. "You are known, though. Not by everybody, but there's enough information out there for people to piece IDs together if they want to. We're not supposed to be able to get online here–all the networks are closed for official use only–but one of the Spares, she can hack into any network. And, I mean, obviously we were kind of invested in learning about the first twins that found each other. She turned up footage of you both, from security data at a mall?"

Her voice rose in a slight question. Elissa nodded, not yet able to speak. The mall that security guards had chased her and Lin through, the mall where they'd emerged onto the roof only to see police flyers screaming down toward them.

"Someone's linked it all up," said Sofia. "That footage– you're in disguise, but they've cleaned up the images with false-ID software. And they've got it linked to your name, and that's linked to your family connections, and the pilot whose ship you were on, and *his* name . . ."

"Okay," said Elissa. Her voice only just didn't shake.

Sofia watched her anxiously. "But you must have known that, right? You must have known you couldn't keep your identities secure from everyone?"

"Yes." She had known that, of course she had. But it was one thing to know it in theory, from a safe place on Sanctuary or on board the *Phoenix* . . .

"What *kind* of famous?" Lin asked. Her voice didn't sound

as if it were anywhere near shaking. She sounded nothing but fascinated.

The yellow-T-shirted boy's smile returned. "Urban-heroes famous," he said, getting up to come around the end of the couch. "I mean, seriously, we'd put up a monument if we weren't living in secret. The *minute* we're relocated, though, I *swear* . . . I'm Samuel, by the way. That's—"

"I'm Ady," said the long-haired boy. He glanced down toward the end of the couch, where, Elissa saw now, someone else was sitting on the floor, mostly hidden by the couch. As the boy spoke his voice softened, became careful, as if he were speaking to an animal or a child. "Hey, Zee, come meet some heroes."

Elissa followed his gaze as yet another boy appeared, standing up so they could see him. He was exactly Ady's height, with a build identical to Ady's and the same light skin, brown hair, and thin, bony face. His hair was much shorter, as if it had been cut very close and was growing out, and he moved as if he didn't want to stand up straight, or as if he were continually afraid of being hit, shoulders hunched, head ducked forward.

A Spare. Another Spare. The first one, apart from Lin, whom Elissa had ever met.

"This is my . . . twin," said Ady, stumbling just the tiniest bit over the word. "We call him Zee." He stood, putting an arm over his twin's shoulders. It should have been a friendly, companionable movement—Elissa had seen it a million times among boys her age—but with Ady, it came across as a gesture, not of easy companionship, but of protection.

"Isn't Zee a name?" said Lin, speaking across Elissa as she opened her mouth to say hi.

Zee glanced toward her. The light caught the side of his face, and scars sprang into sudden shocking visibility. Not just bruises, like Lin had had when she escaped the facility, like Elissa had become used to seeing on her own face after each nightmare vision. Scars, the sort that might come from knife wounds or burns. *Is that what the later procedures do to them? Is that what would have happened to Lin if she hadn't gotten away in time?*

His lip, too, was scarred, mangled-looking, as if it had been repeatedly bitten. "It's a letter," he said to Lin, his voice husky, deeper than Ady's. "The first letter of my code."

"Oh." Lin looked at him, her face interested. "We only had numbers."

Zee returned her gaze but didn't seem to find it necessary to say anything in return. Elissa realized she was staring at him, then back at Lin. Probably *way* too obviously, but she couldn't make herself look away.

They're so similar. She hadn't thought to wonder what other Spares would be like—God knew, Lin had been odd enough to get used to. But Zee, just like Lin, seemed to be lacking the social impulses Elissa had always thought came as automatically as breathing. Like responding out loud when someone told you something. Or like speaking in order to prevent a silence from stretching out and out . . .

Her eyes caught Ady's, and he sent her a half grin that suggested he was aware of the very same thing.

"You can meet the rest of us in the morning," Samuel said.

Elissa nodded. "Is everyone here with their Spares?"

"Well, Ady and Zee, obviously," said Samuel. "And Sofia, and me. It's been just us since we got here three weeks ago, so when we heard new people were coming we all kind of wanted to wait up to see, but mine and Sofia's Spares, and Amaryllis—they all got too tired."

"Amaryllis is a Spare," added Ady, "but she's the only one here without her twin." A shadow crossed his face as he said it, and Elissa didn't ask why the lone Spare seemed to have a real name. Or why her twin wasn't with her. That was easy enough to guess. Her own first reaction to Lin had been shock more than anything else, and an instinctive revulsion she was ashamed, now, to remember.

"In the morning sounds like an excellent plan," said Mr. Greythorn. His voice was deliberately patient, like Cadan's got sometimes. "I understand we're getting a visit from Commander Dacre then as well. I don't imagine she wants to talk to everyone, but those she does talk to could do with an undisturbed night. So let's get to bed, okay?" A second's pause. "That means all of us, Samuel."

"Yeah, I got you. C'mon, guys." Samuel flashed a quick grin at Elissa and Lin. "See you in the morning, okay?"

Five minutes later, Elissa was climbing into the highest of the triple bunks in the room she, Lin, and Felicia were to share, and Lin was giving her face a hurried wash in the tiny corner basin. The seamless join of walls and floor and the bases of each bunk, the smooth roundedness of every corner, were other indicators of the nature of the accommodation they were in. The whole apartment had been molded in a single piece, then slotted into the shell of the tower block. Apartments made that way were cheap, characterless—and quick and easy to both empty and scour clean if the occupants were convicted of one of a whole host of possible antisocial crimes. Practically all of Elissa's life she'd been aware that the lower your rung in Sekoian society, the more likely you were to be convicted of an ASC. For the first time it came home to her that this housing, created for the absolute lowest classes, had been built, not with the knowledge that the occupants might commit crimes, but with the expectation that they *would*. The people Mr. Greythorn had meant by "the criminally predisposed."

That's not okay. I never bothered to think about it before, but it's not okay. It's like declaring the Spares nonhuman, and then treating them in a way that does its best to get rid of their humanity. It's assuming people are one way, and acting like they're only ever going to be that one way. . . .

That's how we thought. That's how we all thought. Like Felicia said—most Sekoians think everyone's divided into two groups: decent people and criminals. No wonder people are so angry that IPL's treating everyone like *criminals*. Then, with a shock, something she hadn't thought before: *No wonder we fell into chaos so quickly.*

At least, after all the blank walls in the rest of the building, it was a relief to see that this room did have a small window, set into the smooth surface of the wall opposite the bed. All it showed her right now was the bed's reflection, three pale stripes of mattresses and covers, off-white against the off-white wall.

Lin scrubbed her face dry with a square of paper towel from the dispenser and clambered into the bunk below Elissa. "Shall I turn the lights off?" she asked, and the overhead light blinked out.

Despite fatigue and what felt like a million different things to worry about, Elissa laughed out loud at Lin's cross, surprised exclamation of, "I didn't mean— It was a *question*."

"I think the programming must have just recognized that

phrase anyway," said Elissa. "Look at everything else—it's all pretty basic."

Lin huffed out an irritated breath. "Well, fine, it can stay like that now." The last word disappeared in a yawn.

For a moment Elissa hesitated. They were sharing with Felicia—at some point she'd want to see where her bed was. But exhaustion dragged at her eyelids, and her thoughts came slowly, like treacle pouring. Felicia would work it out.

Below her, Lin said, "More twins."

"Yeah, I know," Elissa murmured, hearing her words slur.

"Is it weird?" asked Lin.

I don't know yet. She might have said the words out loud, or she might not. Dark and endless, sleep swallowed her.

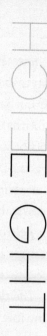

ELISSA WOKE to heat and light. She opened her eyes into sunlight flooding through the window, and familiar desert heat, concentrated in the tiny, unair-conditioned bedroom. Even for her, it was almost too hot. She wriggled, kicking the cover off. But the light was wonderful, and the bed just that bit bigger than the bunk she'd had on the *Phoenix*. She stretched, enjoying the unaccustomed space, and for a moment there was nothing but warmth and light and peace.

Then, like cold stones thunking one by one into her stomach, everything from the day before came back to her. Hearing what the Spares were being threatened with, what Lin had done, the way Cadan's parents' faces had changed . . . Other things too. Sofia's voice saying, *You must have known that, right? You must have known you couldn't keep your identities secure from everyone?* The marks on Zee's face—on his lip. *It's been weeks since the takeover, and he looks worse than Lin did when she first escaped.*

She sat up and leaned over the side of the bunk. Lin still slept, spread-eagled across the bed, her face buried in the pillow, a bare foot poking out from under the cover.

Elissa climbed carefully down the ladder, noticing that Felicia, too, was still asleep, and washed as quietly as she could. Cadan was an early riser, she knew. If she could just talk to him, find out what impression he'd gotten from his parents, maybe get reassurance that she was just being paranoid . . . It would only be one out of a whole list of anxieties in her head, but anything was better than this feeling of being buried in them so deeply that she felt as if she would smother.

The door whispered open, and she slid out into the windowless corridor. She couldn't go looking for Cadan in his bedroom. Even if he weren't sharing with other people, if his parents saw her doing that . . . But if he was up, maybe getting breakfast? The kitchen was that door, wasn't it? The one Mrs. Greythorn had pointed out last night?

She got it right. The door opened on a long narrow room, complete with the familiar appliances. A window at the far end threw sunlight onto every shiny plastic surface.

Cadan stood by the window, coffee cup in hand, fair hair gleaming in the light. As he saw Elissa he broke into a smile, put down the cup, and strode toward her. "Hey, I hoped you'd be up soon. I've been hanging around in the kitchen waiting for you."

"I'm sorry. I just woke up."

"No, that's okay. You must have been wrecked." The smile lingered in his eyes as he put his arms around her waist, looking down at her. "I was missing you, that's all."

He kissed her, and she shut her eyes, aware of the scent of his skin, his lips warm against hers, the heat of the sunlight lingering in his hair when she slid her hands up into it. For a moment, again, there was nothing but warmth and light, and heat building like electricity where his body touched hers. After just a few weeks, the feel of his hands, his mouth, had become familiar—wonderfully familiar, like a safety she hadn't known she wanted—but, too, every time he touched her it felt new, as if in between times her body didn't know how to remember something so intense.

After several long, golden minutes he lifted his head, but only so he could pull her closer to him, his face against her hair, her cheek next to the smoothness of skin above his shirt collar. "Yesterday was all kinds of crazy," he said. "How are you doing now?"

All kinds of crazy. Yeah, she thought that pretty much summed it up. She laughed a little, the sound mostly smothered in his shirt. After wishing desperately, last night, for just a tiny bit of time with him, here she was, and he'd just given her the perfect opening.

All at once, though, she didn't want to ask. What did it really matter? Nothing had changed between them, *nothing.* Cadan had been out from under his parents' roof for years— he didn't need them to like everything he did. Elissa was way younger, and it wasn't like *she* cared about getting approval of their relationship from *her* parents.

Yeah, like that's the same.

Oh, whatever. She didn't *want* to ask. Didn't want to spoil this moment with being insecure and demanding—the needy schoolgirl he would have looked down on.

She might have left it, might have shrugged, said *I'm okay,* and reached up to kiss him again, if she hadn't suddenly been struck by last night's memory: the memory, not of the expression on the faces of Cadan's parents, but of the expression on Cadan's own.

She pulled back a little so she could see his face. The smile was still in his eyes, a smile that he gave only her, a smile that, like his touch, seemed new every time.

"Cadan?"

He ran a hand up her back, fingers spreading between her shoulder blades. "Yes?"

And now she didn't even know how to *say* it. "Um, your parents . . ."

His face changed. The smile froze and disappeared. "What about them?"

Elissa pushed loose hair behind her ear. "They . . . Last night, I . . ."

"Look, Lis, like I said, last night was crazy. Give them a bit of time, okay?"

Frustration—and an edge of resentment, that he *had* known there was something wrong and that he'd made her *ask*—stiffened her spine, pulled her out of his arms. "Give them time for what? What is it?"

His eyes moved just a little so they no longer met hers. "They . . . Look, they weren't expecting us—you and me—to be together, that's all."

She'd known it, but all the same she went cold. "They don't like me."

"No. *No*, Lissa. It's not that. Not at all."

"Then *what*?" Frustration took over. "For God's sake, Cadan, just tell me! This is so unfair, leaving me guessing. I was freaking *out* last night—"

"I'm sorry about that. Last night—there wasn't a chance to talk to you by ourselves—"

"And now there is and you're *still* not talking." She only just stopped herself stamping her foot. "Tell me what's going on!"

"Okay. Okay." He put up his hands, looking so deeply irritated he might have been a different person from the one who, five minutes ago, had kissed her. "It's not that they don't like you. It's that . . . the way you and I used to think about each other, the way I, you know, misjudged you . . . ?"

Oh. Of course. Back before she'd known the source of the head-splitting pain, blackouts, and weird visions, Bruce, embarrassed by his freak sister, had let Cadan believe she was suffering from nothing but the occasional headache—and Cadan, who already saw her as pretty but shallow, had assumed the mysterious illness that had made her give up swimming and driving lessons, and sent her grades sailing further and further down, was a combination of laziness and attention seeking.

She should have realized he'd have said something of that to his parents. Should have realized that was what they'd be thinking of her too.

She and Cadan hadn't been together then. He'd thought of her as spoiled, and she'd thought of him as arrogant. They'd both made mistakes, both misjudged each other—it shouldn't feel like a betrayal to find this out now.

All the same, it did.

"Did you tell them?" Her voice came out small, a voice that belonged to the girl she'd been years ago. "Did—did you explain that I—I'm not really like that?"

"Lis, trust me, they can *see* you're not like that. They know now where the pain came from—they know you saved your sister. What my mother said to you—she wasn't making it up. It still stands."

Elissa wrapped her arms around herself. "But she—they—they're still not pleased we're together."

Cadan shrugged. He looked tired, and years younger, like he always did when something smashed the confidence that normally seemed so untouchable. "It's just . . . for them, it's come out of the blue. They never got any hint that I might fall for you. I mean, even you and I—we both know it happened so fast, from the moment you came on board the *Phoenix* to when I knew I'd fallen for you."

"So? *Everything* happened fast. One minute Lin and I were getting kidnapped by pirates, the next minute the hyperdrive was broken and SFI were attacking us—"

"That's why."

"That's why *what*? Your parents—" She broke off. Realization came to her. "They think it happened because of that," she said, and her voice wasn't quite steady. "They don't think it's real. They think it just happened because of the . . . the situation, because it was all, like, heightened emotion and danger and stuff."

"Yeah." He leaned back on the counter behind him, hands braced on its edge, looking down, his voice heavy. A cold weight fell into Elissa's stomach. It was bad enough that his parents thought that, bad enough that they didn't approve. But if now *Cadan* was thinking that as well . . .

She'd thought he'd been as clear as she about what had happened. She'd never expected anyone else's opinion—even that of his parents—to instill doubt in his mind. But there it was.

"You think they're right." Her voice came out harder than she'd realized it would.

He looked up at her. "No, I don't. I don't think they're

right. It's just"—he rubbed a hand up over his face—"they're not thrilled I let it happen. When everything's so crazy anyway, they . . . they think I could do without the distraction."

For a moment Elissa couldn't speak, and when she did her voice didn't sound like hers. "That's what I am? I'm a *distraction*?"

Alarm flashed across Cadan's face. "God, no, that's not how I meant it to sound. It's not *you*—it's *us*. Our relationship. They—my dad . . ." The next words came out like a quote, and for a moment Elissa could hear his father's voice overlaying his. "He thinks I should have had the sense to hold off until I was in less volatile circumstances."

"And that's what you want?" Her voice still didn't sound like hers, but now it was because it had gone so flat it sounded as if she were speaking through a machine, as if all emotion had been digitally removed from the words. "You want us to . . . hold off?"

"No," said Cadan. The word should have been reassuring, but he said it slowly, not looking at her, and she thought she could see doubt in his face. "No, Lissa, I don't. I'm just . . ." He gave half a laugh, and all at once Elissa could have smacked him. He could *laugh* when she was standing here dying of insecurity? "I'm not used to my parents disapproving of me. I'm kind of thrown. And although I *know* what I feel, trying to trace back exactly when and how, when it feels like I've felt like this about you forever . . ."

He looked up. His face had a lost expression, but it wasn't so much doubt as confusion. "But I love you," he said. "That hasn't changed."

The tight knot in her chest eased a little. "I'm *sorry*. I just . . . I'm freaked out. I never expected them to mind one way or the other. I never expected them to *disapprove*.

"And I'm an idiot. I didn't think to tell them in advance. So they weren't even slightly expecting it. I guess . . ." He hesitated, and what might have been the faintest flush crept up into his face. "The thing is, I've never brought a girl home before. Not that this was bringing a girl *home*, exactly, what with the whole lot of us being displaced persons . . ." His eyes met hers again. "I guess I wanted to do it properly, you know? Not on the phone. Not from a whole other planet."

Where the sunlight streamed in behind him, it caught the edge of his jaw, outlining it in brightness. His eyes were their familiar summer-sky blue, steady where they held hers. But the tiny muscles around them were, just visibly, tight with tension, and he didn't say anything else, standing with hands clenched on the counter behind him, waiting for her to speak.

"Never?" said Elissa.

"Never." His eyes flickered for a moment as, incurably honest, he made sure to qualify so she wouldn't misunderstand. "I mean, I'm not going to say there haven't *been* any girls. There were pretty strict rules when we were training, but in the vacations, when we were permitted to socialize . . ." He stopped, met her eyes again. "But, yeah, there was never anyone I wanted to bring home. Just you." His hands shifted on the counter, a little almost-nervous movement. "Is that . . . okay?"

In this new world, the wreckage of the old one they'd helped bring down, it seemed crazy that little things—like that—still came weighted with meaning. But they did. For some people it wouldn't have been a big deal one way or the other. For Cadan—and so for her—it was.

He'd been at college for years, flying up the ranks, him and Bruce, superstars among the cadets. She'd known he must have dated—and she was pretty sure there'd been plenty of girls to choose from. But now here he was, with her, saying, *never anyone I wanted to bring home. Just you.*

Just me. Out of everyone there could have been, just me. And he's asking me if it's okay. She looked at him across the bright warmth of the kitchen, here at the beginning of a new day. All at once his parents and what they thought seemed a million miles away. She had to fight against the smile that was trying to break out all over her face—she didn't want him to think she was laughing at him. "You really can't have spent *much* time with girls if you're asking me if it's *okay* that I'm special enough to be the first."

He put his hands up, a *you got me* gesture. The color had edged higher in his face. "Yeah, all right. But . . . look, I just wanted to tell you." He swallowed. "It doesn't mean . . . it's not like I'm expecting it to be the same for you. I know you're—" He broke off, restarted. "You don't have to be at the same place I am."

But of course I am! She was on the verge of saying it, but then those last few sentences got through to her. *I know you're* . . . what? Too young? Too inexperienced? He could say he wasn't expecting her to feel the same way, but from where Elissa stood, it sounded like he was taking it for granted that she *didn't.*

His parents made him question whether it's real for him, and now he's questioning that it's real for me, too?

The kitchen no longer seemed quite so bright, so filled with warmth. She crossed her arms. "So what place *am* I at?"

The words came out full of insecurity and squashed-down

anger and resentment she didn't want to let herself feel, a mixture that edged them like ground glass, and Cadan's face changed as they struck him. "Isn't that for you to tell me?" He took his hands away from the counter and folded his arms, an all at once forbidding-looking position.

"Well, yeah, *I'd* have thought so," she said. "But it sounds like you've already assumed you *know*—"

"Lissa, for God's sake!" Real irritation sparked through his voice now. "What's going on with you? I'm not 'assuming' anything. I was giving you the freedom not to say you felt exactly the same. I mean, call me stupid, but I thought girls, oh I don't know, *liked* their feelings to be respected—"

"And this is respecting my feelings?"

Cadan threw his hands open. "Okay, fine, clearly not! Do I get any credit for *thinking* that's what I was doing, though? Suppose you tell me what I'm supposed to say instead?"

They glared at each other. Behind Cadan, the angle of the sunlight had changed a tiny bit, just enough to make it shine straight into Elissa's eyes, forcing her to squint against the dazzle. Her eyes prickled with a sudden feeling like needles.

A few weeks ago everything had been super simple. He'd said he loved her, and nothing else had mattered. Now, though, with Cadan not being able to imagine them being together before they'd been forced together on the *Phoenix*, and with his parents disapproving, and with him not even knowing how she *felt* about him . . .

"You're supposed to *know*," she said. The needles had gotten into her voice as well, making it sound thin and scratched.

"Lis . . ." His face was still exasperated, but he spoke gently. "Come on, how can I know? Isn't that exactly what you don't want me to do—assume I know what you're feeling?"

He leaned over, ran a finger down her hairline, over her cheek. "It's okay. Whatever it is, whatever stage you're at—with me, with us—it's okay. I don't even need to know if you don't want to say. Not yet. Not right now."

She turned her face in to his hand. Her throat was tight. *Can't you tell this is serious for me, too?* She didn't even know why it mattered so much, she just knew it did. Knew she didn't want to have to *tell* him, didn't want to have to spell it out. *I wouldn't be doing this just for fun. Not with you.*

"Lis? What is it?" His voice stayed gentle, and all at once she was angry with herself. She didn't *want* to be this sort of girlfriend. Needy and clingy and *if you don't know I'm not going to tell you.* She'd handled things that none of the girls at her school had ever had to deal with—she didn't need to turn into someone weak and whiny just because she had a boyfriend. This was a *grown-up* relationship. Couldn't she, for God's sake, be a grown-up about it?

But she didn't get the chance to find out. The door gave the very faintest of squeaks as it opened, and they jumped apart. Cadan whisked his hand away from her face. Elissa took two quick steps toward the drinks machine, turning her back to the door. And then the room was full of people, and the precious few minutes she'd wanted were gone.

Breakfast was waffles—nutri-machine waffles, made from a nutritionally balanced prepackaged mixture that tasted pretty good when the waffles were still crisp and hot, and like damp cardboard as soon as they started to cool down. The kitchen wouldn't hold everyone, so once people had collected their waffles and dialed their drinks, they moved across the hall into the sitting room Elissa had inadvertently entered the night before.

Cadan was swiftly absorbed into a group consisting of the *Phoenix* crew—Felicia was up now—and his parents, and Elissa found herself and Lin perched on one of the couches at the other end of the sitting room, surrounded by the interested faces of the boys and girls they'd met on their arrival.

Plus others, the three Spares they hadn't met. Sofia's and Samuel's twins were still pretty much nameless: If someone needed to get their attention, they called them "El" and "Jay"—like Zee, using the first letter in the facility codes they'd been allocated.

The lone Spare, a slight girl with espresso-colored hair, introduced herself as Cassiopeia. At which Samuel gave a loud, dramatic groan, flopping backward to a semi-supine position next to Jay on the other end of the couch where Elissa and Lin sat. "Seriously? That's worse than Amaryllis."

Cassiopeia shrugged. She was very thin, her collarbones a sharp ridge under her T-shirt. "You chose your own name, right?" she said to Lin. "That's what I'm doing too."

"Except she chooses a new one every day," said Samuel from the depths of the couch. "And they're always *really long* ones." His tone was friendly, and there was nothing but mild teasing in the look he gave Cassiopeia, but she just shrugged again and moved to sit on one of the beanbags over by the window.

What did it do to you, Elissa wondered, to grow up as a Spare, to escape—to be rescued—but to *not* end up reunited with your twin? Had Cassiopeia even met her twin? Did she have anything left of the kind of link Elissa and Lin shared, or had it, as it was intended to, died off in her infancy? And if she did have that link, and she'd met her twin, and her twin had rejected her, what would that have done to a psyche already damaged by the years in the facility?

El and Sofia, both tall, slim, and identical in feature, still managed to look as different as Elissa and Lin had when they'd been on the run and in disguise. Sofia's hair was sleekly blond, falling like a pale waterfall down her back. Her skin had the airbrushed sheen Elissa associated with the really well-off girls at school, the product of continual beauty treatments. Her eyelashes were unnaturally long, tipped with gold, and her eyebrows arched in thin, perfect lines over her dark eyes. In contrast, her Spare, El, had hair that stood out in a wild copper flare around her head, her skin was a mass of freckles and her eyebrows straggly and unplucked. It seemed incredible that it would only take time and money and a bunch of specialist grooming products to make her look like her twin.

Well, almost like her twin.

It wasn't just the physical differences that made it clear which was Sofia and which was El. Now that Elissa was, for the first time, seeing Spares other than just Lin, she could see that there was a similarity between them, too—a similarity that, unlike the one between twins and Spares, had nothing to do with similarity of build or feature.

It was maybe something about the way they moved, with small, economical movements, as if they were used to a lot less space than their twins had grown up with. And carefully, too, like . . . *Like bad actors. Not really terrible actors, just ones who you can always tell are acting. Ones who never make you forget they're moving around a movie set, leaning against fake walls and opening fake doors and stirring fake food on stoves that don't work.*

Now that Elissa had noticed it, she could see it in Lin, too. Less pronounced, maybe—after all, Lin had spent longer with her twin than the other Spares had—but still there.

None of the Spares spoke much, either—of all of them, Lin was by far the most talkative. And whenever anyone else was talking, each of the Spares focused intently on that person, as though they weren't used to being part of a group, as though they had to pay close attention in order to get every scrap of meaning from the words.

Had they not spent any time together in the facilities? Lin had said they'd been educated normally for their preadolescent years—surely that had included group classes? Had they been split up once the so-called procedures started, then? Kept in some kind of solitary confinement?

Of the four Spares, Zee's injuries, which Elissa had noticed last night, might have shocked her, but at least they were well on the way toward healing. The others were hurt too, and looked a lot worse. El's shoulder seemed to have been dislocated and was cocooned close to her body in a sling. She was sitting a little way away from the others, where the wall curved around below the window to make a seat big enough for one person, with Sofia sitting cross-legged on a beanbag a few feet away. Jay's ribs were strapped up, and a long cut all the way down the side of Cassiopeia's face and neck was covered with quick-heal plasti-strips that didn't match her skin tone.

Elissa didn't want to ask—the injuries looked *awful*, and it *so* wasn't her business—and tried not to look, either, but after having to force her gaze away yet again, she inadvertently met Ady's eyes.

For a moment his gaze held hers. Heat climbed into Elissa's face. She felt obscurely ashamed to have been caught staring.

Ady's eyebrows came together in a frown—not an angry one, but one that looked as if he were debating something with himself.

Then he said, "Their flyer was attacked. When they were being brought here."

Lin, unperturbed and curious, flicked a glance from where Ady and Zee sat on a second couch, to Sofia, then sideways to Samuel. "You others weren't on it as well?"

Zee's face froze for an instant, an expression that was brief but so blank, so bleak that it struck Elissa with cold. Then Ady was speaking again, leaning a little forward as if to shield Zee from anyone's gaze, drawing attention back to himself. "Most of us were here already. IPL officials came to our houses and asked us if we gave consent to meeting our Spares. Then they asked if our *parents* gave consent—not that that made any difference, it turned out, it was just to log who was opposed. If any of the twins, or any of the Spares, didn't want to meet, then that was it, no one was going to try to make them. So *then*, for those of us who *did* want, they brought us here so we could meet in a 'secure, neutral environment.'" Ady shifted, resting his elbows on his knees. "They didn't want our parents with us to start with—the psych people told them it should be just us. But"—he rolled his eyes—"they didn't want to set up houses full of teenagers with no adult supervision, either."

"Sex-and-drugs parties," interjected Sofia.

"Yeah, that. So they mixed all the parents up and put them in the houses too, as long as they weren't with their own kids. At least, if they had other kids—other underage kids—they got to take them, too. Which is how we ended up with . . ." He nodded across to where the Greythorns stood. "I guess being *his* parents puts them as close to the top of the hit list as all of us."

"Not his sister, though," said Elissa, thinking aloud.

"He has a sister? Older, right?"

"Yes. She's married."

"Yeah, she won't be major priority, then. Especially if it was her, not her husband, who changed names. I mean, obviously people *can* connect them, but it makes her less of a target. And, you know, not everyone *wants* to be swept off into evacuation."

Sofia leaned forward. "They said—to me, anyway—they were going to move the parents around to put them with their own kids, to meet the Spares, after a bit. But then the threats started, and then the attacks, and they decided they didn't dare call attention to the safe houses by shipping people back and forth. They were still planning on a whole gradual integration into society, though, once everything sort of settled down."

Samuel snorted. "Yeah, 'cause *that* was going to happen."

"Well, it could've, couldn't it?" Sofia looked back at Elissa and Lin. "Then the attacks got worse. That first terrorist attack, did you hear about it? It was, like, some group called Keep Sekoia Safe or something. People said they were targeting what they thought was a safe house for Spares, although as it happened it wasn't. I mean, jeez, can you imagine—they ended up killing ordinary Sekoian citizens, exactly the people they said they wanted to protect, which was *obviously* super clever."

Elissa blinked. Sofia's tone was so . . . flippant, as if she were talking about a movie or something that had happened way back in history. As if it weren't real, as if real people hadn't been killed. *It's like she's just enjoying having all the latest gossip or something. I guess, if she didn't see any of the attacks, if it was just newscasts and stuff . . . it's not real to her, not yet. When I*

used to hear about disasters on other planets, human rights abuses,
they never seemed totally real to me, either. Not until it was me and
Lin they were happening to.

"Anyway," Sofia continued, "so *then* they said that we
couldn't be reintegrated into Sekoian society with our
Spares, 'cause it's too obvious what we are if we're together.
And apparently, for some of the Spares, contact with their
twins starts to strengthen their psychic abilities, so they start
to show more, and that makes them even *more* obvious. So
they were going to relocate just those of us who wanted to
stay with our Spares. Moving all the Spares was always going
to be a *massive* operation, they don't have anywhere near
enough personnel to do it easily."

She shrugged, leaning back, shifting her shoulders to a new
position against the wall. "But things just kept escalating, and
info kept leaking out about when Spares were going to be
moved from one place to another, and the safety of a couple
of the safe houses was compromised—they're being *so* careful now, it's completely irritating. So now all the Spares are
being relocated, whether they're with their twins or not."

She made a face. "And we're going to end up with a big
reunion once we're off-planet. Fun. I've been keeping away
from my mother and social events for years. Now there'll be
no escape."

"So all of you—you did *want* to meet," Lin said, the
moment Sofia stopped speaking. She leaned forward to look
past Elissa, eyes intent on Ady.

Ady's gaze brushed briefly over Cassiopeia, but she was
stirring her coffee, looking all at once as if she'd withdrawn
herself from the conversation. "Yeah. All of us who're here.
I mean, I thought I was an only child—my parents weren't

cleared to get a license for a second—and I always thought I'd like a brother. Finding out I *had* one—well, okay, I was pretty curious as well, so even if I hadn't wanted a sibling, I'd have wanted to *meet* him, I guess. But when they told me, when I realized, all this time, I'd had a brother—a brother *my age*, who I should have grown up with . . ." He looked self-conscious suddenly. "It's like finding out about something that you didn't even know was missing, you know?"

Elissa nodded. She did know. "Did you have any idea before?" she asked. "I mean, the link . . ."

"The telepathy? Oh, of course, you have that, don't you? The news reports—they said that's how you found each other. Zee and I don't."

Elissa blinked at him. "You don't? Not at all?"

"Nope. Either we never did, or it died off so early I don't remember. I mean, neither of us remember, do we, Zee?"

As Zee shook his head, Elissa curbed her impulse to look immediately toward the other Spares. Somehow she'd thought, of all the twins in the room, Ady, with his obvious concern for Zee, the way he spoke for him, shielded him, must be one of those for whom the psychic link hadn't faded with the separation. But if Ady and Zee didn't have a link, did any of the others?

She and Lin had returned to Sekoia ready to use the combined electrokinetic power of their link to power hyperdrives, but when it came to restoring the whole of Sekoia's space force, what they had to offer was nothing but the tiniest drop in the ocean. *Really* restoring it—and, with it, Sekoia's collapsing economy—would take hundreds of other pairs of Spares and their twins. All the Spares had been chosen because their brains had psychokinetic potential—they were all capable of powering hyperdrives. But it was the telepathic link with their twins that would enable them to do it without unbearable pain—and, eventually, death.

The link had been supposed to die off years ago. She'd known that, for some of them, it would have done so. But surely it couldn't have died off for *all* of them?

It must still exist. It stayed for me, despite all the treatments that tried to kill it off. And for my dad. We can't be the only ones. That wouldn't make any sense.

She became aware that Zee was watching her. His face was thin, bony, and, unlike his twin's, curiously static. Without the distraction of changing expressions, his hollow cheeks and the burn marks on his skin were thrown into almost-painful relief.

"They don't either," he said, and his gaze shifted toward Sofia and El before returning to Elissa. There was something a little unnerving about that steady regard, and as soon as she could do so without being rude, Elissa looked away.

"We think we used to, though," Sofia said. "When I met El, it was like meeting someone I'd known years ago. I didn't *remember* her, exactly, but it felt like I should remember. And you felt the same, didn't you, El?"

El nodded.

"And Samuel and Jay—" began Sofia.

"Are *freaky*," Ady interrupted.

The word "freaky" made Elissa flinch a little, but when she looked, an anxious reflex action, at Samuel, he was grinning.

"It's not freaky, it's *superpowered*, right?" he said, and Elissa relaxed.

Ady leaned back, arms behind his head, gaze on the ceiling. "There's really *very little* superpowered about *synchronized eating*. I mean, how useful is that going to be in the zombie apocalypse?"

El giggled, sounding, for the first time, like a normal teenage girl rather than someone acting the part of a normal teenage girl.

"Oh God," said Sofia. "Please not the zombie apocalypse again." She sent an amused look toward her twin, then a grin across to Elissa and Lin. "Ignore him—he's going through withdrawal. How many hours a day did you spend plugged into Zombie Uprising, again, Ady? Before all this happened and you had to face the real world?" She put a hand to her mouth, mock-whispering. "Don't say anything, but I actually think he's hoping that the government were breeding zombies as another of their little secrets."

Ady shot upright. "Yeah, yeah. Mock all you want—"

"Oh, we will," interjected Samuel.

"—but if there is a zombie apocalypse, your chances of surviving have moved *way* up just by being in the same building as me. When they rise, you'll be eating your words—"

"Nah," said Samuel. "I'll let myself get bitten just for the pleasure of eating your braaaaiiins." He bared his teeth, lunged sideways across the couch toward Ady, and knocked a leftover half waffle off Lin's plate.

"Guys," said Cadan's father from across the room.

"Oh my God, Samuel," said Sofia. "Civilized society, remember? And also *need for quiet*?" She sent Elissa and Lin another smile as Samuel threw himself back onto the sofa, not looking even a little abashed. "I'm so glad to have more girls, you have no idea. We have *not* been enjoying being outnumbered. Have we, El?"

The genuine warmth in her expression reached Elissa,

and she smiled back. It struck her suddenly, like a fan being switched on, like misty windows clearing to sunlight, that this was not only the first time she'd been with people who were like her sister, it was the first time she'd been with people who were like *her*.

She still had a million things to worry about, but although they were all still there, some of their weight seemed to evaporate from her brain.

Lin picked up her discarded waffle and dropped it onto her plate. She gave Samuel and Jay a curious look. "So what do you do that's freaky?"

Which was another good thing about being with people like her—Lin could say something so denuded of social niceties that it was pretty close to being rude, and whoever she was talking to had already met enough other Spares to not even think twice about it.

Samuel shrugged. "Freaky is so totally in the eye of the beholder. We just have this thing—we end up eating at exactly the same rate, and Ady noticed and . . ." He laughed. "Okay, it *does* look a bit weird. But Ady's kinda slow at catching up with the whole telepathic link thing—he thinks it's weird that I knew Jay before I knew about him. Even Sofia and El don't quite get it, but I . . . I just always had this . . . like this sense in the back of my head, of someone else?" He broke off, a grin lighting his face. "Well, I guess I don't need to describe it to you guys, do I?"

His smile was infectious. Elissa laughed too, more worry evaporating. Samuel and Jay *did* have a link. It *wasn't* just her and Lin. "Not so much."

"Well, there you are," Samuel said. "When it all came out I was like, 'Oh, *that's* what that was!'"

Ady cleared his throat ostentatiously. "Ah, full story, please? What *I* say is freaky is that he thought Jay was his imaginary friend."

Lin blinked at him. "That's not freaky. At the facility, they told us that's what little children do. That's what was supposed to be happening to our twins—any memories they had of us, they would identify as just memories of having imaginary friends."

For a moment, the familiar hot, sick rage washed through Elissa. Her stomach and jaw clenched.

"*That's* normal, all right," said Ady. "Sam, though . . ."

"Oh jeez." Samuel swung a cushion up to throw, saw Cadan's father was looking over at them, and let it flump onto the ground. "What he means," he said, "is that I kept my imaginary friend. I got older, and I knew—I thought—he couldn't be real, but he was so much a part of my life by then that I just couldn't get out of the habit of talking to him. And I"—his face went suddenly so bleak he looked like a different person—"I didn't get on well when I tried to block him out, when I stopped talking to him and tried to stop listening as well."

Next to him, Jay leaned a tiny bit closer. He didn't say anything, and his arm didn't quite touch Samuel's, but all the same Elissa could see the other boy instantly relax. "So I kept him. I didn't, like, *tell* anyone, and I thought—privately, you know—that I was probably a bit insane."

"Didn't that bother you?" said Elissa.

Samuel's face warmed again into his usual smile. "Nah. All great artists are insane."

Ady snorted.

"*Are* you a great artist?" said Lin.

Samuel lifted a shoulder, deadpan. "I could be."

"Oh please," said Ady.

Laughing, Sofia leaned over to shove his arm. "Be nice. He completely *could* be. He *draws*, doesn't he?"

"What about the procedures?" Elissa said, not stopping to think whether it was a horribly tactless question, just wanting to know exactly how much of a link Samuel and Jay had. "If you're linked that much, what happened when they began?"

Sofia stopped laughing. Silence seemed to drop over them all, despite the sound of conversation from the other side of the room. Elissa's face burned. "I'm sorry," she said. "It's not my business—"

"It's all right," said Samuel. The bleakness didn't return to his face, but his expression stiffened a little, and he leaned close enough to his twin that their shoulders touched. And it *wasn't* all right. She should never have asked.

"Honestly," she said, "I'm sorry. I should know better. I don't like to think about what happened to me—to Lin. I only got it secondhand, but when something hurts like that it's horrible even just remembering it, I know—"

"Hurts?" said Samuel, frowning.

She broke off and blinked at him. "Yeah. I thought that's what you were— That's what I meant—"

"You're saying it hurt *you*?"

"Yes. Lin worse, of course, I'm not claiming it was anything like as bad for me—" She stumbled again, confused and kind of embarrassed by the way they were staring at her. "What? What is it?"

"The pain—of the procedures they did on the Spares—it got through to *you*?" asked Ady.

"Yes." Frustration prickled over her. "What are you staring at? What about that doesn't make sense to you?"

Ady spread his hands. "The bit where you felt your sister's pain? That's . . . I mean, it'd be out of my experience, anyway, 'cause we don't have the link. But I never heard about *anyone*. And Sam . . . you didn't, did you? Not at all?"

Samuel shook his head. "More to the point," he said to Elissa, "you *did*. All the time—all the three years or whatever since it started?"

Elissa nodded, watching the horror dawn in their faces. She didn't deserve that reaction. It had been Lin, Lin for whom it had been true horror, Lin who, trapped and helpless, had felt the pain firsthand. Unlike Elissa, she hadn't even had the luxury of thinking it would get better. She'd only survived, only held on to her humanity at all, by reaching out to Elissa, by sharing—although she hadn't intended it—the pain with her twin. If Jay and El and Zee—and Cassiopeia?—hadn't had that, how had *they* survived?

But although the curiosity burned within her, she couldn't ask that. Couldn't ask them to go back into those memories.

"It happened to my dad, too," she said instead.

Sofia stared. "Your *father* was a twin as well? But . . . his Spare?"

Elissa swallowed. "He died. Like, way back. There's an operation they did, if the link never burned out, if it was—you know, causing pain, interfering . . . They did the operation on my dad. They were going to do the same—" She broke off. All at once she couldn't say it. Her hand, almost of its own accord, reached out and found Lin's.

"What are the odds?" Ady's voice filled the sudden little silence. "I mean, of having one in each generation like that? And the same . . . strength of the link, I guess, if you felt Lin's pain, and your dad felt *his* twin's?"

"Please, how is that surprising?" Sofia gave Ady a patient look. "Maybe it runs in families. It's not like freaking SFI was all aboveboard, is it?"

Ady flushed a little. "Oh. Yeah, okay, good point."

Samuel laughed, buoyant again. It wasn't like he was *impervious* to all the bad stuff, thought Elissa. But he seemed super resilient. Was that what it did to you, if you'd deliberately held on to the link with your twin, if you hadn't even tried to dismiss it, if you'd let it become at least a version of the relationship it would have grown into if the SFI had never interfered?

And growing up with that, with the relationship they should *all* have had—was that why Samuel, more than any of the rest of them, seemed like someone at ease in his own skin? And why he and Jay seemed so comfortable together? They showed none of the awkward overcaution that marked Ady's behavior toward Zee, that Elissa knew had characterized the first period of her relationship with Lin.

What Samuel was saying interrupted her thoughts, drew her attention back.

"Wow, you two, you really are like the superheroes among us all, aren't you? What are you even *doing* here? We're all just waiting for the transport to take us off-planet. But you guys *got* off-planet. Why did you come back?"

Lin grinned, lighting up like she always did when this topic came up. "We've come to—"

To help. To save Sekoia. Elissa didn't know exactly what Lin was going to say, but she interrupted, fast, acting on sudden impulse rather than anything premeditated. "Some of the crew have family still here," she said. "My family got transferred to Philomel already, but not Cadan's or Felicia's. And we have a spaceship—at least, Cadan has a spaceship. We can at least help with transport." Her hand tightened on Lin's, trying to send an unspoken message, and it must have gotten through because, although Lin slanted a bewildered look at her, she let whatever she'd been going to say drop, unspoken.

Elissa would have to explain it later, why it had suddenly seemed so important not to go into all the brightly optimistic details of the plans they'd made, and she didn't even completely know herself. All she knew was that they were here, among real Spares and their twins and, despite all the similarities, they were different from her and Lin, their stories were different, their relationships, even their experiences of what had been done to them. And until she and Lin understood all of that better, they had no business offering what they'd—naively?—felt was their expertise.

As well, they might have gotten the whole thing wrong. If most of the twins didn't have a link with their Spares—and if even Samuel and Jay's link was so much weaker than hers and Lin's—then maybe there was no use even thinking about them voluntarily powering hyperdrives.

She'd spoken so quickly, so unthinkingly, though, that she hadn't considered her own words carefully enough, and the next moment she realized that.

"An SFI spaceship?" said Sofia. "The one you escaped on in the first place? But what use is that? It was on the newscasts—the hyperdrive—the Spare—" She hugged herself, suppressing a shudder.

"It's still a working ship," said Samuel.

Sofia lifted a shoulder. "Yeah, but Sekoia's got a million *working* ships. Remember, that IPL guy explained? They could pack us all onto ships if they just wanted to get us off-planet, but without hyperspeed they'd be making us even more vulnerable than we are here. So they're having to do it all slow and stealthily so we're not supereasy to track." She looked at Elissa and Lin. "I get why you'd want to come back to get people from your crew's families. But I don't get why *you're* here. I mean, your family's safe already. And why would you think your ship is going to help with transport?"

But we do have hyperspeed. When Lin and I link, we can power the hyperdrive. But she didn't want to say that yet. It was too soon, all these Spares and their twins were too different. *And I don't know how to say it in a way that's not horrifying. They know what they were intended for, what they've been saved from—I don't know how to say we want anybody to try doing it voluntarily.*

"It's still a working ship," she said, borrowing Samuel's words in the absence of a better explanation, hoping they'd do.

"Okay." Sofia leaned back against the wall, the movement conveying flat disappointment. She'd been hoping for something more, Elissa realized, and like an echo she heard Ady's words: *Hey, Zee, come meet some heroes.* It had been said jokingly, but maybe it hadn't been just a joke. *Maybe they really were hoping for heroes.*

Oh God, and even with what we can *do, we're not that. We're not heroes.* She looked away, feeling horribly inadequate, and once again caught Zee watching her.

His eyes were such a light gray they looked colorless, like a sky so filled with high white clouds it seems to have been bleached into nonexistence.

"That's not true, is it?" he said.

Guilt, both hot and cold, flared in Elissa's chest. "What?"

"Zee!" said Sofia. "You can't *say* that to people—"

Zee's eyes didn't move from Elissa's. "I'm right, though. What she's saying—it's not true. There's something else."

The impact of that colorless stare, the guilt burning inside her, fused into a flash of defensive anger. "I don't know what you mean," Elissa said, her voice coming out high and indignant. "I—"

"Not *true*." Something sparked in Zee's gaze, something familiar. The heat in Elissa's chest fell away, leaving only the cold. She'd seen that spark before, in Lin's eyes. In her memory, metal shrieked, balls of fire exploded against a dark sky.

"Spares are taken for their psychic potential," Zee said, his eyes still on her. "You know that—we all know that. But did you know there are different types of psychic power—Spares don't all develop the same way?"

Elissa swallowed. "I . . . I could have guessed it, I suppose. But I don't see—"

"Shut *up*. Shut *up* with the lying!"

"*Zee!*" said Sofia, at the same moment as Lin, fury leaping into her voice, said, "No, *you* shut up," and as Samuel said, "Zee, chill, okay?" and as behind Elissa, the conversation across the room stopped dead.

But Ady's face was suddenly as rigid as Zee's. "He's right," he said. "Our link—our telepathy—died off. But his psychic abilities didn't. He's empathic. He told me. Aren't you, Zee? Go on, tell us, what is it?"

When Zee spoke, his voice was starting to quiver. "I don't know. I don't know what it is. I just know she's lying, she's *lying*, and it's something bad, it's something she doesn't want to say because it's bad, it's bad, it's bad—" The quiver became a shake, and his voice rose at the same time, shaking so badly it seemed as if he were shaking too, as if he would break apart.

There were tears in his eyes, a shine over their colorlessness, not falling only because he hadn't blinked all the time he'd been talking. He was just staring at Elissa, poised right on the edge of panic, sensing everything she hadn't said, everything she'd wanted to keep for a better time, for a time when they knew her well enough to not freak out at what she was going to suggest.

It was too late for that. Whatever the reaction of the Spares and their twins would be, she couldn't control that now. She had to tell them the truth before Zee's panic caught them all. *Four Spares, all with psychic powers I don't know about, freaking out about something I'm not telling them . . .*

She leaned forward, looking into Zee's face, and spoke as clearly as she could. "I was lying. I'm sorry. I'll tell you the truth. I'm sorry."

With a leftover edge of her attention, she was aware that Sofia's and Samuel's eyes had widened in a look of hurt and betrayal. *Oh God, I've done this all so badly. I thought they were going to be my friends, and I've screwed it up. . . .*

"We can make the hyperdrive on the ship work," she said to Zee, her eyes steady on his. "Lin's electrokinetic power—when she and I link up, she can plug into the hyperdrive. It doesn't hurt her. It doesn't. So we thought . . . some of the other Spares and their twins, if they still have their links . . . the other spaceships . . . we thought—"

She didn't get to finish. Cutting across, drowning out even the faintest sound of the last word she'd said, Zee began to scream.

NINE

ZEE'S SCREAM cut like a blade across Elissa's words—across her voice, too, drying her throat so instantly that she couldn't have formed another sentence even if she'd been able to think of one.

Everything stopped, everyone shocked cold like Elissa was shocked cold. For a long instant there was nothing but the cold, fizzing on her skin, dragging up every hair on her scalp, freezing her eyeballs wide open. The cold, and Zee screaming.

Then movement. The grown-ups and Cadan striding around the end of the couch, Zee's hands flying up to ward them off, Ady shooting to his feet, arms out. "Leave him! I'll handle it! Zee, it's okay, it's *okay*."

"He needs to stop that screaming," said Mr. Greythorn, his voice stern. "*Now*, or he's going to have to be sedated. Do you hear me, Zee?"

Ady was holding his twin's upper arms by now. "He's not *hysterical*—he's just freaked out. Give him a minute—"

"We don't have a minute. Listen to me—the neighbors can hear you, Zee. You have to stop *now*."

Zee stopped. He was cheese-pale, still shaking, his hands clenched at his sides. Ady kept hold of him, staring into his eyes, their two faces, so similar, fixed in such different expressions, close together. "We'll get out, okay? Okay, Zee? We'll get out."

"Not outside the apartment," Mr. Greythorn said immediately.

Ady gave him a look filled with so much impatience it looked like dislike. "I *know*. Jeez, we're just going into another room, okay?" Arm on his twin's shoulders, he turned them both, steered Zee across the room and out through the door on the far side.

As if strings had slackened, Elissa slumped back onto the couch. "Oh God." The words came out as not much more than a whisper. "I'm so sorry. I messed that up so much." The apology was for everyone, but she found herself looking at Cadan's father—and at his mother, standing farther back.

"Not to worry," said Mr. Greythorn, but his voice was curt, and he was already turning to the door that led out to the entrance corridor. "Excuse me. I have to go do some damage control. What the hell anyone would have thought if they heard that screaming . . ."

Across the room, Ivan said, "Comes with the territory, doesn't it?"

Cadan's father gave him an irritated, baffled glance. "What?"

"If you're going to house a bunch of traumatized children in a residential block, I mean. Do you even know what psychic powers they've got between them? And what's your plan for if it goes wrong—you going to drug them all?"

Elissa jerked a quick, surprised look at him. There was dis-approval—almost condemnation—in Ivan's voice. When most of the crew of the *Phoenix* had left the ship, he'd stayed. She remembered Lin asking him why. She remembered his answer. He had daughters. They were grown up now, but she and Lin reminded Ivan of them. That had been all his answer—all his reason for staying when most of the crew had fled.

When Cadan's father answered, his tone was clipped, deliberately controlled. "You assume we've had any time to plan at all," he said, and disappeared into the corridor.

Ivan moved back against the wall, folding his long gorilla arms, his face unreadable.

Cadan leaned over the back of the couch. "Lissa, are you okay?"

"Me? I'm fine." She'd glanced up at him when he spoke. Now she put her hands to her face. "It's Zee who's not. Oh, I messed that up so *badly*."

"Yeah," said Cadan. His tone wasn't condemning, but all the same the word felt like a slap. She looked up at him, not wanting to take down the shield of her hands. He was smiling at her, faintly, and his eyes were sympathetic. "But he's in a bad state, you can see it. I think anyone would find it easy to mess up talking to him right now."

"It depends what they *say*." Sofia's voice was sharp, and when Elissa looked up her stomach clenched under the impact of the other girl's chilly gaze. "What's wrong with you? You think you can come here, among a whole bunch of Spares, and start talking about asking them to go into SFI's *freaking torture chambers*?"

"I'm not *asking*," said Elissa. "I'm just saying it's possible.

We did it, Lin and I, and it saved our lives—"

"Fine, yeah! For all I know Zee could do it if it was to save his *life*. But you're asking him to do it for—*why?* As useful transport? As some kind of *convenience?*"

"No," said Elissa.

"Then what?"

Elissa opened her hands, feeling helpless, feeling unable to explain well enough, but before she could try, Lin broke in.

"Stop making such a fuss," she said. "You don't have a link with your Spare anymore. It wouldn't be *you* trying it anyway."

"That's right." Samuel sounded more unfriendly than Elissa could have imagined. "It wouldn't be Sofia and El. It would be me and Jay. Like he hasn't gone through enough?"

Lin rolled her eyes. "Like *you* know what he's gone through."

"I know as well as I can!"

"As well as I do?" Lin shot at him. "Look at you—both of you—you're speaking *for* the Spares. You haven't even stopped to see how *Jay* feels. I *did* this, I did it voluntarily, and I survived—"

"So what? Like your sister said, that was to save your life!"

"Yes," said Lin. "And this would be to save our world!"

Her words fell into the room, and silence followed, creating a space for them to swirl and echo.

After a long moment filled with nothing but that echo, Lin said, "Sekoia can't survive without its space force. If we don't do something, it's not going to exist as a proper society anymore. We'll all get relocated, and we'll be refugees forever."

"But," said Sofia, her voice blank rather than angry, "why do you care? Our world—our 'proper society'—did terrible things to you. Why do you want to save it?"

Lin looked at her as if she were almost too stupid to bother answering. "Because Lissa wants to."

Elissa felt herself flush. Not for the first time, she thought, *I shouldn't matter that much to her. No one should matter that much to someone.* And then, with a pang of guilt, *After the fight at the base, I should have forgiven her right away. I shouldn't have made her wait, not even for a minute. I should have forgiven her right away.*

Sofia had sent one look across to her twin. El was sitting quiet on her beanbag. She didn't say anything, nor did she meet Sofia's eyes.

Sofia looked back at Lin. "But . . . Okay, I get that, I guess. But being refugees . . . does it matter? You're—okay, look, I'm not trying to be rude, but you—all the Spares—aren't you all basically refugees already? You've all been declared Sekoian citizens, but you've never been let out in the real Sekoia—it surely doesn't seem any more like home than . . . well, than Philomel will. Does it?"

El looked up. "Yes," she said. And from her seat over by the window, Cassiopeia said, "Yes," as well.

As if of one accord, everyone turned to look at Jay. He shrugged. "Yeah."

"*Why?*" asked Sofia.

"Because of the memories," Jay said. "Okay, so I've never lived out here, but at least I have memories of Sam doing it."

El nodded, a silent agreement.

On the windowsill, Cassiopeia brought one knee up, hugged it to her chest, and stared over it. "I don't have memories," she said before anyone could ask her. "But I'd rather live in a society where everyone feels bad about what they did to me than one that feels good about itself for taking me in."

Huh, thought Elissa, *that's something I didn't think about.* It made sense, though, she guessed. Unbidden, her gaze moved to where Felicia stood at the far side of the room. Native of the dead planet Freya, which had suffered from postcompletion terraforming failure, Felicia had been a refugee half her life. Not *legally* a refugee, of course: All Freyan citizens had been given interplanetary citizenship, which was supposed to give them a right to settle on any planet in the star system. In practice, so Felicia had explained to Elissa and Lin, it didn't work out that way, and Felicia's whole working life had been spent proving that she was equal to any native-born Sekoian.

As if Lin had had the same thought, she, too, glanced at Felicia, then away.

Sofia was biting her lip. "You—all of you, then, you'd *rather* stay on Sekoia? And you—if you could—you'd be willing to try what they're saying they've done? To get the space force working again?" She shook her head, her face troubled and incredulous. "Jay? Sam? You'd actually try that? And the other twins who are still linked, the ones who might be able to do it too, you'd be okay with asking them as well?"

Before she'd finished, Jay was nodding, followed by El and Cassiopeia. Lin grinned, looking so pleased with herself that the word "smug" came to Elissa's mind. "You see," she said to Sofia, "you *didn't* ask them what they wanted."

Oh Lin, for goodness' sake . . . but, thankfully, annoyance flashed for only a moment into Sofia's expression. *"Okay,"* she said, with only a trace of *thanks, I got that already* in her voice.

Lin, of course, didn't pick up on even that trace. "See?" she said, cheerful and exuberant. "If they feel like that, then there'll be more of us who feel like that too." She turned to

Elissa. "Shall I go explain it to Ady and Zee now?"

But whatever had been on Zee's face, whatever hideous memory had surfaced to cause those terrified–terrifying–screams, Elissa was sure it wasn't something that could be fixed by talking, like the others had been talking just now.

She got up, not wanting to put herself in the firing line, not knowing how she could expect anyone else to do it. "It was me who made Zee react like that. Can I go try to explain myself to Ady first–explain exactly what I meant and how I–I'd never–I mean, even if he and Ady were still linked, I'd *never* ask Zee–or anybody–to do something he can't cope with. Is that"–she found herself looking up at Cadan's father, who'd come quietly back into the room in the last couple of minutes–"is that okay? Can I try?"

Mr. Greythorn opened his hands a little, tipping them up. "We can't afford that kind of reaction too often, Elissa. I meant what I said–if he puts us all in danger by doing that, we'll have to sedate him."

"No, I know. I just want to try talking to Ady, that's all."

"All right." Then, as she hesitated, not sure if that was per-mission, "Yes, go on, then. They're sharing a room, though, just to let you know. It's the third door."

"Thank you." She opened the sitting room door and slipped out into another corridor, almost identical to the one into which the front door opened, but from the look of the doors, with fewer rooms standing off it.

She tapped lightly on the third door down. From inside came a murmur of voices, then one voice, closer. "What?"

"It's me," she said. "Elissa. I've come to try to explain. I made it sound so much worse than I meant to. I–"

The door slid open. Ady stood inside, his arms out,

preventing her from seeing farther into the room. Tension showed in the tightness around his eyes and mouth.

"You can't talk to Zee. Not yet."

Elissa dropped her gaze. "That's okay. I understand. I don't need to. If I can just explain to you . . ."

"Hang on," said Ady, and hit the button to close the door. As the bland white surface slid across in front of him, she heard the murmur of his voice again, directed away into the room. A minute crawled by. With every few seconds Elissa's insides seemed to tighten a little more.

The door opened again and Ady stepped out, shutting it behind him as soon as he'd crossed the threshold. His face showed none of the earlier friendliness or good humor. "Okay, go on."

"We're not working with anyone." She forced herself to meet his eyes. "It's just me and Lin and the four *Phoenix* crew members. We're not working with IPL. We're *definitely* not working with anyone to do with SFI. We just came back, honestly, to try to help."

Ady's expression didn't change. "What was all that about the hyperdrives?"

Elissa swallowed. "We're not asking anyone to do anything. We're not trying to make them. But Lin and I found out that it doesn't hurt. It's not dangerous. And if—*if*—other people wanted to try, and if it worked the same, we could have a functioning space force on Sekoia." She realized she'd automatically looked away from him, and made herself look back up. "If Sekoia doesn't recover, we'll be refugees the rest of our lives. I'm completely not trying to make anyone do anything, but if they wanted to try, if they wanted to help rebuild Sekoia . . ."

His expression still hadn't changed, and faced with that, she ran out of willpower and had to stop.

"Your sister forgot to ask where Zee came from."

The statement seemed to come from nowhere, and for a moment Elissa just looked at him, waiting for it to make sense. "What?"

"When we told you about Jay and El and Cassiopeia getting attacked on the flyer, she asked if we all came on the flyer. And I said how we—us non-Spares—were already here. Which left Zee unaccounted for."

Elissa thought back. "Yes. I guess . . . I sort of got the impression you didn't want Zee to have to talk about it . . . ?"

Ady leaned back against the wall, arms crossed. "Yeah. Guess why."

"How would I know?" But the beginning of an idea came, creeping up around the edges of her mind, and she realized it would have been more accurate to say *I don't want to know.*

"Take a guess." Ady's face was bleak, merciless. Anger sparked through Elissa, jerking her spine upright, lifting her chin. She was *over* this kind of mind game. And whatever she'd done wrong, whatever awful hidden wounds she'd stamped all over, she didn't deserve to be treated like the enemy.

"I said I don't *know.* If you want me to know, you tell me!"

"Fine," said Ady. "A month ago Zee was on a spaceship. *In* a spaceship. In one of those specially locked chambers, with wires poking through him and liquid all around him so he couldn't even scream."

"No." Elissa put her hands up—a stop sign, or a shield. "No, no. Don't."

"Why not? That's what you want to send him back to—"

"I do *not*!" Although, from the moment he'd said *Guess*

why, she'd kind of known, hearing it spelled out suddenly felt like more than she could bear. She closed her hands and brought them down to her sides, as if by doing so she could keep hold of her self-control, stop it from breaking.

"As good as! I don't know how he's going to be able to get on a ship for relocation, even, and you come here with your glib 'oh, it doesn't hurt.' *Your* twin escaped—you don't have to deal with knowing she had to go through them doing that to her. I've got all these horrific images in my head—and for all I know the reality was even worse than what I'm imagining. You have no *idea*—"

"I *do* have an idea!" Elissa shouted at him, self-control not so much breaking as exploding. "You think you're the only one with mental images you can't get rid of? I saw a Spare it had happened to! I saw a Spare who died of it!"

Ady stared at her, whatever he'd been going to say halted in midsentence.

Elissa's hands were shaking, nails digging into her palms. She forced herself to speak quietly. "You don't know what we've been through either. You've got the most basic details from the public newscasts or from whatever you've found out for yourself—you have no idea what it's been like for me and Lin." He didn't look as if he was about to interrupt, but she didn't pause, not wanting to give him the chance. "I *know* that works both ways, and I *said* I'm really sorry I freaked Zee out like that, but . . . look, we all must have different horrible experiences—I mean, Cassiopeia doesn't even have her *twin* with her, and I can't imagine what that must be like for her—it's not fair for any of us to assume we've had it worse than anyone else—"

Ady did interrupt now, but not with any of the angry

responses she would have expected. "What did the Spare look like?"

"What?"

His face was haunted. "The Spare who died. You saw him . . . in th-the cell?"

"Yes."

"Did he—did it look like it h-h—"

"Hurt him?"

Ady nodded, temporarily beyond speech, arms tight across his chest.

For an instant Elissa considered . . . not lying, exactly, but prevaricating, an impulse born of both mercy and of cowardice, of a desire not to have to deal with Ady's pain as well as her own. Then she opened her mouth and told him the truth. "Yes."

"*Oh God.*" The words were a choked sound. Ady screwed his eyes shut, his body rigid, as if by staying perfectly still he could ward off the pain.

It looked like it was over quickly. I don't think he knew much about it. The hopeful lies came into Elissa's mind. She couldn't say them. They—all the twins—had been lied to their whole lives. No matter how awful the truth was, it *must* be better than more lies. *Mustn't it? Oh God, it doesn't feel better. And there's nothing I can say to make it better.*

"I should have known." Like Ady's previous words, these, too, were almost inaudible.

Not knowing whether he'd shake her off, Elissa reached out to put a hand on his folded arms. "How could you have known? If you and Zee never had a link—"

Ady opened his eyes, like someone with a migraine forcing his eyes open to sunlight, his every muscle looking as if it were braced against pain. "That's why. If we'd had a link, if I'd *known* . . ." He shut his eyes again. "I . . . I just feel so guilty."

"But it's not your fault you don't have a link."

When he looked at her once more, she could see her words had hardly registered. "But what if it is? I mean, wasn't that the point of taking the Spares? That *every* pair of twins has some kind of psychic ability, and it's just a question of taking the one with the strongest?"

"But you said—Zee said—we're not all the same. Zee doesn't have telepathy. He's empathic, you said so."

"With other people, yes. But I'm his *twin*—there ought to be more than that between him and me. *Shouldn't* there? A proper link? Like you. And Samuel and Jay—they have one, and Sofia and El at least know they *used* to—"

She wasn't sure what he was getting at. He couldn't think he was culpable for his lack of telepathy with Zee—it was so illogical, he *couldn't* think it. But all the same, that was what he seemed to be saying. "Oh come on," she said, trying for reason, "that's six people out of all the hundreds of pairs of twins there must be. It's not a representative sample, is it? And what about Cassiopeia?"

"That's what I'm scared of." There was that look of being haunted back in his face again. "Her twin rejected her—wouldn't meet, wouldn't even try. She doesn't talk about it, but once, just after we all got here, she said something. . . . I think her twin rejected her before. Back before any of us knew all this stuff. I think her twin found a way to kill the link for herself. And I—" His face creased again as if he'd been struck by a spasm of pain. "What if I did that to Zee? What if, all those times when I was a kid, when I had a nightmare and told myself it wasn't real, when I found myself daydreaming and snapped out of it to go play or something—what if any of those times, what if I was actually in touch with Zee and I cut him off? What if I could have known? What if I could have helped him—somehow, like you helped Lin escape? What if it's *my fault* he ended up on that ship?"

A million arguments tumbled through Elissa's head. *I did try to cut off the link—I tried for three years and I could never do it. What makes you think you could have done it, when you don't even remember trying to?*

But when she met his eyes, felt the tremor run through where her hand lay on his arm, she forgot all the arguments, she saw only how much he was hurting.

"Ady," she said, "isn't it bad enough that they got away with torturing half of us? Do we have to torture ourselves as well?" She let go of his arm, stepped forward, and put her arms around him.

For a moment he stayed rigid. She'd thought he was shaking, but it was more as if he were vibrating, as if he held on to forces almost stronger than he could control. Then another tremor went through him, he dropped his head on her shoulder, and cried.

Elissa had one shocked split second of wanting to pull away. She hadn't expected him to cry—hadn't known boys her own age *did* cry, not like this, not with such awful wrenching sobs that sounded as if they were physically hurting him.

Then the thought came: *This must have been eating at him for ages, ever since he found out about Zee. And he's been in an unfamiliar place, without the family he actually grew up with, having to cope with the weirdness of Spares and the on-edge emotions of the other twins—and not even being able to make too much noise in case it means they're discovered and attacked. . . .*

He hasn't cried before. And the crying—okay, it did sound awful, but it also sounded like something he needed.

Ady got himself together much sooner than Elissa thought she would have managed, dragging a crumpled tissue out of his jeans pocket, wiping his face, and thunderously blowing his nose. The tissue proved almost entirely inadequate and he fumbled for a dry corner, his face down, an embarrassed hunch to his shoulders, until Elissa found one in the pocket of her hoodie and handed it to him.

"Thanks." It was a mutter. He blew his nose again, then dropped both tissues on the floor. But as in the kitchen, the auto-clean wasn't on, and they lay limp and motionless rather than being sucked efficiently away for disposal. He muttered again, what sounded like a swear word this time, bent to pick them up, Elissa's arm slipping from his shoulders as he moved, and shoved them away in his jeans pocket.

It seemed like now might be the time to leave him to recover—*and, oh God, to let him go and talk to poor Zee who's just in there waiting for him to come back*—but now that the storm of anger and grief had passed, she couldn't quite think how to do it.

Ady pushed the tissues down out of sight in his pocket, then raised his gaze to hers. Battered and tearstained, he looked younger than he had before. An instant of nausea swam over Elissa. *So much pain. How are we ever going to get over it?*

"I'm sorry," he said.

"Oh, it completely doesn't matter—"

"For yelling at you, I mean. I shouldn't have done it. I just . . . if something freaks Zee out, I . . . well, I already feel so bad about not being there for him. . . ."

Elissa managed to smile, although, given the nausea and the sinking feeling of helplessness still dragging at her, it probably wasn't her best effort. "Oh come on, you think I don't understand that? Honestly, you don't need to say sorry."

"You get the guilt too, huh?" His smile didn't look much better than hers.

Elissa laughed, surprising herself with a flash of genuine amusement. "Do I ever. When you think of what our lives have been like, compared to theirs . . . I mean, how could you *not* feel guilty?"

"Yeah, okay." His shoulders relaxed a little. "Jeez, therapy our whole lives, I bet."

"If there are any therapists who know how to handle us." It was weird—but welcome—how the warmth of laughter took away that feeling of nausea.

"God, yeah, you're right. That'd be some special training, wouldn't it?" As the rest of his body relaxed, he leaned against the wall, letting his head tip back to rest against it. "Look, Lissa . . ." His eyes met hers again. "Thanks, okay?"

She hadn't really done anything he needed to thank her for, unless it was just being with him while he cried. But she wasn't going to argue. She smiled at him, the smile coming more easily than before. "Okay." And then, because the word by itself seemed too bald, and because she didn't have anything to add to it, she leaned forward to give him a brief, second hug.

He responded similarly this time, wrapping his arms around her shoulders, putting his face down, not against her shoulder but against her head. She felt the warmth of his cheek through her hair. He was kind of sweaty, the sort of scent she associated with fear and stress—she'd smelled it on herself often enough during her and Lin's escape—and for a moment pity drew her throat tight.

Back along the corridor, the door hushed open. Elissa pulled away from Ady, feeling exposed. Years of concealing what you were feeling didn't exactly make you comfortable being all emotional with people you'd only just met.

Knowing her embarrassment was showing in her sudden stiffness, her awkward stance, she looked to see who'd come through the door.

It was Cadan.

His eyes met hers. His were expressionless, a look that had once been familiar to her but that she hadn't seen for weeks. *Why's he looking at me like that now?*

Then, as one reason blinked across her brain, she felt heat—betraying, misleading heat—climb into her face.

"Cadan," she said. "I was explaining some stuff to Ady—what I meant about the hyperdrives—"

Cadan nodded, a single movement of his head. "That's what we assumed. Can you come into the main room now? Commander Dacre's on her way."

"Of course," she said, knowing it sounded too eager, too bright. "Um, all of us? Zee as well?"

Cadan's gaze moved to Ady. "If he's able to?"

"I expect," said Ady. "You want me to find out? Bring him along if he's up to it?"

"That would be helpful, thanks." Cadan's voice was calm, courteous . . . a shade colder than usual?

Ady ducked his head in a brief nod as the door sprang open in response to his hand on the sensor panel, sent a fleeting grin to Elissa, and disappeared into his and Zee's room.

"Cadan . . . ," said Elissa again.

He was already turning back to the doorway he'd come through. "You coming, Lis?"

"I was . . . I really was just explaining to Ady . . ."

His eyebrows rose a little. "Yes. Like I said, that's what we assumed."

"He—there was some stuff about Spares that really upset him, so I hugged him. I mean, that's why I was hugging him."

"Okay."

"Cadan . . ."

"Lissa, I said okay. I mean it. I believe you. I could see he looked upset."

"Oh." Her cheeks, which had been cooling, flamed again. Here she was explaining herself, explaining something that didn't even *need* explaining, and now it turned out Cadan didn't even think it needed explaining either.

And now he was smiling at her, a smile that, she thought, might be affectionate or might be simply amused. "It's okay, Elissa. It's not like it's my favorite thing, seeing my girlfriend wrapped up in some other guy's arms, but jeez, I don't really have the right to demand you not touch other people, do I?"

Yes. No. No, of course he didn't. A million teen zines and pop psychology channels would have made sure she knew that, even if she couldn't have worked it out for herself. But all the same . . . Okay, she *didn't* want him to demand anything that extreme, but she wouldn't have minded a bit more of a flash of jealousy.

You said this was serious for you. You said it mattered. Why does it not matter enough for you to get jealous? Especially if you don't know whether I feel the same way?

Was it just that he was—*oh, here it comes again*—older, better at being self-contained? Then another thought seemed to appear from the blue. Was it that, serious or not, he was assuming that what was between them was already coded with its own expiration date?

Even as the cold dropped into her stomach, she realized the thought *wasn't* from the blue, it wasn't from a clear, storm-free sky. The thunderclouds had been massing before, from the moment he'd said he couldn't imagine them having gotten together during her previous life on Sekoia, gathering thicker when his parents showed they didn't approve.

No. This was crazy. *She* was being crazy. He'd never wanted a girl to meet his parents before, he'd *said* so. He wouldn't have said that if he was thinking of this as a temporary thing. She needed to hold on to what he'd *actually* said and stop getting in a whole panic about what he hadn't—

"Lissa?" He was watching her, and his expression had changed. "What's wrong?"

But there was no time now. She couldn't ask him about it with Commander Dacre on her way, with everyone waiting in the next room—with Ady and Zee about to come out into the corridor. And—*again*—she didn't want to be *that* girlfriend, the one who was always crying and needing reassurance and being so clingy the guy eventually dumped her out of pure impatience. . . .

"Nothing." She gave him the best smile she could manage. "It's okay."

The smile must have been good enough, because he returned it, dropping a kiss on her hair as she went past him to open the door into the sitting room. But despite the little gesture of affection, the cold remained inside her, a weight she couldn't shift. *Is that what it is? Is he not expecting it to last?*

TEN

WHILE ELISSA had been gone, someone had moved the various couches and beanbags to the perimeter of the room, creating more of a meeting area than a sitting room. Lin sat, cross-legged, against the far wall, her eyes smudged with fatigue. When she was tired, the only color that remained in her face was the fake tan. She remained a version of Elissa herself, but a version left out to fade in the sun, a version in which the color had been washed out.

With a flash of imagination so vivid it felt like memory, Elissa saw Lin in a hyperdrive cell, wired up and strapped down, lip bleeding beneath her teeth in a grimace of pain, energy being torn from her, as agonizing as if every nerve ending were being set on fire. *Oh God, if I'd found Lin and they'd done that to her . . .*

There was a space on the floor next to Lin, and Elissa went quickly to sit next to her, pushing the image from her brain, blocking it out. Lin had escaped. She'd been through a hell of a lot, but, thank God, it had never been *that*.

Lin flickered a look sideways as Elissa settled next to her. "Zee?"

"I only talked to Ady. He's talking to Zee now, though. I think they'll be here."

Lin's gaze sharpened. "What's wrong? What did he say to you?"

Oh God. She hadn't planned on telling Lin about Zee—not yet, not without planning how she could lessen the impact. But if Lin had noticed there was something wrong, she couldn't leave her guessing. And she couldn't lie to her.

She leaned close to her twin's ear, dropping her voice. "He told me that when Zee was rescued, it wasn't from a facility. It was off a ship."

Lin's face went still. Her eyes widened, the pupils shrinking to shocked pinpricks. As clear as if the image were reflected within them, Elissa could see that Lin, too, was being spun back in time to the *Phoenix*, to when they'd prized open the sealed hyperdrive chamber and found the dead Spare.

Elissa put her hand out, finding Lin's, tightening her fingers around Lin's, noticing how cold they'd gone. "Lin? God, I'm *sorry*, I didn't want to tell you with no warning like that."

Lin shook her head. "It's okay. But"—a tiny shudder went through her—"how is he still alive?"

"Or still *sane*. God knows. I can't even imagine it."

A few minutes later Ady and Zee entered.

Now she knew, Elissa couldn't help her eyes going to the healing burn mark on his neck. His hair was just long enough to fall across, obscuring it, but under the hair the mark would stretch around to the back of his neck, to the hole that had been drilled in the back of his skull, the hole where the hyperdrive plug had fitted. Lin had that too, as did all the Spares; Lin had experienced the agonizing pain of the machines they'd used to test her psychic levels. But she'd never reached the stage of being wired up to a ship's hyperdrive, left trapped and helpless in a world of lightless pain. Zee had.

And for how long? How long had he been there? How long was it until he was rescued? She couldn't ask–she couldn't even ask Ady, let alone Zee, but she was suddenly desperate to know, desperate to know exactly how bad it had been. *Please let it not have been that long. A day, a couple of days* . . . She couldn't conceive of it lasting any more time than that–how long would someone be able to stand it before their mind cracked like a blown egg?

The door slid open, and Commander Dacre came briskly in. *She's not in uniform today?* thought Elissa, then felt silly. Of *course* officials weren't going to visit the safe houses in IPL uniform, advertising their presence to the security cams mounted at every corner of every building–security cams that could, at any point, be relaying information to hostile eyes.

Uniform or not, the commander still had her gun, holstered at her belt within easy reach. And Elissa caught the discreet gleam of a com-unit on her wrist, its earpiece clipped neatly over–no, *through*–the upper lobe of her ear. Someone must have offered her a drink, as if she were a normal guest, because she held a coffee cup in one hand, but nothing else about her demeanor suggested that she was here in anything other than an official capacity.

Her gaze skimmed the room, making only the briefest pause at Lin, then she walked across the no-color carpet to stand just past the window, a vantage point where she could see outside to the weirdly traffic-free sky.

Her gaze skimmed over them all again. This time it snagged briefly on Zee before moving on. When she spoke, her voice was as colorless as the carpet, as flatly calm as the sky.

"You're being relocated today. All of you. We've arranged clearance for Captain Greythorn's ship—the *Phoenix*—to take you and your families off Sekoia and to Philomel. You'll be leaving this evening."

Some of the faces in the room lit up so fast it was as if a single wave of smiles had broken across them. Sofia, Ady, Cadan's mother. Others—like Felicia's, El's, Cadan's—became entirely still. And Lin shot upright, vibrating with indignation.

"No," she said. "We're *not*. We're *not*. Cadan already *told* you what we came here for."

"Be quiet, please," said Commander Dacre, and Lin closed her mouth with an almost audible snap, looking as if she'd taken herself by surprise. Elissa fought down a ridiculous giggle. No matter how unpleasant the commander had been so far, it was kind of impressive to see *anyone* be able to shut Lin down like that. She managed to suppress the giggle, but then she looked up, caught Ivan's eye and saw exactly the same expression of suppressed amusement on his face, and she had to fight the laughter back down all over again.

The commander's gaze moved from Lin, to Cadan, to Elissa and the rest of the crew. "You appear," she said, "not to have grasped the full gravity of the situation. Allow me to help you."

She set her coffee down on the windowsill. "As you'll be aware, Sekoia still has a space force, but it's had to be brought entirely under IPL's control. Nearly all your higher-ranking officials have been grounded while we investigate to see how much inside knowledge they had about the use of Spares. We've drafted in most of the pilots—and ships—to help our own with the evacuation process. Except without any access to hyperspeed, the process is still painfully slow, which has left us without the flight power for orbital patrols. Which means the planet is at constant risk of pirate attacks."

Her eyes shifted for a moment to the window. "And this is before the next outbreak of Elloran flu. Which is due at some point over the next six months. And if Sekoia's infrastructure isn't in better shape by then, the consequences could be serious."

Complete understatement. Elloran superflu wasn't usually fatal to anyone in normal health, but it was super contagious. And if it spread through a population that had lost the ability to buy in mass stocks of antiviral drugs . . .

Elissa crossed her arms. *If I'd known, right at the start of it all, what this was going to do to my whole world, would I have made the same decisions?* The answer was yes, of course—it *had* to be yes, because of Lin, because of what SFI had been doing to the Spares. But all the same, the thought kept circling back. *If I'd known the consequences, if I'd known it meant people were going to die . . . what would I really have done? How easily would I have made the decision to sacrifice them all?*

"What about IPL's own ships?" asked Markus.

The commander looked a little surprised to have been asked anything, but she answered. "We're using them, of course. But IPL forces are needed all across the star system—once the take-over was accomplished, we had no authority to keep them serving Sekoia when other societies stand in greater need."

She sipped coffee. "We're operating a triage system for the evacuation. The top priority is, of course, Spares and their families, plus staff from the former SFI facilities."

Staff from the . . . ? Elissa was still sticking on that, her brain telling her it couldn't mean what it sounded like, when Lin spoke, her voice sharp with incredulity.

"*Staff?* Staff from the facilities? *They* need relocating? You're *rescuing* them?"

The commander set her coffee down again. "Hardly. They're being taken off-planet in prison ships to await trial— on Philomel, mostly."

"But they're being moved?" said Lin. "They have the same priority as *Spares*? You're *spending money* on getting them off-planet?"

"Off-planet to prison," said the commander.

"To safety!"

"If you choose to see it that way."

"I don't *choose* to see it that way. That's how it is!"

Fury shook her voice. Elissa put out an anxious hand. "Lin . . . Don't freak—"

Lin slewed around to face her. "You think this is *okay*? Taking them off Sekoia before they've even gotten all of *us* out?"

"*No.*" The word came out with more emphasis than she'd known she was going to give it. The idea that the people who'd put restraints on Lin, who'd drilled a hole in her head and plugged cables into the back of her skull, who'd put Zee in the bowels of a spaceship, trapping him alone in agony-filled darkness—the idea that *they* were being given priority, that they were being taken from a dangerous planet to a safe one ahead of other people, *innocent* people, like Felicia's family, who hadn't even known about Spares, was like a mockery of the justice IPL had talked about, the justice Lin had been promised.

"No, I don't think it's anything *like* okay," she said to Lin, and her voice, like Lin's, was shaking.

"The course of justice doesn't depend on what you think is okay." Elissa turned at the sound of Commander Dacre's words, to see her looking straight at her and Lin, her expression chilly. "Unfortunately for *your* sense of fairness, IPL adheres to a policy of innocent until proven guilty."

"Oh it *so* does not!" The words came on a wave of heat that blazed through her, like flames bursting from the punctured hull of a spaceship. "IPL's treating *everyone* like they're guilty! You're treating *everyone* like they're criminals! You wouldn't even let Cadan bring the *Phoenix* here, although you can see how useful it would be. With your whole military law thing, it's probably *your* fault everything's gone so crazy! You're treating everyone like criminals so they're *behaving* like criminals, but when it comes to real criminals, people who did horrific things to the Spares, you're all 'blah blah blah, innocent till proven guilty,' when it's *obvious* they're not innocent."

"You have no idea what you're talking about," said the commander. Her voice was as chilly as her expression, and now Elissa realized that everyone was staring at her, that everyone else had gone quiet.

"I can see what you've done to my planet!" she said, holding on to the flare of defiance that had allowed her to talk like that to an official, a *grown-up*. "I can see you're doing it all wrong. People on Sekoia—they *like* keeping the law, they *like* being law-abiding. They don't need curfews and rationing and military law. And those—those people from the facilities—they're not innocent. They're criminals. Not just potential criminals, *real* criminals. They don't deserve special treatment."

"You'd advocate summary execution, maybe?" said Commander Dacre.

"No," Elissa said, irritated. "I just don't see why they get *priority*. You could leave them here—like, lock them in the facilities or something—until the people in the most danger have been taken to safety."

"People in the most danger?" For the first time, the commander laughed. Her eyes still lacked all warmth. "You don't know what happened to the staff they did that to, do you?"

Like I care? "What?" said Elissa, folding her arms, glaring. The commander was wrong. *IPL* was wrong. If they could only *see*—

"It was one of the aboveground facilities," said the commander. "We'd reached it, and we were extracting the Spares. We'd been extracting staff, too, up until that point, but as timing got tighter we made the decision to give the Spares priority. So this time—this time only—we left the staff there and locked the place down from outside."

Her eyes flicked across Lin's face, then across Elissa's. "There was a security breach. A leak. People found out, both that the staff was there and that they couldn't get out. A mob took off from the nearest city."

Her voice lost the last traces of expression. "The security cameras at the facility were still running, so the people inside saw the mob coming. They couldn't lock any of the doors—external or internal—from inside, but they managed to barricade themselves into the staff lounges. They held out for eighty-two minutes."

Elissa wrapped her arms around herself. Something prickled up her back, onto her neck. If she could, she would have taken back what she'd said. Not because she hadn't meant it but because it had led to this story—this story she was all at once 100 percent certain she didn't want to know. *If she's just going to tell me they were killed, I can cope, I don't care. But I don't think they were just killed. I think something worse happened to them, and I don't want to hear it. I don't want to hear.*

Across the room, Cadan's face was set. Markus was squinting, as if by doing so he could withdraw himself from what he was about to hear.

"The mob tore them to pieces," said the commander. "Twenty-nine of them. They showed that on the newscasts, too—not the events themselves, but what the place looked like afterward." Her eyes met Elissa's. "You don't like that IPL's instituted military law? We hadn't, until that point, until we saw what sort of things your *law-abiding* population is capable of. And we have no desire to allow criminals to escape justice. But what happened to the staff in that facility wasn't justice."

Silence fell, heavy in the room. Elissa felt sick. Thoughts battered against the inside of her head. *But Sekoia is law-abiding. It is. Things like that don't happen here. People don't form mobs, don't . . .* Automatically, her eyes squinched closed, as if by shutting them she could shut out the images in her head.

Cadan spoke into the silence, his voice tight with self-control. "Commander, the *Phoenix* is entirely at IPL's disposal to relocate anyone who needs it. But I have to request that IPL allows a crew of volunteers to return the same way. As you say, your forces are overstretched. I've been getting caught up since five this morning, and if you'll give me ten minutes I can explain what we can offer to aid IPL in—"

Commander Dacre turned cold eyes upon him. "Out of the question."

Flushing, Cadan opened his mouth again, but she held up a hand, cutting him off as effectively as she'd done to Lin.

"Let me finish, please. Your . . . information source"—her eyes turned for a moment toward Cadan's father—"is correct. We are, as you say, overstretched. And if it were just you and your adult crew, we would find you extremely useful."

She paused for no more than a few seconds. But even that short pause was enough to make Cadan look as if he'd been slapped, enough for Elissa to realize that the commander could have said nothing more angled to make Cadan feel terrible. *If he and the crew had come alone, if he'd refused to take me and Lin, he'd be able to help people now.*

For a moment she felt the drag of guilt, familiar, unwelcome, then anger sparked through her. *She said that on purpose. She said that to make him feel bad. However much they disagree with what we've done, she didn't need to say that to him.*

It seemed like Commander Dacre didn't mind turning the knife a little either. "If you'd wanted to help," she said, her voice expressionless, "you should have left your extra passengers on Sanctuary and come back with an entirely adult crew. As it is, you've got two teenage girls—one of whom is still dealing with the aftereffects of a lifetime's imprisonment—and you're expecting us to use them in a situation that's scarcely suitable for untrained adults."

Another little pause, as vicious as her words, as vicious as the twist of a knife, and the anger flared, bright and hot, within Elissa. "However, as you didn't leave them, IPL is permitting you to use your ship for one relocation journey. Your own family members and your crew, plus a number of already existing candidates for relocation, including the inhabitants of this apartment. Also, of course, your two underage passengers. But you should understand that's all. Once you get them off this planet"—the merest flick of her eyes left Elissa in no doubt as to whom, specifically, she meant—"you will not be permitted to bring them back."

Cadan's jaw was rigid. "Are there rules for where I can take my ship after leaving the passengers at Philomel, too?"

"Not as far as IPL is concerned, Captain. Our agreement with the Philomel authorities does ensure that there's a place for you there, should you wish to take advantage of it." Her voice was still utterly indifferent. "The majority of the refugees have been taken there, of course, so if you still want to . . . help . . . by offering any particular understanding you have, to aid in their rehabilitation, you are all, of course, entirely at liberty to do so."

Elissa supposed she should feel glad about that, feel that at least they were being given something. If they were condemned to being bundled back off Sekoia, to be the perpetually rootless refugees Lin had talked about, at least they could do one of the things they'd wanted. At least they could try helping the other Spares.

But if it had been meant to pacify them, it was too little, and too late. Commander Dacre had behaved as if she was nothing but contemptuous of Cadan, of the decisions he'd made, she'd spoken as if she blamed him for the decisions that had been made by Elissa and Lin, not by him at all. She'd ignored what they could do—what they could offer. She'd treated them like nothing but kids, out of place and in the way.

I might not have minded before all this happened. When all I knew was living at home, being looked after, being told what to do. But when you've had to do everything I've had to do over the last few weeks, when you've faced pain and danger and death—no one should be treating you like a child anymore.

And I don't want to go to Philomel. Already her stomach was clenching, like a spring being wound tighter. The people who'd worked in the facilities were on Philomel. They might be imprisoned, but all the same, sharing the same planet with them felt too close, as if it were a violation to be breathing the same atmosphere.

That's silly. We won't even necessarily be on the same continent.

I don't care. It's not silly.

Her eyes caught Cadan's, and she knew the plea showed in her face. *Don't let her dismiss us like that. Don't give up yet.*

"Commander," said Cadan. "With respect, I don't believe you've got all the details of what we're offering. When I arrived at IPL headquarters, I gave them a full rundown on exactly how we were able to escape from the SFI forces that were sent after us. If it hadn't been for Elissa and Lin and what they can do, my ship would have been blown to pieces before it ever reached Sanctuary. You do have that information, don't you? You do know what they did? And you must have a report from the base, from last night? Lin destroyed two flyers—she probably saved the entire base."

"I'm aware of both those incidents, yes. However, IPL does not use teenagers as power sources. Or as weapons." For an instant there was something other than chilly calm in her voice, a tone as if Cadan were forcing her into distasteful proximity with something slimy, stinking of decay.

"Yes, I understand that." Cadan's voice was full of bitten-down frustration. "But why wouldn't IPL allow said teenagers to volunteer the power they control? No one's been *using* Lin. We're not talking child soldiers here—or Humane

Treatment Act violations. This is voluntary. All along, this has been voluntary."

Except for me. Elissa pushed the thought away. That was over. Lin had promised not to do it again. And that wasn't what Cadan was talking about, anyway.

The commander was looking at him as if it were he who was the stinking and decayed thing. "IPL isn't allowing it for the same reason IPL doesn't allow child soldiers, even when they are—supposedly—voluntary." There was an edge to her voice now. "You're talking about a seventeen-year-old destroying two flyers—taking lives—as if that's acceptable. As if, as long as you were happy to let that happen, we should be too. IPL finds nothing acceptable, Captain Greythorn, in you permitting—*encouraging*—a teenager to kill."

"Oh for God's sake," snapped Cadan. "When did you start your combat training, then? Did IPL hold off training you till you turned twenty?"

"That will do! It's not your place to put personal questions to an IPL official—"

But Cadan hadn't finished. "Because I know *I* was in combat training when I was fourteen—just like I would have been if I'd joined the space force of half the planets in the star system."

"Then you should also know you were being trained for *defense*—"

"And that's what *Lin was doing*! That's what *I* was doing. I killed people in those fights too. Is that okay just because I'm not a teenager anymore, or because I did it with my ship's firepower rather than with electrokinesis?"

"Captain Greythorn, I said that's *enough*. This is not a classroom debate. If you're frustrated by IPL's code of ethics, perhaps I should remind you that maybe it's a little more stringent than the government you're used to."

"Whoa," said Samuel, sotto voce. *"Scorch."*

Sofia giggled, muffled but still audible. And something rippled through the room, an eddy of half-hidden rebellion that reminded Elissa of being back at school. No, not through the whole room—just through the nine twins and Spares.

The grown-ups, too, might be angry and frustrated, but in the glances they shot Samuel's way there was nothing but distracted irritation. Not the delighted, covert amusement that Elissa saw flicker across Lin's, Ady's, Cassiopeia's faces.

What happens if we say we won't go? If we really do rebel, if we force the commander to listen to us? If the IPL forces were so overstretched, how could they stop them? And with a million more important things to focus on, how much effort were they going to put into trying? Mr. and Mrs. Greythorn might think they should leave—even Ivan and Markus and Felicia might, when they'd been told and *told* how dangerous it was for her and Lin to stay. Could they really *make* them leave, though? Did they have enough power to do that?

Cadan was starting to say something else when Commander Dacre put her hand up, a peremptory demand for silence. There was a distracted line between her eyebrows.

After a split second of confusion, Elissa registered the almost imperceptible tilt of the commander's head and realized she was listening to the earpiece fastened through her ear.

"What? *What?* Yes, I'm here— You're not coming through." Her voice rose. "I'm not getting you. Try another ch— *Hell.*" She put her finger to the earpiece, her eyebrows now slanting close together, then clicked twice, three times, on the side of her wrist-unit. "Greythorn, are you running masking?"

It was Cadan's father who answered. "No. You are—IPL is."

"I'm not talking about the standard blackout!" She shot him a look like a razor. "Anything extra, I'm asking. There's interference on every channel."

"Then no. No masking. The interference isn't coming from us."

The commander swore again, threw what looked like a glance of fury at the whole room, and flicked something on her wrist-unit.

The voice exploded into the room at top volume. Several people clapped their hands to their ears.

"Commander Dacre, do you read? Come in, Commander Dacre. Emergency in the immediate vicinity. *Commander Dacre—*"

"*Yes.*" The commander still had her finger on the wrist-unit, and after a second the voice fell to a bearable volume. "I'm hearing you, Control. Go ahead."

"There's unauthorized activity heading toward the tower you're in. A group of twelve, on foot, three different directions, and all the street-corner cams are detecting concealed weapons—"

"Give me the coordinates."

The voice obeyed. The commander tipped her head to hear, eyes crinkling in concentration.

Unauthorized activity? Concealed weapons? No. No! This is meant to be a safe house.

Lin had gone very still next to her. Across the room, Zee was suddenly shivering, and El's lips were white.

"We'll need an extraction," Commander Dacre said. "Send

a team in. I'll get the occupants to the roof for a pickup in five minutes—"

"We don't have a team." The voice crackled across hers. For the first time Elissa realized it was a man's voice, harsh with something more than urgency, something closer to panic. "There's no other team close enough. Yours is the only one in the area—"

"They're not." There was no interference scrunching at the commander's voice, but all at once it sounded equally harsh. "I'm here solo. I logged it all in before I came out—I assigned my team to the fire in Sector C. It's on the records in front of you, for God's sake!"

"You—" The man sounded blank, shocked. "You don't have your team with you?"

"Check your records! This isn't *my* negligence. Get me another team. I don't care where you get them from. Pull them out and send them here."

"Commander, I don't have anyone." It was definitely panic in his voice now. "I don't have *anyone*. They're all in three-bar emergencies—I can't pull anyone out. If you're there solo, you're the sole personnel in the whole area. Commander—"

The commander bit out an expression Elissa's mother had told her no nice woman would ever say, and cut the connection.

She began dialing through names on her wrist-unit. Within seconds it was blinking amber, the speed of the flashes indicating the number of people she was calling. But that was all. It didn't flash green; no voice broke through the charged silence in the room.

The commander swore again, but Elissa wasn't listening anymore. There were people coming to attack them. People with weapons, who must have found out that there was a safe house here—a safe house filled with vulnerable, hated Spares, and their twins, and the people protecting them.

There was an ear-crackling burst of interference, then the voice came through once more. "Commander, your ground-level exits are no-go. They're at both sides of the tower block. They're hacking into the entrance codes—they'll be in the tower within five minutes."

"Then you'll have to find an extraction team," the commander snapped.

"We don't *have* one. The nearest one is twenty minutes away—"

"Then tell them to get here as soon as they can! We'll panic-room the pairs. I've got armed personnel here—we'll hold them off until your damn team can reach us."

The voice was saying something else, but the words broke up into electronic squeaks and burbles, and the commander cut the connection again. Her gaze swept to Mr. Greythorn.

"Panic room," she said. "We can hold out until the rescue team gets here."

Panic room? Since when does low-income housing have panic rooms?

The next moment Elissa and Lin, as well as the other Spares and their twins, found themselves being hustled into the corridor Ady and Zee's room led off, then through the first door. It was just a bedroom—Cassiopeia's bedroom, Elissa guessed, when she saw that only the bottom bunk had been used. The bed in the top bunk was still as perfectly made as if it had slid that moment from the pressing rollers of a housekeeper-bot.

Mrs. Greythorn hit a button by the little window, and a steel shutter rattled down to clunk into the slot at the bottom of the window. A metallic scrape and slither told Elissa that bolts had shot out to secure it.

The twins were pressed against the bunk bed and against the opposite wall. There was room for all nine of them, but only just.

And this isn't a real panic room. There's no food and water supply, there's no washroom, the air-conditioning isn't separate from the rest of the apartment.

Commander Dacre swept them all with a look. "The code word is 'morello.' You need to remember it. Use the internal door locks. Don't open them for anything other than the code word, you understand?" Her gaze included Mrs. Greythorn and Ivan.

They're staying in here as well? But what about the others? What about Cadan?

The next moment she had the answer. Mr. Greythorn's, Felicia's, and Markus's hands were on their holsters, and Cadan was zipping up his uniform jacket. It was blaster-proof, she knew that much from the fight with the pirates who'd gotten on board the *Phoenix*. *But the people coming to attack us—they won't be using just blasters, they'll be using real guns.*

"What are you doing?" said Lin, her voice higher than normal. "What's going on?"

Elissa reached for her hand. "They're leaving us in here, where it's safest. They're going to go fight off the—the attack."

"Markus and Felicia and Cadan?" Lin's voice went even higher. She looked incredulously at the commander. "They're not IPL. They're not supposed to have to fight, not with *people!*"

It sounded crazy, the way she said it, but her voice revealed all the outrage Elissa was feeling. Fighting with a ship, the way Cadan had back at the base, that seemed fair—scary, but fair. It was what he was trained for. But this awful, cornered, rats-in-a-trap last-stand defense . . .

The commander gave Lin an impatient look as she turned to go back out. "Do I have time for this? They're all experienced with combat. I have no team here, and eleven civilians to protect."

And so now they're good enough for you? Elissa thought furiously, knowing it was unfair, not caring. So the commander would talk to Cadan like he was a fool, but then she'd ask—no, not even ask—*expect* him to risk his life to help her with the job *she* was supposed to do? Without even—*does he even have a real gun? And his jacket—is it bullet-proof, too? Oh God, it has to be.*

She couldn't freak out now. She couldn't. It wouldn't help anyone, least of all Cadan. He'd dealt with a million things like this—okay, he was primarily trained for space and air combat, but he *was* trained for hand-to-hand, too, and she knew he was more than competent at it. She didn't need to start panicking.

She clenched her hands so tight she felt her nails jab points of pain into her palms, bit the inside of her cheek to keep her face steady, and looked across the room at him.

His eyes met hers, but this time there was no private little smile in them, no look that told her that no matter what she feared, *he* was sure he was going to be okay.

He's not sure. He knows this is stupidly dangerous, but he's doing it anyway.

Cadan's mother was looking at him too, from him to his father. Her face was white. "No," she said. "No. Twelve of them. *Twelve.* You'll get yourselves killed."

"Emily–" Mr. Greythorn came toward her, tried to put his arm around her, but she jerked away and turned on Commander Dacre.

"What are you *doing*? This is halfway to a suicide mission. What's wrong with you?"

The commander's gaze seemed to skim over Cadan's mother rather than rest on her. "I'm left with eleven civilians here–nine of them underage. Would you like me to leave you all to be killed?"

"I'd like you to save us more intelligently!" snapped Mrs. Greythorn. "Rather than forcing my husband and son to get killed along with them. For God's sake, there *must* be someone else nearby."

Commander Dacre's hand went up, a gesture that, in less than an hour, had become all too familiar. Elissa thought that anytime she saw someone make it in the future she would be filled with the same frustrated anger she felt now. *She's not listening. She didn't listen to what we could do, and now she's not listening to what we can't. Cadan's mother is right–this is too high risk. They'll get killed. The man at Control–he said there was a team only twenty minutes away. We should all lock ourselves in the panic room. We should all just wait.*

But the man hadn't exactly sounded definite about the team. And the "panic room"–it wasn't a real panic room. The approaching attackers, if their weapons were good enough, could be inside it within minutes.

It was an animal's terrified instinct, she knew, that made her want to bolt into the smallest, most secure-feeling place, lock herself in with the people she loved best, shut her eyes, put her hands over her ears, and wait for rescue.

Rescue that might never come.

Cadan had been fastening the collar of his jacket. Now he took his hands down, leaving his collar unfastened.

"She's right," he said. "It's a suicide mission."

The commander swung around on him. "What did you *come* here for? What did you *think* we were dealing with? You've been burning my ears off with your demands to help, and now you have the opportunity–"

"Hey." Cadan put his hands up. "We're going to help. But we're going to help in a way that makes sense." He looked across at Lin. His eyes had the flat blue blaze Elissa had seen before.

"The fire escape goes to the roof," he said. "All the buildings near us, they've got external fire escapes as well as internal. If we get up there, can you get us across?"

Lin was squeezing past the bodies in front of her while Elissa was still working out what he meant. "Easy."

"Then let's go. Commander, we can get to the roof, get across to the next-door building then down to the ground. It'll buy us some time before the extraction team can get here. Lis"–his eyes went to her, and now there was a tiny smile, like a spark, within them–"you coming?"

Excitement burned suddenly through her as what he meant came clear in her mind. The metal fire escapes that jutted above every roof, the narrowness of the alleys between the tower blocks. If they had time and tools, they could bridge the gap even without Lin's help. But with her help, with her electrokinesis, it would take minutes.

They were at the door when the commander stepped in front of them. She put her arm out to stop them going out into the corridor where Cadan waited. "No," she said, not to them but to Cadan. "For God's sake, did you hear nothing I said, you stupid boy? You can't do this."

Elissa could almost hear the clash as Cadan's eyes met hers. "Move out of the way," he said.

"Don't even consider it, Captain." The commander's gun was in her hand. Elissa would have thought it was in preparation for an attack, except it was pointing at them. At her and Lin. "You're not in control here."

"Seems like you're not much in control either," said Cadan. "Like you said, time is tight. Let us through."

The commander didn't move. "I said *no*."

The back of Lin's hand brushed Elissa's. Heat rose all at once through her, a haze like vapor lifting over water. But a haze that seemed to blur only part of the room, leaving other bits very clear. The look on Commander Dacre's face, the set of Cadan's head.

She's not listening. She's not listening to Cadan, or anyone else. She's not paying attention to the fact that Lin and I can move a spaceship. This isn't even her world, it's ours, and she's not letting us make any attempt to save it.

"And we're saying yes."

For a moment Elissa thought it was she who'd spoken, then she realized it wasn't. It was Lin.

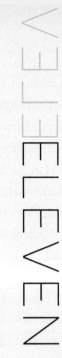

ELEVEN

LIN WAS staring at the commander, her chin up and her eyes bright with a look that made Elissa automatically think *danger*.

"*We're* saying yes," she repeated. "We came here to help and you're not going to stop us."

Commander Dacre gave her a look that almost seemed like one of hatred. "Oh, for God's sake. Do you think I take orders from teenagers?"

Lin narrowed her eyes. *"Too many."*

"What? Too many what?"

"Too many times you've said 'teenagers.'" Lin smiled at her, a look that would have been almost kind had it not been for the flat gleam in her eyes. "Maybe you'd understand stuff better if you stopped being so worried about our age?"

Out of place though it was, a ripple went through the room. A ripple of not-quite-audible amusement.

"That's enough! I'm not here to argue with—" The commander broke off.

"Teenagers?" said Lin, her smile wide and bright.

"*Civilians.* I'm warning you, girl, step away."

A sudden prickle, a feeling of the hairs lifting, ran along Elissa's arms, up the back of her neck. She shot a look at Lin and saw her sister's eyes still fixed on Commander Dacre, her hands whitening as they clenched.

"No," said Lin.

"Who do you think you are? You don't get to say *no* to IPL."

"*I do.* I get to say no to *anyone.*" Something edged Lin's voice. Not quite a tremble, more like the prickling shiver that had run over Elissa's skin. The haze rose further through her head. There was heat in her chest now, burning, and in her hands, too, making them tremble.

Attacking the ships back at the base . . . that was something she hadn't consented to and hadn't wanted. But this was different. Elissa reached out, curled her hand around Lin's. *Make her stop.* She didn't know which of them the thought came from, but she did know that the sudden flare of energy came from both. It sprang from their joined hands, licking up Elissa's arm like invisible fire, burning in her throat like strong alcohol, in her face as if she'd thrown open an oven door.

The commander's gun jumped from her hand, flew across the room, and hit the far wall. It bounced off and fell to the floor.

Make her stop!

Elissa's hands prickled, every nerve humming, a sensation

like superstrong pins and needles. The fingers of her free hand curled. There was a feeling of weight in them, a feeling of grasping something. . . .

The commander staggered against the side of the doorway as suddenly as if she'd been pushed. She made a half-choked sound, something that might have been a cry if it hadn't been strangled by the shock Elissa could see in her face.

Lin giggled, and at the sound some of the haze cleared from Elissa's brain.

We're not going to hurt her! Lin, we can't hurt her!

Jeez, I know. Elissa wasn't looking at her twin, couldn't see her expression, but all the same she knew she was rolling her eyes.

"Okay," said Lin. "We're going to the roof. You"—she pointed at the commander, as imperious as the conductor of a full symphony orchestra—"can come too if you want, but you have to walk behind everyone else. And if you try to interfere we'll move you all the way back here." Her voice was calm and strict—the voice of a teacher or a law officer—but underneath it, like an undertone only Elissa could hear, there was amusement. Far too much amusement.

Elissa was unexpectedly reminded of an early memory, so early she scarcely had the words to frame it, of going into Bruce's room and finding him leaning out of his window with a magnifying glass, systematically frying the bewildered trickle of ants that had been threading their way up the side of the house. She'd screamed and cried, and her mother had come in and scolded Bruce for being cruel, for taking advantage of being so much bigger and stronger than the ants.

Horrified denial swooped through her. That was nothing like Lin was doing. Lin wasn't even *hurting* anyone. And using force on the commander, in this emergency, it was so *beyond* justified it was insane that Elissa was even thinking about it. She pushed the thoughts into oblivion, and when Lin glanced at her she smiled at her twin and squeezed the hand she was still holding.

They went through the corridor into the sitting room, then out into the entrance corridor. Cadan, Felicia, Markus, and Mr. Greythorn, all with their weapons out, then Elissa and Lin, hands clasped tight, then the others, a huddle of the Spares shepherded by Mrs. Greythorn and Ivan. Then, finally, Commander Dacre.

Cadan hit the front door panel, and it sprang open to let them through. They went back through the corridor they'd come through last night, out to where they could climb the staircase. Elissa hardly felt the stairs beneath her feet, was hardly aware of when they rounded the first corner, then the second, climbing from floor to floor. She was aware of Lin's hand in hers, of a feeling like static electricity on her skin, like a buzzing she felt rather than heard.

A few more seconds, and she realized that she and Lin, as they'd done once before—or maybe more than once, and she hadn't noticed—were walking in perfect time, as if joined by invisible rods. Another few seconds went past and she realized something else.

"Oh!"

Cadan didn't slow his pace or look back, but his voice was sharp. "What's wrong?"

"Nothing. Nothing's wrong. I just—Lin, back there, we were *talking to each other*."

"I know." There was a smile running all the way through Lin's voice. "Useful, huh?"

Unexpectedly, Elissa found herself laughing. Her head was spinning, but in a good way, a kind of post-adrenaline euphoric rush. A trickle of an underneath thought came: *Maybe it wasn't even amusement in Lin's voice back there. Maybe it was just this—this light-headedness that comes from using our power.*

"What are you talking about?" said Felicia, ahead of them. "If you mean you were communicating telepathically, what's new about that? Isn't that what you've done your whole lives?"

"No." They said it simultaneously, which made Lin giggle and Elissa choke back a burst of wild laughter. It was insane: They were in so much danger and the world was falling apart—*again*—around them, and yet somehow, right now, this discovery she and Lin had just made was the only thing that mattered.

"No," said Lin again. "We could read each other before—pick up stuff, kind of hop into each other's minds. We never managed to consciously *talk* before, though."

Elissa laughed again, knowing she sounded a little drunk, not caring. "Even when it would have been so *useful*."

A door rose before them. They'd reached the top of the stairs.

The euphoria dropped away. Elissa's heart was all at once thumping in her ears, high in her chest.

External fire doors were usually low tech, in case a fire knocked out all the electricity in a building. Cadan leaned hard on the bar across it, and the door swung smoothly open. Sunlight poured in on them, bright and hot, golden as syrup.

"Wait," said Cadan, and went out first, gun in hand, scanning the roof from behind the partial shelter of the open door. *He should have a real gun. The others—the people coming after*

*the Spares—they'll have real guns and all he has is a blaster that's
okay on the ship but it's not enough out here. . . .*

Then, as he glanced over his shoulder, gestured them to
follow him, she saw the weapon in his hand and realized
she'd been wrong. Either his dad had given it to him, or he'd
had it before and just hadn't been able to use it on the ship,
but either way, the weapon he was holding wasn't a short-
range blaster—it was a real gun.

They came out onto the roof. It stretched out before
them, flat and gray, striped with sharp black shadows from
the shoulder-high railings around its edge. Tall poles, topped
with solar panels that rotated and tilted to follow the progress
of the sun across the sky, stood at each corner, and halfway
along one side of the roof, the railings' shadow-stripes were
sliced into curves and crescents by the shadow of the spiral
fire escape where it jutted up just beyond them. It ended in a
caged platform, from which a short flight of metal steps led
back down to the roof.

Cadan pointed. "That building's the closest. Can you do
it?"

"Please." Lin's gaze skimmed the roof. "It's easy." Where
the skin of her palm touched Elissa's, static electricity built
again under Elissa's fingernails, running hot through the
veins in her wrist. The fire escape quivered, filling the air
with a low metallic sound. "Lissa . . . ?"

"Yes?"

"I can do it myself. If you don't want—I mean, I didn't ask . . ."

Elissa shot her a smile. "No way. I want to help."

Her smile was reflected back at her from her sister's face,
as bright as the sunlight. Another quiver ran along the fire
escape. Elissa felt it run through her hands, too, as if she were

physically holding the handrail that followed the spiral of its steps, as if the smooth metal were actually touching her skin.

Then, with a shock she felt all the way up her arms into her shoulders, the platform snapped away from the steps that led to the roof. The brackets securing it pinged loose.

The fire escape bent away from the railings, away from the roof, curving out over the empty space between their building and the next. The caged platform clanged against the railings on the far roof. Elissa felt it bounce, vibrating up through her hands. Except she *wasn't* feeling it through her hands, she was nowhere near it, she was just standing in the middle of the roof with Lin's hand in hers.

She'd linked with Lin before, to fix the *Phoenix* after it was damaged, and later, to make those hyperspeed jumps. But now, for the first time she was doing it fully consciously, not out of blind instinct, not just reaching out as if to steady her twin but giving her whole self to the effort. And for the first time she realized how hard it was, how *physical* it felt.

With the only bit of her mind she had to spare, she thought, *Lin did this sort of thing over and over when we were escaping. She was exhausted and terrified, and she just kept doing it.*

Then she had no bits to spare at all. Another instant of focused effort, moisture breaking out on her forehead, between her shoulder blades, and the bars of the cage tore away from the platform. More brackets came loose, screws clinking as they scattered over the metal surface of the platform, then rolled to fall off the edge.

Are you okay? The question came half like her own thought, half as if she were hearing Lin's voice out loud.

Yes. It wasn't totally true—the sweat was trickling down her back, and her hands were aching as if she really were moving the metal with them—but she was okay enough. And it was worth the discomfort. She was being useful . . . *being super-powered*.

As she refocused on what they were doing, as she willed herself to be okay, to finish the job, an image flashed up in her mind. The next thing they had to do. She clenched her teeth—and, somewhere in the distance, her hands—then she and Lin bent the broken edges of the railings that had enclosed the platform, curling them around the bars of the farther fire escape, weaving metal with metal, making the bridge steady, making sure it wouldn't come loose.

The last thing was to flatten the spiral of the fire escape they'd bent across the gap. A feeling like squashing an empty can between her hands—but an empty can that fought her, that tried to spring back into shape under her sweating palms.

As they finally managed it, as the fire escape flattened into a surface that could be safely walked on, the connection between them fell apart. Elissa's hand, slippery with sweat, slid from her sister's. An instant of nausea swept over her. The sun didn't feel hot any longer, and the air seemed icy on her skin.

"Lissa?"

"Elissa?"

"Lis? *Lis?*"

For a moment the voices swirled around her, unconnected to anyone. Then the nausea withdrew. The sun was suddenly boiling hot again, and the sweat on her skin warm rather than cold.

"I'm fine." She looked up, seeing black shadows on a gray roof, and bright sunlight bouncing off the bridge—the bridge she and Lin had made—lying waiting for them to cross. "Oh

God, we have to go. We have to get across. That took way too much time—"

Cadan threw a quick, amused look at her. "You're joking, right? It took less than a minute. But yeah, you're right, we do have to get across." He looked at his father and Felicia. "You can lead, right? I'll bring up the rear. Guys"—his gaze swung to the rest of them—"go quickly, okay, but carefully. Lissa and Lin got us a few minutes' grace—we don't need to risk our necks."

As Felicia took the first step onto the steel of the fire-escape bridge, Elissa had a moment of throat-closing conviction that she and Lin had missed something, that it would collapse and fall beneath Felicia's weight, that she'd go plummeting into emptiness—

It didn't. Her feet, then Mr. Greythorn's, then Sofia's and El's, clanged, echoing, as they started across.

"More like *half* a minute," said Ady, behind Elissa and Lin as they followed Sofia and El onto it. "Can I just say? *Seriously* impressed."

"Honestly?" said Elissa. "Half a minute?"

Lin shook her head. "I don't know. It felt longer to me, too." She shot a shining grin over her shoulder to Ady. "Seriously impressed, did you just say?"

Another wave of nausea hit Elissa. She concentrated on walking, trying to ignore it. Sweat sprang out again on her back, tiny points of prickling ice. She'd blacked out one of the first times she and Lin had linked like that, when, driven by terror for her sister, she'd linked with her to make that first hyperspeed jump, but afterward, she'd never felt so . . .

The sky spun, a tornado spout of blue, far too bright. Beneath her feet, the bridge tipped and slid.

"Lissa!"

Cadan's shout hit her at the same moment as Lin's hands closed on her arm. The world stopped orbiting around her.

Ady came up on her other side, and she felt Zee press close behind her.

"You're just hungry," said Lin. "Remember Cadan said electrokinesis uses up energy?"

Nausea clutched again at Elissa's throat. *I don't have time to be hungry.* Prickling all over with irritated frustration, she concentrated on putting one foot in front of the other, step after step, concentrated on not snapping at her sister. Or at Zee, who was crowding so close he was pretty much *breathing* on her.

Her next step hit concrete, rougher than the steel, wonderfully solid beneath her shoe, and then she and the others were hurrying across the roof toward the beginning of the fire escape that spiraled down the outside of this tower block.

"Captain." It was Commander Dacre's voice.

Elissa was waiting her turn to start down the fire escape, trying to control the nausea, the black spots swimming across her vision, the insane impulse that kept telling her to push through the others blocking her way, to get down the steps, to get out of the way of their pursuers now, now, *now*. But the note in the commander's voice pulled her head around to look at where she stood at the back of the group.

"I've told Control we'll be at the nearest communal square," the commander said to Cadan. There might have been a slight betraying note—compunction? guilt?—in her voice, but her face was as clear-cut, as expressionless, as it had been when they first met her. "There's space there for the rescue flyer—and no slidewalks to get in the way."

"How long?" said Cadan.

"Fifteen minutes." For a second the muscles crinkled, a movement like a flinch, at the corners of her eyes. "We hope."

"Let's hope it'll do, then," said Cadan.

There was space now for Elissa to follow Sofia down onto the fire escape. The first turn around the spiral brought her back to face the roof, and she caught another glimpse of the commander's face.

An unwilling admiration woke within her. The commander was keeping herself together under a whole bunch of stresses. *And it wasn't like what Lin and I did really helped with that, although we were right to go and she was wrong to try to stop us. But we gave her a whole other thing to deal with, something she wasn't prepared for, and she did deal with it. And now here she is, back trying to save everyone's lives all over again. She's . . . kind of*—the thought came as reluctantly as the admiration—*like Cadan.*

They made their way down the stairs, into the shadow between the buildings, feet echoing on the steps, all of them moving with a hurried quietness that every moment seemed to threaten to break into panicked running. The feeling of urgency, of the need to speed up, to run, to get down the stairs, far away from the building, boiled inside Elissa's veins, prickled her nerve endings. Any fire escape to one of these endlessly high tower blocks would take a long time to get down, but this one felt a hundred times longer than it really was. Elissa's ears kept straining for noises that would tell her that people—the would-be attackers—had gotten up to the roof, were crossing the bridge.

We should have pulled it down. Not left it there for them to use. But—this as she went around another spiral and her knees went weak beneath her—*ugh, I don't think I could have.*

Finally, they reached the ground. Cadan was speaking, clearly but not loudly, before he'd stepped off the fire escape. "Guys, listen. We're getting to the nearest communal square for the rescue flyer to pick us up. Commander Dacre has the route, so we're following her. When we reach the square, we're splitting into four groups. Felicia, you're taking Lissa and Lin and Cassiopeia. Dad . . ."

He divided the others quickly, naming Felicia, Mr. Greythorn, himself, and Commander Dacre as the four leaders. "At the square, stay in your group, at your side, using its cover, until you get the sign from the flyer itself—*not* from me, not from anyone else on the ground—that it's safe to cross the square. Is that clear?"

Elissa found herself jostled close to Cassiopeia, and gave her a smile that tried to be reassuring, but that she knew probably wasn't. Cassiopeia's face was pale, a little blank. How many times, now, had she been hurried from place to place, without any say in when or where?

"Lis," said Cadan, as everyone divided into the designated groups. He was, just for a moment, standing close enough to speak to her alone. His lips moved, shaping the words rather than saying them out loud. "You okay?"

She bit the inside of her cheek hard as she looked up at him, keeping her eyes steady, refusing to let her mouth tremble. He'd seen her cope with worse than this; she wasn't going to fall to pieces now. "I'm fine," she said, low.

"Doesn't surprise me at all." Just the tiniest smile crept into his eyes, and his hand brushed once, lightly, across her elbow, but it was enough. She was glad she hadn't let her fear show. *Maybe I can get through everything without letting him see how scared I am. Then what he'll take away from all this is what Lin and I did up there. That'll be his image of me—someone powerful, in control. Grown up—grown up enough that he won't have to doubt that what's between us is going to last.*

"Okay," said Commander Dacre, quietly, and Elissa left Cadan behind her as she followed Felicia out into the alley between the building they'd just climbed down and its nearest neighbor. She hunched automatically, aware of the presence of danger stories above her head but not daring to look up. *There are people with guns—up there somewhere, looking for us.* If they'd already reached the roof, all they'd have to do was come to the edge, aim, and fire. The alley was narrow, no room to dodge—and even if the shooters missed first time around, the bullets would ricochet, turning the alley into a death trap, a slaughter house.

Who are they? she thought for the first time. And: *What do they want?* Were they one of the groups who wanted to abduct Spares, or did they just want to kill them? The idea that they might want to abduct Lin was almost too horrific to think about, but at least it made an obscene kind of sense. Wanting to *kill* her and the other Spares . . . even in the minds of people who blamed the Spares for the state Sekoia was in, what would that accomplish? What was the *point*?

They moved along the alley in almost-silence, feet gritting on the sand-dusted ground, past another alley that led away into dusty shadows, then along the side of the next tower block. In this type of housing, there was one communal square about every eight tower blocks, Elissa recalled vaguely. There'd been more before the overcrowding got so bad, before the government had filled some of them in with more housing blocks. In the last few years the decision not to do the same with the ones that remained had come under increasing criticism.

Past the third tower block, at the end of the alley, sunlight flooded into the space beyond. It glinted on the scattered sand grains, on the fine dust floating down through the air. When Elissa stepped out into it, her eyes snapped automatically shut and she had to force them open, blinking till her vision cleared.

The square opened around them, its walls the grubby off-white fronts of the tower blocks. At its center a set of plastic playground equipment stood on an expanse of springy safety-surface. Benches surrounded it, each of them, like the slides and climbing frames, molded in one piece, everything made without sharp-cornered edges that might be a threat to children if they bumped their heads.

The whole place spoke of safety, of the city's commitment to keeping its children safe from any possible danger. Rows of enhanced security cameras, required by Sekoian law for all children's play areas, gleamed from tall supports all around the area. The supports were tamperproof, each made of a paper-thin scroll of super-steel, the structure ensuring that each support was free of handholds and almost entirely impossible to climb.

And there were people there. For a moment Elissa saw them only as blobs of shadow against all the shiny plastic, then, as the shapes resolved into figures—five or six parents, a handful of children, an older couple sitting on one of the benches—she realized that since she'd been back on Sekoia, it had become, to her, a planet of officials and refugees. She'd almost forgotten that among all the turmoil and crises were ordinary people trying to live their lives. And now, it seemed crazy that in the midst of this everyday scene, she and the other twins were running from people who wanted to kill them.

She couldn't see Cadan's group yet, so they must be working their way around to the far side of the square, but Mr. Greythorn's group were over to the left of the square, and at the right side, Commander Dacre stood in the shadows of an alley. By the look on her face, the presence of other people hadn't been at the front of her mind either.

If it was me in charge, I wouldn't know which to do. Risk calling attention to the group by telling the playground people to move, or risk their safety by letting them stay where they are.

The next surge of dizziness, though, wiped the thoughts from her head. She felt herself sway, and put out a hand to the rough plaster edge of the nearest wall.

"You have to *eat*," said Lin's voice, coming out of the blur at the edge of Elissa's vision.

"I *know*. You said. But I don't *have* anything—"

"I do." Lin pushed something into her hand. Elissa blinked, clearing her eyes, and looked down. It was a chocograin bar.

At the sight, Elissa was all at once ravenously, frantically hungry. Her fingers shook as she tore the bar open and bit into it.

The taste of chocolate flooded her mouth. One swallow, and her nausea disappeared as if it had never been. Chocograin bars were the product of a few years' back special initiative by the Sekoian Health Ministry. Elissa had always found this particular attempt to blend health food and treat food pretty unsuccessful, but right now it tasted like the most amazing thing she'd ever eaten.

She bit off another mouthful, then stuck out her tongue to catch a crumb of loose chocolate before it fell. Lin had unwrapped another bar and was halfway through it already.

Elissa had to suppress laughter. "Have you been *stockpiling* these?"

"I like them," said Lin.

"Yeah. Clearly." She tried to chew the next mouthful slowly, but now that it had been fed her body was clamoring for more food and she couldn't slow her pace at all. Another few crumbs fell to catch in a fold of the wrapper, and she blotted them up with her fingertip so as not to lose out on even that tiny amount of calories. This side effect was *super* unexpected. She'd helped Lin with her electrokinesis before. And plugging into the hyperdrive on the *Phoenix*, moving the entire *ship*, surely that would have taken more energy than just bending some metal bars?

Today, though, this was the first time I ever worked with her consciously, using our link to do something, not just letting it happen, letting her use me as an anchor, as a power source. This was the first time it was both of us doing it.

Which was—nausea and sudden crazy appetite aside—pretty cool.

"It's getting stronger, isn't it?" said Lin quietly beside her, holding out another chocograin bar.

Elissa looked up from her crumb salvage and took it, just managing not to snatch. She ripped it open. "Yes. Using it like that—and the *talking*. That's new."

In the alley at the right, just past the one the commander stood in, a movement in the shadows caught her eye, told her that Cadan's group had reached their destination.

Which was a relief, but . . . *Any minute now, those people are going to notice us. And creeping up like this, we look* like *a threat, not as if we're escaping from one.*

Swallowing her mouthful of chocolate, she cast a look up toward the sky, despite knowing perfectly well that she'd hear the rescue flyer before she saw it. But the sky stretched flat and blue and empty above the rooftops. If the flyer was already on its way, it was nowhere near them yet.

The rooftops were empty too—or at least as far as she could see from where she stood. No sign of pursuit.

If the flyer comes soon, we can get out before anything else happens. Get somewhere safe . . . somewhere actually *safe.*

"Is it . . . okay?"

Elissa looked back at Lin, confused for a second as to what she was talking about. Her twin had finished her bar and was holding the empty wrapper, folding it over and over, one neat crease after another. She wasn't looking at Elissa, and hesitation, uncertainty, dragged at her voice.

She was asking about the link. She was asking if it was okay that it was . . . *stronger*, she'd said, but to Elissa it felt as if the link wasn't just getting stronger, but *tighter*, drawing their minds closer so they were no longer picking up just echoes of each other's thoughts, but the actual thoughts themselves.

It was, to be honest, a little scary. But she wasn't going to say that to Lin, not now.

"It's completely okay." She kept her voice firm. "We *saved* everyone, Lin. That's not just okay, it's *amazing*."

Lin looked up, a smile lighting her face. "Really?"

"Really."

Far above them, the sky darkened. Elissa's muscles tightened—*the flyer!*—and she shot a look upward. But it was only a half-invisible skein of cloud, passing across the sky, briefly filtering the sunlight.

She looked away, dabbing up the last bits of chocolate from the wrapper of the second bar, but now her muscles wouldn't relax, and she found herself tipping her head back up toward the empty blueness, scanning the edges of the rooftops, aware of danger all over again. Beside her, Lin, too, watched the sky. And Cassiopeia. Only Felicia, gun in hand, kept her gaze moving from place to place.

It struck Elissa that despite her earlier euphoria at what their shared power could do, despite the fact that, as she'd said to Lin, they'd effected an escape for everyone, here they were, *again*, running away.

Even after the two bars, her stomach still felt empty, and now fatigue dragged at her limbs, together with a sudden feeling like despair. If this was what life on Sekoia was going to be like, it wasn't any wonder that IPL's answer was to move people like her and Lin off-planet.

Should we just give up and do what we're told? Give up and go?

No. She set her jaw, straightening her shoulders and trying to relax her spine. *Not when we've just forced the commander to accept what we can do. Not when we've just saved not only ourselves, but seven other Spares and twins—and probably Cadan's parents, too.*

She might listen to us now. I don't know how to fix Sekoia, but I do know that IPL's getting it wrong. I know—

Something arced through the air. Something that glinted dull gray in the sunlight, curving up from where it had come, from one of the alleyways, down toward the center of the square.

"Get down!" Felicia's voice, rising on a shout so urgent that it bypassed Elissa's conscious mind, throwing her flat on the ground as if Felicia had physically pushed her there.

The glinting object hit the ground near the center of the square, just past the playground. It exploded in a burst of fire.

The noise seemed to split Elissa's head apart. A sound like a thunderclap, like the sky tearing open.

The shock raced through the ground, through the building behind Elissa, into every bone of her spine. Her eardrums went as numb as if someone had slammed giant hands over them.

The people at the playground—children and adults—were thrown to the ground by the blast. The plastic slide gave a shudder, and Elissa saw the topmost part of it slip sideways, its edges dripping where something hot had sheared through the plastic, melting it on impact.

She couldn't hear anything beyond a massive rumble that seemed to go beyond sound and into sensation.

"What was that?" Cassiopeia shrieked. She was lying close to Elissa, but again, Elissa couldn't hear her; she could only see the wide vowel shapes Cassiopeia's mouth made as she screamed. Then she realized that members of the commander's group were screaming too, silent mouths opening, silent lips stretched in ugly terror.

With an odd little fragment of her mind, she realized that she didn't want to scream. Once you'd heard that kind of explosion when you were on a *spaceship*, when it could mean the hull itself had been torn open and you were going to be sucked out into airless space, it wasn't quite so terrifying anywhere else. She *really* didn't want it to come again, though—

But it did come again. Another of the glinting gray objects sailed up from somewhere within one of the alleys. Flat on her belly, Elissa raised her head just enough to follow it, unable to pull her gaze away, feeling her eyes stretching so wide they felt as if they'd never shut again. *A bomb? A grenade? And if they've found us, if these are the people we're running from, why aren't they coming out in the square?*

The explosion was just as huge this time, although now Elissa's ears were so numb it couldn't numb them further. In the playground, parents had been struggling to their feet, clutching for their children. The explosion threw them flat once more.

Around Elissa, people grabbed onto one another or lay frozen, arms over their heads. Only the commander, Felicia, and Mr. Greythorn moved, rising to crouches, weapons drawn, each of them turning to scan the square, the entrances to the alleys.

Farther down the square, the sunlight blazed suddenly from Cadan's hair, jumped in glints from the gun he held. He wasn't out of the alley he'd come through. His arm blocked his group from coming farther; his whole body was tense, poised for action.

The commander moved, her gaze swinging past Cadan, past Mr. Greythorn, then halting, suddenly intent, on the alley behind Felicia's group, past where Elissa lay. *"Down! Keep down! Take cover!"* For all Elissa could hear, the commander might as well have been mouthing the words, but her lips moved clearly, and they—and still more, the frantic look on her face—got the message across. Elissa threw her arms across her head, pressing her face to the ground, knowing that beside her Lin and Cassiopeia were doing the same.

This time the explosion seemed to shake the world. A hundred darts of pain scattered across Elissa's bare hands and arms, pinged less painfully over her hoodie-covered shoulders. Her mouth opened in a gasp she felt but couldn't hear, and she huddled tighter to the ground, clasping her arms over her head. *Cadan.* Was he okay? He'd been standing there, almost out in the open, when the commander shouted at them to get down. With terror that went through her like a knife, she thought, *It hit him. It hit him and he's dead.*

She was shaking when she raised her head to peer over the shield of her arms. *Cadan? Oh God, Cadan, please don't be dead, please don't be—*

The first thing she saw was blood.

THERE WAS debris, too, broken bits of the off-white plaster of the buildings, pale jagged chunks of the pavement where something had hit it, splintering it all across to show the dark-ocher-colored earth beneath.

But it was the blood that filled Elissa's vision. The blood that drew her eyes, demanded her attention so exclusively that for an endless minute she couldn't see past it to anything else at all.

It was splashed across the ground in front of her, lipstick bright, lipstick shiny. Too red to be real. *Too much* of it to be real. That much—it was horror-movie blood. Not real life. You didn't see that much blood in real life. You *never* saw that much blood in real life. Not unless—Not unless someone—

Her heart stopped, her breath, even her own blood in her veins. She couldn't look past that splash of red, couldn't look farther to see where—*who*—it had come from. *Cadan was there. If he ran toward me as it happened—if he was running when the blast came . . . And Lin was next to me, right next to me. It's one of them. The blood—it's one of them. I have to look to find out who.*

She couldn't. She stayed flat, hands pressed on the ground without being able to feel the roughness beneath her palms, knowing she had to drag her gaze up from the blood, knowing she had to find out who she'd lost, which hole in her life she was going to have to face. Knowing, and yet not able to do it.

Then she looked up, and it wasn't Cadan or Lin.

Lin lay next to her, hands over her head, and Cadan was yards away still, just getting up from where the blast had knocked him over. The blood was coming from Felicia.

She wasn't dead. She was lying on her back, one leg crumpled under her, and as Elissa raised her head she saw Felicia's chest rise and fall in one long, labored movement. The blood came from her shoulder, wet and red where her sleeve had been ripped to shreds and skin showed around the deep wound, shiny-dark on the material all around it. It pulsed, a steady rhythm, flowing out and out. And—mercifully mostly hidden by the blood—the flesh of the wound lay open, like raw meat.

For a moment Elissa's whole body went into a spasm, like a giant hand clenching over her stomach, her bowels, her lungs and chest and throat. Sickness heaved through her in one huge wave, as if she were going to vomit up every scrap of everything she'd eaten for the last week.

She's going to die.

The next thought came, very cold and clear, as if from somewhere disassociated from the reeling nausea that had taken over Elissa's mind. *If I don't do something she's going to die.*

And with that thought, the nausea receded.

Then I have to do something! This is Felicia! This is Felicia, and she's going to bleed to death while I watch!

Elissa scrambled to her feet. Pain woke, stinging, all over her hands and arms, and when she looked down she realized she was bleeding too, in dozens of tiny cuts all over her unprotected skin. It looked like the way she remembered her knees and the heels of her hands looking when, as a child, she'd been taken to Reservoir View Park and had fallen on one of the paths. Unlike most of the city parks, Reservoir View had gritted paths to help with the draining of rainwater into the reservoir. The seven-year-old Elissa hadn't come across such paths before, hadn't thought to be careful. She could still remember how the grit had jabbed through her skin in hundreds of little sharp points, how each pinprick of blood had swelled into a shining bead.

The stuff that hit me—was it shrapnel? From the bomb? Is that what hit Felicia, too? For the first time, then, she consciously saw the debris, the crumbs and shards of stone pavement and concrete building blocks, that lay all around her. *Not just shrapnel. Something exploded in the square—a bomb? Grenades? It—they—hit the pavement and exploded. If they'd hit Felicia direct, if they'd hit any of us . . .*

The thoughts rattled through her head, an unhelpful distraction as she hurried across to where Felicia lay.

I have to help, but I don't know what to do. She's going to die, and I don't know what to do to stop it.

Felicia looked up at her, her face gray, her eyes murky. Her lips moved, and Elissa didn't know whether she was actually speaking or whether it was just that Elissa still couldn't hear. "Pressure."

Apply pressure. Apply pressure to the wound. Elissa could have smacked herself. She *knew* that. They'd been taught basic first aid at school—she *did* know what to do.

She dragged off her hoodie. Her hands stung, and the fabric stuck in little points of prickling-cold pain along her shoulders. Then she folded it, over and over, fingers fumbling with haste, trying to resist the desire to just crumple the whole thing into an ineffective ball and cram it over that horrible pulsing gash in Felicia's shoulder.

Lin was next to her, clammy fingers touching Elissa's arm to get her attention. As she looked up, she saw that Lin's lips were moving but she hadn't heard her, and realized that she was still deaf from the blast. Lin was stripping off her own hoodie, folding it in imitation of Elissa.

Elissa turned back to Felicia, aware vaguely that there were other people around them now, that Cadan was coming to one knee beside her. Her stomach lurched as she pressed the folded garment onto Felicia's shoulder. Felicia's body jerked and for an instant—*oh God oh God I'm hurting her!*—Elissa wanted to snatch the hoodie away.

She just managed not to do it, and then, warm and steady, Cadan's hand came down over hers, pressing her palm to the pad. His arm was equally warm and steady against her shoulder, and he wasn't dead, he wasn't even hurt, and he wasn't going to let Felicia die.

There was a high sound in her ears, continuous and shrill, not a ringing but close. Like the flood of panicked, confused thoughts, it was a distraction, something she had to push aside as she pushed down on the pad over Felicia's shoulder, feeling wet warmth begin to come up through it, knowing it was Felicia's blood, knowing that unless it stopped Felicia would bleed to death, and it was up to her to stop it and she wasn't going to be able to . . .

Her thoughts were spiraling into panic again. She dragged in a long breath that shuddered in her chest, clenched her jaw, and continued to press down onto the pad. It was soaked all the way through now, Felicia's life pumping up through it, up onto Elissa's hands. . . .

"Lin," she said, and couldn't hear her own voice. Either because she only thought she was talking, or because her ears still didn't work. *And if my ears don't work—*God, every thought apart from the panicked ones was coming so slowly, as if her brain were trying to run too many programs at once—*if my ears don't work, then Lin's ears probably don't work either, and even if I am talking she won't be able to hear me.*

Lin, she tried instead, speaking within her mind, using that weird new ability they'd only discovered today, *Lin, can you hear me?*

Lissa! Lissa, your hands—Is she—is Felicia—

She's still bleeding loads, Elissa thought . . . or said . . . or whatever it was that she was doing. *Give me your hoodie. Push it down on top of mine as I move my hands.*

They managed it with a little fumbling, Lin's icy fingers touching Elissa's, a sudden panic sweeping through her that it wouldn't be enough, that Felicia would continue to bleed and bleed until all the red life within her had soaked through everything they used to try to stanch it. *How much blood can you lose before you die? How much blood do you have?* She'd learned it once, in some lesson that seemed a million miles away from anything useful, from anything she'd ever actually needed, but she couldn't remember it now.

The shrill sound in her ears had become louder while they worked, more intrusive, less easy to ignore. And now, all at once, as if she were coming up from underwater, it jumped a level, becoming louder—and as it became louder, she realized that the sound wasn't ringing, it had never been ringing. It was screaming.

At the same time Cadan's voice came through to her. He must have been talking all along, knowing she couldn't hear him—probably not even being able to hear himself—ensuring that the first thing she would hear was his voice, low and steady in her ear, repeating, "Take no notice. Don't look up. Just focus on Felicia. Focus on Felicia. Take no notice. It's nothing to do with you."

But she had to look up. Once she heard the screaming, she had to look up.

It wasn't just Felicia whom the explosion had left bleeding or injured. Two of the people over at the playground were hurt too. A man was hunched over an arm that looked as if it had been broken—by a flying chunk of masonry, by being thrown off his feet by the blast itself? Another—a little boy—had been pinned under one of the benches. It had been pulled off him by two of the adults, but his face was a sickly greenish-white and he was lying gasping and whooping for breath, as if the weight had driven all the air from his body.

Sofia was the only other one who was bleeding badly, and that was where the screaming was coming from. Not from Sofia herself, but from El. Sofia was kneeling—not as if she'd gone to her knees deliberately, but as if her legs had folded and deposited her there—her face half-covered in blood, her hair soaked with it. Emily Greythorn knelt next to her, one arm around Sofia's shoulders, one hand holding something to the side of her face. It looked horrible, but no way near as serious as Felicia's wound—except to El, who stood, the hand not in a sling tight against her face so that it seemed as if she were trying to keep herself from flying apart, mouth open in a shriek of horror so extreme, so uncontrolled, that it made her look insane. Cassiopeia had pressed herself against the nearest wall, her hands flattened against the plaster, as still and pale as a paper doll.

"Lis," Cadan said, his voice coming through clearer now, and her gaze flew back to him. "We can't do anything for them. Not right now."

Elissa nodded, her head moving jerkily, pushing the sound of El's screams away into the background, trying to make them become nothing but the tinnitus-like ringing she'd thought they were before. *The people attacking—I knew they wanted to hurt us. But if ordinary Sekoian citizens get in the way, they're willing to endanger them, as long as they can still hurt us. How can they? How can they hate us that much?*

Hate crime. She'd heard the term before, in the news, in ethics lessons and organized debates at school. She'd thought of it the way she'd thought of all violent crimes—robbery, piracy, assault, terrorism—as something you did only if you were halfway to crazy. Something that normal, decent people could never relate to, something that they could only stare at or talk about with incomprehension and horror.

But although this *was* crazy, it wasn't just like all other violent crimes. These people weren't chasing the Spares to get something from them, or to try to force an unwilling government to change some law they didn't agree with. They weren't driven by ideals or greed. They were driven by hatred. Hatred so blind that to them, even people who weren't Spares, who weren't so much as *associated* with the Spares, were nothing but collateral damage.

You can't argue with that. You can't fix it. If it's just hate, if it's not need or greed or ideals, if it's just total, mindless hate, how can you ever change it? How can you ever make them stop?

Lin held out another garment, folded to a pad. Elissa hadn't seen where she'd gotten it. "Is it time for this one?"

Cadan's gaze had dropped back to where his hands pressed next to Elissa's, on the second pad. The blood hadn't soaked through this one yet, Elissa noticed vaguely, which had to be a good sign, didn't it? He answered without looking up. "In a moment, okay? I'll nod when we need it."

"But the flyer?" Lin's voice was urgent. "Won't the flyer be here soon?"

"Any minute. And they'll have med equipment on board. She'll be okay. They'll all be okay."

The words came out with patented Cadan-calm, but all the same there was something, the very slightest hesitation, maybe, just the edge of a tremor as he said "okay," that made Elissa not believe him. And now, for the first time, as her focus widened from Felicia, from the groups of injured people around her and in the playground, she realized that Commander Dacre and Mr. Greythorn weren't helping the injured. They were standing at the corners of two of the nearer alleys, guns at the ready.

That last explosion, the one that had hurt Felicia and Sofia—and probably the others—that had been the last. Why hadn't there been more? Because of the commander and Cadan's father, because they were defending them?

But they can't defend this whole square! There are entrances all around it—they don't have a hope. Any minute they're going to attack again. If they've got a whole bunch of those grenades, they don't even need to risk coming into the square themselves. They can just keep throwing grenades till we're all blown to pieces.

And, like a weight dropping into her stomach, she realized why she'd heard that hesitation in Cadan's voice. They were under attack. Not right this second, but there'd been one attack, and any minute now there'd be another. The flyer might be only minutes away, but by the time it arrived, it could be too late.

"Cadan . . ."

His eyes came up to hers. He must have read the realization in them, because his own moved, just slightly, a side-to-side flick like a head shake. *Don't say anything.* His look couldn't convey any more than that—it wasn't *Cadan's* mind she could read—but she didn't need it to. She could see as well as he what effect it would have if everyone around them knew there might be no hope, that they might not get out of this alive.

Her arms were hurting from the pressure she was putting on Felicia's wound. Speckles of dizziness raced across her vision, and she set her teeth in the soft inside of her lower lip, trying to draw on whatever reserves of strength or stamina she still had. Felicia was still breathing, her chest rising in one painful, labored heave after another. She might not—*oh God, I can't be thinking that*—she might not survive until the flyer arrived. *But it can't be my fault if she doesn't. It can't be because I gave up too soon.* Back weeks ago on the *Phoenix*, when Elissa's decisions had put the whole crew in danger, when most of them had left and the *Phoenix* had been damaged, when Elissa had been in shreds about what she'd brought upon them all, Felicia had told her to stop looking guilty, told her that she didn't bear the responsibility for what the crew had decided to do.

She can't just die. She can't just die like this.

Her ears filled with sound, not ringing this time but a high, thick whining, like swarms and swarms of insects, their wings whirring. Her vision darkened, not in specks but as if a cloud had covered the sun. *Oh damn it all, no, no, I'm* not *going to faint.*

Then the sound and the sudden dimness came together in her head, making sense. She looked up.

Overhead, a smooth dark shape against the blaze of the sky, blocking out the sunlight, the flyer was descending. The sound filling her ears was the whir of its propellers.

Lin's face lifted, lit with relief, and for a moment that same relief swept through Elissa, too. It was here. It was here in time, and they were going to be okay.

Then the next attack came.

She saw the grenade as it was hurled from the far side of the square. This time it didn't explode on impact, but bounced, once, twice. Elissa had time to crouch over Felicia, her hands flattened between them, feeling Cadan's body cover her own, knowing that Lin and Cassiopeia had thrown themselves facedown on the ground, not knowing what Sofia and El— *and oh God, Cadan's mother*—were doing, not having time to see, screwing her eyes tight shut against what she knew was coming—

The grenade blew up. She heard the crack of the pavement exploding beneath it, felt something whiz above her and Cadan's heads with a rush of hot air, a smell of burning, managed to think, *It's not as close as the last one. I can still hear. Please don't let there be another. Don't let me go deaf again.*

She didn't go deaf, but when the next explosion came it cracked through her ears so painfully she almost wished she had. In the moment of horrible quiet afterward, she lifted her head, and the angle she crouched at took her gaze straight to the brightly colored play area. The slide lay on its side now, a couple of women in its shelter, their children huddled in their arms. The little playhouse was still standing, but flying shrapnel had melted great gouges across the blue-and-red stripes of its roof, blown straight through one corner so two of the little windows had become one big window beneath a sagging plastic ledge. Some parents and children were sheltering behind that, too, but the parents at least must know it was next to useless.

They'd do so much better running for the shelter of one of the security-cam supports. But they're all around the sides of the square, the idea of running across all that empty space must be just too much to cope with.

Then the silence suddenly registered in Elissa's brain.

El. El was no longer screaming. Elissa threw a terrified look toward her. *They can't die. None of the Spares can die, not when they've only just gotten free.*

El was kneeling beside Sofia, her long limbs in a graceless huddle. She wasn't hurt, at least not physically. Looking at her, though, Elissa was suddenly scared that this last escape, the attack, the danger and violence suddenly bombarding them were all too much for an already fragile mind. El's eyes were wide and blank. Her fingers pressed into her face as if she were trying to push herself out of existence.

And above them all, the flyer had stopped descending.

"What's wrong?" Lin's voice was a whisper, as if shock would not allow her to raise it. "Why isn't it coming down to get us?"

Elissa threw another look up. The flyer wasn't an IPL craft, but a standard Sekoian emergency vehicle. On its sleek side, just visible from where she crouched, the trident-caduceus symbol showed. Her whole body seemed to sink as if she'd gotten caught in a high-grav field.

"It's med-services," she said. "They sent a med-services vehicle. It's not armored. They can't come down."

"What?" The relief drained from Lin's face. She cast one disbelieving look around them, at the shocked and injured Spares and twins, at the terrified people trying to shelter behind the ineffectual shields of plastic slides and swing sets. "But they *have* to. People are hurt."

"They still can't," said Elissa, despair making her careless, making her forget to guard her words. "They can't risk getting hit."

"They can risk it more than we can!" Lin's voice rose, a shrill edge to it that hurt Elissa's ears. "If one of those things hits us, we're dead!"

Elissa felt her shoulders begin to slump. If it hadn't been for Felicia, still breathing under her hands, she'd have let them slump, let her whole body crumple. "If a grenade hits the flyer, if it punctures the fuel tank, we're all dead anyway. It'll go up like a fireball, Lin." She shut her eyes for a hopeless moment. "They can't land without getting themselves, as well as us, killed."

When she forced her eyes to reopen she found Cadan looking at her. His shoulders had the same defeated slope to them she recognized in her own.

"*Why?*" she asked him, despairing disbelief in her voice. "Why would they send an unarmored flyer? The commander said it was an emergency. She *told* them."

Cadan moved his head in what was almost a head shake. "She didn't say that we were under direct attack, though.

She couldn't: We weren't. I . . . God, I don't know. I'd have thought they'd have guessed how close we were to danger." He shook his head again. "They're overstretched, we know that. If they didn't have a police flyer free . . ."

"So what are we going to do?" Lin demanded. "If they start throwing those grenade things again? If the flyer can't come down to get us? What can we do?"

And it was that, the panic in Lin's face, in her voice, that shook Elissa into realization. Here she was on the verge of giving up, when less than half an hour ago she'd been congratulating herself on the power she and Lin had discovered.

Her spine stiffened. Her head came up. "You tell me," she said. "We moved a *spaceship*, Lin. We shouldn't be asking what *can* we do. We should be asking which thing are we going to *choose* to do."

Something rose, blazing, into Lin's face. Her head came up too, and she swept one look around the square. "The people attacking us—they're not in vehicles or anything, or I'd be able to feel where they were, we'd be able to do something to their vehicles."

"What about the people themselves?" said Cadan, his voice pitched low so it wouldn't carry.

Lin cast Elissa a cautious look. "Lissa said she doesn't like me killing people. . . ."

It was true. She had said that. But right now, with Felicia's life oozing away beneath her fingers, with a square full of hurt and frightened people who hadn't done anything, who were just trying to survive in a world gone mad, she couldn't remember why it had mattered so much.

Trust me, I can make exceptions.

She nearly said it out loud before she bit down hard on

the words, forcing them back, trying to unthink them before Lin picked up on the thought. Right now she *felt* that, but she couldn't say it, not to Lin, couldn't confuse her that way. "They're trying to kill us," she said instead. "They're not trying to negotiate or *anything*–they're just a hate group. We can let them kill us, or we can defend ourselves. And if we can only do that by attacking back–"

Lin was shaking her head before Elissa finished speaking. "But I can't see them. If I can't see them and can't touch them, I can't do anything."

"Not even knock them out?" Cadan said. "Like on the *Phoenix*?"

Lin had done that, had rendered the *Phoenix* crew unconscious long enough to take control of the flight deck, plug herself into the hyperdrive, and make that death-wish leap that had saved them all. But now she shook her head again.

"Not without touching them. I just can't." She was biting her lip, driving the blood from it with the pressure of her teeth. Every time she spoke she released it and the blood rushed back in, making the skin bright red, swollen and sore-looking.

"*Fine,*" said Elissa. "We'll do something else." She cast a look around, trying to crush her own rising dread. What did they have? What weapons to use? What kind of protection? Her gaze swept over injured people, and others terrified into immobility, over Spares who might have something like Lin's electrokinesis, but who, if so, hadn't yet discovered it, and weren't going to do so in time to help them now. Over Mr. Greythorn and Commander Dacre, their hands full with trying to defend the square. No one could help. It was her and Lin or no one.

She scanned the square again, and this time her gaze caught on the burned, half-melted trail across the playhouse roof, on the mothers and children sheltering ineffectually by the overturned slide. The play equipment. It was just plastic, it wasn't even reinforced with anything stronger. But what else was there? What else was there that could be used as a shield?

She'd thought it a few minutes ago, thought that they'd be better running for . . .

For the security-cam supports. Supports that were made, not of flimsy plastic, but of super-steel.

"Lin."

Lin followed where she was looking. "What? Those things?" Then, quick as a spark, understanding leaped. "You mean we can defend the square? Long enough for the flyer to come down?"

"It's you who's the heavy lifter," said Elissa. "Do you think we can?"

"*Yes.*" Lin's voice was all emphasis. "How do we tell the flyer pilot, though?"

"Cadan?" said Elissa. "The commander—she'll have communication, won't she?"

Cadan's shoulders were no longer slumping either. He nodded, a quick jerk of his head, then shot a glance over to Cassiopeia and raised his voice. "Hey, can you keep applying pressure here while I get over to the commander?"

Cassiopeia's eyes were so wide the eyelids seemed to have disappeared. Although she was staring at Cadan, nothing registered on her face. She was looking at him, but not seeing him.

"Cassiopeia? *Cassiopeia?*" Nothing. Cadan swung his head

to where El knelt. "El, listen, I need someone to take over here. . . ." This time his words trailed off as he recognized that El was going to be no more use than Cassiopeia, and his eyes went to Emily Greythorn. He raised his voice a little. "Mom?"

It was just Emily's head that moved. Her arm stayed close around Sofia, her other hand still pressed tight against the bloody pad on Sofia's head.

"Are you safe to leave her?" Cadan said.

Emily glanced at Felicia, at Cassiopeia's fixed, wide eyes, at Elissa and Lin. "If it's vital."

"It's vital. Felicia's still bleeding badly. If you can leave Sofia, I need you to come deal with Felicia."

Emily withdrew her arm from Sofia's shoulders, took the girl's hand in hers, and guided it up to the pad on Sofia's head. She spoke to Sofia, quietly, her voice steady, and after a moment Sofia's fingers spread to hold the pad in place. As Emily got to her feet, though, Sofia's eyes followed her as if she represented the only safety anywhere.

Emily came over to where Felicia lay. For a moment her gaze brushed Elissa and Lin. Her expression was neutral enough that Elissa couldn't read what Cadan's mother was thinking, but all the same she thought it was something pretty much like, *What the hell are they doing, then, that stops them helping you?*

"Mom," said Cadan, and Emily's eyes went straight to him. "Here."

Emily knelt, sliding her hands under Elissa's onto the folded hoodie. She didn't look at Elissa as she did so, not as if she were deliberately ignoring her, just as if Elissa was no longer relevant to what was happening.

"Mom, you need to press harder than that—" Cadan broke off as his mother shifted her hands, pressing down as firmly as he'd been doing. She slanted him a look that was very slightly amused.

"I know first aid, Cay. Go, do what you need to before they start their next attack."

As Cadan stood, Lin put her hand out for Elissa's. Elissa reached out, then stopped as she saw the lines of her own palm, the crease at the base of each finger, the crescents beneath her nails all lined with blood. It was no longer bright, fresh scarlet, but it wasn't the unalarming color of old blood either. *It's her life on my hands. Felicia's life, Felicia who stayed on the ship with us instead of leaving like most of them, Felicia who was kind to me and told me to stop feeling guilty. Is that still what she'd tell me, now, with her blood drying on my hands?*

"Lissa." Lin's hand slid into hers, covering the blood, bringing Elissa out of the sudden onslaught of horrified thoughts.

"Okay." Elissa turned her head to look at the nearest of the supports, feeling rather than seeing Lin do the same.

Pushing at the base of the support wouldn't do anything, wouldn't even come close to knocking it over. It was thickest at the bottom, designed so that would-be vandals or criminals couldn't knock it down to smash the row of cameras it held. *But if we push halfway up . . . And we'll have to do them one after another, as fast as we can, or all we're doing is warning the attackers what we're doing and giving them time to move from alley to alley and attack again.*

She didn't realize she'd been thinking it *at* Lin until her twin's reply sounded in her mind. *Okay. Let's go.*

If they hadn't done something very similar with the fire escape earlier, Elissa didn't think they'd have been able to manage this at all. As it was, she didn't feel the weight of the metal in just her hands, but throughout her body. Dragging on her shoulder sockets, stabbing pain, real pain, through the muscles down the sides of her spine. *I'm going to bruise this time. This isn't just some sort of creative transference thing going on in my imagination, this is actually taking physical strength.*

But they did manage it. Slowly, slowly, the breath burning in Elissa's chest, they forced the metal strip to bend.

"Now," said Lin, and Elissa heard it like an echo, doubled in her ears and her mind. "Now." *Now.*

A whip-crack-short agony of effort, a shock of pain that sliced knifelike through her palms, and the support snapped across its base. It fell, clanging, to bounce on the ground.

After that, it felt almost easy to flip it up, push it into the mouth of the nearest alley. It went in diagonally, curving to fit along the sides of the alley, forming—not a complete barrier, but half of one.

Now another.

I know. If Elissa had had to say the words out loud, she would have sobbed it. Her muscles were screaming, and her hands throbbed so badly she didn't dare look at them for fear she'd see her own blood welling up from her ruined, mangled palms, to mingle with the dried blood from Felicia's wound.

They moved on to the next support, bent it over and over until they could break it, stuffed it crosswise into the mouth of the alley. It was no less difficult this time, and no less pain shrieked along Elissa's nerves, making her wish for enough leftover energy to cry out, but at least this time they knew what they were doing.

The support clanged and scraped into place. There was still

a gap above and below the makeshift barrier it formed with the first support, but it meant that anyone wanting to throw grenades into the square would have to come a lot closer to the alley entrance.

Let them come closer. Let them get themselves *shot!*

For a flicker of a moment, at the very edge of her attention, she was aware that Cadan had taken over the commander's place guarding one of the many still-unblocked alleys, that the commander had retreated to the edge of one of the tower blocks and was speaking into her wrist-unit.

Then she and Lin were focusing on the next support, and the next, and the next, and she had no attention left for anything other than turning to look at one support after another, forcing the metal to bend beneath their will. No attention left for anything other than making barriers across entrance after entrance, knowing they couldn't hold forever, hoping they'd hold just long enough to allow the flyer to descend.

But after the fifth support, or maybe the seventh, or maybe the thousandth, she had no attention left for hoping that, either. She had scarcely attention left for anything other than trying to hold herself together against the pain, trying not to let it win, no longer even remembering why she mustn't give in under it. Every time she had to look at the next support, had to focus on it with her eyes in order to focus on it with her mind, it blurred and wavered before her, like something seen through a heat haze.

Eventually, after minutes . . . or hours . . . or days . . . it was the sudden storm of the descending flyer's propellers that pulled her out of the haze enveloping her. And it was Cadan's voice that pushed her into movement, half blind as she was, caught inside her own mind, lost in a blur of pain.

"Lissa, go! Run for the flyer!"

She made an automatic step, realized she couldn't see and didn't remember which direction she was supposed to be running in, and stopped.

"Lissa!"

She shook her head, trying to clear her vision, terror sweeping over her. "I can't see. Cadan? Cadan?"

Someone grabbed her arm and spun her. She reached out, almost stumbling, finding nothing to grab, and then she was running, sand and the grit of broken masonry scraping beneath her feet, her free hand out in front of her, her eyes screwed up against the fear she was going to crash straight into something she couldn't see, the terror between her shoulder blades driving her on.

Whoever was holding her slowed, pulling her to a stop. Something seemed to clear from her eyes and the sleek silver side of the flyer rose in front of her, its side door open, hands—Lin's and Ady's—reaching out to pull her in.

"Up you go," said whoever had been holding her, and as she scrambled up into the body of the flyer, she recognized Mr. Greythorn's voice.

"Cadan?" she said, suddenly frantic.

"He's coming. Look." Mr. Greythorn had climbed up beside her. He put his arm around her shoulders, turning her back toward the flyer's entrance.

Cadan was running flat out across the square. There was blood on his face, his gun was still in his hand, and behind him one of the supports was just crashing to the ground. A shot zinged over it as it fell. Not a grenade but a bullet.

Elissa saw Cadan's face change as he registered the sound. He slewed sideways, then back, running in a zigzag pattern.

"Good boy," said Mr. Greythorn next to her.

The other support clanged to the ground. There were people in the mouth of the alley—people with masks pulled down over their faces, weapons in their hands. One of them drew an arm back. In his hand an oval something gleamed dull gray.

"*Cadan!*" Elissa shrieked.

The grenade flew up against the pale backdrop of the buildings, then curved, falling in an arc, horrible and slow. Cadan was running beneath its trajectory, set on a collision course with it. Time slowed. The world stopped spinning.

Cadan. Cadan, oh God, no.

The grenade hit the top of the flyer with a clang. Every cell in Elissa's body went still, waiting for the explosion to end it all.

The explosion came, thunderous, world shaking, but from behind the flyer. The grenade had bounced off it, struck the ground before it exploded.

Every last bit of strength went from Elissa's knees. She started to crumple, and Ady caught her. He pulled her away from the doorway and lowered her to the floor.

Then Cadan was there, swinging himself up into the flyer. He reached up, hit the door button, and the door clamped shut, sealing them all in.

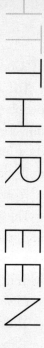

THIRTEEN

THE PROPELLERS raced above them. Elissa's stomach dropped with a violent lurch as the flyer rose into the air.

"Lissa." Cadan went to one knee in front of her, shoving his gun into its holster.

"Oh God, Cadan, I thought . . ." She couldn't say it. She rose to her knees, reaching for him.

He shifted position so he was on both knees too, drawing her into his arms. She put her arms up around his neck, feeling him safe and whole against her, feeling his hands shaking where they touched her, warm through the back of her T-shirt. "Lissa, God, when I told you to run and you didn't move . . ."

"I tried to. I couldn't see."

"Jeez, not blaming you." He pulled back enough to look down into her face. His eyes were blazing, the bright blue of a sunlit sky. "That was incredible. What you and Lin did.

We'd never have gotten out if it hadn't been for you."

The sunlight seemed to go all through her, lighting her up from inside. "I didn't think we'd manage it. It was the hardest thing *ever*."

"Yeah, I believe you." His lips curved in a smile. "You're amazing, you know that?"

"Not just me."

Cadan flicked a quick look up. Above them, in the jumble of people, no one was paying them any attention. He looked back at Elissa, the smile creeping into his eyes, and lowered his voice, for her ears only. "Mostly just you."

He pulled her tight against him and kissed her, harder than he'd ever done before, his fingers threading through the hair at the back of her head, his hand tilting her face to his. Her heart picked up, thundering against his body where he held her. Her arms locked around his neck, her mouth opened under the insistent pressure of his lips, and the world disappeared.

Except not really. A long way off, someone cleared their throat. Cadan pulled away, leaving her dizzy. She put a hand up to cover her tingling lips, ducking her head, swept by shyness.

Cadan looked a little dizzy too. He glanced up, a flush coloring his face.

His father was standing close by. He looked down at Cadan, raising one eyebrow, and Cadan's flush deepened.

"More important things at hand, son?"

Cadan rolled his eyes a little. "Jeez, can't a guy get half a minute?" He looked quickly back at Elissa, and suddenly there was a slight hesitation in his face, as if he'd been brought back to the moment, back to the life where he was supposed to stay in control at all times. "You okay? That wasn't—I didn't . . ." He trailed off, leaving it unspoken. *That wasn't too much? I didn't go too far?*

She was breathless, heart still thumping, not to mention nerve endings all over her body. "I think we should risk our lives more often," she said, low enough so that only he could hear her.

His eyes met hers, and a spark seemed to jump between them. "I'll remember that," he said, and the grin he gave her made her blush from forehead to toes.

When he stood up he moved a little awkwardly, pulling his jacket down with what seemed like unnecessary care. Elissa looked at him for a puzzled moment, then—*Oh.*

A burst of almost-shocked giggles rose within her. *That* must have happened before today—okay, she hadn't done a ton of dating, but she wasn't an idiot—but it was the first time it had happened so *obviously.*

Her skin tingled all over again, as if a shower of warm sparks had fallen over and through her. It wasn't just . . . *that.* It was the way he'd touched her. The urgency in his hands, in the feel of his mouth, was all new, as if seeing her in danger had forced him, just for a instant, into letting go of all his usual careful control.

The flyer tipped, making her sway sideways, bump against the wall. It brought her out of the bubble of glowing warmth to which the world had momentarily shrunk. Above her the flyer's propellers beat the air, and all around her were refugees, shocked and wounded.

Felicia! Oh my God, what's wrong with me?

She scrambled to her feet, steadying herself with a hand against the wall. The body of the flyer, separated from the cockpit by a clear barrier, stretched out before her, easily big enough to hold all the passengers plus two crew members, a man and a woman, both dressed in light blue shirts and pants, the trident-caduceus showing on their right sleeves.

Felicia had been lifted onto a pull-down bed, and both crew members were bending over her. Her shirt had been cut off, and the female crew member was holding a clean white pad to her shoulder while the male crew member hooked her up to an IV unit.

Sofia was lying on another bed, Emily Greythorn attending to her head wound. Her movements were calm and steady, betraying no urgency. *Head wounds bleed a lot anyway,* thought Elissa, the snippet of random information entering her mind from nowhere. Despite the gray look to Sofia's face, and the expression of barely controlled panic on El's, it didn't look as if Sofia's wound was anywhere near life threatening.

It was Sofia getting hurt that freaked El out so badly, then. It wasn't just getting attacked—it was her twin *getting hurt.* From how Sofia and El had interacted back at the safe house, Elissa wouldn't have thought there was enough of a bond between them to make El react like that. *I should have known better, though. Once I'd gotten over the weirdness of meeting Lin, it hardly took any time before she mattered more than anything. . . .*

Everyone else who'd fled the safe house was sitting or standing around the flyer, holding on to grab handles to keep them steady as the flyer banked in the air.

And not just the people from the safe house. As Elissa's brain caught up with what she was looking at, she realized that the parents and children from the playground were on board as well, grouped at the end of the flyer farthest from the cockpit. When had they gotten on board?

"They all ran for the flyer when we did," said Samuel's voice behind her. Elissa turned to see him sitting, his back against the wall, his shoulder close to Jay's. "That big guy who came with you—Ivan? He pulled them all on board. The commander said they didn't have refugee clearance, and . . . well, he didn't pay much attention." He grinned. "It was very cool."

Elissa shot a look down to the other end of the flyer, where the commander stood, speaking to Cadan and Mr. Greythorn. "Jeez, I should *hope* he didn't pay attention. Those little kids, with grenades and bullets flying—you couldn't just leave them there! But what are they going to do with them now? I mean, they're not up for relocation, are they?"

"They're putting them back down," said Lin. She was kneeling beyond Samuel, next to where Cassiopeia huddled. Cassiopeia's face was hidden on her knees. After a second Elissa noticed that Lin's hand was on the other girl's shoulder, as if she was trying to comfort her but wasn't quite sure how to go about it.

That's new. Although Lin had wanted to come back to Sekoia in order to help other Spares, this was the first time Elissa had seen her do anything so normally human as offer comfort to anyone—apart, of course, from Elissa herself.

Big change. Was that the effect of escaping immediate danger, or was it just a natural development of meeting people like herself?

Belatedly, Elissa realized she hadn't responded to Lin. "Back down? Near where we were?"

"I guess so." Lin slid a glance at the unmoving Cassiopeia, putting her free hand up to her mouth to chew on the edge of her thumbnail. Her look at Elissa had some appeal in it.

I'm trying, her expression said, *but I don't know what I'm doing.*

Elissa choked back a giggle. It was really cool that Lin was trying to look after Cassiopeia, but it was a bit like watching a robot follow some kind of preselected "empathy" program. The right gestures, but performed in a way that made them a little alien.

"Cassiopeia?" she said. "Are you okay?"

A dark swathe of hair slid back from Cassiopeia's face as she turned her head to the side to look at Elissa. "I . . . don't think I'm hurt." Her voice came out as a croak, and she stopped and swallowed. "I . . ." A shudder took her, making her teeth chatter together.

"It was pretty freaky back there," Elissa said, speaking as gently as she could. All at once she was remembering the first time she'd seen Lin, filthy, shaking with fever, tipped out into a world she didn't understand, a world that had no welcome for her. "You're probably kind of shocked."

"Oh," said Lin suddenly. "Where's my hoodie?"

Elissa cast a quick look at her. Had that been all the empathy Lin had to spare? Seriously? She tried not to let her voice show disappointment. "Over by Felicia or something, I guess. It'll be all bloody, though, Lin—they won't let you get it."

"Okay." Lin looked back at Cassiopeia. "Sorry. I had some chocograin bars, but I can't— Oh, wait!" She delved in the pocket of her trousers, and after a few seconds produced the familiar wrapped bar and held it out to Cassiopeia. "I forgot I put one in there." She looked at the bar critically. "It's a bit squashed."

Elissa found herself smiling, wanting to reach over and hug her twin. "She's right," she said to Cassiopeia. "We're all pretty shaky, I bet. Chocolate does kind of help."

Cassiopeia took the bar, fumbled to tear it open, and bit off a piece.

Lin watched her eagerly. "It's nice, isn't it?"

Cassiopeia swallowed and bit off another piece. She nodded, and Lin beamed. Then, after a moment, Cassiopeia lifted her head fully. "It was you two who saved us down there," she said. "Wasn't it?"

Elissa felt herself flushing. It was one thing to have Cadan praise her; it was somehow less comfortable to have the others comment on it. She wasn't sure why. Maybe it was just that she and Lin—oh, they'd been so *lucky*, really, although it hadn't felt like it at the time. The fact that their link was powerful enough to save themselves, to save *other people*, felt almost embarrassing, like it was good luck on top of good luck, and none of it really deserved.

Lin didn't seem to feel any of the same reticence. "Yes," she said, a smile spreading across her face. "That was us."

From over by Zee, Ady spoke. "What you guys can do— it's amazing." He gave a rueful grin. "And kinda unfair. All the Spares were taken for the same reason—at least, as far as we know. We should all have that kind of power, don't you think?"

"No," said Lin seriously, missing the humor in his tone. "People's minds are different, even when they have telepathy or electrokinesis."

Just the corner of Ady's mouth curled. "Yeah, you're right," he said, deadpan.

Past him, Samuel started to laugh, then covered it by turning his head to speak to Jay.

Jay dug into his pockets as Lin had done, coming out with two bars—not chocograin but a couple of varieties of chocolate and dried fruit. Elissa had always thought those mixes worked even less well than chocograin. Samuel took them, unwrapped one, and started breaking it into pieces, dropping them back into the wrapper as he glanced up at the others. "Do you want to share? There's not enough for, like, everyone, but we could save a bit for Sofia and El?"

"That sounds fair," said Ady, reaching to pluck a bit from the opened wrapper.

Elissa shook her head. She felt shaky, but nothing like the ravenous hunger from before. Maybe some of the energy from the bars she'd eaten then was still in her body? *How much energy does electrokinesis use up, anyway?*

Lin nibbled a corner of her piece. "I never tried this one. We didn't have it on the *Phoenix*." Then her eyes went to the far end of the flyer, where the parents and children sat, huddled and silent. "Should we . . ." She hesitated. "Some of those children were crying. Do you think they'd like some?"

Jay followed her gaze, a reluctant look appearing on his face. "But we don't have much. And they're my bars."

Lin narrowed her eyes at him. "You can get more. And those children are really little." She leaned forward, took the second bar from Samuel's hand, and stood. "I'm going to give them some." *So there,* said her tone of voice.

Elissa smothered laughter, turning to watch as Lin made her way across to the far end of the flyer. Beside the laughter, affection for her twin glowed, warm within her. Those kids weren't even other Spares. They were just people, ordinary Sekoian citizens. She'd asked Lin, once, what people like that were to her, and Lin had said, *Just nobody. They're not anything.*

And now, here she was, looking at them and seeing people who'd been frightened and upset, people who might find chocolate as comforting as Lin did herself.

The glow inside Elissa wasn't just affection. It was pride.

One of the mothers looked up as Lin neared where they sat, and—suddenly, weirdly—something seemed to freeze in her expression. She moved her hand to touch the man next to her. The man looked up too, then, with the back of his hand, he touched the shoulder of the man next to him.

By the time Lin reached them, all the parents were watching her. A couple of the toddlers, too—one of them with his eyes fixed firmly on the snack bar she was holding.

"Hi," said Lin. Only three of the parents responded, and with nothing more than awkward-looking nods. Although they were looking at Lin, none of the parents' gazes seemed to focus steadily enough on her face to indicate that any of them were meeting her eyes.

The warmth inside Elissa ebbed a little. *What's going on? If they're blaming us for getting them caught up in the attack, that's completely unfair.* She stood, steadying herself against the wall, and began to walk over to join her sister.

Lin held out the bar to the nearest woman. "Would your children like some? It's chocograin—no, I mean"—she turned the bar to look at the wrapper—"oh, chocoraisin. I think it's good, though."

The woman shook her head, a polite smile flickering over her face, then disappearing. Too quickly, Elissa thought, to actually be polite at all. "No thanks."

Lin took half a step back, looking suddenly unsure of herself. "Okay. Um, would anyone else—"

A dark-haired woman, one of those who hadn't replied at all to Lin's greeting, spoke. "No *thank you*," she said, the words emphasized.

Elissa was next to Lin now, and she saw her twin's face go momentarily still. Lin often didn't pick up social cues, but the ice in the woman's voice was impossible not to notice.

"It's just chocolate," she said, her voice uncertain. "We thought—back down there, it must have been really scary for your children. We thought they might like . . ." She trailed off, still holding out the bar, and Elissa saw her throat move as she swallowed.

What's the matter with them? Like she said, it was really scary, and it would make sense if they were all shocked like Cassiopeia, but this isn't shock. This is . . .

This is hostility. But she stuck on the word. Okay, that was what it *seemed* like, but it made no sense. The parents had seen what had happened; they must know that it was Lin and Elissa who'd saved them.

At that point the toddler who'd had his gaze fixed on the choco bar apparently decided that the grown-ups were all taking too long getting him his share. He lunged forward, escaping from his father's arms, one chubby hand grabbing for the bar.

Lin's face lit in a smile as she put her own hand out to stop the toddler staggering into her legs. "Hey, do you want some?"

His father snatched him away. The dark-haired woman stood with a fast, jerky movement that made Lin step back. "We said *no thank you*, okay?"

Lin stared, bewildered. Elissa put a hand on her arm. "Lin, don't bother. It's just . . . whatever, they don't want it. They—"

But Lin wasn't moving. "What's *wrong*?" she said, looking at the man who'd snatched his son away. "It's just chocolate. You don't have to have any, but your little boy—he'd like some."

"That's because he doesn't know any better." The dark-haired woman's voice was bluntly belligerent. She stepped sideways, between Lin and the other parents, speaking past Lin to Elissa. "We said no, we said it politely, now can you stop her harassing us?"

"I'm not harassing you!" Lin's voice rose, sounding squeaky and indignant. "I'm being really nice! We already saved you back in the square, and now I'm sharing chocolate with you. That's not *harassing*."

But now understanding came to Elissa. *Can you stop her,* the woman had said. She'd spoken not to Lin, but *about* Lin to Elissa. As if Lin were some badly behaved child. Or not even a child—an animal. As if Elissa were her keeper.

They can see the difference between us. They can see I'm the "real" one, the one they can treat like a normal human. Somehow they've noticed those weird little differences, the things that make her look as if she's not quite familiar with the world she's living in. They know what she is. They know she's the Spare.

"Lin." She tugged on her sister's arm. "It's not worth it. Leave it." She had to get her away before Lin realized what exactly it was that she was meeting with—and why. She hadn't yet picked up that the woman had addressed Elissa, that she was treating Lin as if she didn't even want to acknowledge her presence. She hadn't yet picked up what that meant.

Lin had come here brimful of good intentions; Elissa didn't want to see her face change when the truth hit her, didn't want her to be left hurt and exposed in front of these horrible, ungrateful, freaking *stupid* people. "*Lin*, come away."

Lin threw her a bewildered, angry look. "But she's crazy. I'm not *harassing* them. Lissa, *you* tell her."

"It's not you, Lin. You didn't do anything wrong. She

probably is crazy. Let's just leave them alone—"

"Oh, *I'm* crazy?" It was naked enmity in the woman's face now. "You think we don't know what she is? You think we want her near our kids?"

And that was when it hit Lin. Her face went still, the stillness of someone who has sustained a bad blow and freezes, as if keeping motionless will stop the pain from getting through. "You mean Spares," she said, her lips hardly moving.

The woman had drawn back toward her friends as if they'd provide some kind of shield. "You shouldn't even be out in the population," she said. "You're supposed to be shut away."

Fury licked up through Elissa, a wave of heat like sheet lightning. "She's *not*, she's supposed to be in a *safe house*. No one's supposed to be shutting her away—she never did anything!"

"You call that down there nothing?"

"That was *both* of us," Elissa said, enraged. If this woman was freaking out because of what their electrokinesis had done, then at least she should be freaking out about both Lin *and* Elissa, not just one of them.

"Oh, and you were doing it *before* IPL put the two of you together?" The woman paused just long enough for Elissa to do exactly what the woman was obviously expecting, which was to say nothing. She'd have said *yes* if she could: *Yes*, I was already electrokinetic, *yes*, I'm the freak here.

"IPL," said the woman, the word colored with contempt. "Taking over, ruining our planet. Treating Spares like they're the only victims here. Putting them and their doubles back together. They should have *investigated* it, they should have thought about what it might do. Anyone could have warned them they needed to be more careful. All those reports of what they can do! Reading people's minds, psychokinetic abilities, for God's sake—they should *never have been let out*." She was shaking as she spoke. At first Elissa thought it was just anger—like *she* had any business being angry. But then something—the overrigidity of the woman's lips, the screwed-up crinkle at the outer edges of her eyes—told her that if it was anger, it wasn't *just* anger. The woman was afraid.

And it was Lin she was afraid of. She'd seen what Lin and Elissa had both done, but she was only afraid of Lin. She thought Lin needed to be locked up. As if she were danger-ous, as if she were a criminal.

Somewhere at the back of Elissa's mind, a voice, born of the unease of weeks ago and the fear and fury of the day before, whispered, *Well, she is dangerous.*

I don't care! She didn't do anything this time. She saved them. She saved this stupid woman and her stupid friends and their stupid children!

She opened her mouth to say something like that—except maybe with some *really* bad words tacked on—but at that point a cold hand slid into hers, cold fingers closed around her own.

"It's not worth it," said Lin, her voice without expression, echoing Elissa's words as if, for the moment, she had none of her own. "Come away."

Actually, telling this woman what Elissa thought of her seemed *completely* worth it, but when Elissa turned her head and saw her sister's face, the words died on her lips.

The brief, blunting edge of shock had worn off. Now the pain had reached Lin. Before, when people had shown they thought of her as subhuman, like some kind of weird full-body clone, Lin had been angry, but not hurt. But back then, she hadn't expected anything different. She hadn't expected anything of legal humans, hadn't, at first, even expected anything of Elissa. But this time . . .

She thought they'd accept her like they would accept me. She thought she could offer them chocolate and they'd take it like Cassiopeia did, like it wasn't a big deal.

And instead, the woman had slapped her away, treated her like some—*thing*—they didn't even want to get near. And because this time Lin had expected it to be different, this time it hadn't struck her with anger, but with pain.

Elissa looked at Lin's face, her pressed-together lips, her stricken eyes, then turned her gaze to the people who'd hurt her twin. For an instant her anger seemed to bleach out everything, turn it into a white haze. And it must have shown in her face, because the dark-haired woman took a big step backward, so fast that she almost stumbled over one of the toddlers.

Then Ivan was there, his big arm around Lin's shoulders, his other hand on Elissa's back. "Like she said, sweetheart, it's not worth it. Not with these types." Elissa felt his gaze go over her head and meet that of the dark-haired woman. The woman's chin went up, defiant. There was fear in her eyes, but a whole lot less than when it had been Elissa looking at her.

I scared her. Good. Good. I wish—

But then Ivan was turning her and Lin around, steering them away across the floor of the flyer, and the wish slipped away before it could become entirely verbalized in her mind.

The others had witnessed enough of the little scene to understand what had happened. Ady was giving the refugees a look like a laser, and as Lin got within reach and stepped away from Ivan, Samuel came to give her a huge hug. Past Lin's head, Samuel's eyes met Elissa's. His move toward Lin had been so calm that Elissa was almost shocked to see the blaze of fury within them.

"Screw them," he said, loud enough to carry across the flyer. "Slow learners, that's all. They'd be in itty-bitty pieces if it wasn't for you guys."

Elissa gave a choke of laughter, so unexpected that it hurt her chest the way a hiccup would have. She looked at the back of Lin's head, her gaze moving from the place where the dark roots faded to pale blond, to the place where her skull curved down and where, under her hair, a hole had been drilled in through the bone. Lin was standing still, not moving out of Samuel's hug, not returning it either.

"Lin?"

Lin stepped away from Samuel's arms. She looked as if every muscle in her face had tensed, pulling the skin tight over the bones. As if she were holding herself together.

Elissa's stomach cramped. Lin wasn't supposed to look like that, not now, not anymore. "You did the right thing," she said. "They're idiots, and they're scared and they're stupid, but everything you did—it was the right thing to do."

Lin shrugged, not speaking. She wasn't just holding herself together, she'd closed herself off. Again rage bleached up through Elissa's head, fading the world, scalding the back of her throat.

The flyer banked, not sharply, but enough to make Elissa reach for a grab handle. They were descending to whatever safe place the pilot had decided on to put down the group of inadvertent refugees.

Good. Let's dump them. Forget about them. We shouldn't have bothered with them in the first place. Back when Lin was newly escaped from the facility, when she'd said that kind of thing, Elissa had been horrified. But now, anger scorching through and through her . . . *I get why she said it, I get what she was feeling.*

She didn't *mean* it, not really, not with all the bits of her brain that were still rational, but it was a kind of sour comfort to tell herself she did, to let herself give in to the vicious thoughts. *People like that—they're not worth even thinking about, let alone helping. And they'll bring their kids up to be as dumb as they are—what's even the point?*

The flyer descended only a short distance before touching down. Through the glass slits around the top of the passenger cabin, Elissa caught a glimpse of tower block roofs, the dazzle of sun on metal railings.

They'd landed on a roof. Of, Elissa guessed, yet another tower block, although she'd lost all track of where they were. Still one of the residential areas, probably. The indoors route down wouldn't be accessible to anyone without the entrance codes for the block, but their unwelcome passengers would be able to get down to street level via the external fire escape.

As for which sector they'd ended up in, which way they'd have to go to get to the square where they'd been attacked, Elissa didn't have a clue.

Not that it would be a problem for the refugees. They'd all have phones or myGadgets, and there were mapscreens displayed at nearly every street corner. It'd take them all of thirty seconds to figure out how to get back home.

Unless the mapscreens had been turned off when the lights were? Unless the citywide communication channels were all down so their phones wouldn't work?

She was jerked from her thoughts as the door beeped, letting them know the lock was off. Markus opened the door, and the unwanted refugees filed past.

The moment the last of them had stepped out, Markus hit the doorpad to shut the door. The propellers picked up, vibrating through the roof above Elissa's head. She glanced back and saw Lin watching the closed door. Her face was still tight, her lips bloodless.

If the mapscreens are off, thought Elissa, furious all over again, *if their phones won't work, well, serve them right.*

Then, flaring in her head, hot and vicious, came thoughts so strong she felt them all through her body, as if it were her veins acting as their conduit. *Let them be lost and scared and not know where to go! Let them have to run from people who want to hurt them. Let them have just a taste of what it was like for me!*

The thoughts—and not only the thoughts, but the emotions—were so clear, so *immediate*, that it was several seconds before she realized that they weren't all hers. She and Lin weren't touching, there was no crisis to shock them into telepathic connection, neither of them was trying to communicate with the other, and yet, for that instant, she'd heard her twin's thoughts as clearly as if they were her own.

The link's getting stronger. Cold sifted through her, like flakes of crushed ice slipping down through water. She'd thought that earlier today, and had felt—mostly—nothing but awe and triumph. But what they'd done back then—communicating telepathically—it had been deliberate. And she'd known all along which thoughts belonged to whom. *This is different.*

The Spares and twins had moved out of the way as the refugees went past. Now, as they moved back, filling the space, Elissa caught sight of Zee.

Zee's eyes were fixed on his brother's face, but not as if he saw him. Not as if he saw *anything*. His expression was empty. Elissa was suddenly aware of her heart beating in long, slow strokes, as if counting out the time that Zee stood, blank eyed, motionless, his eyes on Ady's face. *Something's not right. He's . . . what? Gone into shock? Something like that? Something worse?*

Then Ady moved, turned his head a fraction away, and Zee's face came immediately awake. Ady glanced at him, said something, and Zee answered, his whole expression entirely normal once more.

What was that? It can't have been shock—not real shock, or he'd never have snapped out of it like that.

The flyer lifted into the air. Suddenly needing to be away, for a moment, from all the Spares, Elissa went to the far end of the flyer, where there were two windows slightly bigger than the narrow, high slits around the rest of the cabin. The flyer was not quite directly above the rooftop now. The refugees were filing onto the fire escape that Elissa could see spiraling down the side of the tower block.

The crackling whine of a communicator made her jump, then the crackle became words. "Alert. Alert. Come in, Commander Dacre. Come in, Flyer A-Eighty-two."

Elissa swung around as, in the cockpit, the flyer pilot put his hand out to the communicator on the dashboard, and as Commander Dacre spoke into her wrist-unit. "Commander Dacre here. You need to call someone else. I'm not equipped to handle any–"

The voice came through clear and urgent. "*No.* Danger coming your way. We intercepted an exchange near your sector—one of the terror groups has got hold of details of the nearest safe houses, and you're near one of them now—"

"For God's sake, don't *say* it out loud—" Exasperated anger rose into the commander's voice.

"No, listen! They think you're delivering a group there now! They've got a ship. You need to get out. Flyer A-Eighty-two, get out now!"

Beneath Elissa's feet, the floor tipped as the pilot took the flyer up in a steep climb. She grabbed for a handle, panic fizzing all over her skin. *A ship? A ship with weapons? But we're not armored!*

"Wait," said Cadan. "If a terrorist group thinks we've just dropped off Spares, Commander, it's not us in the most danger—"

Elissa jerked back toward the window. The refugees were all on the fire escape now. Between the metal bars were flashes of movement, here-and-there glimpses of the color of a sleeve or pants leg, where the parents and children climbed down toward the ground. *Some group—some hate group—thinks they're Spares. We put them out of the flyer and now someone thinks they're the Spares, not us—*

Then a shriek cut across every other sound in the world, and the ship came like a lightning bolt out of a clear sky.

It cut low across the buildings, a silver bullet streaking through the air, and fire rained after it, shattering edges of roofs, sending dust and smoke boiling up in clouds.

Elissa shrieked herself, hands clamped over her ears, the sound tearing through her brain, terror like ice and fire wiping out every thought. The flyer lurched. She saw Lin's face, a pale blur in front of her, Lin's eyes, shocked wide open.

The flyer lurched again, not climbing this time but ducking below the level of the rooftops. The wall of one of the tower blocks rose before the window she was staring out of.

Above them, the ship came back in an ear-shattering shriek. But not in pursuit of the flyer. It was focusing its attack on the tower block from which they'd just taken off. The tower block—*oh God oh no no no*—where they'd left the parents and children.

And we can't do anything! The flyer can't help. It doesn't have armor or weapons—it can't do anything.

She turned, frantic, from the window—*but we can't just leave them like that!*—into Cadan's hands as he reached for her.

"Cadan," she said, knowing he couldn't hear her over the ship shrieking through the sky somewhere above their heads, over the roar of their own propellers as the flyer's pilot took them farther down into the shelter between the buildings, knowing he'd have to read her lips to understand her at all.

His hands closed tightly on her upper arms. "I know." His lips moved to form the silent words. "I know, Lis. But we have to keep the people on this flyer safe. We can't help."

There was something like despair in his face, but all the same the touch of his hands steadied her, swept away her own horrified despair. *We can't help,* he'd said.

Except we can.

She twisted out of his hold to look back through the window. It was a storm of dust and smoke out there, rolling down between the flyer and the tower blocks they were moving past. But she could still see the flash of the ship as it made another pass, raining destruction behind it.

Acting on instinct she hadn't even realized she'd learned, Elissa screwed her eyes up, focusing on that far-off glint of the attacking ship. Focusing on it both with her eyes and her mind.

Lin—and I—blew up ships like this one. But we've moved *things too—we don't have to destroy. If I can just take hold of it, slow it down, force it away . . . just long enough to give them a chance to escape. We escaped, they can too. . . .*

She reached, focused, feeling her fingers curl up so her nails dug into her palms, reached to take hold of the ship. . . .

And didn't. It was like trying to seize a hologram. The fingers of her mind closed on emptiness, went through the image of the ship as if it were made of nothing but air and pixels.

She tried again, her physical fingers tightening until cramp jabbed through their joints. But this time she couldn't even reach halfway to the ship. It was like that moment in a bad dream when you realize your legs won't move, or your hands fumble endlessly over some simple, everyday task.

But I've done this before! I did do it, did it myself. *I wasn't just watching Lin. I was there, I was involved.*

She tried for a third time, and this time her mental image of the ship wavered and flickered, and then disappeared. She hadn't even been really reaching for it in the first place. Whatever power her mind possessed, she hadn't been accessing it. Not this time. Not at all. It had been nothing more than her imagination.

The ship made another air-splitting pass above them. Exploding masonry showered and rattled all across the body of the flyer.

Eyes still fixed on the spark-netted dust seething outside the window, Elissa reached out a hand. *Lin. Lin, help me.*

No answer came. No familiar hand clasped hers.

Elissa turned. Lin was there, next to Cadan, fingers locked on to a grab handle. She was as white as if all the blood had left her body. Her eyes were huge. *She's shocked. But it's okay—if she helps me, if we help them, we can fix this, we can make it okay again.*

"Lin," she said, speaking out loud, knowing that if Lin didn't manage to read her lips it wouldn't matter, because she'd still hear the words in her mind. "Help me. I can't do it by myself. I can't save them without you."

Lin's eyes met hers, and they weren't shocked. They weren't shocked at all. They were as calm as the sky had been before the ship had exploded out of it.

"No," she said.

Elissa stared at her, uncomprehending, her hand still stretched out. "Lin, they're going to *die.*"

"I don't care."

"*Lin.* There are *people* there." For an instant the words echoed in her mind, sparking the beginning of a memory.

"I know." Lin shook her head, still calm. "I'm not helping them."

"But they're *people*—" She broke off. The memory came clearly now. The memory was from when she'd found out that it had been Lin who'd set the fire that had enabled Elissa to escape the bedroom where her parents had locked her. Once again she heard her own voice, shrill with horror: *There are other people in that building. There's safety measures and all that stuff, but people die in house fires all the time. You could have killed them!* Then Lin's voice, confused, not getting why Elissa was upset: *Why should I care about that?*

That had been the first time Elissa thought the word "psychopath." The first time she'd looked at this strange image of herself she'd just met and found the question appearing in her mind: *What if there's a very good reason they kept her locked up?*

But she's changed! Elissa thought now. *She's different. She doesn't see other people–non-Spares–as different from herself.*

"Lin," she said, helpless, desperate, the world as she thought she knew it cracking to pieces all around her.

Lin shook her head. "I'm sorry, Lissa." She held up her hands, and Elissa saw that despite her calm they were shaking. For a moment she thought it was distress, and hope flared through her–*she doesn't mean it the way I thought she did, it's just that she's really upset, of course she's going to help me*–before she realized the tremor of her sister's hands wasn't distress, but only fatigue.

"I would do it for you, because you wanted me to," Lin said, "if it wasn't going to hurt me when I did. I've been saving people all day. I hurt all over. And half of them weren't even"–for a moment the calm of her expression broke like masonry cracking, and pain like dust, like smoke, clouded her face–"*grateful.* I'm not going to keep on *hurting* myself for people who wish I'd stayed in the facility. I'm not hurting myself for *them.*"

The ship screeched past again. Although she knew it was impossible, Elissa seemed to hear other shrieks beyond it– human voices, children's voices, screaming for help. Other sounds followed it, sounds she couldn't really be hearing but that were no less horrible for being in her imagination only: the grinding of metal as the fire escape broke, as it ripped away from the wall and fell in a clanging tangle, fragile human bodies being carried with it.

"Lin," she said again.

And again her sister shook her head, stepping back, stepping away. "No. No, Lissa. Not this time."

A last shriek through the air, a last clattering and shattering of brick and cement, a last cloud of dust that blocked out the sunlight. Then the ship had gone, streaking into the distance, and there was just the roar of propellers as their flyer rose from where it had sheltered, rose from the dust and the smoking buildings, rose away into the sunlight and the clear blue sky.

Elissa didn't want to look back. She told herself not to, repeated it furiously to herself, even put a hand up to her eyes as if to try to force them not to see. But her head turned as if of its own accord; her hand dropped down. She looked through the window, back down to the building from which they'd taken off. She *couldn't* really have heard the fire escape fall, of course she couldn't, not over the noise of the ship— but she'd been right all the same. It hung, a ruin of twisted metal, from halfway down the tower block. She could no longer see anyone on it. And now the ground below it was not only obscured by swirling clouds of dust, but hidden under piles of rubble.

FOURTEEN

SHE LEFT them to die.

It was late afternoon, and Elissa was alone for the first time in hours, walking down one of the shiny-white, sterilized-clean corridors of the city spaceport hospital.

The flyer had gotten them to safety at the spaceport several hours ago, but it wasn't until now that she'd had the chance to seek out a few minutes alone with Cadan.

Sofia and Felicia had both been taken to the hospital the moment they arrived at the spaceport. Sofia had been bandaged up, given an antibiotic injection, and was resting, El waiting in a chair next to her bed.

The rest of the group were in the hospital too, although they were in the waiting rooms, not the treatment wing. Unlike normal hospitals, the spaceport hospital had been built underground, and right now was about the most secure place they could go.

Felicia's condition had been a whole lot more serious

than Sofia's, but she, too, was recovering. Her wound was clean and stitched, she'd been given a blood transfusion and pumped full of anti-infection drugs and healing accelerants. The rest of the *Phoenix* crew had been allowed to see her as she lay pale and tranquil in drug-induced sleep, and everyone had told Elissa how well she—Elissa, not Felicia—had coped. Everyone, too, had told Elissa and Lin how well they'd both done, how amazing they'd been, how fantastic their linked powers were. It was the recognition, the praise Elissa had thought she'd wanted. Now, though, every time anyone said anything about it, she felt as if she were once again breathing in the dirt and dust from back in the square, feeling it sting her eyes, clog her throat, lie bitter on her tongue.

She left them to die. I asked her to help and she wouldn't. The thought seemed to burn through her brain. She pushed through a swinging hospital door, letting it flap shut behind her, glancing up at the exit sign on the clean white wall.

As soon as they knew Felicia would be okay, Cadan had left the hospital. He'd gone in the shuttlebug with Markus and one IPL official, back to the base where they'd left the *Phoenix*. Commander Dacre had organized clearance, and he'd been going to fly the ship back to the spaceport. That had been several hours ago. He'd sent a message through IPL channels to say he'd gotten back safely, but Elissa hadn't seen him. He'd stayed aboveground with the *Phoenix*, overseeing its preparation and refueling for the twenty-four-hour journey to Philomel.

For our evacuation.

Well, what did I expect? I should never have let her come back in the first place.

They'd known it was a risk, known they were returning to

danger. But—and now Elissa couldn't believe she'd ever been so naive—it hadn't crossed her mind that the risk would be not to Lin's safety, but to her humanity.

By returning to Sekoia, she'd brought Lin back to the world that had declared her nonhuman, the world that had treated her like a lab animal, that had wanted her imprisoned—and if not imprisoned, dead. How could Elissa have thought it would end in anything other than disaster?

She turned a white, featureless corner, into the white, featureless corridor that lay past it.

I should never have come back either. In the world beyond her home, and then out in the vast reaches of space that lay beyond Sekoia's atmosphere, she'd become somebody she liked. Somebody she could feel almost . . . proud . . . of being.

At the time she'd felt as if all she was doing was stumbling from crisis to crisis. Looking back, though, she saw someone who'd managed to make decision after difficult decision, someone who'd coped with fear and pain and danger. She'd not only protected Lin but had helped her to learn how to live in the world outside the facility.

But now . . . God, the worst mistake she'd made must have been bringing Lin back to Sekoia. Now, when it was too late to change it, it was horribly obvious that it had been too much, too soon, had crushed the empathy—the *humanity*—Lin had been developing.

Back when she first found me, I realized then that I had to get her away from Sekoia because I was afraid she was a sociopath. Why didn't I know better than to bring her back?

The next door opened on a flight of stairs, as impossibly clean and white as the corridors. The hospital elevators were all shut off, conserving energy here as in the rest of the city. Elissa started up them. Heaviness dragged at her as she climbed, as if artificial gravity were being used in the hospital as it was on the *Phoenix*, as if it had been turned up just that uncomfortable fraction too high.

Well, at least this time I don't have to figure out how to get Lin off-planet.

They wouldn't be able to come back. Given everything that had happened, she didn't think Lin would even want to. Not now, not anymore.

They would go to Philomel. She and Lin still had a whole lump of their compensation fund—they could move on where they wanted, go to college like they'd been half planning. *Lin can train to be a spaceship pilot if that's what she wants.*

But whatever they did, wherever they went, they would have to stay away from Sekoia's shattered society. That was no longer even a question. If they ever came back, if something else happened . . .

*I'll lose her. If we keep being faced with danger, on this world that did such terrible things to her, if she keeps being pushed and pushed . . . she's going to end up doing something awful, something so bad I won't be able to forgive her. Something so bad—*Elissa flinched; oh God, even the thought was a betrayal—*that I'll end up wishing they'd left her locked up.*

The stairs led to a little landing. Elissa crossed it and took the next flight of stairs, continuing to climb.

So they'd go, because they had to, and they wouldn't return, because they couldn't. They'd forget that they'd come to Sekoia full of high hopes—of changing things, of giving aid to their world. They'd figure out a life for themselves somewhere else.

But what about Cadan? Will he do that too? Inside her, something twisted. Cadan had mostly wanted to come back to see if his family was okay. But now he'd seen what was happening to the planet he'd been trained to protect. Once he'd gotten the ship's load of passengers to safety on Philomel, would he want to return to Sekoia? Would he want to come back to give the aid Elissa and Lin couldn't?

What was there to keep him on Philomel? His parents would be there, but he was twenty-one, and he'd been living away from home for years—their presence wouldn't keep him on a planet to which he had no other tie.

But there's me. I'll be there.

Yeah, but was she kidding herself to think that was anything like close to enough?

This—everything he can offer the IPL on Sekoia—this is the kind of thing he trained for, after all. And he'd be useful—truly useful. Even Commander Dacre said it would be different if he'd come here without me and Lin. He wouldn't even need our money to refuel the Phoenix *for him. If he told Commander Dacre he wanted to come back, she'd arrange for IPL to fund him, I know it.*

Extremely useful, the commander had said that morning, endless hours ago. Not Elissa, not Lin—they were burdens, both of them, too young, too fragile, too much of a liability—but Cadan and the *Phoenix* and the—*adult*—crew.

If he did return, his parents would approve. They would know, this time, that he was doing it because it was the right thing, not because he'd been manipulated into it by his girlfriend. And Cadan would know it too. He wouldn't have to have doubts anymore, wouldn't have to struggle with not being sure whether his motives were all clear and right the way he always needed everything to be.

He doesn't like gray areas. He especially doesn't like thinking there might be gray areas in himself.

The next thought came from nowhere. *IPL could call Bruce back from Philomel too. Give him his career back. Put them both on the* Phoenix *to work together, pilot and copilot like they were meant to be before Bruce had to go into quarantine and missed his chance.*

Then, borne by a vicious stab of jealousy: *And won't that seem just like old times, with no irritating little sister around to whine and cry and mess things up?*

No. She was being stupid. That might be how Bruce would think about it, but it wasn't how Cadan saw her. It *wasn't*. And there must be half a million things for a trained space pilot to do—and plenty of them that his parents would approve of. There was no reason to assume he'd want to come back to Sekoia when there was a whole star system of opportunities out there.

But the idea was there now, the twist tightening in her belly, moving up into her lungs so for a moment it was difficult to take in enough breath to keep her climbing the stairs.

If Cadan comes back to Sekoia, I'll be scared the whole time. Every minute I'll think he's been killed.

And nearly as urgent as that fear—she despised herself that it *was* so urgent, but she couldn't help thinking it—was the fear of what would happen between them.

If she and Lin stayed on Philomel, and Cadan came back here, what would happen to them, to him and Elissa? Would what they had survive a separation of—God, maybe months, with scarcely any contact? With Elissa not knowing from one day to the next whether he was even still alive? With Cadan in the midst of a combat zone, civilian preoccupations fading further and further from his mind?

She reached the top of the stairs. The door in front of her was a normal sliding one rather than a flappy hospital door.

Elissa opened it and went through into an entrance lobby. It wasn't one of the main hospital entrances, so although it had a reception desk, the current understaffing situation meant that the desk wasn't staffed, and the only person she could see was an armed IPL guard standing just outside the doors.

Even as she noticed him, another person came into her line of sight. Cadan's mother, her hair ruffled by the dusty wind that swept almost constantly across the plateau, walking toward the hospital door. The guard nodded as she reached where he stood, and she smiled at him as he put a hand up to hit the doorpad and open the door for her.

The door whooshed open on a gust of air as hot and dry as if it came from an oven, and Elissa instantly tasted dust and sand and rocket fuel, smelled dead, baked-dry grass. Her skin welcomed the wave of warm air even as her nose wrinkled at the smell.

"Elissa?" said Cadan's mother. "Whatever are you doing up here? Did you get lost?"

"No. No, I'm fine." Infuriatingly, she found herself stammering slightly, nerves tying her tongue.

Emily Greythorn came toward her as the door swooshed shut. "You really shouldn't be up here, though. I know it's guarded, but—well, you're already well aware of the threats we're facing, aren't you?"

Elissa shook her head. "Oh, I know. I'm not going to stay long—I just wanted to see Cadan."

Mrs. Greythorn's eyebrows lifted. "Ah . . . Elissa, it's probably not the best time for that. He's up to his elbows in prepping the ship. I'm sure you'll get a chance to see him later, when he's not so busy."

Elissa bit her lip. She didn't want to be rude to a grown-up—and *really* not to Cadan's mother—but she'd waited for hours already. And she and Cadan had managed their relationship for weeks without needing advice. She made herself smile, hoping that it didn't betray the edge of resentment she was feeling. "I won't interfere. I know he's super busy. I just have to see him for a minute."

She took a step toward the door, and—to her bewildered surprise—Emily Greythorn put a hand out and laid it on her arm, halting her, gently but inexorably.

"I really don't recommend it," she said. "He won't thank you for interrupting him, not right now. Take my word for it, my dear."

The bewilderment morphed into something much simpler. Heat flickered into Elissa's cheeks. She lifted her chin and stepped back so that Mrs. Greythorn's hand fell from her arm. "Cadan's pretty much always happy to see me."

"I'm sure he is." Mrs. Greythorn's voice remained utterly calm—and kind, like she thought Elissa needed reassurance or something. "And I'm sure that when he's next at leisure he'll be happy to see you again. Right now, though—" As if she'd caught the flicker in Elissa's expression, her voice changed to firmness. "Elissa, he's at work."

The heat spread through Elissa's veins. "Wasn't he at work when you came to see him too?"

Mrs. Greythorn's eyebrows lifted again, and under them her eyes were suddenly the cold blue that Cadan's could go. "I am his mother."

Elissa folded her arms. "Okay. Well, I'm his girlfriend."

"Oh good Lord." For the first time impatience lent an edge to Mrs. Greythorn's calm tone. "I don't think it's really the same, do you?"

"Well, it's not like he's *flying* the ship right now. If he doesn't mind *you* interrupting him—"

"I didn't 'interrupt' him," Emily Greythorn said sharply. "I've been an SFI mother for a long time, I know better than to disturb him when he's working. I had business there—I was arranging for his skybike to be fitted in the cargo hold. There are no slidewalks on Philomel, and Cadan can't be of as much use if he's grounded."

Her manner had that not-quite-conscious pride Elissa's own mother had always shown when she mentioned *her* SFI son.

"Well," Elissa said, and it came out with more of a snap than she intended, "I know better too. I *grew up* with him—him and Bruce. It's not like I don't know what he does. I'm not going to *interfere*."

"Really?" said Cadan's mother.

"*Yes!*" Elissa stopped. "What? What do you mean, 'really'?"

Emily Greythorn sighed. "Look, Elissa, don't think I don't understand the attraction. You and Cadan—you've been thrown together under some really stressful conditions. And of course it probably didn't help that you had the world's worst crush on him when you were little—"

"*What?*"

"Elissa, please. You think we didn't notice? And he's grown up . . . well"—again that look of pride colored her smile—"I'd be surprised if you could spend all that time with him and not be . . . tipped a bit off balance. Especially with the pressure you were both under. And, of course, you're a very pretty girl—I can see the attraction for him, too."

"*Jeez,*" said Elissa, all at once furious, "thanks for the compliment."

Mrs. Greythorn gave her a patient look, a look that said she'd noticed Elissa's anger, but that she was choosing not to pay attention to it. "You say you're not going to interfere. What do you think you're already doing?"

Hearing it said like that, actually stated rather than implied, was like being hit in the face.

"I—I'm not—" She was stammering again. She stopped, staring at Cadan's mother, shock and hurt taking away all that heat of anger she'd felt a minute ago.

"Well, I'm afraid you are." Mrs. Greythorn's voice wasn't unkind, but it was unrelenting. "He's thinking about you when he needs to have his attention undivided. After we escaped from the square, he came to you first of all, when he could have been—"

"We—we'd only just escaped! I'd thought he was—"

"I know." Mrs. Greythorn spoke over her, cutting her off. "I thought he was too. Elissa, listen to me. I'm not *opposing* you here. You're a sweet girl, and you've coped with an awful lot. I'm impressed, truly. And goodness knows, I'm not against Cadan dating!"

"It's not just . . ." She trailed off. *It's not just dating.* She could say that, but what reason would his mother have to believe her? And, really, despite what Cadan had said, despite what Elissa herself felt, it had been only a few weeks. It might not *feel* like just dating, to either of them, but all the same, that was pretty much what it was.

Mute, feeling like her defenses had been, very neatly and gently, taken away, Elissa stared at Cadan's mother as she continued to speak.

"I just think, Elissa, that now probably isn't the right time for it. Don't look so stricken! I'm not trying to stop you seeing him." Mrs. Greythorn laughed a little. "I've brought up two teenagers—I'm not so stupid. I'm just saying maybe . . . ease off a bit? Spend some time with the other young people. Make some other friendships. You can't afford to depend on just Cadan—and he can't afford to have you doing it."

She sounded so . . . *sensible*. Like the voice of a million teen advice websites and magazine advice columns. And everything Elissa could say, every argument she could make, would just make her sound like the insecure girls who e-mailed those advice columns. *But we love each other. But he doesn't want us to ease off any more than I do. But I'm dealing with more than I can cope with alone. But it's not just an ordinary teen-age relationship. . . .*

"And he's a good bit older," said Cadan's mother, still the voice of an advice columnist. "Oh, come on, don't look at me like that. Again, I'm not *against* it. Trust me, I haven't forgotten being seventeen myself, and I can imagine I might have been swept off my feet if someone Cadan's age had been interested in me!"

She paused for a moment, as if thinking whether to say her next words. Her gaze met Elissa's, and although there was still an edge of coolness to her expression, her eyes were kind. That made it worse, really. If there'd been spite showing in them, or if Elissa could think Mrs. Greythorn was being the clichéd possessive mother of books and TV shows, at least then she'd have had good reason to ignore her. To fight back. To say to Cadan, *Do you know what your mother's been saying to me?* and have him leap to her defense.

Cadan's mother sighed again. "Look, I'm not blind. I can see how close the two of you have become. I can tell he cares about you. But honestly, Elissa, I have to ask: How much do you think the two of you really have in common?"

Elissa's lips went cold. All this stuff, everything his mother was saying—it wasn't like the thoughts hadn't come into her head before this. It was what she'd been scared of. What she'd been scared of all along, the stuff she'd wanted Cadan to reassure her about, help her dismiss.

But oh God, hearing it . . . hearing it said out loud—and by Cadan's *mother*—it was so much worse than when it had just been silent fears in her own head.

"I—" she said, and couldn't think of anything else to say.

Mrs. Greythorn stepped away from her. "I'm sorry, Elissa. I don't usually comment on Cadan's relationships. If life was as it was before the takeover, I'd let things take their own course. But as things are . . ." She lifted a shoulder. "Well, I won't patronize you. You know the situation as well as I do." She moved a step toward the stairs up which Elissa had come. "Look, I'm going back down now. You're old enough to make your own decisions. And it's not like I have any authority over you—I'm not going to try to stop you seeing him if you're set on it."

She moved farther, out of Elissa's line of sight. Elissa didn't move her head to follow her. She couldn't bear to meet her eyes again. Couldn't bear to see all that dispassionate, adult wisdom—that look that said Emily Greythorn had witnessed this kind of thing before, that this time wasn't anything out of the ordinary, that—*whatever* it felt like—it wasn't anything different.

Cadan's mother's footsteps tapped across the floor. The door to the stairs slid open, then shut. She was gone.

Elissa put her arms around herself, not so much as a comfort as because of a feeling that if she didn't, she would break apart. *If I ask Cadan, he can tell me it's not just because he thinks I'm pretty, it's not just because we were thrown together and everything around us was going crazy. It would have happened anyway. It would.*

He wouldn't tell her that, though. Someone else might say what she needed to hear whether they were sure or not. Someone else might take a leap of faith—*yes of course it would have happened anyway, no of course it wasn't just right place, right time.* Cadan wouldn't. He wouldn't say it unless he was sure. And that hours-ago talk with him (was it really only this morning?) had told her he *wasn't* sure.

It was more than that too. His mother—probably both his parents—didn't think she was good enough for him. She hadn't *said* it, but then how could you say something like that without sounding like some crazy-awful snobby cliché? But no one talked the way she had to the girl they *wanted* their son to end up with. *How much do you think the two of you really have in common?* she'd said, and Elissa hadn't needed to read between the lines to know what she meant.

She came out here to talk to Cadan. Was she saying this kind of thing to him, too? Does he know she thinks I'm not good enough for him? Does he . . . even a tiny bit, does he agree?

The door to the spaceport opened on a rush of hot air. Elissa's fingers gave a guilty twitch—*I shouldn't be here, I don't have a good reason*—and her head jerked up to look.

It was the guard who'd opened the door. He'd left his hand on the panel to stop the door closing, and although he was still clearly on alert, he'd turned enough toward the lobby to be able to look across at Elissa. "You're wanting Greythorn?"

Elissa nodded. "*Cadan* Greythorn?" There wasn't any reason for Mr. Greythorn to be out there, but she *really* didn't want to go straight from the conversation with Cadan's mother to one with his father.

"He's on his way."

"Oh, he's finished?"

The guard smiled at her. "No. I told him you were here, that's all. Pretty girl, I said, dark hair, and he was happy to drop what he was doing."

The twitch of guilt turned into a spasm like a giant hand closing on her stomach. The words *What do you think you're already doing?* and *He's thinking about you when he needs to have his attention undivided* rang in her ears. And the word "pretty," which always before she'd have been super pleased to hear, suddenly sounded like an accusation.

"Oh God, I didn't mean to *interrupt* him. He doesn't have to come—tell him I can wait till he's done, or taking a break, or whatever—"

"That's an awful lot of backtracking, Lis," said Cadan, coming in through the doorway. His fair hair was ruffled—the same way, Elissa noticed, his mother's had been—and there was sweat and dirt on his forehead and staining the edges of his shirt collar. "Are you sure you weren't actually hoping to see Markus?"

His eyes laughed at her, and for a moment warmth crept through her like the warmth blowing in from outside, relaxing her muscles, warming her cold lips and hands. *It doesn't matter what his mother thinks. His mother's not here, she doesn't know what it's really like. She's only judged from the outside—she doesn't know, she doesn't understand.*

She reached out for the reassurance she was still—mostly—sure he could give her. "Is it okay for me to be here?" Then, as insecurity took over, "I can go away again if you're busy.

I completely didn't mean to interrupt you."

"You haven't." Cadan nodded a thank you to the guard and came across to pull her into a hug. He smelled dusty and sweaty, but underneath she caught the scent of his skin. And although his hands were rough with dust, they were warm and steady on the small of her back as his arms closed around her. "At least, I guess *technically* you have, but I can promise you it's not a problem."

He smiled down at her as the door shut, leaving them alone in the chill lobby. "The ship'll be ready to go in another couple of hours." He let out a breath. "I have to say, Lis, it'll be a relief to be off this damn planet. I'm half-ashamed to admit it, after everything we hoped to do, but . . ."

He shook his head, and relief and hope bloomed within Elissa. *He's not going to want to come back. I'm not going to lose him to a combat zone.*

"But at least on Philomel we'll get a chance to regroup," he continued. "There *must* be things we can offer IPL, for God's sake. I'm hoping, Lis"—his arms slackened a little as he moved back, his face alight with enthusiasm—"that the IPL officials on Philomel won't have quite such an . . . on-the-front-line firefighting mentality, you know? If they're able to think a bit more strategically than the people down here, who're just lurching from one crisis to the next, then talking to *them* might actually get us somewhere. What do you think?"

She nodded, numb. "Yeah, I guess so."

"And you and Lin—once they see it's a *gift* you're offering them—" He broke off. "What is it?"

You and Lin. The instant he spoke, that anxiety had swooped back over her, eclipsing the more recent worries.

Her eyes burned, and her throat, too, as she tried to hold back the tears. His mother's words—*more* of his mother's words—sounded in her brain. *You can't afford to depend on just Cadan—and he can't afford to have you doing it.*

But who else am I going to talk to? Who else understands what Lin is like, who'll listen and who won't instantly see her as a monster?

"It's Lin," she said.

As understanding dawned in his face, she knew she wouldn't need to explain further, and the knowledge was such a relief she went weak.

"It's what happened on the med-flyer?"

She nodded, blinking back tears, feeling her nose sting. "She let them die, Cadan. I asked her. I asked her to help me save them, and she . . ." Elissa shook her head, not wanting to spell out the details, not wanting to relive that horrible moment when she'd realized her sister wasn't going to step in like she'd always done before. "She let them *die*."

Cadan drew her over to sit on a narrow white bench standing at the side of the lobby, then took a seat next to her. His eyes were bleak. "We all did that, Lis."

"But only because most of us couldn't do anything else! Because if you, or Commander Dacre, or the pilot had tried to save them, you'd have gotten yourselves killed. But Lin . . ." She couldn't look at him as she said it. She put her hands up over her face. "She *could* have done something. She almost . . . kind of . . . considered it, because she knew I wanted her to. But she decided not to because—because she said it would *hurt* her." She drove her fingers into her hair, pressing hard against her forehead as if to press the realization away. "When those children . . . those *little kids* were . . . I thought, when I looked down, I thought I could hear them. . . ."

"Lis," Cadan said, his voice very gentle, "there was a hell of a lot of noise. You couldn't have heard them, not really. You must know that."

"I know." She spoke into her hands, her breath warm and damp against her palms.

"And we didn't see what happened to them. They might have gotten down."

"But they were on the fire escape. It was hanging out from the building, didn't you see?" Behind her hands, her eyes screwed shut as if, too late, they could protect themselves from the image that was burned into her retinas.

"I saw it. But I didn't see *them*. And you didn't either. They might have managed to get down before it went."

She took her hands down, looked at him. "But do you think they did?"

His eyes met hers. "No." A pause. He was trying to find a way to soften it, a way to make it better. But of course there wasn't anything. Nothing he could say, nothing he could do. She knew that, and after a few seconds she saw that he knew it too. "I'm sorry, Lis," he said.

A sob rose in her chest, like a balloon filled with grief and horror, emotions that swelled like expanding liquid. She felt the feelings pressing against her lungs, ready to rise into her throat, to sweep through and drown her.

If she gave in, if she let herself start crying, she wouldn't be able to stop until she was drained of tears, until she'd sobbed herself sick and empty. It would be a relief . . . maybe.

But even as she thought it, sudden cold iced her veins. All at once, it came to her that she didn't dare. She didn't dare give in to tears.

Those emotions—*Lin's* emotions—that had reached her on

the flyer: She'd had no warning of them, and for a few seconds not even any indication that they weren't her own.

Yesterday she dragged me into doing something I'd said no to. I resisted, I tried to stop her, and she was still able to do it. Today I've been feeling her thoughts as if they're mine.

Lin was stronger than her. Elissa knew that, she'd always known that. It was Lin with the electrokinesis, Lin who'd been able to drag Elissa into her mind, forcing Elissa to share Lin's experiences, to see through Lin's eyes. The link worked both ways, but its strongest pull—its gravity—was always in Lin's favor.

If, now, the link was getting stronger still . . . *and it is, there's no "if," it is getting stronger* . . . then it meant, it must mean, that Lin's power over Elissa was getting stronger too.

Elissa shivered, an involuntary shudder that prickled over her from the nape of her neck down to behind her knees. *Now, if I let my guard down the tiniest bit, if I give in to my own emotions, let alone hers, if I let myself get just a little out of control . . . what will that give her the power to do?*

"What is it, Lissa?" Cadan was watching her, his eyes too intent, too observant. She had wanted—needed—to talk to him. But now . . . *I can't. I can't talk to him about this.*

It wasn't just her fear of what Lin might be able to do. It was worse. In that moment of chill clarity, Elissa had remembered, all too clearly, what she'd thought as she'd stood in the flyer as it descended to let the families out, knowing that beside her Lin was rigid with hurt.

Let's dump them, Elissa had thought. *Forget about them. We shouldn't have bothered with them in the first place. People like that—they're not worth even thinking about, let alone helping.*

If she could, she'd put the blame for those thoughts, too,

on Lin. But they hadn't been Lin's thoughts. They'd been her own. She had looked at the people who'd hurt Lin, and she'd hated them. She had wanted them punished.

What if, this time, it was the other way around? What if it was Lin who was hearing my thoughts? My thoughts that tipped her over into not caring at all, into being able to stand aside and watch those people die?

It had been Elissa who, all along, had taught Lin what it meant to be human. It had been her horrified reactions that had shown Lin it wasn't okay to hurt people, it wasn't okay to threaten people to get what you wanted, it wasn't okay to risk innocent lives. And Lin had learned. She'd learned empathy—enough to make her willing to sacrifice herself, not just for Elissa, but for the whole crew of the *Phoenix*.

But what if she never really learned it? What if she was just . . . unconsciously mimicking me, just doing what I was trying to do, what I wanted from her?

I can control my behavior, if that's what she's going to copy, if that's what I need to do. But I can't . . . whatever I do, however hard I try, I can't control my thoughts!

"Lis?" said Cadan.

Her eyes came up to his, horrified at what he might read in her expression, horrified at the idea of telling him—oh God, any of this, *any* of it.

If his mom talked to him, if he's already thinking I'm not good enough . . .

If he found out that it was her thoughts—her out-of-control, vicious, shameful thoughts—that had affected Lin, had caused the deaths of those people, what would that do to what he thought of her?

She shook her head. "I can't. I can't talk to you about this."

"What? Lis, of course you can. Look, I get how horrible it is for you. . . ."

Concern filled his face. His eyes were sympathetic, observant—one of which she didn't deserve, the other which she couldn't afford.

This last twenty-four hours had taken something from her. She was afraid of her sister now, the sister she'd given up everything for. Afraid, too, of the link between them, the link by which she'd begun to define herself. If she told Cadan what she was scared of—if she told him and it turned out to be true . . .

I can't lose him. If I've lost what I thought I had with Lin, I can't lose Cadan, too.

"I'm sorry," she said. "I just can't. It's not your fault. It's me. I'm . . . oh God, I'm just a mess."

"Like I'm going to agree with that?" There was a note of gentle mockery in his voice. He put his hand on her upper arm, and its solid warmth came through her sleeve. For a moment, more than anything she wanted to lean into him, into his warmth, into the comfort he was offering, and spill everything. How scared she was—scared of what Lin had done, of what she herself might have done. Scared of how out of control their world had become, how impossible it seemed that they might ever be able to do anything to fix it. Scared of losing him.

But as she let her body relax just the tiniest fraction, as she leaned a very little toward him, that sob swelled again inside her, the feeling that if she let go even the tiniest bit she'd lose control of everything.

"Cadan," she said, miserably, a plea for him not to push for what she couldn't say.

"Okay." He brushed a strand of hair off her face, a gentle, one-finger touch, then took his hand back and leaned away from her. "Do you want to talk to someone else, then? I'm not pressuring, Lis. I just—you're in kind of a state and, okay, of course you don't have to talk to me, but maybe you need to talk to someone?" He lifted a shoulder in half a shrug. "I don't know . . . my mom?"

"No," she said, with more emphasis than she'd meant to, not getting a chance to moderate her voice, to make the word come out less rudely.

Just a flicker in Cadan's eyes showed that he'd registered her tone. "Okay," he said, calm, expressionless. "I'm not sure, though, who else . . . When Sofia's recovered a bit more?"

All the suitable women, Elissa thought. Then, on a note of half-hysterical amusement: *At least he knows better than to suggest Commander Dacre!* He was trying his best, God knew, thinking she needed a nice kind female friend to talk to.

But, oh God, it would be a relief to talk to *someone.* Someone who'd have at least a chance of understanding the whole mess of fears and confusions in her head. Someone who could relate, at least to some extent, to the . . . the utter, disorienting *weirdness* of having a Spare, someone who was both a total stranger and yet more familiar than anyone else in the world.

Sofia would understand some of it, she thought, but like Cadan had said, Sofia wasn't exactly in a fit state to be talked to right now. Samuel, too—he'd grown up, as she had, with an awareness of his twin.

But she didn't want to talk to Samuel—nor to Sofia, either, not really. It wasn't that she disliked them or anything, but she didn't really feel she knew them either. Of all the people she'd met since returning to Sekoia, it was only Ady she'd felt any real connection to. Ady, who *couldn't* understand the link between her and Lin, because his link with Zee had died out years ago.

He does understand the complicatedness of it, though. She remembered, now, the guilt and torment in his face. *I feel so guilty,* he'd said. And *What if it was my fault?*

It wasn't the same, the things tormenting him, but at least . . . again, it was the word "complicatedness" that came to her. The wretched, messy mass of emotions she'd never had to feel before, the responsibility, the guilt, the fear . . . the *resentment* that she was only seventeen, for God's sake, and she was having to deal with a whole bunch of things most *grown-ups* never had to think about.

"I could talk to Ady," she said. "I think."

"Ady."

"Yes." Relief didn't exactly *sweep* through her as she said it, but there was a lightening within her, a feeling that she was no longer in danger of breaking out sobbing.

Talking to Ady . . . well, it wasn't like she wanted him to be appalled by her either, but if for some reason what he was going through with Zee didn't force him to understand, at least . . .

At least it won't be Cadan's expression I see change as he realizes what a mess I've made of everything, as he realizes it was my fault those people died.

Maybe, too, when his mother saw Elissa making other friendships, talking to the other twins, taking her advice, maybe she'd start approving of her a bit more.

"Yes." She found herself saying it with more certainty this time. "I'll go in a few minutes to see if I can talk to him now."

Buoyed by even that little bit of relief, she leaned in to Cadan as she'd wanted to do before, his presence a comfort rather than a dangerous temptation to weakness.

He put his arm around her, but after a half second of hesitation that made her glance up at his face, thrown off balance.

"Cadan? What is it?"

He looked down at her, a slight, unexpected hardness to his mouth. "You can't talk to me, but you'll talk to Ady. Who you met all of a day ago."

She leaned a little away from him, feeling as if he'd pushed her. "Yes, but . . . He has a Spare."

"He might as well not, though. They don't even have a link!" Sudden frustration stabbed through Cadan's voice. "I don't get it, Lissa. I'm here, I'm trying to help, and you're saying you'd rather talk to some guy you didn't even know before yesterday."

Elissa pushed herself right away from him now, and he didn't try to hold on to her. "Hey, you just *asked* me if I wanted to talk to someone else!"

"*Yes*, someone who might actually have some real support to offer you—"

"Oh, like *your mom*?" Once again, it came out with more of a bite than she'd meant to give it, and this time Cadan did react.

"Okay, you don't get to talk about my mother in that voice. She's been nothing but nice to you—"

"Jeez, wow, I suppose I should be just completely *grateful*?"

Even as the words left her mouth, she knew she'd gone too far. Her throat locked up at the idea of telling Cadan about the conversation with his mother, but she couldn't say something like that and not let him know why. She opened her lips to try, somehow, for an explanation, but he spoke before she could manage it.

"Be grateful or not, your choice. But you can damn well be polite." He stood, folding his arms.

She was still about to try apologizing, but when she met his eyes, they were like ice.

Okay, so she shouldn't have said it, but he had no business giving her that look. She was super upset, and dealing with six hundred things all at once, and now he was defending his mother *against* her?

"Well, *you* can stop swearing at me!" she snapped.

Cadan laughed, a hard sound. "You call that swearing at you? Step into the real world a moment."

"*The real world?* What world do you *think* I'm in?"

He gave her a look of utter exasperation. "You tell me. For God's sake, look, I have to go finish prepping the *Phoenix*. We've got a full complement of passengers we're taking to Philomel, plus what possessions they've been able to bring. I'm just trying to help here—"

"Well, you're *not*," she snapped at him.

"Clearly." He took another step back, his hands up, a gesture of abdication. "Fine. You do what you want, okay?"

"I'm going to! You're not fair, Cadan. You *asked* me who I wanted to talk to, and I said Ady, and now you don't want me to—"

"Have I said that?"

"You didn't need to! It's so completely obvious!"

"Oh for God's *sake*, Lissa." His voice seemed to explode into the room. "And you're telling me *I'm* not fair? Look, am I thrilled my girlfriend would rather talk to some guy she's known five minutes than to me? No, not really. But jeez,

Lissa, it's not like I own you. I don't have the right to try to stop you talking to whoever you want."

All at once, everything about what he was saying—his tone of voice, the way he refused to see why she might have a problem with confiding in his parents, the fact that, just as his mother had, he seemed determined to emphasize exactly how temporary their relationship was—was more than she could bear to listen to.

She shot to her feet. "You're right," she said. "You don't."

She turned on her heel and marched across the lobby to the internal doors. Cadan said nothing. He didn't try to call her back, and she didn't look around. She slammed her hand on the doorpad, the doors sprang open, and she walked through them without even glancing back.

The corridor walls were so shiny white that Elissa's reflection, a shadowy shimmer in the slight curve of each wall, kept pace with her as she marched down flight after flight of stairs, down one corridor after another.

The fury stayed with her, a heat behind her eyes, a burning in her hands, all-encompassing. It left no room for anything more than just a suggestion of coldness sinking through her stomach, the merest hint that there were emotions much worse than anger waiting to envelop her.

Cadan had *asked* her who she'd like to talk to. He'd *asked* her, for goodness' sake! Elissa stuffed her hands in her pockets, a swift, jerky motion. The stupid irony of it all was that it was he who'd have been her first choice even as short a time ago as this morning. And the *other* stupid irony was that she'd *wanted* him to be jealous, had wanted the reassurance that he cared that much.

But not when I need him not to be!

Elissa shoved her hands farther into her pockets, not caring if she wrecked the seams. *Fine*, so she wasn't being totally rational here. Who would be? After this day from hell, and then getting all that patronizing advice from Cadan's mother—*no one* would be rational after that.

If you'd told Cadan, if he knew what his mom had said to you, he'd never have suggested you talk to her.

And great, so now a bit of her mind *was* being rational—and apparently determined to be fair to Cadan, too. Because it was true. She might be furious with him right now, but she knew that he wouldn't have suggested she talk to his mother if he'd had any idea of the talk they'd already had. *And if I'd told him, he'd have understood why I was so upset.*

Struggling with contradictory thoughts, and with the nasty feeling that as well as being angry with Cadan and his mother, she might need to be angry with herself, Elissa kept walking, shoulders hunched, head down.

She was most of the way along the last corridor and nearly at the double doors leading to the main waiting area, before she realized someone was standing outside them. Her brain registered who it was while she was still lifting her head to look.

No. Not now. Really not now. She said it out loud, feeling the need to speak the words whether it was actually necessary or not. "Not now, Lin."

She hadn't yet looked up fully when Lin spoke. "*Yes* now."

Elissa met her sister's eyes, surprise jolting through her at Lin's tone. If she'd expected anything, it would have been the tears and remorse of the previous day. But there were no tears in Lin's eyes. And no remorse, either. Instead they were blank and blazing with rage.

Oh for goodness' sake, what's she got to be angry about?

But Elissa didn't get any more time than that to wonder.

"You're not to talk about me to him!" Lin's voice shook. Again, not with distress, but with absolute, consuming anger.

Elissa put up a hand. "Lin, I don't want to *talk—*"

"Then don't! Don't talk to him! Don't tell him about me!"

"Oh, for God's sake," Elissa snapped. "You mean Cadan?"

"Of course I mean Cadan!"

"And I'm not supposed to *talk* to him?" Elissa pulled her hands out of her pockets so she could fold her arms, a wave of fresh irritation sweeping over her. God knew she didn't *want* to talk to Cadan right now, but it wasn't Lin's business either way.

"Not about me!" Lin's voice quivered on the edge of a shriek. "I don't want to be shared! I'm your twin, not his! You're allowed to be angry and upset with me—he's not. He's not *allowed*!"

Elissa gave an exasperated sigh. She was so seriously out of patience with having to handle Lin's emotions. *If it's not bad enough I've got to deal with my own . . .*

"Jeez, Lin," she said, "talking to him about you doesn't mean you're his—" She stopped.

Just now, she *had* been talking to Cadan about Lin. About being angry with her, about being upset—God, more than *upset*. But how did Lin know? It wasn't the first time Elissa had gone off to be alone with Cadan. How did Lin know that this time it had been to talk about her?

A fresh rush of anger rose inside her. "You were *listening*? You were listening to *me and Cadan*?"

There wasn't the slightest bit of compunction in Lin's expression. "How else am I meant to know if you're talking about me?"

The one last thing that might have tempered Elissa's anger—
the possibility that Lin's listening in had been inadvertent—
evaporated. Blind fury rose through her like sheets of flame.
When she looked at Lin, her eyes were so blurred she could
no longer see her sister's face. "You did it *deliberately*?"

Lin shrugged. "Like I said, how else am I meant to know—"

"You're *not* meant to! You're *not meant to know*! When people
are alone they're supposed to be private, what they're *talking*
about is meant to be private. That's the *whole point*! If I'm
talking to someone and you're not there, you don't listen in!
You don't spy on me!"

Now Lin's voice rose all the way to a shriek. "But you were
talking about *me*! You're not supposed to talk to him about
me!"

Elissa threw her hands out, so furious she felt she'd explode
if she couldn't express it in movement as well as words. And
now she was shouting too. "I'm not the problem here! It's
not *me*. It's *you*. You're not meant to know *what* I'm talking
about!"

For a moment they both stared at each other, locked in
an equal outraged lack of understanding. *It's like trying to get
through to an alien.* The thought rose through Elissa's brain, as
thick and black as the smoke from burning rocket fuel. *Like
trying to talk to someone . . . God, someone who's not even human.*

"What?" said Lin.

Her gaze clashed with Elissa's, furious and outraged. And
now, as well as anger, there was hurt there too. Hurt as deep
as if Elissa had stabbed her.

*Oh, so now she's hurt? She drags me into killing the people she
wants to kill. She refuses to help me save the people I want to save.
She listens in to my private conversations with my boyfriend—and*

*into my Private. Freaking. Thoughts—and then it's her feelings that
get hurt by finding out what she wasn't even meant to know in the
first place?*

She didn't try to hide what she was thinking, didn't try to
soften the impact of what Lin had just read—was still reading—
in her mind.

"You heard me," she said.

For a long moment everything stilled. Hurt rose like a slow
tide in Lin's face. All the blood seemed to drop from under
her skin. Elissa watched the pain pour into her sister's eyes
and didn't care, didn't *care*, it was only fair that Lin should
get hurt as well—

Then all at once it was as if the pain had bled far enough
to reach Elissa, too. She was still angry, but this was *Lin*, her
sister, her twin. She swallowed as much as she could of her
anger, managed to reach a hand out toward her. "Lin, look,
I'm sorry—"

Lin flinched. Actually flinched, as if the touch of Elissa's
hand would bring further pain. Her face was blank with hurt.
She didn't say anything. She shook her head, backing away,
then turned and walked off down the corridor, the way Elissa
had come. She moved clumsily, as if her feet, her whole
body, had gone numb.

"Lin," said Elissa, but her sister didn't turn around. Her
feet stuttered once on the shiny-clean floor, as if, whether
she willed it or not, she couldn't help but respond to Elissa's
voice, but she continued walking, down the corridor and
around the corner at the far end.

Elissa took a step back, found the wall behind her, and
slumped against it, dragged down by a weight of misery so
strong it felt like exhaustion.

It'll be okay, she told herself. *I'll sort things out with Lin, I'll make it better. She has to forgive me, she always has to forgive me, just like I always have to forgive her. And once we're off-planet . . .*

As it had once before, the idea seemed like the only bright light in wastes of darkness. Getting off-planet. Getting onto the *Phoenix,* breaking out of Sekoia's atmosphere into the cold, clean, safe emptiness of space.

Here, on Sekoia, she and Lin were being continually forced to use their link. And every time they did, every time one of them reached out to the other, to communicate, to tap into Lin's electrokinesis, the telepathy that had drawn them together wound itself still tighter. Like the strangle-grass that grew in patches on the desert outside Central Canyon City, that you had to burn to the roots if a patch of it seeded itself in your garden or window boxes or even in an edge of dirt collected in a crack between wall and window . . .

Once we've left, once we're not dealing with crisis after crisis, we'll stop reading each other's minds like this. We'll stop passing emotions back and forth. If the link was meant to die off with distance and disuse, it must be that it's getting stronger just because we have to keep using it.

The image of burning a patch of strangle-grass came to her. It was a native Sekoian plant, back from before the planet had been terraformed. If you touched a lighter to the tips of its lethal, spikelike blades, it would burn down to the ground, but it was super resistant—even fire would leave its root cluster unharmed, and within days it would be growing again. To kill it off entirely you had to run a narrow, sharp-ended tube beneath the base of the plant and pour a capful of acid into the funnel at the top of the tube so it would soak, smoking, into the ground and destroy the plant from the roots upward.

It was a legal obligation to do it, and there were strict penalties if you let a patch go, but the process was easy enough, and you could order the kit online—tube, funnel, acid, protective disposable gloves and goggles.

And it was a relief, knowing you'd done it right, knowing the plant wouldn't grow again.

Elissa moved her head sharply, shaking free of the image. *That's not what I'm thinking about, though. I'm not thinking about destroying the link. I wouldn't think about doing that, not ever. But this—what's been happening since we landed on Sekoia—this has to stop. I can't handle it anymore. I need my mind to be just my own again.*

Having an identical twin was one thing. She'd been shocked to start with, but she'd gotten used to it, she'd adapted. This, though, was a whole other nightmare. She was starting to feel . . . *Ugh, what do I mean? What do I feel like?*

What she meant came to her all at once, in frightening clarity. *This connection between us: It doesn't feel like just a link, something that can be made and unmade, something that's in the control of both of us—and of neither. It feels like it's hers. It feels like she's taking me over.*

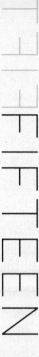

FIFTEEN

AS ELISSA stepped out of the spaceport passenger shelter to cross to where the *Phoenix* waited on the flight pad IPL had cleared for Cadan's use, hot wind, gritty with sand and full of the scent of rocket fuel, swept across the plateau and into her face, dashing dust in her eyes, edging her tongue with an acrid taste. Although now the sun was sliding, a white-hot coin, down the fathomless blue of the sky, the plateau had been soaking up its heat all day, and every gust of wind was like the breath from a dragon's throat.

She screwed her eyes up, raising a hand to protect them, and at the corner of her vision saw Lin, like a mirror image, perform exactly the same gesture.

A hand made a pretty ineffectual shield. The dust blew past Elissa's fingers, crept under her eyelashes. Her eyes began to water, and she had to force herself to let the tears come, force herself not to instinctively scrub at her eyes, to let the liquid wash the dust away.

It seemed like she wasn't any better at making a mental shield than she was a physical one. She hadn't spoken to Lin in the two hours since her sister had walked away from her, was avoiding looking at her now, trying not to notice what she was doing, trying not to listen when she spoke—and Lin seemed to be doing exactly the same. But all the same, Elissa kept getting gusts of Lin's emotions, bitter and laden with pinpricks of hurt like blowing specks of sand.

She'd planned on finding Lin, talking to her before they left the hospital to board the ship, but Lin had more or less disappeared the whole time, appearing just once, and only then when so many other people were around that Elissa couldn't face trying to talk to her.

Sofia and El were back with the others now, Sofia bandaged up and looking pale but okay. Felicia had regained consciousness but wasn't being allowed to walk: She'd been stretchered on board the ship a short while ago and was going to be traveling in the med-bay, with Ivan—was there anything he *couldn't* turn his hand to?—watching over her during lift-off.

Next to Elissa, Ady said, "Are you okay?"

She looked at him, biting her lip. She still felt he was the one among all the other twins who'd have the best chance of understanding what she was going through, but if she talked to him now, Lin would know. And would experience it like another betrayal. A weird, uncomfortable mix of loyalty and pride held Elissa back too. She and Lin had come back to Sekoia so full of noble ambitions, hopes for saving their world, and they'd screwed up everything so badly. She didn't think she could bear to articulate how stupid they'd been, how unreasonably idealistic. She was ashamed of what Lin had done, and scared it had been her fault, but also, she was ashamed of how she, Elissa, had treated her sister.

I'm so freaking bad *at relationships. It's like I forgot how to do them in those three years when I was ill.*

"Oh, you know," she said vaguely. "Stuff . . ."

"Yeah," said Ady. He was looking ahead to the upright squid-shape of the spaceship, his eyes narrowed against the blowing dust. His voice sounded as if he was, not sympathizing, but identifying.

Elissa glanced at him, a little puzzled. His jaw made a hard line, as if he was gritting his teeth.

"Are *you* okay?" she asked.

Ady gave a little snort, half laughter, half not. "Not really. I'm worried about Zee." There was no hesitation in his voice—he hadn't been agonizing over whether to tell her. In fact, Elissa thought, he'd probably been *waiting* to tell her.

She looked ahead to where Zee walked at the edge of the original group of Spares and twins, a little separate from the larger group of further Spares, twins, and carers who had been assigned for evacuation on the *Phoenix* and who had arrived in the last hour. As she did, she realized that was where Ady had been looking too, rather than toward the towering shape of the ship, colorlessly flaring in the sunlight.

"What about?" she said.

Ady's gaze skated to hers for a second. "I'm not even sure. That sounds crazy, right? I mean, if it was anything . . . *concrete* . . . I'd talk to Clement or Emily. They told us about, like, post-traumatic shock and the stuff to look out for, and they said it wasn't our job to, you know, try to do therapy on our twins. They said to just refer any concerns to the people in charge of our group."

"Shouldn't you, then? Anyway—whether it's concrete or not?"

Ady lifted a shoulder. "But like I said, I don't even know if it *is* anything. How much of a douche am I going to sound if I say I don't like the way he looks at me? Not even all the time, but it's only been in the last couple of days. I don't think he was doing it at all before." He shrugged again. "But even now, it's only sometimes, not often—and there's not even anything *wrong* with what he's doing. . . . And God, you know, he's been majorly traumatized and I've had everything, and . . ." He trailed off, and the look he gave Elissa showed he was pretty sure that whether he finished the sentence or not, she would get what he meant.

She did. Within her, a despairing voice asked how any of them were ever going to manage normal relationships with their Spares while each one of them bore this guilt. This guilt of having had a normal life when their twins were being strapped onto torture tables and told they weren't human.

"What do you mean, you don't like the way he looks at you?"

Ady's shoulders slumped, as if he were already giving up the hope that she'd understand when he told her. "He . . . I don't know, maybe it's not even at me . . . I . . . it's like he goes into a fugue state?"

Elissa blinked at him. If it had been Cadan who'd used the term, she'd have been instantly trying to work it out from the context, trying to avoid admitting she had no idea what it was. With Ady, though—according to him, she and Lin were already heroes; she didn't exactly need to try to impress him all over again. "I have no idea what that is," she said.

"Oh, sorry. It's this weird psychiatric thing when someone

just, like, checks out of their normal consciousness. A kind of temporary amnesia? Then they come back to themselves, without any memory of what happened—or what they did—during the fugue state. It sometimes happens as a response to major stress. I mean, I haven't *asked* Zee, so it might not be anything like that. But major stress would totally apply, and that's kind of what it looks like . . . the checking out, I mean." He sighed. "Okay, that sounds crazy. Does it make any sense at all?"

The description had sparked memory. "Yes, actually. I'd forgotten, but back on the med-flyer, I thought he was going into shock or something. It was just like you said—he went all blank and starey, then he snapped out of it. And I forgot, with everything else that was going on."

They'd come into the endlessly elongated shadow of the *Phoenix* now, and were climbing the slope of the cargo-bay ramp, drawing a little nearer to where Zee and Cassiopeia walked.

Ady dropped his voice, but she could still hear the relief in it. "So it's not just me. God, I'm so glad, you don't even know. Not that I *want* something to be wrong with Zee, but at least something like that . . . with what he's been through and everything, it makes *sense*. I was"—he gave her an almost shamefaced look—"I thought I might be imagining the whole thing, that it might be something going wrong with *me*. Like . . . paranoia or something? A reaction to all the weirdness and the . . . well, the whole guilt thing I told you about?"

She nodded. "I understand."

He gave her a friendly little nudge with his shoulder. "Well, yeah, of course you do. Thanks, okay? At least now I know there *is* something. I will talk to Clement. I mean, not this evening, obviously! But tomorrow, you think?"

She nodded. "Yeah." She laughed a little. "You're right, I can't see him being grateful for *more* stuff to think about tonight, not after . . . oh jeez, everything. But it's not like he'll have a ton of stuff to do tomorrow, not until we land."

"And once we're on Philomel they can, like, run tests or whatever, can't they? Do all that psychiatric help they've been talking about offering us?"

They were too close to Zee now to continue the conversation, and Elissa didn't want to risk answering. She nodded again, and it seemed like it was enough. Ady didn't say any more, just flashed her a brief, grateful smile.

They went up into the chill shadow of the cargo hold, then climbed the long flight of steps leading to the walkway that would take them to one of the corridors into the main body of the ship. After a quick word to his father, Cadan, accompanied by Markus, drew swiftly ahead of the rest of the group. They would be going straight to the flight deck, to the controls of the ship.

Entering the *Phoenix*, her home for the past few weeks, Elissa's first instinct was to go to her cabin, which had come to feel as if it were really *her* room, her own space, not just a temporary resting place like a room in a motel. But of course it wasn't just hers, it was hers and Lin's. She couldn't go there and be sure of being alone. She needed to put things right with her sister, should have done so before they left the hospital. But now, with Lin clearly avoiding her, it seemed so difficult she didn't even know where to begin.

So she followed the group as they, in turn, followed Mr. Greythorn along the bluish-lit corridors, then into the amber-lit corridors of the passenger section, and finally into the passenger lounge, with the viewing window that made up its exterior wall. Someone–Cadan? Mr. Greythorn?–must have decided that was the best place for them all to be during liftoff, and of course it was the area–aside from the flight-deck–where you got the best view. Now, though, the idea of standing on the *Phoenix*, with fractured relationships all around her, watching Sekoia, the place she'd thought they could save, the place where they'd failed–where *she'd* failed–dwindle behind them, did nothing but fill Elissa with a cold weight of misery.

The glass window gleamed in front of them, filling the entire wall and curving slightly into floor and ceiling. It looked out on the side of the *Phoenix* facing away from the sun, into the shadow the ship cast across the flight pad outside. With the lounge lights on, the group's reflections stared back at them, shimmery and indistinct, seeming to swim between the ground and the slightly concave surface of the glass.

Sofia hurried to one of the little tables fixed to the floor, choosing the one farthest from the viewing panel. "I seriously hate this bit," she said when she caught Elissa's quick glance. "And please *don't* tell me how illogical that is, okay?"

There was a panicky edge to her voice. Elissa shook her head, sending Sofia a hopefully reassuring smile. "I won't."

"It's not actually illogical," said Jay behind her, his voice calm and interested. "I was reading about it on Sam's book-screen just last night. Statistics show that the most dangerous point in the flight is during liftoff."

Sofia snapped a look up at him, and he must have taken the expression on her face as one of interest, because he continued, "It's not just because of accidents due to technical failure or pilot error–the book said it's also the time when passengers are most likely to inadvertently injure themselves, and to have what are believed to be psychosomatic nose-bleeds, brought on by the knowledge that the air pressure outside the ship has changed, even though there's no physical change within the actual ship—"

"Oh my *God*," said Sofia. "Do you think that's even a *bit* helpful?"

Jay stopped, his face surprised, and Samuel laughed. "Hey, you said you didn't want to be told it was illogical. Jay's totally helping you out."

"He's really not," Sofia said, her voice tight. "Jeez, you two are *linked*, he should be *more* socialized than Zee and El, not less."

The grin fell from Samuel's face. "Hello? Let's not talk about people like they're not here, yeah?"

Emily Greythorn hurried toward them. "Guys? Is everything okay?"

The low thunder of the engines rumbled through the room, the steel auto-safety shutter slid across the glass, and Sofia's face went rigid, her fingers locking together in her lap. Emily took a seat next to her.

"Breathe, Sofia. It'll be over in minutes."

The ship took off with that stomach-swooping rush that the best antithrust cushioning couldn't entirely eliminate, and Sofia went faintly green. Over by the shutter, Lin stood, her fingers spread on it as if to feel every vibration of the accelerating ship as it blasted through the envelope of Sekoia's atmosphere. The first time they'd done this, her face had lit with the first expression of pure happiness Elissa had ever seen on it. This time, though, she reached out as if for comfort, as if to touch the thing that, despite everything else, had remained constant. She'd done everything wrong, couldn't be a real human after all, but at least engines still roared, ships still flew. Outside the world that hated and feared her, the world she'd never be able to understand, space was still black and endless and . . .

Just as it dawned on Elissa that she had, once again, tapped inadvertently into her twin's thoughts, the acceleration eased. The lights of the room dimmed as the shutter lifted away into the ceiling. Outside, green and blue and white, Sekoia shone against a background of space, a background that was black and endless and . . .

. . . *filled with more stars than you can ever count. Stars that make everything else small.* The words came into Elissa's head, but she didn't know whether they were her own thoughts or her sister's.

As she slid a look toward Lin—*I'm sorry. God, I'm sorry. I messed up, I never meant to make you feel less than human*—her gaze caught on Zee.

Like most of the others, Zee was standing near the window. Elissa remembered Ady saying *I don't know how he's going to be able to get on a ship for relocation. . . .* It looked as though it wasn't a problem after all. Maybe the experience of being on this ship was so different. . . .

Then she noticed how Zee was standing.

He was motionless, motionless as if he'd forgotten how to move—as if, Elissa thought, looking at his face, he'd forgotten that a concept like moving even existed. *Fugue state. Like Ady said, he's checked out of his normal consciousness.*

His face was still turned toward the window. *Is it really a fugue state? Or is it just that's he* is *struggling, that he's standing so still because he's trying to hold it together?* Elissa moved so she was looking at the sheet of glass from the same angle as he was.

Although the lights had dimmed when the shutter lifted, an automatic setting to allow the lounge occupants an unobstructed view of the planet they were leaving, the strips of amber safety lights at the edges of the room had remained lit, creating little oases of reflected images. Zee wasn't looking at the stars. He was looking at his twin's reflection.

That's how he looked at Ady on the flyer. That's how Ady said he's been looking at him. This time, a chill went over her. *It's not okay. It's really not okay. There has to be something wrong with him for him to look like that.*

Over by Sofia's table, Emily Greythorn got up from her chair. The movement brought her in front of the bit of strip light that was reflecting in the glass, and the glowing, floating sphere of Sekoia replaced Ady's reflection.

Zee didn't move immediately, at least not that Elissa could see, but all the same his body lost that statuelike appearance, and even before he turned away from the glass, she knew he'd relaxed, knew his eyes had lost that blank, fixed stare. Knew he'd—what was the term Ady had used?— checked back in.

The whoosh of displaced air caught Elissa's attention, and she turned to see the door to the lounge dilating, each panel sliding smoothly away into the wall. Ivan came in, sweeping a glance across the room—a glance that maybe wasn't quite as casual as it seemed. "Lissa. Lin. Felicia's asked to see you."

"Both of us?" Lin's voice was spiky with reluctance. She didn't take her hand from the glass.

"Yep," said Ivan. His expression and voice were both perfectly relaxed, but all the same they left Elissa unable to refuse. She'd tried not to let it be obvious that she and Lin weren't speaking, but she guessed it wasn't surprising that the *Phoenix*'s crew members would have picked up that something was wrong. *I don't want them interfering, though. I don't want more advice.*

She left the viewing panel, her eyes flickering instinctively toward Zee before she did. *I don't know what's wrong with him—God, given what he's been through, for all I know it could be any one of a million different psychiatric conditions. But it's something. Something that needs to be dealt with. If Ady hasn't talked to someone by tomorrow morning, I'm going to do it for him.*

Ady sent her a brief smile as she turned away, and from the back of the room Sofia looked up, catching her eye as she went past. The crew—Ivan and Felicia and Markus—had started to feel like family after they'd survived their third . . . fourth? . . . crisis together. The other Spares and their twins . . . okay, not all of them felt that way to Elissa, not yet. But Sofia was getting there, and Ady . . . and even Zee, despite that edge of unease Elissa had felt when she saw him staring, empty eyed, at his twin's reflection. He was damaged, probably even more damaged than Lin, but all the same . . .

He's one of us. For the first time the thought came to her: *The Spares are different from ordinary people, everyone knows that. But we—their twins—we're different too. Either because we are twins, or just because of our connection to them. The Spares aren't normal humans. And neither are Sofia or Ady or me.*

She and Lin reached the door at the same time. Elissa paused, letting Lin go ahead of her. For half a second, her sister's eyes met hers, and all at once Elissa felt as if she were falling. As if gravity had been taken away and she were tipping, slowly cartwheeling, helpless, above . . . below? . . .

within? . . . an endless void. Lin's face held so *much* pain. It wasn't just that it hurt to see it: It felt as if it had snatched away Elissa's surroundings.

Ivan was already walking away down the corridor. Elissa moved through the doorway, a couple of steps after Lin. The door snapped shut behind her, and they were suddenly more alone than they'd been since that horrible fight in the hospital.

"Lin," she said, low, urgent, not even knowing what she was going to say but knowing it had to be *something*.

Lin looked back, her face bleak, her eyes haunted, and the words came to Elissa before she needed to think them.

"Listen," she said. "I'm lost, and terrified, and angry, and I don't know how to deal with any of the stuff that's been happening. But it doesn't change anything. It might"—she gestured, a helpless movement—"it might change stuff about you—or me. But it doesn't change *us*."

Lin's face quivered. She set her teeth hard in her lower lip, and Elissa saw the blood leave it. "Everything's wrong," she said, her voice a defeated whisper. "I can't . . ." She shook her head. "I don't know how to live in this world. I . . . I'm not sure I know how to live on any world."

"Lin . . ." Elissa reached out automatically. Her twin's hands were cold, unresponsive in hers. The idea that Lin was blaming herself for the stupid, messed-up society Sekoia had developed went through her like pinpricks of ice. "That's the *world's* fault, not yours."

"Yes." For a moment Elissa thought that her sister's response meant Lin was listening to her, accepting her argument. Then Lin's eyes came up to hers again. "I know," she said. "I know it's not my fault. Those people down there—you wanted to come back and help them. I don't know why. They're not worth it."

Elissa's insides lurched. "Lin, no. You met some really crappy ones—that doesn't mean they're all like that. And—"

"And they're people, and we should care about them just because they're people." The words sounded tired, recycled, as if all meaning had been crushed out of them. Lin shut her eyes, exhaustion all over her face, and leaned against the wall next to her. "No. I'm done. I can't do it. I don't want to do it. They don't care about people like me, and I don't care about people like them." Her eyelids lifted, as heavy as if invisible weights were tied to her lashes. "It's no good, Lissa. You want to make me like you. I'm not like you. I'm not going to be."

Then what are you going to be like? If you won't care about people, what sort of person will you be?

"Girls?" said Ivan, at the end of the section of corridor, his hand on the doorpad. "We haven't actually reached the med-bay, you know."

Lin pushed off from the wall and moved down the corridor toward him as he opened the door and stepped through it.

Elissa made herself hurry after her sister. "Lin," she said, her voice low, "*Ivan's* 'people like them.' And Cadan, and Felicia, and—"

"I know." As she walked, Lin crossed her arms, as if for warmth, or comfort, or to hold herself together. "They're different."

"But if you're willing to admit *they're* different, then that shows not all people are . . . like, bad, uncaring." Elissa's words were tumbling out now, driven by sudden panicky desperation to convince Lin that she *had* to see the rest of their species as worth caring about, no matter how lousy some of them were. *She's not naturally a sociopath. She's* not. *She can't decide to* become *one!*

"No," Lin said again. This time there was impatience in her voice. "They're only different 'cause they *behaved* different. It doesn't mean I have to see every person as a potential Ivan or Cadan. I'll care about them if they make me. I'm not going"—and now not just impatience, but anger, stabbed through her voice—"I'm not going to *try*, Lissa. I'm not going to try to care about people who'd like to see me back in the facility!"

They went through another door, and it snapped shut behind them. Even as Lin walked, she kept her arms wrapped tightly around herself, and when she looked back at Elissa her face was set in tense lines. "So?" she said, and the word would have sounded belligerent if her eyes weren't so terrified. "*Does* that change us?"

For a split second Elissa shut her eyes, an instinctive movement to cut herself off from what Lin was saying—from what she was asking of Elissa. "I don't know. I don't know yet. I'm . . . it's too much to process."

It's still me.

For a moment she thought Lin had said it out loud, then she realized the words had sounded not in her ears but in her head.

"I know," Elissa answered. "But I . . ." *I'm scared. You already did some pretty awful stuff, while you were still trying not to be a psychopath. Now, if you're not even trying . . . I'm scared. I'm scared of what you might do.*

She knew she wouldn't manage to censor her thoughts, knew Lin would pick them up anyway, so didn't even try.

But what she hadn't expected was for her sister to pick up the thoughts she *hadn't* verbalized, the underneath, too-painful-to-look-at fears she couldn't help.

"You're scared I'll hurt *you*?" It was a cry of betrayal. Lin stopped dead in the middle of the corridor, the faded color in her face ghastly in the bluish lights, every line in her body seeming to vibrate with shock and pain. Ahead of them, Ivan halted with his hand halfway up to the next doorpad, his head jerking back to look at them in alarm.

"Lin—"

"*No*. You *said*, you said back when you'd only known me a few days, you *said* you trusted me not to hurt you!"

"Lin, I'm still *processing it*. I *told* you—"

Lin shook her head, her eyes huge and panicked. "You said, you *said*—"

"I know what I said—"

Lin was still shaking her head, not listening, lost in fear and distress. "You said, you told me"—the words came out with just the inflections Elissa recalled using, as if Lin had not so much remembered as recorded them, holding them in her brain like a guarantee of safety—"you *told* me: 'Whatever you do, it doesn't make any difference.' You can't just take that away. You—you—"

Her voice cracked. She was shivering all over now, hugging herself, her fingers digging into her upper arms.

Elissa looked at her in despair. She'd reassure her sister if she could, but she was so screwed up herself, she'd never be able to lie with any conviction—and even if she did, Lin would read her mind and know. "I'm not taking anything away. Lin, I'm just *trying to work it out*."

"Lin." She hadn't noticed Ivan come back toward them.

"Sweetheart, come on now. Give your sister a minute."

Lin was crying now. Every nerve in Elissa's body shrank from the sound. Ivan put his arm around Lin. "Okay, calm down. What's going on? What are you girls doing to each other?"

Elissa couldn't tell if there was accusation in the question, but, every emotion scraped raw, she responded as if there were. "I can't *help* it, Ivan! I can't tell her something that's not true even if it'll make her feel better!"

Ivan's face stayed calm; all his voice betrayed was an unperturbed amusement. "Your telepathic twin? Well, of course you can't."

"I'm not *asking* her to tell me something that's not true. But she said, she *said* . . ." Tears choked Lin's voice, making her stop.

"Come on," said Ivan. "Let's just get as far as Felicia's room, okay?"

Arm around Lin, he steered her down the corridor, through the next few doors and into the glossy-white med-bay.

Felicia was sitting in an egg-shaped chair, tipped back and hugely padded. One of her arms was free, but the other was strapped carefully immobile. Webbing ran over her bandaged shoulder, and a monitor in the side of the chair bleeped quietly and steadily.

She looked a whole bunch older than she had doing yoga in the cabin of the *Phoenix* less than two days ago. Her already pale skin had lost so much color it looked as if it were thinner than usual, and under her eyes and her lips were the same alarming shade—a bruised-looking slate blue.

Reassuringly, there was nothing faded about the bright, alert look she gave them as they entered. She started to speak, then broke off. "Lin? What's happened? Lissa, what's wrong with her?"

Ivan steered Lin into a chair close to Felicia's and nodded to Elissa to pull out another for herself. "Issues," he said. "You talk to them. I'll get hot chocolates."

Felicia sent him a smile. "Yes please."

"You're not going to throw up on me, are you?" Ivan eyed her suspiciously.

"Not if I can have a hot chocolate. If I don't get anything in my stomach soon, though, I might throw up just in protest."

Ivan shrugged, going over to the nutri-machine in the corner of the room. "You know your body best, I guess."

Felicia laughed. "After forty-two years, I ought to." Her gaze moved to Lin, who was shivering and hunting through her pockets. "Tissues are behind you, sweetie. What's going on? What's gone wrong?"

Lin had started to wipe her face, but at this another sob shook her. She clenched the tissue in her fist, shoulders bowed as if she were carrying a weight so heavy it was painful. Her voice came out so obscured by tears that Elissa could hardly understand her, and she was amazed that Felicia seemed to.

"She thinks I'll hurt her." Another sob choked Lin as she spoke. "Lissa—she thinks I could hurt her. I *couldn't*—couldn't *ever*—"

"Lin," Elissa said, despairing and exhausted, left without any of the right words or thoughts . . . or *anything* . . . to make things better, to fix the damage she—they—had caused each other and themselves.

"Okay," said Felicia. "Just hang on a few minutes." Then, as Lin began to choke out something else, "Just a few minutes, okay, Lin? Give yourselves time to breathe. Let Ivan work his magic on the nutri-machine."

She took a breath herself, leaning her head back against the padded surface of her chair. "I didn't ask to see you so I could make you cry, by the way. I wanted to say thank you. And good work. Both of you." She grinned. "Not that I noticed at the time, but afterward, when they'd patched me up . . . Oh, and I don't know what the malls are like on Philomel, but I hope they're halfway decent, at least. I owe you each a hoodie."

The nutri-machine hissed steam, and the smell of chocolate rolled out into the room. Ivan twirled the cup he was holding, forcing the foaming stream of hot chocolate to make a curly shape on the surface of the drink.

When he brought it over to Lin, Elissa saw the shape he'd made was a looped *L*. Lin put her hands around it, her shoulders still shaking with sobs, bending her head as if to breathe in the steam and heat and scent of the sugar-laden chocolate. Her hair swung forward so Elissa couldn't see her face.

Ivan handed the next cup to Felicia, and the third to Elissa. Elissa's had another *L* drawn in the foam. She was an *E* really, of course, but she'd been Lissa to everyone on the ship for nearly as long as she'd been on board. Had been Lissa to friends and family most of her life, too. It was the name Lin had known her by, the name Lin had based her own name on, back when all she had was a numerical code. She'd called herself "Lissa's twin." As if that in itself were a name. As if she only existed as a real person through her connection to Elissa.

Then, when she'd escaped, she'd come to find Elissa. Not asking for anything, not even expecting to be allowed to stay with her. Just wanting to see her, the twin sister whose existence had formed so much of her life.

Elissa had lifted the cup to her lips, but not yet taken a sip. Which was just as well, because as the thoughts came to her, her throat closed too tight to let her swallow.

She looked at Lin through the wisps of steam. "I do trust you not to hurt me."

Lin's head came up. Her face was tear smudged and muddy-pale, her eyes looking bruised. *Really?* Her lips formed the word, but Elissa wasn't sure if she actually said it or if, once again, she heard it through their link.

"Yes. Like Ivan said, it's not like I can lie to you even if I wanted to."

Lin's bruised eyes fixed on hers—and for an unnerving flicker of a moment Elissa was reminded of Zee's blank, blind stare. "I wouldn't *ever* hurt you."

"I know. I know. It's okay."

"You had to think about it." Her fingers tightened, bloodless, on her cup. "You shouldn't have had to think about it. You're supposed to *know*."

"I do know. I wasn't thinking about it, not really. I was just . . ." She shook her head. "God, Lin, it's just so much to deal with, you know?"

Over at the machine, Ivan turned a knob to clean the drinks nozzle, and steam hissed. Elissa found herself staring kind of blankly at what he was doing, tiredly glad of something to focus on that wasn't words and emotions and the impossible, heartbreaking complexities of a relationship that mattered more than anything and yet that she couldn't seem to see how to handle.

"But when you did think about it, you did know?" Lin's

voice sounded as tight and bloodless as her fingers had looked, drained of everything but the need for reassurance.

Elissa reached out and put her hand over her twin's. "Yes. Of course I knew. Of course I knew you wouldn't hurt me."

Lin's hand turned, and her fingers curled around Elissa's. "And you don't . . . hate me?"

"I don't hate you." Her eyes met Lin's. "I swear." She swallowed, afraid to hurt her again, needing to say it all the same. "But that doesn't mean everything's okay. You deciding that people don't matter—that's not okay with me. Letting those people die, not helping me when I asked you—that's not okay either."

Lin's face went tight again. "I can't change. You're not fair to expect me to. Those people—" A sudden shudder went through her. "If it had been me in danger, they'd have let *me* die. If they'd seen me, back when I was in the facility, they wouldn't have cared what was being done to me—"

Elissa felt the shudder, not just through Lin's hand into hers, but through her mind. The memory of pain was showing in Lin's face, in the tense lines of her body, but as that mental shudder echoed through Elissa's brain, she remembered something she'd once read about the experience of abuse survivors, and she realized something she hadn't realized before.

It wasn't just memory. Lin wasn't just remembering those years of SFI-sponsored torture; some part of her was *reliving* them.

Horror tipped Elissa's stomach over. *Oh God, she's so right. I haven't been fair. The* Phoenix—*it was a little safe haven for the past few weeks. Of course Lin seemed to be recovering while she was on it. Of course she seemed normal.*

Then, an underneath thought: *It was a haven for me and Cadan, too. This is the real world now. If we can't survive the real world, then what we had was never real to start with.*

But this, right now, wasn't about her and Cadan. She pushed the thought to the back of her mind. "I'm sorry," she said to Lin. "I was wrong. I know you can't change."

"But you said—"

"Yeah, I know. Listen, Lin. I said it wasn't okay with me, and it's still not okay. People—they need to care about other people. They—they just *need* to. And one day you'll need to as well. But you can't do it now. And that *is* okay. It's not your fault and I don't blame you, and I don't think that it means you'll end up hurting me, or Cadan, or any of the people you *do* care about."

Lin nodded, slowly, biting her thumbnail. "But one day . . ."

"One day you'll need to care. Just because"—she fumbled to put into words what she felt so clearly but had never had to articulate—"because that's what people are *supposed* to do."

"They don't all do it," said Lin.

"No, I know. But that's because there's something wrong with them—or because they've chosen to *let* there be something wrong with them." Without planning it, without realizing it was going to happen, her voice became suddenly definite—both definite and defiant. "There's nothing wrong with you, Lin, and we're not going to let anything *be* wrong with you."

This time Lin's nod was less uncertain. A faint flush had come back to her cheeks, making her eyes look less bruised. "Okay."

"Okay," said Elissa, and, suddenly worn out, took a sip of her hot chocolate. The underneath thoughts returned. *I have to talk to Cadan. If we're going to make this work, we have to talk.* Her shoulders slumped. *It's not like I'd want us to be telepathic too, but with not knowing what his parents have said to him, not knowing exactly what he's thinking . . . I* don't *want telepathy with him, I really don't, but . . .* But this was her first real relationship ever, and although she didn't want telepathy, she *would* like a cheat sheet.

"You have to talk to Cadan," said Lin.

"Yeah." Elissa took another sip of the hot chocolate, too tired to feel resentment that Lin had picked up another of her thoughts that she hadn't intended to share, one that was supposed to be private. "I . . ." Her shoulders slumped farther. The idea of *that* talk seemed too daunting to even attempt. *And if he really does think I'm not good enough for him . . . God, he's probably right.*

"He's not."

Elissa gave a little laugh. "It's nice that you still think so."

Lin shook her head. "No. I don't mean he's not right. I mean *he* doesn't think that."

Alarm went through Elissa like a snap of electricity. Surely Lin hadn't started reading *Cadan's* thoughts? "How can you know?"

Lin smiled a tiny bit, responding either to the alarm on Elissa's face or the shock waves reverberating from her mind. "Not that, I swear. I can't read anyone else's thoughts—I can't read his. It's . . . It's just that, God, Lissa, haven't you seen the way he *looks* at you?"

From her chair, Felicia held her cup up to Ivan. He gave her a look, but took it all the same, then went back to the nutri-machine to refill it, moving quietly.

"I . . . I don't know," Elissa said. "I mean, obviously I see his face when he's looking at me. . . ."

"But you haven't noticed *how* he looks?"

Felicia had her face turned toward Ivan, and Ivan's attention seemed to be solely on the cup he was refilling. All the same, Elissa found herself flushing. She picked up the stirrer that came clipped to the side of the cup and poked it into the froth on her drink. When she pulled it back out, the froth was stuck to its handle in tiny chocolate-ringed bubbles. "I don't know. I . . . How does he look?"

"Like nothing else exists," said Lin. Her voice, uninflected and unemotional, seemed to give the words more impact than if anyone else had said them. "Like someone's turned all the lights off and you're the only thing that's left lit up."

Oh. Elissa's lips parted, but when no words came out, she closed them again. *Like nothing else exists. Cadan looks at me like that?*

"His mother notices too," said Lin. "She keeps looking at him looking at you. I don't think she likes it."

"She . . . talked to me. Earlier."

"I know."

"Oh, right." That feeling of being invaded, *taken over*, resurged within Elissa. "So I guess you know what she said?"

Lin shook her head. "I was talking to Cassiopeia and Jay and Samuel. I didn't pay attention until I felt you get upset . . . and then it was all blurred and I couldn't hear what she'd said to you." Her eyes met Elissa's. "It was 'cause you were upset that I listened in to you talking to Cadan. I was . . . scared."

That's not okay either. I'm going to have to make her see she can't do that, no matter the reason, she just can't.

But right now the need to tell someone about Cadan's

mother took over her still-present resentment of Lin's invasion of her mind.

"She's said stuff to him," Elissa said. "She said we have nothing in common. She—*both* of them, probably—they don't think I'm right for him. They . . ." When she articulated it for the first time, the bitterness she'd been trying to suppress flooded the words. "They don't think it's going to last. *He* doesn't think it's going to last. Like I'm too young to have genuine feelings or something. Like it only happened 'cause we were on the ship together, and if we hadn't been—if life had just stayed normal—he'd never have noticed me."

Lin was shaking her head, confused. "Which?" she said. "I mean, which one are you upset about?"

"*All* of it! They think I'm too young, and it's not serious, and it's just some temporary thing, and I'm not good enough and I'm just distracting him from what he's supposed to be doing—"

"Balls," said Ivan.

Elissa jerked a look at him, shocked into momentary silence. "What?"

"Balls. Garbage. Nonsense."

"It's *not*. His mother, she said—"

"Yeah, his mother said. But if you're telling us *Cadan* said those things to you, then he's not the man I thought him."

A flush rose uncomfortably into Elissa's face. "I . . . No, he didn't *say* them. . . ."

"Then I'm betting you he doesn't think them."

Irritation threaded through Elissa's embarrassment. "He *does*," she said stubbornly. "He said so—he *does* think it might not have happened if we hadn't been thrown together—"

Ivan laughed. "Not really the same thing, is it?"

"I—" She broke off. "It—it *is*. If he thinks it wouldn't have happened, then it's because he thinks I'm too . . ." She trailed off this time, trying to think what Cadan *had* said, and what he'd sort of said, and what had gotten mixed up in her mind with what his *mother* had said. . . .

"That's a bit of an assumption there," said Ivan. "You sure he thinks you're too . . . ?"

"All *right*," Elissa snapped, frustrated. "But he did say he didn't know if it would have happened if—"

Ivan shrugged. "Well, how can he? How can you? How do you know what would have happened if things had been different? Why does it matter?"

All at once, Elissa knew she was about to burst into tears. "It *does* matter!" she said, hearing her voice go humiliatingly shrill, out of control. "It *does*! If it *wouldn't* have happened anyway, how do I know it's going to last? How do I know he's not going to get bored of me?"

"Why would he get bored of you?" Felicia's voice was quietly curious.

Elissa swiped furiously at her eyes. "Because—" *Because I'm not superpowered or highly skilled or trained or clever. Because for years I was just Bruce's little sister. Because . . .* "Because I'm just me!" she burst out. "And he—he's *Cadan*."

Lin thrust a handful of tissues at her. Elissa pulled one from her sister's fingers and blew her nose, then grabbed another two to mop her eyes, feeling her face scorch, knowing she'd betrayed all sorts of things she'd been trying to keep hidden, wishing it wasn't so obvious, hoping that maybe they hadn't worked it out.

But, of course, because Lin was there, and because Lin had no social filters . . .

"It's not *Cadan* who doesn't think you're good enough," she said, in a voice of pleased discovery. "It's you."

Elissa grabbed another tissue and blew her nose again to avoid answering. Or looking up. Or even having to acknowledge that she was still in the *room*.

"You should *definitely* talk to him," said Lin.

An unexpected laugh got mixed up with Elissa's nose blowing, and she kind of snorted into the tissue. "You *think*?"

"She's right, though," said Felicia. "And, you know, Lissa? Cadan—he likes things to be . . . clear, exact. He's learned to deal with shades of gray, but he's not any more comfortable with them than you are. If you haven't told him how *you* feel, then"—she shrugged her unhurt shoulder—"well, it might be helpful."

"Oh jeez, he *knows* how I feel."

Felicia looked at her.

"No, honestly. He *must* know. I mean . . ."

"Guys aren't always all that secure either," said Ivan. There was a glint of mockery in his eyes.

"I *know* that. I've *read* stuff. I . . . just . . . this is *Cadan*."

Ivan smiled at her, and the mockery had gone. "Yeah, we know," he said. "But trust me, honey. Tell him, all the same."

SIXTEEN

THE FIRST time Elissa had walked up the long spiral of the main corridor leading through the center of the *Phoenix* and up to the flight deck in the nose of the ship, she'd been a fugitive, on the ship because she and Lin had nowhere else to go. And she'd been tense all over, unwilling to see Cadan and sure he would be anything but pleased to see her invading the captain's space.

A million things had changed since then, but still, here she was once more, butterflies in her belly, nervous sweat prickling the palms of her hands. It had been easier—maybe—when she was sure she knew exactly what he thought of her, and when she'd at least been able to pretend she didn't care.

She wasn't even sure what to say to him. *I'm sorry* would be a start, she knew—she shouldn't have walked out on him in the hospital lobby—but *oh*, it all felt so much more complicated than the sort of ordinary fight she remembered having with friends, or the brother-sister bickering she and Bruce had done. *And telling him what I feel, what I want . . . opening up to him the way Ivan and Felicia said I should . . .* She didn't just feel nervous. She felt kind of sick.

The overhead door to the flight deck came into view at the end of the corridor, set into the ceiling at the top of a short flight of stairs. Cadan had kissed her here once—the first time he'd ever kissed her, the first time he'd said he loved her. The ship had been under fire, the shields deteriorating moment by moment, and for a few seconds it hadn't even mattered.

The corners of her mouth twitched suddenly downward, and the back of her eyes stung. *For God's sake, Lissa.* At the point she was thinking about, she and Cadan—and Lin and the crew as well—had been *this close* to being killed. It was *stupid* to remember those few moments with longing.

She blinked until the stinging in her eyes dissolved, gritted her teeth, and touched the doorpad that would open the door and let her through onto the flight deck.

The door snapped open, like the iris of a silver eye widening to nothing but a thin, gleaming rim. Above Elissa, star-filled space showed through the glass walls and ceiling of the flight deck, providing the giant eye with a pupil like a bottomless well full of dark, silver-glinting water.

She climbed up. Her head emerged, and the first vertiginous moment of feeling that if she let go she would fall and fall into that endless sky gave way to the correct perspective as the flight deck spread out around her. The bridge stood in front of her on its shoulder-high platform: the platform that was the exterior of the chamber that housed the now-defunct hyperdrive—and had imprisoned the tortured, dying Spare who had powered it.

A glass barrier rose to the ceiling all the way around the

bridge. Treated to eliminate reflections, it was almost as invisible as a force field. A short flight of steps led to a security-locked door in it. Elissa climbed the steps, butterflies flipping and flapping inside her, and pressed the buzzer to get Cadan's attention.

He and Markus were sitting at the wide control panel, on the other side of the safety rail that ran along the back of the row of seats. It was Cadan who turned to see who their visitor was, and the moment he saw Elissa he pushed the button to let her in.

Some of the butterflies seemed to leave Elissa's body on an involuntary sigh of relief. She'd half thought he might tell her to go away—he was, after all, *busy* flying the ship.

There was some reticence in his eyes as they met hers, a slight stiffness about his mouth, but he smiled all the same. "Hey." He turned to Markus. "You could take a break now. Lissa can keep me company."

Unlike Ivan would have, Markus didn't offer any comment. He grinned at Elissa as he got up and came around the end of the safety rail. "The others are still in the lounge?"

She nodded. "Ivan was going to take them doughnuts."

"Doughnuts, huh?"

Even through her nerves, she managed to smile at him. "Lin was helping him. If you want one, you're going to have to go fast."

Markus laughed. "Yeah, and I've got no one to blame but myself. I should never have introduced that girl to the realization she has a sweet tooth."

As the flight-deck door clamped shut above his head, Elissa turned, her hands clenching nervously in her pockets, to look at Cadan.

But before she could gather the words she needed to say, he spoke. "I'm sorry. I wanted to say it the minute you'd gone. I should never have talked to you like that."

She felt herself flush. She hadn't expected him to give such a comprehensive apology. Hadn't even been sure if he'd feel he should apologize at all.

She walked over to the end of the safety rail. It was cool and smooth beneath the sweaty palms of her hands. "I came to say sorry to you."

A smile flashed over his face. "Thanks." And now he flushed too. "I didn't have any right to act jealous of you. I knew I shouldn't have done it, but I . . ." He gave an uncomfortable shrug. "I'm sorry. That's all."

Tell him what you feel. Guys aren't always that secure either. She swallowed. "Cadan, me talking to Ady . . . it's completely not 'cause I, you know, like him better than you or something. . . ."

Her voice trailed off, but Cadan was already waving a dismissive hand. "Lis, it's okay. Like I said, I don't have any right to object."

Not that secure. Yeah, right. He's so secure he not only doesn't need reassurance, he can't even stand to hear it! A frustration that over the last couple of days had become all too familiar bubbled within her. "Well, you kind of *do*," she said. "If I *did* like him better, I mean. Given that I'm, like, dating *you*, not him."

Cadan shrugged again, looking even more uncomfortable.

"What?" The frustration leaked into her voice. "What's wrong with that? *Why* are you disagreeing with me?"

"Well, it's not like I own you, is it?"

"No. But, jeez, it's not about owning. We're *dating*. Doesn't that—" A sudden plunge of fear turned her stomach over.

"Hang on, what do you even *mean*? Is there someone *you* like more than me?"

The shock that flashed instantly over his face made her feel better. "God, Lis, no. Absolutely not. There's no one."

"Well then, what's going on? I mean, we're dating, but you—you acted like it was more than *just* dating, you said it was serious—you said I was the first girl you'd brought home. *You* said that. But the way you keep talking, it's like you don't *want* to act like it's a relationship—it's like you want to treat it as some kind of—of temporary hookup."

"I don't." He said that with so much force it almost made her jump. "I wouldn't treat you like that, Lissa."

"Then what's going *on*? I don't understand. It's serious but it's not, and it's not a casual thing but you're not allowed to get jealous? I mean, that doesn't even make sense!"

I don't care what Ivan said. No way *am I going to tell him how I feel when he keeps doing this!* She glared at him. "You just keep contradicting yourself, and I don't know where I am—where *we* are—and I don't know what you're trying to say!"

Cadan shoved a hand through his hair. "Hell. Lis, I'm sorry. I never meant to leave you so confused. Look, the thing is, I don't know where we are either. I don't want to assume you're in the same place I am, or be too intense, or push you into . . . I don't know, something you're not ready for. So I'm kind of . . . flying blind here. I'm trying to . . . I don't want to—"

But that was one interrupted sentence too many. Elissa lost all patience. She caught herself on the edge of stamping her foot the way she would have done a few years ago. "Oh my God, *what* same place? *What* thing I'm not ready for? And you haven't tried to push me into *anything*. Why are you acting like it's a problem that you love me? For goodness' sake, I love *you*, don't I?"

It was the look on his face that brought her up short. "*Now* what? What is it?"

"You never said that before," he said.

"I–what? Of course I have."

"You haven't." His mouth quirked in a half-suppressed grin, as if he knew this *really* wasn't the time to make her think he was laughing at her. "Trust me, babe, I've been watching out for it."

"But . . ." She shook her head, bewildered, sure he must be wrong. "But–but even if I didn't, you must have *known*?"

"Well"–there was that grin again–"I was hoping, yeah. But no, Lis, I didn't know. You didn't say. I may be capable of arrogance, but I'm hardly arrogant enough to assume something like that."

She was still staring at him, still disbelieving, running through in her head all the times they'd been together, trying to remember what she *had* said to him. "I *did* say it, Cadan. I *did*–back when you first told me. I said I'd been in love with you since I was thirteen."

"No," said Cadan.

"I *did*. I *remember*–"

"'I was in love with you when I was thirteen,'" said Cadan, his inflections making the words a quotation. "Not 'since.' '*When*.'"

"But I said–I said . . ." Okay, she couldn't remember now exactly what she had said, but surely . . . "But wasn't it obvious? Wasn't it obvious what I meant?"

"Like I said, I hoped. But jeez, Lissa, it's such early days. Especially for you . . ."

So here they were again. The familiar cold, the feeling of being pushed away, seeped through her.

"What does that mean?" she said, hearing her voice change, hearing the cold seep into it, too, making it stiffen and crack.

"Lis? What's wrong?"

It wasn't cold making her voice crack. It was tears. "You keep saying that," she said. "Like it means I can't feel anything real. Like because I'm not fully grown-up I can't know what's genuine, like I don't even know what I want."

Cadan looked thunderstruck. "Lis, I *never* thought that. I don't even– God, whatever have I said to make you think that's what I think of you?"

She blinked back the stinging in her eyes. "You're always saying it. You act like there's no future for us. Like you can't count on it lasting. You tell me it's serious for you and then you won't let me tell you it's the same for me." She blinked again, furiously. "And *okay*, maybe I should have said it anyway, but it's– This is hard for me, Cadan. I'm not *used* to doing this–I'm not used to having to tell people what I feel."

He put his hands out, palms up, a gesture that was too gentle to–quite–convey *I told you so*. "That's why," he said.

"That's why *what*?"

"That's why I don't want to assume anything. This is a first for you, Lis. I mean, I know you dated when you were younger–God knows you made sure to let me know whenever some guy asked you out!–but then the symptoms took over everything, and all those normal bits of your life, once you were at high school, they didn't happen for you." He spread his hands again. "I mean, tell me if I'm wrong, but that's the impression I got?"

"You're not wrong." Her face burned. It was humiliating

to have to admit it to him. She'd known he knew, really, but to have to spell out how abnormal her life had been . . .

"So this, it's your first . . . real? serious? grown-up? . . . relationship. And"–he rubbed the side of his face, a sudden out-of-character, self-conscious gesture–"it's with me, the only guy anywhere near your own age you met since the symptoms stopped. The guy you were stuck on a spaceship with."

"*That's* what you mean?" Suddenly what he was saying came clear to her. "You mean you think it might not even be just because of the situation, but just because you were *there*?"

"I'm not trying to insult you, Lis. I just . . . if that turns out to be all it is for you, it's not like I can blame you, it's not your fault. But I don't want to . . . take advantage. I don't want to be *that* guy, you know? The one who goes for younger girlfriends so he can keep some kind of upper hand? I–" He broke off. "Since we got back to Sekoia, since you've been making friends, meeting guys that much closer to your own age–I don't *want* to let you go, but I've been wondering if it's only the decent thing to do."

"*Let me go?*"

His eyes met hers. "Like I said, Lis, I don't *want* to. I mean, God, I really don't want to, but maybe I have to let you choose for yourself. Maybe I–"

"Oh my God, *Cadan*."

The exclamation came out with so much force that he stopped dead, looking completely taken aback.

"How can you be so stupid?" she asked him. "Okay, I'm seventeen–that doesn't mean I'm an *idiot*. This isn't some kind of–of"–she waved her hands, trying to find the right words–"*starter* relationship before I go on to something better. I *did* choose for myself. I chose you!"

"Yeah, I know. I know you're not an idiot. But, look, it's so early on, and like you said, you're only seventeen. You can't be sure–"

"Yeah, well, *you* can't be sure either! You might have had a million more relationships than me, but this is a first for you, too. You *said* so, you said you'd never wanted to take any of them home before."

"Yeah." He flushed a little. "Okay, maybe I am being stupid."

"*Yeah*, you are."

Laughter crept into his eyes. "*Okay*, Lissa. I get the message. Except–hang on, a million, really? What are you trying to say about me?"

She didn't bother to reply. She had too much to say to be distracted by him teasing her. "I'm not stupid," she said. "I know it might not last forever. But right now it's real, and"– she put her chin up, determined not to blush–"I love *you*. Not because you're the only guy around, and not because you're some hotshot spaceship captain, and not because we were, like, thrown together when everything was going crazy around us. It's not *convenient* to be in love with you. You're always about to get killed, and we might end up being separated for ages, and your mother thinks it's a silly crush and I should back off and stop interfering in your life." She glared at him, still determined not to blush–or cry. "Trust me, if I *could* fall in love with someone else, it would probably be a whole lot less painful. So there you are–it's my bad luck: There isn't anyone else who'll do. It's you or nobody."

She stopped, out of breath, hot all over, part with anger, part with the embarrassment of having to say all that stuff out loud.

"Say that again," said Cadan.

She stared at him. The laughter had spread from his eyes over the rest of his face. "What?" she said.

His mouth curved into a smile that was full of amusement—and of something else, something that made her heart jerk to a stop, then pick up faster, stealing her breath. "Well, I could stand to hear all of it again. But just that last bit will do."

Her face was flaming now. She met the blue blaze of his eyes, dragging in enough of a ragged breath so she could speak. "I said I love you. I said it's you or nobody."

And then it was just as well she'd taken that breath, because Cadan had swung around the end of the rail and was kissing her, his arms so tight around her that she could hardly breathe at all.

Not that she cared.

Just like always, with them, they didn't have long enough. Even with his arms around her, his mouth on hers, the smell of his skin so close she could breathe him in, she was aware time was moving on without them, a feeling like seconds sifting away, the slow glitter of pixels sliding through an egg timer. He was in sole charge of the *Phoenix*—he didn't exactly have hours to spare. And she . . . things still weren't right with Lin, and she should tell Ady she'd seen Zee do that weird fugue thing again, and if Cadan's mother knew she was here, *interfering* with him when he was supposed to be flying the ship, she'd be all kinds of unimpressed.

Push me into something I'm not ready for, ha. We don't ever get enough time for him to push me into stuff I am ready for.

But when she dropped her hands to his chest, made as if to

move away from him, when his eyes met hers, it wasn't all his waiting duties that had come back to his mind.

"Wait a minute," he said. "What was that about my mother?"

Oh God, please no. She couldn't cope with being flung, *again*, from golden, glowing happiness into yet another fight. "Oh, Cadan . . . I completely didn't mean to be rude about her. I just—"

"No, no, it's okay." His hand was resting lightly on the small of her back, just close enough to the waistband of her pants to make a shiver run up and down her spine. Now his fingers flattened against her skin, pulling her a fraction closer. "We're not going to fight about it, Lis. I just want to know what you mean. You said she thinks you should back off? Is that—do you mean that's just the impression you got?"

Elissa bit her lip. "No, she said it. She said I should stop interfering with what you were doing. She said we didn't have anything in common, and I should . . . I don't think it was back off, exactly. . . . Ease off. That's what she said."

"She said that to *you*?"

"Yeah." Suddenly scared she was misleading him, that she was going to cause all sorts of problems, she started to qualify it. "She wasn't nasty or anything. I—she said she wasn't opposing me, and she wasn't against us dating, and she didn't normally interfere with your relationships. . . ."

"But she said that? To you? That you should stop 'interfering'?"

Elissa nodded.

"When? When did she say that?" His face changed. "It was when you came to see me at the spaceport, wasn't it? You met her on your way there?"

"Yes."

Cadan pushed a hand through his hair. "So that's why you were so edgy. And–" He checked a moment. "No wonder you felt weird about telling me everything that was going on, if my mother had just told you to back off."

"Ease off."

"Whatever." There was a snap to his voice. "God, Lis, seeing you was the one good thing in a whole long crappy afternoon. If I'm ever too busy, if it's an interference–jeez, you must know me well enough by now to know I wouldn't hesitate about telling you!"

She couldn't help laughing at that. "Yeah, I guess."

"And my mother–both my parents . . ." His eyes crinkled in discomfort, and Elissa felt a twinge of pity for him. She'd had to cut the strings tying herself to her parents pretty catastrophically not so long ago, and for her there wasn't ever going to be a going back, a wishing for their approval. But Cadan, despite all his grown-upness, hadn't cut those strings.

He cleared his throat. "She probably meant well–at least she meant well for me. They both do. But . . ." His eyes crinkled again. "They don't *know*. They're judging it–our relationship– from the outside. Okay, my parents aren't stupid–I respect their opinions, I do. But they don't know what it's like for us, how we feel, how it happened without either of us wanting it, without us knowing it was going to. They don't *know*."

It was what she'd told herself, earlier that day, almost an echo of her own thoughts. She looked up at him, the warmth from where he was still touching her spreading over her whole body.

"I love you," she said, not blushing, the words coming out for the first time without any effort.

He bent his head as she reached up, and their lips met in a brief, light touch that nevertheless left her dizzy all over again. He smiled into her eyes. "Right there with you. And this time I'm not apologizing for being intense."

She lifted her eyebrows. *"Finally."*

He laughed. "Brat." Then, "Lis, I'm sorry, I'm not dismissing you—"

She laughed a little. "Jeez, I do know you're flying the ship. *Not* a brat anymore, remember?"

His fingers brushed down her arm, lingering a tiny bit, as he moved away to lean over the controls, then all at once his attention switched away from her, focusing entirely on the communications screen. "What the hell . . . ?"

His hand fell away from her as if he'd forgotten she was there, and he was around the other side of the safety rail almost before she'd blinked, sliding into his seat, hands flying over the controls.

She'd seen him move like that before, seen the focus of his attention narrow so swiftly it shut out everything else that was happening. Although her heart was suddenly thumping, she knew she mustn't distract him by asking what it was, asking what was going on, what new threat they were facing.

But after a moment, although he didn't turn around, he told her.

"There's an incoming message. It's not getting through. I've got our receivers set to their widest, and I can't pick it up."

"Where's it coming from?" Elissa asked, then, catching herself as she realized it was a silly question, "Sorry. I forgot. Of course, the location codes won't be coming through either."

Cadan threw her a mostly preoccupied smile. "Yeah, they're

not. It's coming from the direction of Philomel, though–I can tell that much. So it's a fair bet to say it's coming from their flight control. Or from something in their orbital field." His lips quirked wryly. "I can *also* tell it's got an emergency marker tagged to it. Which of course makes me feel really leisurely and relaxed about picking up the whole of the damn thing."

He pushed a hand through his hair. "You said Lin was in the lounge?"

"Yes."

"Thanks. Okay." He flicked the com-unit open, and the sharp note flattened out of his voice. Anyone listening wouldn't have known there was anything out of the ordinary going on. "Bridge, calling Lin. Lin, are you there?"

Lin's voice came through clearly, sounding surprised. "Yes?"

"Can you get up to the bridge right away, please?"

"Lissa? Is Lissa there? Is she all right?"

"She's fine." Cadan's voice remained calm. *I wish I knew how he does that.* "I could just do with a hand from you, that's all."

"Okay. I'm coming."

A few minutes later Lin arrived on the flight deck and hurried up the steps to the bridge. She looked flushed and bright eyed, obviously riding a sugar-and-chocolate high.

"What is it?" she said as Cadan let her through the barrier.

He explained briefly. He'd tried to get the message again while they waited for Lin to arrive, and again it had come through in a spatter of meaningless pixels on the screen, a disjointed buzz and crackle of static in the speakers. The emergency marker–a tiny, ultrastable block of code designed to make it through nearly any type of interference–blinked on the screen and repeated in a short pattern of beeps in the midst of the storm of static. And on the main viewscreen, Cadan pointed out the broken, blinking line that showed that the message was originating from on or near Philomel. But nothing else came through. No ID marker, no hint of whether the emergency was on the planet itself, or between the *Phoenix* and its destination.

"For all I know they're warning us away," said Cadan, wiping the screen clear and resetting the receivers—yet again—to their widest sweep. "But without knowing for sure, I can't take the ship blinding back out into space. Damn it, Philomel's supposed to be a first-grade planet—what are they doing with this kind of shoddy equipment? For all SFI's faults, we did at least keep our communications going."

Lin had slid into a seat next to him, her gaze intent on the screens. "What do you want me for?"

"Okay," said Cadan. "It's a long shot, I know. But you picked up incoming aircraft down on Sekoia. I don't know which bit of your mind you're working with when you do that—"

Lin shrugged. "Me neither."

"—but if it's tied to your electrokinesis, then it might be that you're sensing the presence of electrical fields. In which case you might be able to read this message before it hits whatever it is that's scrambling it before it reaches us."

Lin was nodding. "Yeah. Okay." She reached a finger out to the com-unit, then hesitated. "Can I touch?"

"Sure. Try not to fry the circuits, though."

Lin grinned, amused, then put her fingertip to the screen of the unit, and her smile was brushed away by a look of intense concentration.

Silence stretched out, second after second of it, ticking soundlessly by, measured only by the blinking, changing numbers of the control-panel clock. Lin shut her eyes and spread her other fingers over the screen, still resting just her fingertips on the shiny surface.

"Oh," she said. "It's . . . very empty."

Vertigo made Elissa's stomach swoop as it came to her that Lin was looking out into space, into all that emptiness, into a dark, airless, lifeless ocean that went out and out and down forever. For a terrifying moment she was afraid Lin, as she had so many times before, would pull Elissa into experiencing it with her, would pull Elissa into staring, through Lin's eyes, into all that directionless dark. A random, out-of-place quote swam into her brain: "If you gaze long into an abyss, the abyss gazes also into you." She couldn't remember where it came from or what it meant, but that was what it felt like—the abyss gazing into her, huge, impersonal and merciless. Her head spun, and she dug her nails into her palms, trying to anchor herself in her *own* body, her *own* consciousness.

"Oh," said Lin again. "That's why it's not getting through. There's a . . . like a cloud of . . . bits, debris. A whole band of it."

"Can you tell what the message is?" said Cadan.

Lin's eyes, already shut, screwed up tighter. "It's such a long way . . . and it's so *empty*."

"Stop it," said Elissa suddenly. "Stop it. It's too much."

"Lissa," said Cadan, "we have to get this message."

"You don't. Lin, come back! Stop trying."

"Lissa—"

"Cadan, she's not a *machine*! You can't just use her like this!"

For a moment his mouth opened as if to snap back at her, then he changed what he'd been going to say. "Okay. You're right. Lin? Lin, you heard what your sister said."

"Emergency," said Lin, her voice expressionless. All of a sudden it was as if she *were* a machine, a speech-robot processing a communication from unspoken words to spoken. Elissa's skin went as instantly cold as if she had stepped physically into that airless, freezing ocean outside the ship. That was *Lin* speaking in that robot voice. Lin who'd gazed into the abyss and seen it gazing back at her.

"Emergency transmission to all ships carrying Sekoian Spares," said Lin. "All Spares and their twins are at extreme risk. Repeat, extreme risk. Spares and twins must be separated immediately—"

She broke off, choked, then spoke in her normal voice. "*What?* What are they trying to do?" She scrambled up and around in her seat, her hands going out to Elissa. "They're wanting to *separate* us? *Now?* I thought we were coming to Philomel because it was *safe*."

"*Lin.*" Cadan had half risen in his seat. "What else did it say? The message, what else did it say?"

Lin shook her head. She was clutching Elissa's hands now, her own tight with panic. "I don't know. I don't know what else. It said that—they want to separate us—"

Elissa's heart was thumping, high in her chest, her throat, her temples, making it hard to think, making it so that she couldn't draw enough breath to speak. *Extreme risk. All Spares and their twins are at extreme risk.* And suddenly it wasn't Lin's face in her mind, but Zee's.

Cadan touched the controls, turning the autopilot on, then got up and came around the safety bar at the back of the control-panel seats. He reached over Elissa's arm and grasped Lin's shoulder. "Lin, listen to me. You're at risk. You and Lissa. That's why they're saying separation. If you didn't hear the rest, then we won't know why, but we're going to have to do it."

"No. *No.*" Lin wrenched her shoulder away from him, her gaze clinging frantically to Elissa's. "Lissa, say something. You said you believed me. You said you knew I wouldn't hurt you. I *won't*, I wouldn't *ever*—"

"And if you want to make sure of that, you'll let yourselves be separated." Cadan's voice rose. "Lin, listen to me. If you want to keep Lissa safe, you'll do as they said."

"But I *won't hurt her*! I *won't!*" Lin's fingers were a death grip now.

"*Lin!* No one's saying you will! It's *both* of you in danger—you read the message yourself. It's not saying who the danger's from, it's just saying in order to be protected you need to be separated. Now for God's sake will you stop freaking out and putting your sister in more danger than she needs to be?"

That, finally, got through to Lin. Her hands dropped. She took a step back, bumping against the edge of the control panel, her eyes fixed on Elissa's face. "Then what is it? What's happening?"

"I *don't know*," said Cadan, a slight snap to his voice. "You didn't listen to all the message. Look, Lis, you stay here for a minute. Lin, I'll take you back to Ivan. I—" He broke off. "God, what am I thinking? The *other Spares*." He lifted his hand, about to switch his wrist-communicator on, but as if he'd broken Elissa's paralysis, her throat unfroze. She could speak, and she knew what she had to say.

"Zee," she said. "If there's danger, it's from Zee."

Cadan's eyes met hers. "You're sure? Just Zee?"

"I don't know. I mean—yes, definitely Zee. But I don't know. The message—maybe it just meant Zee, maybe it meant the rest of us too."

"Okay." He clicked his wrist-unit on. "Attention, all passengers and crew. Attention. This is an emergency directive. All Spares and twins must separate immediately. All Spares, go to the passenger lounge. All twins, go to your cabins. Go immediately. This is an emergency directive from the ship's captain. You must comply immediately. Official personnel will contact you shortly to explain further."

He clicked the wrist-unit again. "Dad?"

"Cadan?" came Clement Greythorn's voice. "What do you need?"

"Isolate Zee," said Cadan. "He's the priority. Get him away from Ady. Sedate him—both of them—if you have to. I need him secured."

"Got it," said his father.

"Where are you now?"

"On my way to the passenger lounge. I'll find them, son, don't worry."

In the background, there was a sudden clamor of voices, loud enough to be heard even through the narrowly focused mic of Clement's wrist-unit.

"What's that?" said Cadan.

"Arguments." His father's voice sharpened. "Possibly resistance. I'm outside the lounge. It sounds like they don't want to get separated. You might want to get down here too, Cay."

"On my way." Cadan strode to the door, then swung around to the twins. "You both come. Lissa, walk in front of me. Lin, come behind. When we reach the lounge, Lissa, go to your cabin, okay? Lock yourself in. Lin, you need to go into the lounge with the other Spares."

Lin didn't so much as murmur an objection. She was silent as they left the bridge, then the flight deck, then went down the corridor through door after door, each snapping shut behind them with a *whoosh* and *clunk*.

They weren't far from the passenger areas now. *Resistance,* Mr. Greythorn had said, but Elissa was sure it wasn't anything as deliberate as that. They'd be panicking, afraid that "separated" meant "separated for good." Maybe appalled, as Lin had been appalled, at the implication that it was they who would put their twins in danger.

She threw a quick glance back over her shoulder—and that one glance showed her that although Cadan didn't yet have his blaster out of its halter, he had dropped his hand to rest near it. He was capable of shooting to kill, she knew it—had seen it—but never before had he used a weapon against anyone other than people attacking *them*.

"Cadan," she said, "they won't be resisting, like, on *purpose*. It's not a mutiny. They'll be freaked out."

"I know." Although she'd flung only one glance toward him, she knew he must have seen her eyes widen when she saw his hand on his blaster. "I'm not going to mow them down, Lis. But they have to be separated for their own safety, and if I need to frighten them into doing it and apologize afterward . . ."

"Yeah. Okay." It *was* okay. Of course that might be what he needed to do—she *did* understand. But all the same . . .

They went through another door, into one of the amber-edged passenger-area corridors.

. . . all the same, if I got it wrong and the danger isn't from Zee— if it isn't from anyone, if we misunderstood and it's something else altogether . . .

And that was when the screaming started.

SEVENTEEN

ELISSA FROZE, all her blood suddenly beating just below her skin, a thrumming all over her body, cutting off coherent thought. *Screaming.* Screaming coming from one of the rooms in the passenger area ahead of them.

Then she was shoved against the wall as Cadan pushed past her. "Keep back," he said. "Both of you. Keep out of the way."

He strode ahead, past one door, another, then paused outside the door of the passenger lounge, where most of the Spares and twins were. His blaster was in his hand, but for a horrible frozen instant he hesitated, hand half up to the panel that would open the door. His face was pale in the overhead lights, and Elissa suddenly knew that he, like she, was all at once hyperaware of everything that could be waiting behind that door. He, being Cadan, probably wasn't considering putting his hands over his ears and shutting his eyes and running to his cabin to bury his head in the pillow, though.

Or—once again his expression hit her—maybe he was.

Cadan moved his hand up to the panel, and the door opened.

The screams hit her like something solid, so loud that for a moment every sense save hearing ceased to operate.

There were lots of mouths the screams were coming from, but the person Elissa noticed first was Cassiopeia. Her eyes were so wide with shock that they seemed to be bulging from her head. She'd been stumbling across the room, and as the door opened she half fell out. She would have fallen onto Cadan if he hadn't sidestepped. Instead she crashed into Elissa. Her hands came up, a death grip on Elissa's arms, and her mouth formed shapes that seemed to have no connection to words.

Elissa's gaze went frantically over her head, trying to see what was happening, trying to scan the room. Cadan's dad had said they were resisting, that was all, that was *all*. What had happened to cause that screaming, to make Cassiopeia look like that?

Cadan was in the room now, pushing through the crowd, snapping commands for them to move back. Then someone lurched into him, knocking him sideways.

A space cleared, and Elissa saw what had caused the screaming.

It was Zee she saw first. Zee, his eyes as blank as a white sky, his teeth bared, and around them, his lips drawn back as far as they would go. His face was empty, but it wasn't just the emptiness—the fugue state—she'd seen on it before. This was the face of someone whose mind had been rinsed of every scrap of sanity.

The next thing she saw was the blood on his hands. On his

fingernails—*under* his fingernails. As if he'd—*oh God, no. That can't be someone else's blood. What can he have done to get someone else's blood under his nails like that?*

Even as she stared, Zee's arms were seized from behind, dragged behind his back. One arm had been grabbed by Samuel, the other by Ivan, and even Ivan looked as if it was taking every bit of his strength. Zee was struggling against them—*furiously*, Elissa's mind supplied, but that word didn't even begin to describe the insane energy powering Zee's limbs as he fought to get free. Samuel's wrist was bleeding, and there was a spatter of scarlet across Ivan's chef's shirt collar. *Oh God, it* was *someone else's blood. He attacked them—Ivan and Samuel. But why? Why?*

And Ady. Where's Ady? If Zee's freaking out, Ady must be able to do something?

Then, as if her mind was deliberately narrowing her field of vision, forcing her to take in only one horrifying thing at a time, she realized where Ady was. Realized what had happened to him.

Ady was standing by the viewing panel, facing Zee. His hands were to his face, and blood was streaming down between his fingers. Blood was smeared around his eyes, too, from where it had poured from long scratches that raked his forehead, hairline to eyebrow. Long scratches that were the marks of fingernails.

"Zee." She spoke out loud without realizing, her voice drowned in the noise of the crowd around her. She disentangled herself from Cassiopeia's clutching hands and went forward, her legs numb beneath her, her gaze fixed as if she were mesmerized on Zee's awful, blank-eyed, snarling face. "Zee. My God, what have you *done?*"

"Don't go near him." Ady's voice was choked with tears, wavery with shock and pain. "Something's gone wrong. It's my fault. I should have known, I should have spoken to someone sooner. His mind—all the stuff he went through—"

But you? He attacked you? Elissa's mind was a fog of horror. Somewhere in the distance she heard Cadan's voice and realized vaguely that he'd been speaking for a while, although she hadn't heard anything of what he'd said.

"Restraints," he was saying now. "Get me *the goddamn restraints.*" Then: "Lissa, get away from him! Get back, everyone. Ady, get away, for God's sake."

Elissa backed away, partly in response to the note in Cadan's voice, mostly from an instinctive, panicked impulse to put as much distance as she possibly could between herself and the blood-streaked creature in front of her that was this nightmare version of Zee.

She crashed into someone, and she must have been moving faster than she realized because whoever it was staggered, throwing her off balance. She trod on someone else's foot, flung a hand out to steady herself, missed grabbing anything, and was only stopped from falling by someone's hands coming out to hold her. She threw a look up, and it was Mrs. Greythorn.

"What's happening?" asked Elissa, her voice coming out so thin she could hardly hear it, then rising and cracking, an out-of-control note that scared her all over again. "What's going on?"

Mrs. Greythorn's voice was flat with shock. "I have no idea. We were starting to organize them into separating. El got upset, and a couple of the others, and I went over to them to talk to them. Then"—she shook her head—"I heard

Ady say his brother's name, and I looked back, and Zee had . . . frozen. And then . . ." She shut her eyes, her face going motionless, swallowed, and reopened her eyes. "Just . . . that. He just . . ."

All the time she was talking, Elissa hadn't been able to look away for longer than a second from where Zee was now being wrestled into wrist restraints. He was shrieking now, on an impossibly high note that sounded as if it would tear out the lining of his throat, and it was taking not only Samuel and Ivan but Cadan and Mr. Greythorn to hold him still enough to get the restraints around his wrists.

He can't be that strong, not naturally. And this—it's not just panic. He's actually gone insane. Oh God, Ady and I both knew there was something not right, and we didn't tell anyone. We didn't think . . .

What if it was too late? What if, after everything he'd been through, Zee's mind had cracked beyond fixing? What if, so soon after finding his twin, Ady was going to lose him all over again?

Faces set with effort, shoulders straining, Cadan and Mr. Greythorn had gotten the restraints around one of Zee's wrists. Now they were struggling to pull his other wrist close enough to lock the restraints around that one too. Just as the second restraint snapped shut, Zee gave a high, ululating wail, and all Elissa's skin seemed to shrink closer on her body, part in terror—no one should be able to make that noise—and part in horrified pity. *Are they hurting him? He's gone crazy, but he's still Zee, and such awful things have happened to him—*

One more awful thing still to come, as it turned out.

The wail hadn't been a noise of pain, but of defiance. So fast Elissa hardly realized what he was doing, Zee braced himself and slammed his head back into Cadan's face. Cadan's head snapped backward, his face stunned and blank but seemingly unhurt for a second—until the bright blood began to gush from his nose.

Elissa cried out. Mrs. Greythorn's hands bit into her arm. *Cadan!* People got killed like that—she'd seen it happen. *Cadan, oh God*—

Cadan blinked. He was alive. But his hands had slackened on Zee's wrist. Just for a moment, but it was enough.

Zee tore himself free from all the pairs of restraining hands. Arms bound behind him, head down, looking as if every second his legs would go from under him and he would crash to the ground, he charged across the room in a staggering rush.

When Cadan had told him to, Ady had backed a little farther away. But not far enough. He was still standing near the viewing panel. He'd taken his hands down from the scratched-up mess of his face, and he was crying, tears streaking the bright blood to pale, soaking it all down into the collar of his T-shirt.

Zee lunged into him with all the force of someone no longer held back by considerations of their own safety or their own pain. Ady flew backward, hands coming up in a futile attempt at defense, and crashed into the side of the viewing panel. The back of his head banged against it.

"Zee—" he said.

Zee had only just remained on his feet. He took one step back now, his balance off, swaying, and for a moment his eyes locked on his twin's face.

"Zee," said Ady. The word was a plea, but there was love there too. Love, and pain at having to watch what Zee was doing to himself.

Zee's hands clenched in the restraints. He braced his feet, and drove forward with his head. It struck Ady in the face as it had struck Cadan's, but this time the splash of blood was instant. Ady's head crashed back against the viewing panel, and, as if the impact had shaken all consciousness from him, his eyes went as blank as Zee's.

Elissa screamed. Across the room, Mr. Greythorn and Cadan both lunged toward Zee. Nearer, a pair of twin girls grabbed for him, their eyes wild with fear and a sudden terrified determination.

Zee reared his head back, then crashed it again into Ady's face. Something crunched, a horrible sound that the human body shouldn't ever make, and more blood splashed, onto Zee's face, onto the panel behind Ady. Through it, the distant stars showed suddenly red, a thousand warning lights, a thousand signs shrieking *danger, danger, danger*.

Cadan was shouting, and other voices, a cacophony with no power to help. "Zee! *Zee!*"

Zee drove his head once more into the bloody ruin of his twin's face, and Ady crumpled, falling backward against the panel. For an instant it held him in a half-standing position. His eyes were open. Elissa caught a glimpse of something that might have been expression in them—or might have been just a glint of reflected light. Light that reflected nothing but red, like the shrieking warning lights of the stars, like the blood.

I will talk to Clement, he'd said to her. . . . *not this evening . . . But tomorrow . . .*

She should have said, *No, not tomorrow.* Should have said they didn't know what the stresses Zee had been under had done to his mind, should have said that the fugue states might be a warning of danger, a red light they shouldn't ignore, that tomorrow might be too late. Should have told him that Mr. Greythorn had to be told right away. Should have said, *Don't wait. Tell him now. Tell him before anything can go wrong.*

She hadn't said that. Hadn't said any of it. She'd laughed, and nodded, and agreed.

Zee lunged again at his twin, but as he did Ady's body slid, a slow collapse, down the viewing panel. He landed at the bottom, on the little lip where you could stand and feel you were flying through endless space, a crumpled huddle, smaller than he'd looked when he was standing up, when he was moving, smiling, taking care of his brother.

And he lay still.

There was sobbing in Elissa's ears. And someone screaming again, but this time in broken, half-choked screams that sounded as if they were running out of breath.

Maybe they would run out of breath. Maybe then they'd be quiet and everyone would be quiet and there wouldn't be so much noise in her ears, in her head, stopping her thinking, stopping her making sense of what had just happened. Because what she thought she'd seen, it *didn't* make sense, it didn't make any sense, so it couldn't be real. Not really. It couldn't be that Ady was dead. It couldn't be that Zee had killed him.

Her eyes were shut. She didn't remember shutting them, but at least in the darkness she could make things make sense, she wouldn't have to look at images that didn't make sense, images she couldn't let herself believe.

Lissa.

But now there was a voice in her head as well as her ears. The one voice she couldn't ignore.

I can't. I can't—

She didn't know what she was saying she couldn't do. Open her eyes? Let herself think? Listen to what her sister wanted?

Lissa. Please. I'm so frightened.

Elissa opened her eyes. But as if they were still obeying another of her brain's commands, as if they were still trying not to let her see, they showed her a world gone blurry. A haze of moving shapes, a far-off reddish glittering mist.

"Lissa."

Lin was blurry too, but that didn't matter, because Elissa could tell where she was. Could tell by the tremor in her voice that even if it *wasn't* true, even if what she'd seen wasn't real—*and it can't be, it can't*—something had left Lin shocked and frightened.

Elissa put her hands out—and the shape that was Lin jerked away.

Don't! "Don't come near me!"

Elissa caught the thought before the words, and they overlapped weirdly, making an echo in her mind. Something else that made no sense.

"Lin? What—"

"The warning," said Lin. "The warning to separate us. That's why. If they'd separated—" She choked on the next word, tried again, couldn't say it. But Elissa knew what it was. The knowledge came relentlessly, inexorably, a swelling tide of unwanted memory. If they'd separated them, that wouldn't have happened. If they'd known in time. If they'd . . .

If they'd separated Ady and Zee.

The merciful blur resolved itself into unmerciful clarity.

The stars were red because she was seeing them through the blood splashed up the inside of the viewing panel. Ady was a crumpled heap because he was dead. Because his brother had killed him.

People were crying. Cassiopeia was still screaming. Cadan, as white as death, knelt over the body.

And Lin was backing away from Elissa because that was what the message from Philomel had been warning them about. It had been warning them about all the Spares. Warning them to separate the Spares from their twins. Because whatever had happened to Zee, whatever insane meltdown had driven him to kill his twin, it could happen to them.

Whatever had happened to Zee could happen to Lin as well.

Zee had been pushed to the floor, and Ivan had a knee between his shoulder blades, pinning him. But Zee wasn't struggling now. His face, blood-smeared, bits of his hair sticking up in red wet points, was turned toward where Ady lay. His expression was still blank, but in his eyes showed something like a returning tide of consciousness. And as consciousness returned, so—like a black slick of oil, stinking and scalding and poisoned—Elissa could see a rising awareness of agony.

He's coming back. He's coming back, and he's going to see what he did.

Lin backed away farther, hit the wall behind her and stayed there, palms flat against it, fingertips white, as if she were trying to drive her fingers into the wall itself. "I didn't *know*," she said. "I said I wouldn't hurt you. I didn't *know*."

Momentarily, instinct drew Elissa toward her—before Zee's insanely shrieking face flashed into her mind's eye. She stopped dead. How many times had she shared a room with Lin? Sleeping all night, unprotected, unaware of danger? How many times could she have woken to see Lin's face, insane, empty eyed, filling her vision, feeling Lin's hands closing on her throat or raking across her skin?

A shudder took Elissa, so deep it seemed to send tremors along the marrow of her bones. She took a step away, and another, her heart beating in her ears, in her temples. Her sister watched her, fingertips bloodless against the wall. "Go," Lin said. "Get away from me. Lock yourself in."

It was only what Elissa herself was thinking, but coming from Lin, the words seemed weighted with threat. As if Lin, like in some awful horror movie, were giving her a chance to run before she came after her.

"Come to my cabin," said a shaky voice behind her. Sofia. "I have to go, I have to get out of here, but I—oh God, I can't be alone."

Elissa nodded. Her hand reached down and found Sofia's. The fingers were cold, as Lin's so often were, but the shape of them was wrong, unfamiliar. Something lurched inside Elissa. She couldn't go near Lin—right now she was terrified just being in the same room as her—but all the same, every cell in her body seemed to be clamoring for the comfort she could only get from her twin.

"*Come,*" said Sofia, her voice quivering on the edge of total panic. "Come out of here."

The door whooshed open behind them. Clumsily, not taking her eyes from her twin's face, Elissa backed through it. Lin was watching her, motionless, her face set. She didn't move a hand to gesture good-bye, didn't smile, didn't mouth words. She just watched, unblinking, while the door contracted shut.

Once in Sofia and El's cabin, the door locked behind them, Sofia slid down onto the lower bunk as if her legs had forgotten how to stay upright. Tears swam into her eyes and clogged her voice. "I *know* her. I know her. She couldn't possibly do that to me. It's not—it makes no sense, it's not *possible*."

Elissa's knees too wanted to fold beneath her, but she couldn't let them. She'd left Lin behind, shocked and terrified, and Cadan dealing with what felt like the aftermath of a massacre. And like Sofia said, it made no *sense*.

Except that they had been warned about it. Warned about it too late, but warned about it all the same. Which meant that to someone, on Philomel or elsewhere, it did make sense.

She couldn't let herself collapse. She had to think.

She braced herself with one hand on the edge of the cabin's little nutri-machine. "Zee and Ady didn't have a link," she said.

Sofia's eyes came up to hers, bright with an unthinking hope that, in the circumstances, seemed so selfish that Elissa wanted to slap her. "You mean that might be why? The rest of us—we might be safe?"

Ady's dead and Zee's waking up to horror beyond horror, and it'll be okay as long as the rest of us are safe?

Elissa gritted her teeth, forcing herself not to reply the way she wanted to. Sofia wasn't being selfish. Not really. It wasn't fair to think it—of *course* she was scared for herself, just as Elissa was. Just as—probably—all the twins were.

"The warning came for all of us," Elissa said. "Not just those of us without a link. But maybe, if not having the link means your mind is more damaged than someone who does have the link, maybe that's . . ." She rubbed her hands up over her face. "Okay. Zee *was* more damaged. He was used in a hyperdrive. He was way more traumatized than the other Spares. Maybe that's why that—whatever it was—happened to him first. And he'd been having those fugue states—"

"What?" said Sofia.

Elissa explained, forcing herself not to flinch when she said the words Ady had used to explain it to her.

"And you *knew*?" Sofia's voice was shrill with accusation. "You and Ady, you knew something was wrong and you didn't *say*?"

"Trust me," Elissa snapped, "if we'd known this was likely to happen, we would have said."

"But you knew *something* was wrong—"

"Yeah, we did. And we didn't say. And now I'm sorry and Ady's dead."

"You could *look* a bit sorrier," Sofia said disagreeably.

Elissa clenched her hands. Anger was easier than grief. She knew that. It wasn't Sofia's fault.

She met the other girl's eyes. "I'll be sorry my whole life," she said steadily. "Right now, I don't have time. If that can happen to Zee, it could happen to Lin, or El. We have to try to think how it happened—*why* it happened—or we won't stand a chance of stopping it."

The door chimed to tell them someone was requesting entry. Sofia jumped a mile, and when she answered, her voice jumped too. "Who's there?"

"Me, Sam. They sent us all to our cabins, but I"—his voice cracked—"I keep seeing his face. And Zee—he's realized now and he's just gone to pieces and he started screaming. . . ."

Elissa touched the doorpad, and the door opened to let Samuel in. His dark skin showed muddy with shock, and the color had gone from his lips.

He squeezed in and sank next to Sofia on the bed. "Wasn't it bad enough?" he said. "What they did, what Jay's having to recover from? Wasn't it *already* bad enough, without this?"

"Zee?" Sofia's voice trailed off even as she asked the question, as if she knew there could be no good answer.

Samuel shook his head. "Meltdown. He started screaming at himself to wake up. Then he started trying to slam his head against the floor. They hauled him off to the med-bay or somewhere."

"The med-bay? But *Felicia*—"

"No, it's okay. They had to sedate him before they could move him anyway. They'll tie him down or something."

And when he wakes, he'll have it to face all over again.

What else could anyone do, though? The warning had just been about Spares and their twins, and Zee's attack had been focused on Ady, but he'd hurt Cadan as well—if someone went as insane as that, nobody could count on being safe.

"But the others?" Elissa said. "Lin?"

Samuel's head dropped as if he were too exhausted to hold it upright. "They're just locking them all in other cabins. Keeping them all separate. Greythorn said we'd be at Philomel in a few hours. The IPL officials there obviously know more than we do, so screw them, let them take over the whole freaking mess."

"Cadan never said that."

"No." Samuel looked up at her. "I say it. This shouldn't be our problem—yours or mine or Jay's. They—IPL—screwed us. They should have known better than to reunite us so soon. They should have put protections in place. They should have done"—his voice shook—"oh God, just *better*."

She couldn't disagree. But again, it came to her: *Anger is easier than grief.* Knowing who to blame, and damn well *blaming* them, was easier, less painful, than thinking what had led to it, what there might be that could prevent it happening again.

She couldn't think how to say it, though, couldn't think how to express it to two people as shocked and grieving—and frightened—as she was.

She looked at Samuel, and he looked back, his face set in a mask of anger and misery. "Zee's never going to recover from this," he said. "They're stopping him killing himself, but they'd do better to let him. How the hell do you recover from murdering your twin?"

Elissa opened her mouth to respond, to make an automatic rejection of what he'd said, and couldn't. Thinking of Zee, poor guilt-and-grief-ridden Zee, being driven to kill himself, was awful.

But thinking of him staying alive, knowing, for endless, isolated years, what he'd done to his twin, to Ady . . . That was worse.

Elissa, Sofia, and Samuel spent the night sharing the same cabin. It was cramped—Samuel only just managed to fit on the floor, and every time he turned over he banged against the lower bunk, shaking Elissa out of any half-waking doze she'd managed to fall into—and, because the air-conditioning wasn't set up for more than two occupants, it was also unpleasantly stuffy.

But they weren't likely to sleep much anyway. And, used to being with their Spares, and with Ady's and Zee's faces in their minds, none of them could face the idea of a whole night by themselves in a lonely cabin.

Lying in the dark, in the bed meant for El, Elissa reached her thoughts out along the corridors of the ship, to whichever cabin Lin had been left in. *Are you there? Are you all right?*

But it was just as before, when she'd tried to use what she'd thought was her own electrokinetic power and found that, without Lin, it wasn't a power at all. Now she sent her mind reaching out for her sister, picturing the narrow corridors, the cabin she and Lin normally shared, but it was nothing more than an exercise in imagination. Left by herself, without the stimulus of physical contact, she, unlike her twin, couldn't make the telepathic connection between their brains. Without Lin providing her greater mental power, without Lin reaching out for her, the link might as well not have been there at all.

And Lin wasn't reaching out.

As the night dragged on, as Samuel stopped throwing his arms about and settled into sleep, as Sofia gave the occasional muffled cry, in her dreams, Elissa, alone in the dark, tormented herself by wondering why. Did Lin think Elissa blamed her for the danger she had unknowingly become? Had she seen the fear in Elissa's face—or, worse, read it in her mind—and did she now think that Elissa would fear their link as well?

Lin. Are you there? Can you hear me?

But there was nothing but the dark.

Elissa dozed eventually, until the sunrise-effect of the room lights sent gold-colored light seeping through her eyelashes, forcing her to full wakefulness.

It was early morning, Sekoian time. The display on the info-screen showed an announcement that touchdown on Philomel was an hour away—and a message from Cadan, telling them that their Spares were all entirely safe and were being held in separate cabins until they'd landed.

"'. . . for both their and your security,'" Samuel read out loud. "Like he needs to tell us that?"

"People resisted yesterday." Sitting on the edge of the lower bunk, Elissa bent to fasten her shoes. Aside from worries about Lin, she'd had plenty of time for other thoughts in the night, for what-if after what-if to stack up in her mind. Exhausted and unwary, she gave voice to one. "I wondered . . . maybe that was what tipped Zee over the edge. The panic—everyone feeling trapped. Ady"—she stumbled on the name—"Ady said he was empathic."

"Oh, so now it's *our* fault?" Sofia gripped the edge of the upper bunk and leaned down to shoot a furious look at Elissa. "If we'd all gone along like good little robots he'd still be okay—Ady would still be alive?"

Elissa bit down on her temper. "I'm not saying that."

"You're not saying what *you* did either. Or what you *didn't* do." Sofia turned her head to where Samuel stooped over the tiny corner basin in the shower cubicle. "She knew there was something wrong with Zee, did she say? She and Ady *knew*, and they didn't tell anyone. They didn't say anything."

Samuel jerked upright, showering water, shock and hurt in his face. "No," he said to Elissa. "You didn't?"

Elissa stood. "Yeah, I did. And now I'm sorry, and I can't fix it, and I'm *sorry*." All at once everything seemed too much. She felt as if a flood of tears were rising to drown her. She swallowed, hard, digging her nails into her palms, drawing a breath in through her nose, forcing the tears away. She'd thought other what-ifs in the night, as well. She hadn't been going to say them, but now it came to her that maybe they needed saying. Maybe, if they were true, the twins and Spares and the people charged with their welfare needed to be aware of what could be going on.

"This isn't just us," she said. "The warning came from Philomel, where they've already got a whole bunch of evacuated Spares. We don't need to be arguing about which of our faults it was—we need to get to Philomel and find out what it is, and what we need to do to stop it."

She opened the door and stepped through it, out of the room, away down the corridor, away from them.

The moment Cadan let her onto the bridge, the moment she saw the expression on his and Markus's faces, she knew something else had happened. She knew there would be no comfort here.

She opened her mouth, then couldn't bring herself to ask.

But Cadan read the question in her eyes and told her. It turned out that the question of whether Zee should be prevented from killing himself was moot. He had died in the night.

"He came around from the sedation," Cadan said, his voice bleak, his eyes on the control screens in front of him. "And he started screaming again. He was strapped down, but he screamed so much he broke blood vessels all over his eyes. He tore his throat membranes too—he spat at us, and it was blood. It was like he"—he shook his head, as if trying to shake the image from it—"like he wanted to destroy himself, and we'd strapped him down so he couldn't, but he was going to find a way to do it anyway. I kept thinking, if we'd only kept him away from Ady for longer, if we'd only held him back until he'd flipped back out of that psychotic state . . ."

He opened up another window on the screen. "When he

stopped screaming—God, it was such a relief. For a second I thought he was calming down, that I'd be able to talk to him. Then when I looked, I realized . . ."

He took one hand from the controls for a moment to rub it over his face.

Oh God. Like Samuel had asked, she found herself thinking, *Wasn't it bad enough? Wasn't it* already *bad enough?*

It could be worse. It could have been Lin. Even the thought of that turned her stomach upside down, swept cold over and through her, but at the same time she hated herself for the selfishness of it. *It's not okay just because you escaped! It's not okay that it happened to them, not you.*

And it wasn't okay that—maybe—she could have stopped it.

She swallowed, wrapping her arms across herself, a comfort and a protection.

"Cadan?"

"Yes?"

"I–" She had to tell him, but all the same the words stuck in her throat and she had to stop, swallow again, then force herself to carry on. "I knew there was something wrong with Zee, and I didn't say anything."

Cadan's eyes left the screens and came up to hers. There was shock in his face, and concern, but none of the anger—the blame—she'd seen in Sofia's and Samuel's. "What sort of wrong?"

She told him, unable to stop her voice shaking, fighting down the tears that wanted to come. Wanted to come partly out of a cowardly instinct to show him that she blamed herself so much that he didn't need to, that he didn't need to be angry with her.

Cadan was swinging back to the screens almost before

she'd finished, his hand going to the com-unit. "Hang on. Bridge, calling Ivan."

Ivan's voice came through, deep and calm, a little gritty with fatigue. "Captain?"

"I need a report on the Spares. You'll need to ask their carers to help you, and their twins if you can do it without panicking them." He gave a quick description of what Elissa had told him. She watched him, miserable with guilt. She should have told him this last night. She should have thought that *of course* it was something he might need to know.

"If anyone's noticed anything like that," Cadan finished, "I need you to make a note, that's all, Ivan. Something to pass to the IPL authorities on Philomel."

"Got it." A moment's pause, then, "Captain, you're busy, I know, but have you spoken to Lissa? She handles whatever gets thrown at her when she's got her twin to think about, but now, with them separated, she's going to be in a pretty bad state—"

"She's here."

"Ah." The relief in Ivan's voice came clearly through the com-unit. "Signing off, then, Captain. I'll report back."

Cadan flicked the unit closed. He looked back at Elissa.

She swallowed, not wanting to meet his eyes but needing to see the expression in them. "I should have told you the minute Ady mentioned it. Or told someone. Or made Ady tell someone. If I had—"

Cadan interrupted her. "No. Don't go there, Lis. A fugue state—like you thought, it could have been no more than that, a temporary response to shock. If you'd said something, the most anyone would have done was keep an eye on him till we got to Philomel and could have a scan taken. No one

was going to anticipate something like . . ." His face tightened, and he didn't complete the sentence. He turned a little
more in his seat and put out his hand to take hers. "And still,
it could be a false lead. It could be nothing to do with what
happened. The warning came through about all the Spares.
Not just Zee."

Her fingers curled around his. She still wanted to cry, but
with relief, a momentary lightened feeling in the midst of the
weight of everything else. But now wasn't the time to cry. She
blinked hard, swallowed the tears down.

"Have you gotten any more messages from Philomel?"

Markus laughed, nothing like a happy sound.

"No," said Cadan. "That debris that Lin said was in the
way? There's bands of the stuff—it's screwing up all communications. Not to mention playing hell with my navigation."
He rubbed his eyes again. For the first time, Elissa noticed
the stack of used coffee cups next to the controls, and when
she glanced at the nutri-machine, she could see the last drink
setting included both extra caffeine and extra sugar. Cadan
hadn't slept.

"So we still don't know?" she asked. "What did that to
Zee? What's going on? Anything?"

"Nothing. Trust me, as soon as we land, first thing I'm
doing is getting all the explanation they have. I won't leave
you and Lin hanging."

She tightened her hold on his hand. "I know." There was
no point asking, but all the same: "I guess I can't go see her?"

"If I thought I could dare to let you . . ."

"Or even just talk to her with one of the com-units? Or
write her a note?"

"Lis . . ." He gave her an exhausted look. "All right, this

could be me being crazy, but I . . . I'm scared of letting you even do that. They said *separate them*, and I didn't, I didn't do it fast enough, and Ady–" He broke off, then shook his head, visibly regrouping. "I'm scared that if I let you have any communication, it might set off . . . whatever the hell that was, again. And I can't risk it. I'm sorry, Lis–"

"No, I know. I get it. I know. I . . . have you seen her? Do you know if she's okay?"

"My mother went with some of the other carers. She's"–his mouth twisted wryly–"she's doing all right, given the circumstances."

He meant it as reassurance–or as much reassurance as he could give. But over the next few hours, as the *Phoenix* neared Philomel, as they touched down on the huge natural plateau in the midst of the mountains that held the planet's main spaceport, as the doors opened and armed IPL guards escorted them through the bright, icy air and into an indoor holding area that was probably normally a waiting room, the words echoed in Elissa's head. *All right, given the circumstances* meant that Lin, her sister, her vulnerable, dangerous, precious twin, wasn't doing all right at all.

Even now, surrounded by a whole bunch of guards with huge guns of a type that Elissa had never seen, or even heard of, the Spares were being kept away from everyone else. Cadan passed the information to their waiting, anxious twins and carers that they'd been taken to a different holding area, but then an IPL official came to summon him away, and he disappeared up a long flight of steps and through some sliding glass doors–and didn't reappear.

There were the usual drinks machines in the waiting room, and it was set out comfortably, with smooth-covered sofas,

low tables, and various music or entertainment channels showing on the screens around the room. And after half an hour,
food was delivered: long platters of tiny pastries, vegetable and
fruit sticks and sushi. Real sushi, according to the illuminated
menu-ticker running along the rim of the platters. Elissa
remembered now that Philomel's oceans, unlike those on
Sekoia, supported life. Although she had had real fish, from
Sekoia's carefully farmed lakes, she'd only tasted pseudo-
sushi—made of seafood-flavored white veggie-protein, or
insects, of which Sekoia *did* have an abundance—and she
wasn't a big fan.

Another time she'd have tried some of the genuine stuff,
out of curiosity if nothing else, but now, as the minutes
trailed by and neither Cadan nor Lin nor any news about
anything appeared, she knew she wasn't going to be able to
eat. She ended up standing at the glass wall at the end of the
room, holding on to the handrail that ran across it, staring
down across the spaceport plateau and to where the mountains rose again at its perimeter, high and sharp edged against
the thin blue-white of the sky.

She and Samuel had asked one of the guards if they could
at least speak to their twins by phone, or even e-mail, and
the guard had said that they—probably—would be able to "at
some point." But he hadn't been able to tell them when that
point might be.

IPL had chosen Philomel as the relocation planet for the
Spares and their twins: It *must* be safe. It couldn't be that Lin
and the others had been shepherded off to be killed or—

She forced herself to switch off the images trying to burn
themselves into her brain. *Nothing* like that could be happening, not on the official relocation planet. And, even if

Lin had somehow closed herself off from the link between them, if anything like that happened, she wouldn't be able to prevent Elissa from knowing. *I felt it before, even when I didn't know she was real. If something were happening now, I'd know. There wouldn't be a way of keeping it from me.*

It didn't *matter* that they'd been on Philomel for—she looked at her watch—over an hour, and Cadan still hadn't come back, and no one had come to tell them anything about what was happening to the Spares. It didn't matter, because *nothing bad* was happening. Nothing bad was *going* to happen. *Because if it did*—she repeated the words furiously, insistently, to herself—*if it did, I'd know.*

The doors at the planet-side wall of the room, which had remained shut and guarded since they arrived, slid open. They moved silently, so it was the reflected flicker of that movement in the glass that caught Elissa's attention.

She turned, her heart jumping with a mix of relief and fright.

The guards at the door were standing down, holstering their weapons. The doors stood wide open, and a crowd of people—all adults around her parents' age—were coming through them.

Elissa stared at them a moment. They weren't the Spares who'd traveled on the *Phoenix*. They weren't IPL officials. So what were they doing, being let into a guarded room filled with evacuees?

"Mom?" Sofia's voice was high with shock. She pushed her way out of a little knot of people who'd been standing by the food table, the plate she'd been holding tipping sideways, forgotten, in her hand. A couple of pieces of sushi tumbled off it, scattering rice. "Daddy?"

Then she dropped the plate entirely, more rice scattering in sticky grains across the floor, and was running to them, crying.

She wasn't the only one. All at once, all over the room, twins were recognizing their parents, hurrying over to them. A wave of noise rose: some sounds of crying, but mostly a growing roar of talk, explanations, a catching up of the last however-many weeks since parents and children had seen each other.

It was a stab of disappointment that Elissa felt first. She couldn't remember what Sofia had said now, but she'd gotten the impression that Sofia wasn't particularly looking forward to seeing her parents. And, somehow, that had been a scarcely recognized comfort, that she, Elissa, was not the only one for whom a reunion would be an ordeal rather than a relief.

I should have known. People—they complain about their parents, but it takes more than a bit of irritation to make you really not want to see them again. It's dumb to be surprised at Sofia—it's obviously me, not her, who's the unnatural one here.

But they lied to me. And betrayed me, and my mother refused to recognize Lin as her daughter—or even as a person. It's not my fault that I don't want to see them, that I wouldn't be glad if I did—

Her thoughts stopped dead. Her stomach plunged, as if she stood in a plummeting elevator. Across the crowd, a head showed above most of the others. Dark hair, which had been closely cropped in the same style as Cadan's but was just beginning to grow out. The lines of a familiar face, clean-cut, good-looking enough that Elissa's friends—back when she'd *had* friends—had gone silly and giggly every time they came over and he was around. Cadan's closest friend. Her older brother, Bruce.

And if Bruce was here . . .

Her stomach plunged again. Next to Bruce, the crowd parted a little as more people found who they were looking for and moved over toward them. Shorter, slighter, and with the dark hair Bruce had inherited threaded all through with gray, her father, Edward Ivory, stood next to his son. And next to him, nearly as tall as her husband, her face composed and unreadable, was Laine Ivory. Elissa's mother.

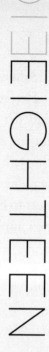

EIGHTEEN

"WE'RE JUST glad it wasn't you," said Elissa's mother.

They were standing by the drinks machine nearest the window. Mr. and Mrs. Ivory were both holding iced teas, Bruce had a soda, and Elissa was clutching a coffee. She hadn't wanted a drink, but after the first hugs—too tight on her parents' parts, stiff with awkwardness on her own—it had seemed suddenly vitally important to have something for her hands to do.

And now, with the news they'd just dumped on her, the kick of the oversugared coffee was very welcome.

"Fourteen?" she said again. "It happened to *fourteen* other Spares? *Today?"*

Laine Ivory set her drink down so she could press a hand to her perfectly made-up face. "We're all still so shocked," she said. "All these teenagers—and children—to be put in so much danger. It just doesn't bear thinking of. And for it to happen just when we'd been told you were on your way here, on a ship in the company of *your* Spare . . ."

Instinctive defensiveness took over Elissa's awareness of the danger she knew she, too, had probably been in. "*Lin* wouldn't ever hurt me!"

Her mother looked at her, and the calm patience in her expression was worse than if she'd snapped back. "Elissa, you can't possibly know whether that's the case. None of them appear to *intend* it. And afterward, when they have that shock to face . . ." She shook her head.

"Why would you care about that?" Elissa said, so stiff with resentment that the words came out sounding sulky. "You don't even think Spares are human."

Laine Ivory spread her hands a little. "Well, and doesn't this bear that out? I know you feel some kind of attachment to your Spare, Lissa—we've been getting some advice since we've been on Philomel, and apparently that's entirely natural—but it's still not human in the way you are. Humans don't randomly attack one other."

"Oh, *please*." Elissa set her coffee down with a little thump, and it splashed over the edge of the cup. "We were attacked back on Sekoia—three times! By *humans*."

Mrs. Ivory lifted an unperturbed shoulder. "I didn't say humans couldn't be violent. I said they don't attack one another randomly."

"Oh, they so do!" Anger scorched up behind Elissa's eyes, turning the world into a bright-edged blur. "Like, *serial killers* are random. And those guys who suddenly go crazy and kill their families—"

Her mother's eyebrows went up. "And you're comparing them to your Spare?"

"I'm saying humans can do awful things without them not being human! And Lin hasn't even *done* anything awful yet!"

"Yet."

"Stop it!" Elissa heard her voice shake and couldn't get it back under control. "You don't even know her. You don't get to talk about her like that. She's in pieces at the thought she might hurt me, *she* told me to get away from her."

Laine's voice rose easily over hers, not because it was louder but because it was so dispassionate that it seemed to flatten out her daughter's. "Really, Elissa, calm down. As I said, no one is suggesting the Spares *intend* to hurt their doubles."

"But they are, all the same." Beyond greeting Elissa, Bruce hadn't yet spoken. Now his voice was grim. "You can waste time explaining how *your* Spare, among all the others, won't, Lissa, or you can accept that, yeah, actually it probably will, and face that you're going to have to deal with it."

"What do you mean, *deal* with it?" She was shivering now, in impotent anger. Her mother and Bruce had been back in her life for less than ten minutes, and already they were stamping all over her and telling her that everything she was doing was wrong. "What am I supposed to do? If Lin *is* going to hurt me, I can't stop her any more than she's already been stopped. We've been separated, what else am I supposed to do?"

"*Jeez,*" Bruce was beginning impatiently, when his father interrupted.

"All right, Bruce, that's enough." He turned to Elissa. All her life he'd looked tired—although not as worn thin as he did now—but now that she knew what had happened to him, she could see that behind the look of fatigue, of distance, lay the grief he'd borne most of his life, ever since the link between him and his Spare had been severed.

She bit down on the furious responses she wanted to give, and listened.

"Lissa, these fourteen—fifteen, now—incidents, they've only occurred between Spares and their twins. Anyone else who's been hurt, they've only been hurt incidentally."

A picture of Zee's head slamming back into Cadan's face came to her. The blood pouring from Cadan's nose. The moment when she'd thought Zee might have killed him.

"Officials—scientists, medical staff—they're at a loss to understand exactly what's going on," her father continued. "But what they are clear about is that this . . . response . . . is triggered by the presence of a Spare's twin. And it appears to happen only after a threshold of at least sixteen days after the Spare and twin have been reunited. It's as if, in this case, familiarity doesn't so much breed contempt as . . . pathological aggression." His expression altered slightly. He was still looking grim—and tired—but for the first time Elissa saw him slide into what she thought of as his lecture-room manner, saw a trace of satisfaction edge his expression as he coined an appropriate term for something he'd been talking about.

She bit down on a surge of anger and disappointment. *It's not some freaking academic theory we're talking about here! This is me, and my sister—your daughter!*

Except this customary detachment was probably some kind of coping strategy that he'd evolved in order to deal with the loss of his own Spare. Elissa breathed in, carefully, then out. It wasn't fair to be so angry with him.

"Yes, okay. But what's that got to do with me?"

He looked at her, sympathy showing in his eyes, waiting for her to catch up as he had so many times when she was small, when he'd explained something to her. And now she saw the expectancy in her mother's face, the look of familiar impatience–*come on, Lissa, get with the program*–in Bruce's.

"Where do they want us to go?" she said, stiff lipped.

"Not you," said her father. "The Spares. There's an island in the southern hemisphere of the planet. It could be made secure–"

She took a step back. "No. *No.*"

Her mother blew out an exasperated breath. "It wouldn't be forever. Just until the officials have gotten to the bottom of whatever's causing this. Your Spare could be in the best place, kept secure, with people observing who know what they're doing. We have an apartment not far away. You can come home with us–"

Home? A home without Lin? "No. *No way* am I leaving Lin! You have no idea what you're saying–you have no idea what that would do to her!"

"Oh, for God's sake, Lissa!" All patience had vanished from Mrs. Ivory's voice. "Think! If it kills you–"

For a moment Elissa heard only the words her mother had used, not the sense behind them. "*She,*" she said. "*She!* Not *it.*"

"Fine. She. If *she* kills you, what's it going to do to her?"

Lin's face flashed up in Elissa's mind. Lin's face, but overlaid by Zee's. By that awful blankness in his expression. By the dawning horror as he came out of his fugue state, as he realized what he'd done. Lin, after everything she'd gone through, left without her twin, left with nothing but the knowledge that she'd killed Elissa.

If anyone else had said it, she might have given way to the horror the image filled her with, might have at least considered complying. But her *mother* saying it–she was only doing it to manipulate Elissa into doing what she wanted, what she'd wanted all along.

"You don't *care* what it does to her," she said, cornered, furious. "You don't *care!*"

"That's right," Elissa's mother snapped. "I *don't* care what happens to your Spare. I care what happens to you."

"We all care," added her father, quietly. "Lissa, we're really concerned for your safety here."

The quiet appeal in his voice caught at her. He'd called Lin his daughter a few weeks ago, when they'd spoken on the interplanetary phone from Sanctuary. He didn't see her the way Elissa's mother did; he *did* see her as a person.

But *no*. No, it was no good. He was still here with her mother, on the same side, arguing against Elissa, not for her.

She took another step away, crossing her arms over herself, feeling her face freeze into defiance. "No," she said again. "You don't get to play the concerned card. You lied to me. You tried to make me have an operation I didn't want." She looked at her mother, and of their own accord, her teeth gritted against one another. "You called the *police* on me."

"*Elissa*, you know very well that was for your own good—"

"I don't care! I don't *care*. It was *wrong*! You don't get to tell me what to do anymore. I'm not doing *anything* before I talk to Lin. I'm not making any decisions without her."

Mrs. Ivory flung her hands up, an exasperated gesture. "How can you be so unreasonable? You can talk to that Spare of yours from a secure place. You can phone, you can e-mail—"

"I'm not talking to her about this in *e-mail*! I have to *see* her. When Cadan gets back, he'll let me—all of us—know what's going on."

"Cadan." Laine Ivory shook her head. "I cannot *believe* he's going along with this. You'd think he'd remember he owes it to Bruce, at least, to keep an eye on your safety." She turned to her son, putting a hand on his arm. "When he does get back, maybe *you* should talk to him. He must know he should never have taken Elissa back to Sekoia—I still don't know what you thought you were *doing* there, Elissa— he obviously should have brought her here."

Bruce shrugged. "I'll be glad to talk to him, Ma. He was kind of landed with her, though, you know? If he had to go to help with the evacuation, and if there wasn't time to make a stop-off here?"

Despite everything, laughter rose within Elissa. Cadan had been *landed* with her, had he? *Yeah, you wait, big brother. He's not just yours anymore.*

The insecurity she'd felt yesterday had evaporated—and remained that way, like a far-off haze of water droplets. If she didn't actually need to worry about his mother's influence, she wasn't going to start worrying about *Bruce's*.

Her mother looked back at her. "Very well," she said. "We'll wait to see what information Cadan has. But you're going to have to make some sort of decision, Lissa. You can't just be waiting around indefinitely. Quite apart from anything else, the Philomel authorities are allowing us to *resettle* here—they're not putting us up as guests. Your father's working, Bruce is on a waiting list for possible jobs. You're going to have to do something with your life as well."

She was right, but everything about what she was saying grated, raw, against Elissa's skin. *It's not us who's waiting. It's me. And whatever I have to do, it's not you who gets to tell me what it is.*

"I know that," she said, her voice mulish.

Mrs. Ivory's eyes sparked with anger. She looked as if she were about to say something, but then a stir across the room caught their attention. Cadan was coming back down the staircase.

His eyes swept across the room and found Elissa. Despite the grimness of his expression, a smile crept into them as he looked at her, and for a moment she thought he would come straight over to where she waited.

He didn't, though. He stopped halfway down the staircase and turned on a mike clipped to his collar. As he began to speak, Elissa realized that as captain of the ship that had brought them all here, he'd been given the unpleasant task of explaining the situation with the Spares.

He didn't have much more information than Elissa had already gathered from her family. Up until the last twenty-four hours, the reunions of Spares and twins had gone fairly smoothly. Not everyone had chosen to be reunited with their double, but those who had, had mostly formed relationships that ranged from a cautious friendship to the intense bond Elissa knew herself, and that she had witnessed with the other Spares and their twins.

Here, under the close supervision IPL officials had provided, other people had picked up on the odd phenomenon that Cadan, like Ady, was referring to as a fugue state: times when a Spare would seem to check out of normal consciousness, flipping back with no apparent awareness that time had passed. As a possible symptom of something more serious, it hadn't been ignored, but it had been seen as nothing more than an aftereffect of the trauma the Spares had been through, or the psychic shock of being reunited with their twins.

Then, the first of the attacks. A fifteen-year-old girl called Amanda had been strangled by her Spare—in the middle of a board game with two other pairs, and with no warning at all that anything was wrong. The emergency staff were dealing with the fallout from that when the second attack came.

Cadan didn't go into detail about that attack, or any of the others. All he said was that there'd been twenty-two attacks in all, fifteen of which had resulted in the death of a twin. And of the fifteen Spares who had killed their twins, six had also killed themselves, and the others were in states of catatonia.

Like Zee. Elissa found her mind trying to shy away from the reality of it all, found herself thinking ridiculous things like *maybe it didn't hurt, maybe the dead twins didn't know what was happening, maybe the catatonia happened before the Spares realized what they'd done. . . .*

Cadan's voice pulled her out of the morass of wishful thinking she knew very well probably wasn't anything like true.

"IPL doctors and scientists are working on finding an explanation for this," he said. "So far they've identified three common factors. First, all of the pairs to whom this has happened have been at least twelve years old. There have been no attacks with the younger age groups, and as far as officials can tell, no incidences of the fugue state, either. Second, it has happened only to those pairs who were reunited at least sixteen days ago. Third"—and now his eyes met Elissa's again, and she saw, not only the smile, but the look of relief within them—"it has happened only to those pairs with no current telepathic connection."

A stir—of relief, confusion, distress—went around the room, but Elissa hardly noticed anyone else's reaction. Relief bloomed in her chest, and warmth spread to every nerve ending. *Lin's safe. Lin's safe. I don't have to let them take her away.*

Cadan looked carefully away from Elissa and resumed speaking. "The IPL team working on this wants me to make very clear that none of these factors provide a guarantee of safety for those outside the specified groups. No one yet understands how this has happened, or why, and the data is insufficient to make a full analysis. For this reason, Spares and twins need to continue to be kept separate while the team continues to work on identifying the reasons behind these incidents."

From all over the room, voices combined in a rising murmur of protest. Cadan held his hand up. "The team understands this is difficult for both Spares and their twins—and for those parents who've been hoping to be reunited with their children. IPL officials, aided by Philomelen police, are going to work on providing supervised contact in the very near future. Also, brain scans are being performed on all Spares, again in an attempt to identify the source of the pathology that causes the attacks. As this can be a distressing experience for the Spares, and as they will be fully restrained throughout, IPL medical personnel are inviting their twins to be present during the procedure."

Lin in a machine. Lin being *strapped down* into a machine. Elissa looked up at Cadan, sick with horror. *You're calling it nothing but a "distressing experience"? What the hell is wrong with you? You know what she went through. You know what they did to her.*

Again, his eyes met hers, a very brief glance. She dragged in a steadying breath. Okay, they weren't Cadan's words. But how *anyone* who knew how the Spares had been treated could minimize what they needed to do to them now as nothing more than "distressing" . . . She curled her fingers up into her palms, drew in another breath. At least she'd get to *see* Lin. And at least Lin would know she wasn't likely to kill Elissa.

What is it that's making the difference? Of all the factors Cadan had mentioned, the fact that it had happened only to the twins with no telepathic link seemed like the most significant. But if the doctors weren't sure, then how could Elissa work out what lay behind it?

Cadan was talking again, explaining that the team of doctors and scientists was going to be performing the first scans on the Spares who had no link to their twins, trying to isolate any common factor in their brains. *Not Lin, then, not yet.* She bit at her thumbnail, watching Cadan as he spoke, waiting for him to finish. *I have to see her. If I can catch up with him when he's done here, maybe he can help me see her.*

It was selfish, she knew, using her connection with Cadan to jump the line of all the twins who were probably as desperate as she was to see their Spares. She didn't care. *I tried to be unselfish. I tried to think about other people and I tried to get Lin to think about other people, and look where it got us.*

Cadan finished talking, and as he came down the rest of the steps he was swamped by a crowd of people, by a jumble of questions and high-pitched anxiety. Elissa waited, every muscle tight.

"Elissa, don't bite your nails."

Elissa looked around, whipping her thumbnail away from her mouth, an automatic reaction that came before she could think. She stared at her mother, incredulous, anger rising in a wave. *You're telling me what to do? Still? Now?*

Laine Ivory met her eyes. "We did it for your own good," she said.

Elissa put her hands up, a barrier between herself and her mother's words. "No. *No.* It doesn't matter how many times you keep saying that. It doesn't make it okay. It doesn't make it better."

"Oh, it's very clear you hate us. But you should still admit—"

"I *don't*," Elissa said, exasperated. "I don't hate you. But I'm not *admitting* anything. You did it all wrong, and you're not even trying to see that!" She flung a hand out toward the crowd. "*Look.* Look what it did, you going along with what SFI was doing. You didn't challenge them, you didn't tell them it was evil and immoral and illegal. *Look* at all these damaged people!"

Fury flashed over her mother's face. "And now you're *blaming* us? We didn't know what they were doing!"

"You didn't *let* yourself know!" She raised her hands farther, blocking out her mother's view of her face. "I'm not *talking* about this."

"*Elissa.*"

"*No.*" Her teeth snapped down on the word. She turned, pushing through the people standing behind her, refusing to look back.

She reached where Cadan stood just as he was extricating himself from another group of questioners. His eyes met hers through a gap between them, and after a moment he managed to excuse himself and come toward her.

"Your parents—I just saw them. Are you okay?"

He spoke at the same time as she said, "Can I see her?"

Then she registered that he'd asked her a question too. "Yes. I'm all right. Kind of mad, though . . ."

He grinned a little. "Yeah. Look, about Lin—"

"Cadan, she's going to be so freaked out."

"Yeah, I know, I know. But like I said, there's no guarantee of safety. They wouldn't let me make it part of the announcement, but the brain scans they've already done? All of them—all of them performed on the over-twelves, that is—they *all* show some kind of abnormal activity. It's more marked in the unlinked Spares, but it's there for all of them. It sounds like you and Lin should be safer than the twins without a link, but no one's going to want to risk—" He broke off, frowned. "But wait a minute, why are you asking? The link, the way it's been developing between the two of you? You don't need to see her to talk to her."

Tears pricked unexpectedly in Elissa's eyes. "She's shut me out. Or she's not cooperating. Or something. I can't get through to her." Frustration and disappointment and worry combined in her voice, making it tremble. "I'm not the superpowered one, Cadan. Everything I've done, I've only managed because I've been doing it with her. If she shuts me out, I'm just—just *me*."

"More than enough," Cadan said, for her ears only, his eyes smiling into hers.

For a moment all other preoccupations fell away. She slid her hand into his and felt his fingers curl around hers to pull her a little closer. She leaned in, just enough that she could feel the warmth that came off his skin, catch his scent. He smelled of sweat and too much coffee, a smell she wouldn't have ever thought she'd have liked. But, of course, it was still him underneath.

"I have to go in a minute," he said. "I'll talk to someone about you seeing Lin, okay? I'll do what I can."

"Okay."

He bent his head, then caught himself. He wasn't going to kiss her in this crowd. But he did pull her closer, just enough so the top of her head brushed his cheek, so the feel of his warmth spread all along her body, so that if she shut her eyes it felt, for a moment, as if they were alone. . . .

"Seriously?" said Bruce.

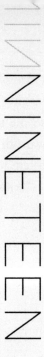

NINETEEN

ELISSA JERKED upright, dropping Cadan's hand. When she turned around, Bruce was standing a couple of feet from them, staring at Cadan.

"No way," he said. "No *way*. Jeez, man, tell me she's freaking out and you're just being kind."

Elissa was still close enough to Cadan that she felt him stiffen.

"Bruce," he said. "It's good to see you."

"Yeah? Suppose you answer my question, then."

There was undiluted hostility in Bruce's voice. Elissa blinked at him, confused. What did it matter to him if she and Cadan were together? *And haven't we all got more important stuff to worry about?* For the first time, she consciously noticed that the dark blue clothes he was wearing weren't the familiar SFI uniform he'd more or less lived in for the last four years, but civilian clothes—dark blue jeans and a T-shirt in the same color. *Does he know he's wearing as close to uniform as he can get?*

Cadan folded his arms. "Have to say, didn't actually notice a question there, Bruce."

"Don't play dumb. Are you"—he made a dismissive gesture, as if whatever terms came to mind weren't ones he wanted to use—"in a *relationship* with my sister?"

"Yes." Cadan's voice was flat.

Bruce took half a step back, folding his own arms. "No wonder she's so freaking pleased with herself, then. Jeez, Cay, what were you thinking?"

"Yeah, not really sure that's your business."

Elissa flicked a glance up at Cadan's face. It was expressionless, the only hint of what he might be feeling in his eyes, cold as chips of ice.

"Not my business? You didn't hear the way she just talked to my mother! God, Lis"—and now he turned on her—"what the hell is wrong with you? She's been worried half to death about you—it only got a bit easier for her once we heard you were with Cadan—and now, just when she thought you were going to be safe, it turns out you're in danger of being beaten to death by the freak double you ran off with!"

Heat rushed up into Elissa's face. "Don't call her that! You weren't there. You don't know anything of what's been happening—you don't know what Lin's had to go through."

"And you don't know what *our mother* has been going through!" The heat in Elissa's face was suddenly reflecting from Bruce's. "Then you meet her again, when she's been beside herself with worrying about you, and you just wave away all the danger you're *still* in. Is this what getting

Cadan has done for you? You selfish little brat—"

He broke off. Cadan had taken a swift step forward, unfolding his arms, and both his hands were clenched into fists.

Bruce barked out an angry, incredulous laugh. "You're going to try beating me up for the way I talk to my sister? Well, hasn't she got you pretty well hooked." His lip curled. "She always did follow you around like a puppy. I guess now that she's with you, there's not much she won't do for you, is there?" The twist in his tone made it all too clear what he meant, and his disdain, the implication of what he was saying, went through Elissa like an electric shock.

"I think that'll do." Cadan's voice was tightly controlled, and his hands hadn't relaxed so much as a millimeter.

Bruce laughed again. "You're not going to hit me, then, Mr. Gallant Boyfriend?"

Cadan let out a careful breath, then shrugged, his hands relaxing, bit by deliberate bit. "Unfortunately, my behavior is constrained. I'm on duty here."

All the laughter drained from Bruce's face. "Yeah, of course. *You* managed to keep your career, didn't you." It wasn't a question. There was naked fury in the glance he gave them both. "You broke every freaking law you came across. *You*"—he sent a vicious nod Elissa's way—"broke our mother's heart, and Cadan's still ended up with the career, and *you've* ended up with the boyfriend you always wanted." He took a step away, about to turn on his heel, and Elissa suddenly realized it wasn't just fury in his face, but misery. "You wrecked our world," he said. "You wrecked lives all over the place, and you don't even care because you got what mattered to you."

He strode away, back stiff, half a head taller than nearly everyone in the crowd, in his uniform that wasn't a uniform, and disappeared through the doors he'd come in by.

Oh hell. Elissa dropped her face into her hands. She'd thought she was done with guilt, but that momentary glimpse into what lay behind Bruce's vicious display of anger had brought it all back, a snarl of tangled feelings like a physical weight dragging at her.

Above her head, Cadan swore. When she looked up at him, his jaw was set hard. He let out a long breath, swallowing anger. Not guilt, just anger. Either he hadn't seen that sudden raw misery in Bruce's eyes, or it hadn't had the impact on him that it had on Elissa.

He was looking at where Bruce had disappeared, slowly unclenching his hands, which had once more tightened into fists. "I'm starting to think there was something pretty freaking wrong with the way SFI trained its cadets," he said, and his voice was bitter. "Stewart—at least he didn't know the full details. And the situation landed on him so fast he hardly had time to process it. But Bruce—he can't *not* know the full god-awful nightmare, and he's still . . ." He trailed off, then his head jerked around. His eyes met Elissa's. "And God, it's his *sister* involved. Not you, I mean—Lin. I know he doesn't know her and hasn't met her, but you'd think . . . his *own sister.*"

Elissa's lip was becoming sore where her teeth were worrying it. She made herself stop. "It's his career. He . . . SFI was everything to him, from the moment he found he was eligible for the preacademy training."

"Yeah, him and me both." Cadan's voice was unforgiving. "There are some things a damn bit more important, though. I mean, God, I *get* how much of a wrench it is, but when you weigh it up next to what SFI was doing to the Spares—"

He shook his head. "You remember you called me arrogant? And yeah, a lot of that's on me—I can't blame anyone else. But all the same, the way they trained us—I look at it now, and think they were training us into *more* arrogance."

He had a point. But all the same, that look on Bruce's face . . . He and she had never been close, really. And once her link with Lin had thrown her into the whole nightmare of inexplicable symptoms, what closeness they had possessed had dwindled as her world narrowed to nothing but surviving the next attack of phantom pain, and as he started to find the sheer weirdness of it all an embarrassment. But although Bruce had patronized her and made fun of her and put her down, he, unlike Carlie and Marissa, whom she'd thought of as her friends, had never made fun of the symptoms themselves, never made her feel she was a freak or a failure because of *them*.

And once, when she was fifteen—she remembered it now, unwillingly—he'd found out that a boy from school had started up a chatpage called Freak Spot for which the entry requirement was a "sighting of Lissa Ivory acting like a big freak." He and Cadan had been right in the middle of revising and training for the beyond-intensive second-year exams—it was the only time since joining the training program that she'd seen him look actually stressed, as if, for the first time, it had struck him that he might not make it all the way through—but he'd somehow gotten a two-hour leave of absence and had turned up to meet her as she came out of school.

"Point him out," he'd said.

"Oh God, Bruce, *don't*. It's not worth it." She still remembered how she'd shrunk, sure he couldn't do anything, horrified at the idea of drawing more attention to herself.

Bruce hadn't listened. "Point him out," he'd said again, and, defeated, she'd complied, then watched as he, taller than all the high school students, strode over and, with one hand on the boy's shoulder, plucked him from among a whole crowd of his friends.

That had been the only physical contact he'd made, and Elissa, cringing over at the other side of the platform outside the school, hadn't been close enough to hear what he said. But she'd seen the boy's expression change so fast he'd looked ludicrous, and when she got home and logged on, not only the chatpage, but every cached snapshot, every mention on the social networking sites the kids from her school used, and every associated link and username had been wiped off the net.

"Lis?" said Cadan now.

She looked up, aware only as she did so that she'd moved on from biting her lip to biting her thumbnail. "I know," she said. "But . . . I guess at least you got to make the choice yourself? I mean, I know I pretty much forced it on you, and it wasn't a *great* choice, but . . ."

"But Bruce didn't even get that?"

She shrugged, not wanting to diminish how hard Cadan's choice—to protect her and Lin by rebelling against SFI and the Sekoian government—had been.

"Fair point," said Cadan. His voice was still grim, but his eyes were no longer quite so hard. "I'm damned if I'm going to excuse him talking to you like that, though."

She couldn't help laughing a little. "Oh Cadan, I grew up with him. He's called me much worse than that."

"Yeah. I bet he never implied you were doing . . . whatever

I wanted . . . before, though, did he?" But before she could answer, he flung up a hand. "No, okay. It was nothing but a cheap shot—against both of us—because he was angry. I get that." The hint of a smile crept into his eyes now. "Jeez, our freaking families, huh? What d'you think, should I go talk to him?"

Every cowardly impulse impelled Elissa to say yes. But, with the anger she could see lingering in the rigidity of Cadan's jaw, the still-icy glint in his eyes, it was pretty clear that wouldn't be a good idea.

Anyway, it was her Bruce was angriest with. The accusations he'd flung at them both came back to her. *No wonder she's so freaking pleased with herself. You broke our mother's heart. You wrecked our world, and you don't even care because you got what mattered to you.*

Letting Cadan talk to him for her: All that was doing was pushing the problem off onto him. It was her brother, her problem, and she should deal with it.

"It's okay," she said. "Let me talk to him first. He's had a few minutes, maybe he's calming down a bit."

"You sure? If he says that stuff to you again—"

Again, laughter caught her. She reached up and brushed a kiss on Cadan's jaw, feeling the tension in the muscles beneath his skin. "Yeah, well, at least he's not likely to hit me."

As she made her way through the crowd, she noticed the guards again, standing at ease but still present at the doors. How tight was the security now? Had they been given orders not to let any of the former occupants of the *Phoenix* through to the main body of the spaceport?

Clearly not. She guessed it must be only the Spares who

were regarded as too dangerous to allow out into the general population. The guards didn't make a move as she approached the doors, and she slipped through them to emerge into another waiting-room-like area.

This one was more or less empty. There were a few guards, and a scatter of twin-and-family groups who, she assumed, had come out here in search of a quieter place for their reunion.

Bruce was nowhere to be seen. Which might mean he'd left completely, gone back to wherever he and her parents lived now. But across the far side of this waiting room, faint vertical lines in the glass wall showed where doors would slide open onto what looked like a balcony outside. From here she could see only pale, endless sky beyond it, but maybe it overlooked more of the spaceport, giving people a place to watch the ships take off and land. If Bruce hadn't actually gone completely, if he was still somewhere in the spaceport . . .

Elissa walked across the waiting-room carpet, feeling its springiness beneath her feet. She didn't remember much about Philomel, but what she had picked up was that it wasn't thought to be as advanced as Sekoia. Or maybe just not as fast-developing? Sekoia, after all, had moved at light-speed once they'd gotten their spaceflight industry working. As far as spaceports went, though, there didn't seem to be any difference.

She reached the wide expanse of window. Now that she was here, she could see that the balcony jutted out over the edge of a cliff—the end of the spaceport plateau. Beyond it the land fell away into the depths of a valley.

Elissa had grown up in Central Canyon City. She knew about heights—had learned to cope with vertigo while she was still in kindergarten. But she'd never seen anything like this. Not because of the height of the valley, but because of its unbelievable *greenness*. Even the upper reaches, where a veil of thin white cloud had fallen, were a mist-muted green, and below the mist, the valley sides were a tangle of long-fronded bracken that gave way only to trees.

Elissa moved a little closer and a section of the wall slid back, glass sliding over glass, creating a momentary optical illusion that the air was rippling in a heat haze. But the air that blew in at her was as cold as water poured straight from a refrigerator. And it even *smelled* green, almost like the pine scent she knew from her home's house-environment settings, but somehow thinner, cleaner, the difference between nutri-machine fruit juice and juice that had been freshly squeezed.

She stepped out onto the balcony.

Toward the farthest end of the valley, the distance-blurred trees seemed so thick, so soft, that Elissa felt as if she could take up handfuls of them. Closer, their thickness meant they looked as if they'd been poured, like leaf porridge, down the sides of the valley, to flow all over its floor, so dense they concealed the contours of the valley itself, turned it into a cauldron filled with green.

Elissa remembered now. Philomel was that rare planet that hadn't needed to be terraformed before it could support humans. These forests were thousands of years old, growing from earth made fertile by millennia-old trees, which had died and rotted and become earth themselves.

She'd known about planets like this, of course—had learned about them at school and seen them in documentaries and movies. But nothing had prepared her for what one would look like in real life.

"Sekoia's never going to look like that now."

Bruce's voice came from farther along the balcony. Elissa looked, the muscles in the back of her neck already tightening, bracing herself. "Sekoia was never going to look like that anyway. Even Sanctuary doesn't look like that."

"Yeah yeah yeah. You're going to rub your interplanetary travels in my face now too?"

So he hadn't calmed down. Elissa took a breath of the cold, sharp air, the green scent almost making her dizzy. "Look, I'm sorry about how things turned out. Honestly. We went back to Sekoia to try to help—we're only here because they *sent* us here."

Bruce eyed her with what could have been contempt—or outright dislike. "Help? With what? Your Spare's brainpower is the only thing that would help—or didn't you remember it had been ruled illegal?"

She knew it was sarcasm, but at even a sarcastic suggestion that it would be okay to use Lin as Zee had been used, she was all at once blind with fury. "Of course I freaking remembered. And if it hadn't been made illegal, I'd never have let them do that to her. She can power hyperdrives voluntarily. If she and I link, it doesn't hurt her—"

Bruce's eyebrows went up, and his eyes were sarcastic and disbelieving. "Seriously? You expect me to believe your Spare *volunteered* to help our planet?"

"I don't care whether you believe me or not!" Elissa snapped untruthfully. "But she *did* volunteer. Back on Sanctuary, she said she wanted to come and help. She *wanted* to. We—"

We were going to save the world.

Yeah, that worked out well, didn't it? Suddenly she had to fight down tears. *It's all gotten so messed up, and I'm scared to keep accessing the link because of what it's doing to us. And even if I wasn't scared, I don't dare—and I'm not allowed—to be close enough to her to try.*

"Kind of screwed now, isn't it? With all the Spares in danger of going psycho?"

She flashed a furious look at him—*you're making fun of me, now?*—before she realized that this time his tone of voice had been neither sarcastic nor disagreeable, but edging toward what sounded like sympathy.

"No," she said, not wanting to admit to it. "It's . . . tricky. But the scientists and people are working on it. They'll work it out. They'll fix it."

"They're not human, you know, Lis."

She'd have flared at him again if his voice hadn't still held that note of sympathy.

"They *are*. You haven't met her, but I swear, she's—"

She'd been going to say *just like you and me*, but suddenly it was as if something had closed on her throat. A stack of images unfolded before her, images she'd been trying to forget.

"She's what?"

Elissa swallowed. "She *is* human. She's just . . . how *couldn't* you be damaged, if what happened to her happened to you? And a lot of it—it's not even her fault. It's the link, with having to use it so often. . . ."

"What's not her fault?" He said it after a pause, but there was still that sympathy in his voice, and oh *God*, it would be such a relief to talk to someone. . . .

"The link keeps getting stronger," she said. "Our thoughts . . . they're starting to get mixed up. I end up having her thoughts, and sometimes . . . there was this one time, I was angry, and I—I think she picked up *those* thoughts, and I can't guard what I'm thinking all the time, I just *can't*, it's not possible!"

"You can't, like, switch it off?"

"*She* can. I can't. She's stronger than me, and she—well, she knew she had the link from when she was really young, while I didn't even realize it was something real, so she has a ton more control than I do."

"Parasite mind control?" said Bruce.

What? She blinked at him a moment before registering the flicker of amusement in his eyes, and then, unexpectedly, she was laughing too.

When they were nine and thirteen, their mother out at the Skyline Club and their father catching up on some work in his study, they'd managed to hack into the family-friendly settings of their home movie system and reset them for the two hours necessary to watch *Parasite Invasion*, the latest multi-horror movie sensation their parents—and all their friends' parents—had vetoed without any pretense at discussion.

They'd both had *major* nightmares afterward, Elissa remembered. Of all the multihorrors the film genre was named for, the one that had bothered her the most was when the parasitically mind-controlled diner owner had fished up a giant worm from the sewers, chopped it into sections, and turned them into ring doughnuts to serve to an unsuspecting diner full of glossily beautiful teenagers. Shortly afterward the mind-controlling parasite had gotten the diner owner to climb into the whirling blades of his own mega-blender, and the resultant screaming, splattered gore, and severed limbs should have eclipsed the doughnut scene, but in Elissa's mind, somehow the horror of thinking you were eating doughnut when actually you were eating *sewer worm* had been the thing that had lingered.

Bruce had had his own nightmares too, although he'd always refused to tell her which of the assorted horrors had invaded his dreams, but somehow their parents had never found out the reason—even when both Bruce's and Elissa's vocabularies suddenly began to include the term "parasite mind control." And when Elissa went off eating doughnuts for a year.

"*No,*" she said now. "Completely not parasite mind control! Jeez, Bruce."

The corner of his mouth turned up in something like a grin. "Okay. Look, don't go crazy, but, Lis, it doesn't sound a *hundred* percent different."

Elissa opened her mouth, then shut it, and turned to lean on the side of the balcony, feeling the cold roughness of the concrete beneath her elbows and, as she leaned out farther, the slight tickle of the safety field along the hair on her forearms.

It felt disloyal to say anything about Lin to *Bruce*—Bruce, who'd said Lin wasn't human. Especially anything that associated her, no matter how slightly, with the monsters from a low-plot, high-gore horror movie. But Bruce's words had brought some of her own thoughts back into her mind. *It's like trying to get through to an alien,* she'd thought just yesterday, staring at her sister. *Like trying to talk to someone who's not even human.*

"You keep fighting for her." Bruce had moved to lean on the side of the balcony too. Out of the corner of her eye, she saw him looking at her. "You met her, what, six weeks ago? Has she really gotten that important so fast?"

A laugh caught at Elissa's throat. "She was that important, like, two days after I met her. She's . . . some of it must be that we were linked for so long, even though I didn't really know it. But"—she lifted a shoulder, shy about sharing so much—"I love her. I know it doesn't sound likely, and if it hadn't happened to me I don't think I'd believe it could happen to anyone. But I just . . . she feels like part of me. She matters more than anything. Even when she does something awful, or when I feel like she's taking over, or when I just want her out of my *head* . . ."

She leaned out a little more, into the buzz of the safety field as it caught her, stopped her leaning farther. Bruce hadn't said anything, and now that she wasn't looking directly at him it was easier to talk, easier to be honest.

"You know how people say love—like, *all* love—is unconditional and everything?" she said. "It's really not. You can love someone, but if they do something really bad . . . they can . . . kill it off, eventually. But with Lin . . . I don't think she could. Kill it off, I mean. I've been so furious with her, and scared *of* her, sometimes, but it always comes back. Like something you can't escape from. Something that's always there whether you want it or not."

"Really," said Bruce. His voice had changed again. Now it held a note she didn't recognize, but that made her glance sideways at him. Something new showed in his face, too. A stiffness, like shock, or anger held under such tight control it hardly showed as anger at all.

All at once she felt foolish, exposed. She shrugged. "Yeah. It's completely difficult to explain, though."

"No. You explained it pretty well." But he seemed distracted. He'd tipped his wrist to check the watch he wore on his right hand, and now he was fiddling with it, running his thumb over the watch face. Elissa wondered, vaguely, with a fraction of her mind, whether his watch, like hers, was still set on Sekoian time, or whether he'd changed it over to match this time zone on Philomel.

Elissa straightened, turning so her side was to the balcony wall, hugging her arms to her chest. "If you meet her, though . . . I mean, I wouldn't expect you to feel like I do, but she's your sister too—and if you met her, you'd see she was human. I swear—"

She stopped short. It wasn't just a watch on Bruce's wrist. She should have recognized it before now: It was the mini-communicator he'd worn when he was training. They could be worn as casually as if they were nothing but watches, without worries about SFI channels being compromised, because of the built-in security. They could be activated only by the thumbprint of the owner.

And now, here was Bruce with one. And he'd just run his thumb across it. He'd just activated it.

Fear shot through her. Fear that, even as her body felt it, her mind told her was irrational. There was nothing out here that screamed danger. But the fear came all the same, riding on a wave of instinct, a fight-or-flight impulse that came from nowhere.

As her senses sprang alert, she became aware that she and Bruce were the only people on the balcony, that the nearest guards were way across the other side of the room she'd walked through to get here, and that during the time she and Bruce had been talking she'd moved, somehow, much farther from the doors than she'd realized.

There was no *reason* why any of that mattered, there was

nothing sinister about Bruce fiddling with his mini-com—without the SFI network it probably didn't even work—but all the same, unreasoning instinct pushed Elissa back toward the entrance to the spaceport.

She moved carefully, not wanting—*again*, for no reason!—Bruce to notice what she was doing.

"You think I should meet her, then?" As Bruce spoke he, too, stepped away from the balcony wall.

Elissa moved a few more cautious inches. "Yeah," she said, almost at random, concentrating on keeping her voice casual rather than on what she was saying. It was crazy, she was just talking to her *brother*, for goodness' sake, but all the same she knew she'd feel 100 percent better once she was back in the shelter of the spaceport.

Bruce laughed. "Lis, what are you doing? You keep shuffling backward. You look like you did when we were playing chase when we were kids!"

"Oh, I thought we should maybe start going back inside?" Her voice came out overbright, and she felt her lips stretch into a forced smile. The reference to their shared childhood added another layer of reluctance to the voice in her head telling her she was being crazy, that this was her *brother*, who she'd *grown up* with. But at the same time, the way he'd laughed . . . there was something off about it, something that seemed as unnatural as her smile.

Bruce moved toward her again, and this time every one of her muscles felt as if they jumped, jerking her away from him.

"Lis, for God's sake—"

He took the last few steps fast, grabbed her arm, and the unease growing within her woke into full-blown panic.

"Let go. *Let go.*"

"Jeez, Lis, we were *talking*. You can't just walk off."

She pulled back against his hold. "Bruce, let *go* of me!" With the panic, memory flared too, screenshot-vivid. She'd been here before, struggling against a family member, someone she should be able to trust but that she couldn't, someone who was acting on instructions she didn't know about, instructions someone else had given them.

Normal conventions had trapped her before—the conventions that said you shouldn't run away from home, you shouldn't push your mother away even if she grabbed hold of you, that you could trust your family, you could trust the government. She was *damned* if she was going to let them trap her again.

She opened her mouth to scream—and Bruce's free hand came down hard over it, crushing the scream as it formed, cutting off half her breath.

No. No! Not again! She jerked backward, dragging him with her, and as he lunged after her, off balance, she kicked out, catching his shin. He staggered, and although he kept his grip on her arm, his hand slipped from her mouth.

She tried to scream, but she hadn't drawn in enough breath and it wasn't anywhere near loud enough. And, of course, the doors had slid shut behind her, and this was a spaceport— the glass would be soundproof so even if she could scream loud enough no one inside was going to be able to hear her.

I should have listened to my instincts. I should have run away the minute I got scared. I shouldn't have come out here with him—

It was all true, and it was all too late. As Bruce grabbed her again, pulled her against him, his hand back over her mouth, his arm like a steel bar across her body, over the edge of the balcony, a flyer rose—a slender, bullet-shaped thing, so black, so unreflecting, that it seemed like a hole in the sky. It made almost no sound—just the thinnest whine at the very edge of her hearing. She'd never seen one in real life before. She shouldn't have seen one at all, shouldn't even know what it was, but way back when Bruce had joined SFI, and before he'd been trained to confidentiality, he'd shown her a picture on his shiny new SFI bookscreen—a picture that later, as the training on need-for-secrecy kicked in, he ordered her, in a panic, to forget she'd ever seen.

This flyer didn't belong on Philomel. It shouldn't have been brought here, must have been smuggled onto the planet in the cargo hold of a spaceship. It was one of a type that was almost silent, unbelievably fast, permanently shielded so it was impossible to track or trace. It was an SFI stealth vehicle.

As it turned, effortless in the air, one narrow black fin passed over the edge of the balcony. Blue sparks spattered as the safety field disintegrated. A slim opening appeared in the side of the flyer. A man, in a close-fitting flying suit and helmet whose seamless blackness matched the flyer itself, stood in it, one hand on a grab handle.

What the—?

Panic wiped most of the coherent thoughts from Elissa's head. She fought like crazy, kicking Bruce's legs, curling her fingers around to claw at his arms, trying to bite the hand that crushed her lips against her teeth.

It didn't do any good. His hold didn't falter; he pulled her to the edge of the balcony. To get her into the flyer, though, he was going to have to lift her up, and to do so he'd have to let go of her mouth, slacken his hold on her. Elissa stilled for a moment, trying to drag in as much breath as she could through her nose, through the cracks in between his fingers. As soon as he shifted his hold, as soon as he gave her the slightest opening–

The man in the flyer leaned out. There was something in his hand, something that glinted bright in the sunlight.

The scream Elissa couldn't utter rose inside her head, and a surge of terror that burned like ice.

In this last extremity of panic, something in her head narrowed, focused. She reached out the way she'd never been able to before. *Lin! Lin!*

No voice answered, but what did come was a sudden rush of panic on top of her own. And fear that was different from her fear, fear that came from a mind not her own.

Lin! There's a stealth flyer! And Bruce. Bruce–!

Bruce's hands clamped tighter on her mouth and body. The man leaned closer, and the needle slid through Elissa's sleeve and into her arm.

And the world went black.

TWENTY

ELISSA WOKE as if from nightmare, jerking bolt upright, heart hammering, mouth sand-dry, breath like hot smoke in her chest. Her eyes snapped open on floods of bright white light, her gaze taking in the sight of objects that her brain couldn't make sense of.

The movement of sitting up made her head spin, a feeling as if something inside it had come loose. Then the same sensation hit her stomach. She doubled over and threw up.

The vomit splashed onto a shiny white floor, farther away than it should have been. The smell, warm and vile, came up to Elissa, and she threw up again, tasting a horrible mixture of acidic sweetness, feeling it burning her throat and the inside of her nose.

Someone pushed a steel pan onto her lap, swiped a damp cloth across her mouth, then handed her a plastic beaker of water.

Elissa sipped, gagged, and half vomited again into the steel pan. She put out her free hand, groping blindly.

A hand whisked the steel pan off her lap and replaced it with a box of tissues. Elissa pulled up a handful and blew her nose, again and again, trying to get rid of the sweet-acid smell, gagging twice while she did it.

"The water will help," said an unfamiliar voice, very loud above her head. Elissa sipped, spat into the pan, then drank, feeling the cool liquid wash both the burning and the sand-dry feeling out of her throat.

Hands—the same hands? different ones? and did they belong with the voice?—took away the disgusting, used-tissue-filled pan, then came back with another cool, damp cloth and wiped Elissa's face. Then pushed another beaker into her hands.

She drank, suddenly aware that she was so thirsty she wanted to cry, shutting her eyes against the brightness that kept making her head spin, that made her afraid she would be sick again.

"You'll be okay in a few more minutes," said the voice, from somewhere beyond the dark of Elissa's eyelids. "You had a bad reaction, that's all. Keep sipping the water—not too fast, you don't want to get sick again. I'll be back in a minute to clean up."

Footsteps—soft-soled footsteps—went away over the floor.

The shiny, superclean floor. The chair she'd been lying in, which had tipped up with her as soon as she moved but was still too far off the floor for her feet to touch it. The readily available steel pan. She must be in a hospital.

But why?

Elissa's eyelids tried to snap open, but she kept them shut. Everything still seemed to spin, in her head, in her stomach, and she *really* didn't want to be sick again.

I'm in a hospital. Why?

There were a million jumbled images in her head, a million images that made no more sense than the bright whiteness she'd opened her eyes on. Faces . . . Lin, Cadan, her parents, Bruce . . .

In a hospital. In a chair. And my arms can move, but my legs . . .

This time she couldn't stop her eyes snapping wide open. Through the swimming of her vision, she looked down at herself, over an expanse of white hospital gown. She hadn't been able to move her legs because they were strapped to the chair. A harness went up over her chest, too, pinning her shoulders to the chair back.

An operating chair. One of the many medical advances that had become standard before she was born. That was why it had tipped with her when she sat up. When the hospital staff chose, it could be moved back down again, opened out to become a full operating table or a recovery bed, tipped back up for when a patient was well enough to sit up and eat.

But why am I in it? Why am I being gotten ready for . . . what? For an operation? For surgery?

Surgery . . . The word, charged as it was with urgency and the beginnings of panic, rang suddenly familiar in her mind. *Surgery. Brain surgery.*

Oh my God. It was just as well she'd drunk all the water, because her hand jerked and she dropped the beaker. It landed on the floor, bounced, and rolled in a half circle before it came to a slightly rocking halt.

That's what they were going to do. They were going to perform brain surgery on her. The brain surgery she'd escaped by fleeing Sekoia. Brain surgery that would burn out the part of her brain that connected her to her twin. Brain surgery that would destroy the link.

It hit her like a blow: shock and fear, then a terrible, rising panic. They couldn't. They couldn't do that to her, not now, not after everything she and Lin had gone through. The weeks of getting to know each other, talking and arguing and fighting and learning how to be sisters.

A helpless, despairing sob rose in her throat. *Lin*. Lin, infuriating and dangerous and more precious than anything. *If they take her, if they take her away—*

Elissa put her hands to her face, trying to crush down the panic and the rising grief, trying to think. *Bruce. Bruce brought me here. If I explain to him, explain how vital the link is, he has to listen, he has to understand.*

Across the room a door slid open. A woman came in, followed by another woman, both dressed in the white uniforms of medical staff. And just behind them, another two figures, one, like the women, in white, the other in a dark color. Elissa tried to see, but her vision was still blurry and the room too bright, and she couldn't make her eyes focus.

"How are you feeling?" said the first woman. From her voice, it had been she who'd been with Elissa when she first woke up.

"How am I *feeling*?" Her voice came out so loud it would have been a shout if it hadn't been shaking so much. "You drugged me! How do you think I'm—"

Then the darker figure moved a little closer, her eyes focused, and she recognized him.

Fury scorched through her, obliterating everything else. "*You*," she said. "*You* drugged me. You—my God, Bruce, you tricked me and drugged me and *abducted* me! What the hell is *wrong* with you?"

"I can explain." An uneasy half grin twitched his lips, the

grin he'd worn when he was in trouble at school and was going to try to bluff his way through it. "Seriously, Elissa, if you listen a minute—"

"You can *explain*? You can explain abducting me? What planet do you even *come* from, to think that's okay? To think that's okay to do to your *sister*?"

"Okay," said Bruce. "Look, it was necessary. Unavoidable."

"*No. It. Wasn't.*" She was too angry to be scared. Too angry to think beyond the outrage of the moment. "What do you think Dad and Mother would say to you? What would they *freaking say* if they knew what you'd—"

Something changed in his face, and she broke off, so appalled that for a moment she couldn't speak.

Would there ever come a time when she would stop being shocked at betrayal?

"They *knew*?" she said. "They knew what you were planning?"

"No, of course not." But he said it too fast, and his gaze, for a second, slipped away from hers.

She stared at him, stiff with shock.

What had he done? What was he involved with? And her *parents*—what had they . . . colluded with? Turned a blind eye to?

Bruce's eyes came back to her. "Dad doesn't know anything," he said, as if he were making a reluctant confession. "Ma . . . she didn't know about this, but she . . . well, she hasn't asked, but I'm pretty sure she knows I'm a member of a covert group. I'm not going to freak her out with the details, but she's not stupid—she knows we sometimes have to take action that's a bit . . . controversial."

Elissa choked over a furious laugh. "'*Controversial*'? You're what, trashing a hotel room?"

"God, *Lissa*, you never listen. Will you just let me *explain*?"

"Oh, please do! I'd love to hear your 'explanation' for why it's okay to *abduct your own sister*."

"Well, if you'd stop *talking* for a goddamn minute—"

"Okay," said the other man. "Enough pleasantries, yeah? Bruce, give your sister the explanation she's asking for, or I'll have to do it."

Jeez, thought Elissa, still furiously sarcastic, *because it makes it so much better to get the explanation of why you've been abducted from the brother who helped with the abduction.*

She looked at him through eyes she'd narrowed to slits. "Well? Do what the man says." A thought struck her. "Oh, but *please* tell me it doesn't include the words, 'it's for your own good.'"

Bruce's eyes flickered again.

"Seriously? God, could you be any more of a cliché?"

"Fine," said Bruce, his voice defensive. "But just because I don't say it doesn't make it any less true. You listen to what I have to say, then *you* decide if it's for your own good to get you away from that freak you're tied to."

"Don't call her—"

"She's dangerous." He spoke over her. "They're all dangerous. That's what everyone keeps trying to tell you. How many deaths will it take before you believe it?"

"Lin is my sister. She's as terrified of hurting me as I am! She'd die rather than—"

"But she won't be able to help it."

And now there was something else in his voice, an added weight—a knowledge.

Elissa's stomach tipped. "What? What do you know?"

"They're all time bombs, Elissa," said Bruce. "We've—our

group—we've managed to access some top-level SFI data. Details of the Spares program. They—the scientists in charge of it—they built a trip switch into each of the Spares' brains."

"A *what*? How can you *build something* into a brain?"

Bruce shrugged. "They were—are—geniuses, Lis. Once they had a brain open, to get it wired up to the energy converters, they could have done just about anything they wanted." A different note had crept into his voice, a suggestion of something she didn't want to hear, something she didn't want to recognize.

He continued, hands in his pockets, voice flat yet still with that undertone to it. "As long as the Spares were secure in the facilities, kept away from their doubles, the bomb would stay defused. The programming is to do with seeing their twins. After a certain number of times—randomly set, it's different with each one—they'll look at their double and it will trip the switch. It'll trigger a psychotic state of extreme aggression—focused primarily against their twin, if he or she is present, against others if not. And when that happens, the trigger won't reset until their twin's dead."

Zee. That's what had happened with Zee. She'd seen it, seen the programming in his brain kick in, seen the switch trip. Seen the bomb explode.

"They made them into weapons," she said, and her voice was nothing but a thread of sound. "They took people and *made them into weapons*."

"No," said Bruce. "That's not what they were trying to do at all. SFI never *wanted* the Spares to meet their doubles. They wanted them for energy, not for weapons. This was a fail-safe, in case the Spares escaped the facilities—or in case some überliberal party came into government and started interfering. They didn't want to lose control of them—"

"Oh *God*, so not true!" Her voice still hadn't regained its strength, but there was enough outrage in it to make Bruce break off. "If they only wanted to stop them escaping, they'd have programmed them to—oh, just self-destruct or something. Making them attack other people—making them attack their *twins*—that's not a *fail-safe*, that's sadism!"

"*Lissa*, you're missing the point. They didn't want to *lose* the Spares. They wanted to get them *back*. Even your typical bleeding-heart clones-rights activists wouldn't be so keen on allowing potential psychos into the community. A few deaths—of Sekoian citizens, not just Spares—and our whole world would have been happy to bundle the Spares back into the facilities. Of course, IPL—helped by you, that is—screwed all that up."

Elissa's stomach seemed to tip all the way over, as if she were going to throw up again. What had happened on the *Phoenix*—Ady's and Zee's deaths—it had been *meant*. It had been *designed*.

"And this is who you're working with now?" she said to Bruce, her voice sounding as nauseated as she felt. "Mad scientists and butchers, who think it's okay to program people to kill other people just so they can stay in control?"

Incongruously, Bruce looked as if she'd insulted him. "We're not working *with* them. I told you, we've accessed some files."

"Oh *please*. You just 'managed' to access some top-level SFI files? These people"—she jerked her hand in a brief wave— "they're not SFI? They're nothing to do with SFI?"

"SFI doesn't exist anymore," the other man said, his voice bland.

"Oh, but their secret files are just randomly lying around? And you're—what are you doing with this information? What's it got to do with abducting me?"

"For God's sake, Elissa, stop saying you've been *abducted*!" Bruce snapped.

Elissa rolled her eyes at him. "I'm *so sorry*. Is that completely insensitive to your feelings? Should I say 'borrowed' instead?" She swung her gaze back to the other man. "So *tell* me. What has this got to do with me? Why did you bring me here? You want to turn me into a weapon—oh, sorry again, Bruce—*fail-safe*, as well?"

"No!" Bruce's voice rose to a shout. "I just don't want you to be tied to one!"

"It's a bit freaking late for that!" Elissa shouted back at him. "What the hell is *wrong* with you? I *told* you how much she matters to me. And you weren't even listening! You were just, what, distracting me until you could call your terrorist friends?"

"I was listening," said Bruce. His voice dropped again, and an intensity came into his face. "The group—they asked me to arrange access to you when we heard you were coming to Philomel. I wasn't sure. I . . . you're my sister, and it might be for the greater good, and it might be unavoidable, but I . . ." He shrugged. "I don't like this new world you gave me, Lissa. I like a world where I don't have to think about breaking the law, because the law is fair."

"The Sekoian laws weren't *fair*—"

"They were to *me*!" Their eyes met, and again, in Bruce's, there was that misery that, despite Elissa's anger and fear, caught at her, made her unable, for a moment, to snap back at him.

Bruce swallowed, getting control again. "Then I talked to you. And you—God, Lis, you keep talking about how you love her, and you don't even know why. She's taking over your head, and she can control you, and you don't even *like* it, and yet you're still talking like it's okay, like it's a real relationship you've got with her."

"*No.*" She stared at him, appalled at how her own words were being used against her. "No, Bruce, that's not how it is—"

"Yeah, it is. It's you who can't see it."

"No. *No.* I—you can't understand what it's like." But even as she spoke, she knew there would be no convincing him. All too clearly now, she heard her own words, convicting herself—convicting Lin. She'd been stupid, and she'd relaxed her guard, and she'd reduced all the complicatedness of her bond with her twin to something that Bruce had mistaken for . . . well, like he'd said, parasitic mind control.

And now . . . *I don't want you to be tied to one,* he'd said. Cold slid through her, sponging away the anger.

"Bruce," she said, "please, listen. You've gotten it wrong. I do love her. I do. It's real. She matters—I swear, she matters more than anything."

"I know," Bruce said, and for a second relief broke over her. But then she heard the note in his voice, saw the look, unhappy but unyielding, in his face. "That's what's not natural, Lis. I promise, we're going to fix it and then you'll realize. Then you'll see things as they are."

Elissa's hands started shaking. "*No.* Bruce, you can't be really planning—God, Bruce, please, *please* don't say you're going to do that operation."

His eyes met hers. He didn't answer, but by then she didn't need him to. By then she already knew.

Elissa screamed. For the next two minutes she lost all ability to reason, or argue, or plead. She just screamed, and fought, twisting and scratching as they closed around her, tipped her back in the chair and forced straps over her elbows and wrists and across her throat.

"I thought you said she'd be reasonable once she understood!" one of the women snapped at Bruce as she dragged a strap tight and stepped back, furiously dabbing at a long scratch down her cheek.

Bruce had helped them pin her down, but he'd backed away now, a white shade to his lips. "I–I thought–God, Lissa, don't do this. It'll be okay once it's over."

"When it's over I'll be *dead*!" she shrieked at him, incoherent with grief and rage. "If you take her away–if you take her–I'll die. I'll *die*, do you hear me? Bruce, *please, please–*"

Misery rose in his face. Misery, and pity, all the worse because it was pity for the wrong thing, pity he shouldn't be feeling for her now.

"It's not real," he said as the woman she'd met first swabbed her arm, leaving a patch of cold. "Lis, what you're feeling–it's not from you."

"It *is*. *It is*." How could he be so blind, so stubborn? "Bruce, don't let them–"

The other man wheeled over a stand with tubes dangling from it. At the far end of the room the second woman was washing up to her elbows in a deep sink. The first woman took Elissa's blood pressure, then tied a tourniquet around her upper arm.

They were talking to each other, but Elissa's brain had closed them off. Bruce didn't want to do this–he'd struggled with it to start with, he was only doing it now because he thought it was for her benefit. If she could get through to him—

But it was too late. One of the others said something to him, and, his face set in miserable lines, he turned away toward the door.

Elissa shrieked after him. "Bruce! Listen to me! *Listen!*"

He didn't look back. He opened the door, went through, and it shut behind him.

A huge, helpless sob rose in Elissa's chest, swelling against the straps, making her feel she couldn't breathe. *Lin,* she sent out, desperate, as she had before. *Lin, I'm sorry. I love you.*

But it was like calling into a void. Either she'd used up all her own telepathic energy earlier, with the frantic cry that hadn't, after all, brought Lin and Cadan to save her, or the stealth flyer had taken her so far across the planet that she was, for the first time, entirely out of range.

I thought I wanted her out of my head. I was so stupid. So wrong. Lin. Lin. Oh God . . .

There was a mask dangling from the stand. A mask with tubes attached. The woman who'd been washing came over now, sliding her hands into thin white surgical gloves, and nodded to the woman who'd been prepping Elissa, who took up the mask and held it ready.

The gloved woman picked up a syringe, snapped the protective end off the needle, and ran it into Elissa's arm. Mist fell over everything. Mist that dulled sight and sound and the disinfectant-and-plastic smells of the room.

Someone tipped Elissa's head back. She felt the mask descend. And then, for the second time since arriving on Philomel, nothing.

TWENTY-ONE

THIS TIME Elissa woke, not as if from a nightmare, but into one.

She was lying in a different room, in the same chair, now tipped back to make a bed. She was no longer strapped down, and there was a pillow, soft as a marshmallow, under her head. A table stood beside the bed, with a transparent goblet of water within easy reach on it. The room's lighting was soft, a gentle, warming amber, and the scent of chamomile and orange blossom floated in the air, overlaying the sharp chemical smell of the hospital.

A whole bunch of things that had been designed—presumably—to provide comfort.

They didn't.

The moment she came to, the loss struck her.

She found herself doubled over beneath it, pain so intense that it took every scrap of breath, leaving her gasping, biting down onto her fist as if that smaller pain could take away some of the greater.

It wiped out everything she'd thought had caused her pain before, reducing it all to pinpricks, gnat bites, stupid stuff that had hurt only her body, hadn't touched her mind, stuff that, compared to this, wouldn't even *be* pain.

This, this screaming sense of loss that went through and through her, scouring the inside of her skull, flaring black lightning in her thoughts and her brain and along every nerve . . . *oh God, if I could swap it all* . . .

Her teeth clenched on her knuckles so hard that an ache stabbed through her jaw, but it didn't help, it didn't distract from the pain, it didn't do anything.

A snatch of thought came–*my father–how did my father ever survive this?*–and went. There was no room for anything but the pain, the abyss of whirling empty blackness rising to consume her, starless and airless and forever.

It wasn't just that, as before, she couldn't reach Lin, couldn't speak to her. It was as if something of herself had been torn away, something that had always been there, that she'd grown so used to she hadn't even been consciously aware of its existence.

Like a backdrop to her mind, a sun that cast everything in its light, a sense–like the sense of taste–that you only noticed when it was gone.

Her whole life, whether she'd known it or not, her sister had been there, sometimes a voice like her own voice, sometimes nothing more than a silent presence in her mind. But always there, only unacknowledged because she was so familiar it would have been like acknowledging part of Elissa's own body, pointing out one of her senses to herself.

No wonder she'd come so quickly to love Lin–it hadn't been like meeting someone new, it had been like opening her eyes to see someone who'd always been there.

And now, for the first time, she wasn't there. Not just silent, not just distant. *Not there.*

The loss stabbed through her again, jackknifing her body against the bed, and the blackness rose, a screaming cloud that blotted out everything.

It didn't recede, it didn't grow any less, but after a while Elissa managed to force her body to unclench. She took her hand away from her mouth, seeing the marks her teeth had made redden as the blood flowed back beneath the skin.

She pushed herself up to a sitting position on the bed and, a little shakily, moved her legs so they dangled over the side. No nausea hit her this time—they must have given her something to suppress it, or maybe the anesthetic they'd used hadn't been so swift acting as the one they'd used to abduct her.

She had to think. What was going to happen now? Having accomplished what they'd intended, were they really going to take her back? Or had they just been saying that, using it, like they'd used the warmth and the scents and the soft pillow, to try to keep her calm? Had they been just trying to ensure she didn't fight?

For an instant, the thoughts—sensible, rational thoughts, devoid of emotion—formed a barrier, a welcome barrier that she found herself clinging to. Maybe clinging too hard, because all at once it crumbled. *Lin. They took Lin away.*

She was staring once more into the abyss. Its darkness spiraled up into her head, making her dizzy.

And within the darkness, grief was building, the blind pain of loss growing into something more focused, something that said *this is forever, this is always, this is what you're going to have to live with the rest of your life, forever and ever and ever.*

But although she felt it, swelling in her chest, behind her eyes, tightening in her lips, making her hands heavy, no tears came to release it. Something within her wanted to scream, but when she opened her mouth the only sound she made was one like a bitten-down whimper.

The soft *whoosh* of a door opening. A voice.

"Lissa? God, *Lis*, what's wrong?"

Bruce's voice. Bruce's stupid, unaware, unrealizing voice. *It's for your own good,* he'd said. *Your own good, Lissa.* And *It'll be okay once it's over.*

She looked up at him, and anger took her so that for a moment she couldn't even see. "What's *wrong*?"

"Does it hurt? Your head? The anesthetic—it's not supposed to leave you in any pain."

My head? She hadn't even thought that that, of course, it was an operation, and operations left physical scars. She raised a heavy hand, patted her fingers over her head—and found a small patch, still numb, where the hair had been shaved off, a tiny seam running through it.

The pain hit her again, as if a huge hand had descended, thumping all the breath from her body. *That's where they took it from. The link. That's where they went to burn it out.*

"God, Lissa, it is still hurting, isn't it?" Bruce's voice was full of compunction. "I'm sorry, they swore it wouldn't. I'll go get someone to give you something—"

Elissa had been moving through pain and grief as if through deep water, but at this rage fired her, bringing her head up to stare at him. "To give me *what*? What do you think your band of terrorists has that can help with this?"

"Lissa, look, I'm sorry it's left you in pain—"

"You took my twin!" she shrieked at him, on her feet, swaying, her head spinning, not knowing how she'd gotten there. "Can they give her back? Can they make the link again? *That's* the pain, Bruce! That's the pain you left me in! I told you, I *told* you and you wouldn't listen!"

For a moment he just stared at her, his face frozen, his mouth just opening on something else he'd been going to say, not turning as the door whooshed open again and two figures entered, wearing stealth-flyer uniforms. "Lissa, no, that makes no sense. It must be just shock from the operation–"

For an instant Elissa thought her head would explode. Rage and grief and horror swept through her. She knocked against the wheeled operating bed, which in turn knocked against the table at its side, rattling the plastic goblet of water. Elissa spun and gave the bed a violent thrust, sending it spinning across the room. The table fell, clattering. The goblet was flung off it, and the water splashed across the floor.

"Shock?" Her voice no longer sounded like hers. *"Just* shock? You have no idea what you're talking about! If you hadn't knocked me out before you did that to me, I'd be *dead* of what you're calling just shock, you *stupid, freaking*–" She stopped, her chest heaving and burning, her teeth clenching so hard her jaw spasmed. There were no words bad enough.

The people in the flyer uniforms were coming toward her now, moving either side of Bruce. She wasn't scared of them anymore. There was nothing they could do anymore. Nothing that could hurt her worse than she was already hurt.

Behind them, by the door, Bruce stood still. Something of her anguish must have gotten through to him: He'd gone a shade paler, and his mouth was set. "Lissa," he said. "Stop.

It's okay. We're taking you back now. If she still matters, if she really does matter that much, you can see her."

You can see her. You can see her. The words echoed in her ears. Bruce didn't understand, he *still* didn't understand, but that wasn't what made what he'd said echo against the inside of her skull, a throbbing, ominous beat as if she were invisibly bleeding to death.

There have been no attacks with the younger age groups, Cadan had said. And Bruce had explained why. The thing they'd done, the horrible time bomb SFI had built into the Spares, they'd only built it into them once they reached thirteen or so. And they'd set it to be triggered by contact with their twins—again, what Bruce had said explained what the IPL scientists had found, that the attacks had happened only with Spares who'd been reunited with their twins at least—what was it?—two weeks ago?

One thing remained, that Cadan had mentioned but that Bruce hadn't. Either because his gang of terrorists hadn't told him, or because they didn't know either.

She remembered Cadan's smile as he met her eyes, and the relief in his face, relief because he knew what he was saying meant for her and for Lin. The attacks, he'd said, had happened only to those pairs with no current telepathic connection.

He'd added, of course, that it didn't guarantee anything, added that all the Spares' brain scans showed abnormal activity. And he was right. Lin, like all the other Spares, had that same time bomb built into her brain. Lin, like all the other Spares, had the potential to go psychotically insane.

But she'd been with Elissa for more than six weeks now, far, far longer than any of the other Spares had been with their twins, and not only had she *not* gone insane, there'd been no traces of the fugue state that Zee and others had shown.

Because of the link. Because of the link that, with us, is stronger than with anyone else we've met, stronger than with any of the other Spares and their twins.

The uniformed people took hold of Elissa's arms, led her toward the door. She went, unresisting. *It was the link that kept me safe. The link that blocked the trigger in Lin's brain. The link they've destroyed.*

They took her through long windowless corridors, into an elevator that rose, whining, past floor after floor. Bruce, silent, followed.

He doesn't know. He thought breaking the tie between us would keep me away from her, would keep me safe.

But the others . . . She gave a quick look sideways at the unreadable face of one of her escorts. *Bruce didn't know. But someone did. These people—I'm not their sister, they weren't going to risk that kind of abduction, plus an illegal operation, out of altruism.*

SFI had built time bombs into the Spares as a safeguard, as a way to get the Spares back into their custody if they should ever escape. *A few deaths,* Bruce had said, *and our whole world would have been happy to bundle the Spares back into the facilities.*

How different would it be now? With so many Sekoian citizens—and Philomelen citizens, for all she knew—still convinced Spares were nonhuman, scarcely different from full-body clones? How many deaths would it take before they'd be happy to hustle the Spares back to Sekoia . . . or into the custody of anyone willing to take them?

And who would those willing people be? As the elevator came to a halt, as its doors opened on chill sunlight and the solid shadow of the waiting stealth flyer, Elissa's gaze slid again toward the people on either side of her. *You didn't just find SFI files,* she thought. *And you're only unwillingly ex-SFI. You want to be current SFI. You want things back as they were, with ships powered by imprisoned Spares. For you, the Spares going crazy, getting more and more people to see them as dangerous—that's exactly what you want.*

But with most of the Spares, the damage they could cause was limited. A death here, a death there. It wasn't enough. Not enough to make a whole planet's population rebel against IPL's edict that the Spares be kept safe, given sanctuary.

But Lin . . . Lin wasn't just telepathic, or empathic. Lin's power wasn't limited to just the link with her twin. Lin could set buildings on fire, bend metal, explode ships. Lin could kill with her mind as easily as ordinary people could with a fighter ship.

If Lin went insane, it wouldn't be just damage she'd cause. It would be devastation.

And—once again, she heard Bruce's voice, explaining what the SFI had done to the Spares, explaining what had happened to Zee—*the trigger won't reset until I'm dead. If that happens to Lin, it won't be just a short-term thing, something we can contain, something that we can fix. It'll be the end, for both of us.*

Elissa didn't know why the link, in itself, should have been powerful enough to block the vicious trigger SFI had put in Lin's brain. But she was sure, beyond doubt, that it had.

And now . . .

And now they'd destroyed it.

The stealth flyer didn't, of course, take Elissa and Bruce back as far as the spaceport. It dumped them out halfway along the side of the valley leading up to it, took off, and its outline had faded away into the sky before Elissa had even begun to get her bearings.

Not that she was managing to do so quickly. She still felt as if she stood on the edge of screaming, empty blackness, the only coherent thoughts in her brain her horrified realization of what the destruction of the link meant. And whenever she looked at her brother, a murderous anger so strong that, had she been capable of feeling any other emotions, would have frightened her.

Bruce had his thumb on his com-unit, reactivating it.

"What the hell is the use of that?" Elissa said, hating him. "SFI aren't going to come for you here."

He shot her a quick look. It was the first thing she'd said to him since the recovery room she'd woken in, and ever since then he'd seemed to find it difficult to meet her eyes.

"It has a standard SOS beacon programmed in," he said. "The spaceport people will be looking out for us by now, anyway. We disappeared from the balcony—Mother will be frantic."

It was the first Elissa had thought about that, and she couldn't summon up much reaction to it. "Way to go on considering her feelings, then," she said.

Bruce's eyes met hers so briefly she couldn't catch the expression in them. "I didn't have a choice." Then: "I—I didn't think I had a choice."

Elissa's knees were beginning to fold beneath her. She let them, sinking to kneel on the moss-covered rock. "If those are doubts, it's a bit freaking late. And why are you coming back too, anyway? If you think sisterly loyalty is going to stop me telling everyone what you did—"

"Of course not!" For the first time he met her eyes fully, and she saw a glimpse of his familiar arrogance. "I wasn't going to disappear and leave Ma worrying about me. I knew I'd have to come back. I knew that was the sacrifice I'd have to make."

Sacrifice? Again, fury rose into her eyes, making her blind. *You call* that *a sacrifice?*

It must have showed in her face, because Bruce didn't say anything for some minutes—not until they heard, far off, the thrum of a flyer. Then he cleared his throat.

"Lissa, listen, what you said, back there—it's not really hurting, is it? I mean, it's not *real*, it's just some kind of mental thing—it can't really hurt you."

Elissa put up her hand, a barrier so she needn't see his face, getting to her still-shaky legs, looking in the direction of the flyer. It was sleek, silver, a shape she thought was familiar. "I already told you, and you didn't listen. When it mattered, when I needed you to listen, you didn't. You think I'm going to waste my breath on telling you again?"

"Lissa—" His voice was half-guilty, half-frustrated, and maybe there was hurt there too, somewhere underneath, and a willingness to believe her.

She didn't care. She turned away from him, walking toward where their rescue vehicle—the *Phoenix*'s shuttlebug—was descending.

"Lissa."

"I wish I had my twin's powers," she said, not looking back, bitterness flooding her voice. "If I did, I'd burn you alive."

And then, finally, Bruce didn't say anything else.

The shuttlebug landed. The door slid back and a tall, long-armed figure jumped out to stride along the ridge toward them, calling her name even before he reached her.

"Lissa, thank God. We've been tearing the spaceport apart." Ivan wrapped her in a hug that took her off her feet, and she felt him look over her head at Bruce. "You've been gone two hours. What the hell happened here?"

Markus had gotten out of the shuttlebug after Ivan and was only a little way behind him. And now a third figure jumped down, fair hair glinting in the sun.

Behind Elissa, Bruce cleared his throat. "I'm a member of a group of freedom fighters. I helped them take my sister away in order—"

"You did *what*?" Ivan's voice boomed in Elissa's ear. "You stupid, wretched boy, what the hell were you thinking?"

Even without looking at him, Elissa could tell Bruce was fighting to make his voice sound certain. "It's the group's belief that the Spares are too dangerous to be permitted to join the general population. With this in mind, we found it necessary to take Lissa—"

"*Lissa.*" Cadan had reached them.

As Ivan let her go, Cadan's arms came around her. "Lissa. God—" He looked down into her eyes, and broke off. His face went still. His hands tightened on her arms and his head moved, just fractionally, up so he could look at Bruce. "What happened? What happened to her?"

"I'm explaining, the group I'm with found it necessary—"

Cadan's voice lashed out like a whip. "*What happened to her?*"

"They burned out her link with her Spare," said Bruce.

Elissa felt the shock of the words go through Cadan's body. Where he held her, his arms went rigid. "They did what?"

"They burned out the link." There was defiance in Bruce's

voice now. "She told me about it, Cadan. The Spare—she's been taking over Lissa's mind. It's no good for her. All it does is put her in danger. The group, we agreed, it would be better if she lost it, if she could go back to being normal—"

"We? This group—you're with them?"

"The boy's a *freedom fighter*, Cadan," Ivan said. He gave a dry twist to the words. "He was telling us a minute ago. He didn't quite get as far as saying freedom from what, or who he's fighting." There was contempt in his voice, and Bruce flushed.

"*You* let them do this to her?" said Cadan. "You *let* them?"

"He *helped* them." Ivan's voice was still dry. "However they got hold of her, they wouldn't have managed it without her big brother's help."

"Cadan, will you listen to me, for God's sake!" Bruce was angry now, his voice rising in frustration.

"Listen to you?" Gently, Cadan let go of Elissa's arms. He turned toward her brother, every movement tightly controlled. "*Listen* to you? Do you have any idea what you did? We thought she was dead!"

"What?" Bruce took half a step back. "Why—"

"Because I thought she was."

Elissa hadn't heard the footsteps on the moss-covered rock, hadn't seen the fourth and fifth figures get out of the shuttlebug. But the voice was as familiar as her own.

Lin.

She spun around. Six feet away, Lin stood as rigid as the rock beneath their feet, her face chalky, her hands behind her back. At her shoulder, Edward Ivory waited. There was a gray look to his face. If Lin had thought Elissa was dead, then he must have thought it too.

But right now Elissa had no room to spare for anyone but her sister. *"Lin."*

"Don't come near me." Lin's lips, nearly as pale as her face, hardly moved. Her voice was flat, and she kept her gaze on the ground. "I thought you were dead. I—"

"You felt the link die."

"Yes."

"Oh God, Lin . . ." She hadn't even thought. Blinded by her own anguish, falling through the abyss, it hadn't even crossed her mind that the loss of their link would have hit Lin, too. And, unlike Elissa, her sister would have had no warning.

"Don't come near me!" Lin's voice stabbed like lightning, and Elissa realized that, without thinking, without meaning to, she'd started to move toward her twin. Still, Lin wasn't looking at her. She was looking past Elissa, into the distance. "I'm not safe. Not for you. I had to come, I *had* to, once they said a message was coming in, once they tracked it to him"— her eyes flicked in Bruce's direction—"but that's all. Once we're back, I—" Her voice cracked. She squeezed her eyes shut as if she could only continue talking if she could shut out the world. "I have to go away. I can't see you anymore."

Oh God. Oh God, of course that's true. It was the only way to keep either of them safe—Elissa from being killed, Lin from becoming her killer. *But we can't . . . We've already lost the link, we can't be totally separated as well!*

It was too much to comprehend, too much, all at once, to even begin to face. Elissa put her hands over her own eyes, shutting it all out, trying to shut out even her thoughts.

"Dad," said Bruce, somewhere, the sound of his voice grating on every one of her exposed nerves. "Cadan . . . Look,

I'm sorry, okay? I didn't mean it to turn out like this. But listen, I did it for her sake. She's been tied to this—this *psycho* for weeks. God, for longer than that! She can't think for herself anymore, she's damaged. She said herself, she wants her out of her head! Okay, drastic measures, yeah, but it's *for her sake*—"

"You stupid bastard, will you shut the hell up?" Elissa had never heard Cadan sound like that before. And when she took her hands down and looked at him, she thought she would scarcely have recognized his face, either.

Behind Lin, Mr. Ivory said, "Cadan, there's no need for—"

Bruce took half a step back. "*Hey*. I don't—"

Mr. Ivory might as well not have spoken. Cadan's eyes, full of contempt, stayed fixed on Bruce. "I said *shut up*." The whiplash cracked again through his voice. "You have no idea what you've done. Carry on explaining yourself to the authorities back at the spaceport. And anyone else you want. No one here has the slightest interest in hearing anything else you have to say."

He turned away from Bruce and put an arm around Elissa. She could feel the suppressed anger like an electric current going through him, but his touch was gentle, as was his voice. "Let's get back, okay?"

Elissa looked toward her sister. "Lin. Someone has to—"

"Someone is." Ivan's voice was as gentle as Cadan's had been.

Edward Ivory put his arm around Lin's shoulders, turning her in the direction of the shuttlebug. It was the way he'd touched Elissa when, as an eight-year-old, she'd gone through a spell of walking in her sleep, every night waking to sobbing panic in different places all over the house. Each time, her father had steered her back to bed like that, his arm around her shoulders, his hand a reassuring clasp on her upper arm.

For an instant, seeing him like that with Lin brought a fleeting comfort. Then, as Lin turned, Elissa saw why she'd kept her hands behind her back.

Lin's wrists were handcuffed together.

She came because she was afraid I was dead. They all came, all the people who love me. And yet, out of all of them, Lin could only come if she was wearing handcuffs. Because otherwise just being near me puts us in too much danger.

I should go to her. Comfort her. Tell her . . .

But there was nothing *to* tell her. No comfort Elissa could offer. And every time Lin looked at her, every time their eyes met, it might be the last time, it might be the trigger that would get Elissa killed. And God knew who else.

Bruce called it a fail-safe. And it might have been meant that way. But that's not what it's done to Lin. It's turned her into a weapon.

At the entrance of the shuttlebug, as Lin moved to climb in, Mr. Ivory's hand under her elbow to support her, Elissa caught a glimpse of her sister's face. Grief and pain rushed over her all over again, choking her, drowning her.

"Lin."

Caught unaware, Lin looked back. For the first time since they'd gotten off the *Phoenix*, their eyes met. Elissa looked into her twin's eyes, and it was like looking into emptiness.

"You said it to him," said Lin.

"What?"

A spasm passed over Lin's face. "You said to him—to your brother—that you wanted me out of your head. Like you said back on Sekoia. Like I"—her face quivered again—"like I *heard* back on Sekoia."

No. That's not how I meant it. That's not the message you're supposed to get.

But the pain and the grief were still drowning her. She couldn't get her thoughts together, couldn't form the words she needed to say. She just stared past her father at her sister, trying to make her lips move, knowing she must look as blank as if she had no emotions at all.

"I–" she managed. "Lin . . ."

For an endless second longer she looked at her sister's face, saw the pain rising, a dark tide, in Lin's eyes. They'd lost so much, but they couldn't have lost everything. There must be something–there must be *something* left–

But she was cold, and numb, and drowning, and whatever was left, she couldn't find it.

"At least you got what you wanted," said Lin. Her eyes left Elissa's. She turned and climbed, her cuffed hands, despite Mr. Ivory's help, making her clumsy, up into the shuttlebug.

TWENTY-TWO

"YOU WILL survive this," said Cadan.

They were back at the spaceport, in a room in the small spaceport hospital. The moment they'd landed, Lin had been whisked away to secure accommodation. She hadn't looked at Elissa again, and although Elissa knew she couldn't just leave it like that, with Lin thinking this was what she wanted, for the moment Elissa had neither the emotional nor mental energy to do anything to help.

Now, from the couch where she sat, waiting for a doctor to come and inspect her, it seemed to take every last scrap of energy to raise her head to look at Cadan.

"You will," he repeated, his voice insistent. "Your dad did."

The last scrap of energy bled away. Elissa slumped. "Hardly."

"That's not going to be what it's like for you. It's not the same. At least you know what's happened."

It wasn't just insistence in his voice. It was fear. And if

she had any emotion left to spare, she'd be able to feel for him, seeing her like this, beaten and empty . . . faded like her father had always been faded.

I can't live like he did. If I could at least see Lin . . . we're still sisters. The relationship we've got wasn't all built on the link. We must be able to salvage something. . . .

She didn't realize she'd said the last sentence aloud until Cadan answered her. "Of course you can. Of *course* you can."

She looked at him. "You think we . . ." But then the loss was on her again, washing everything out of her mind, leaving her with just the blackness. "Oh God, Cadan, they took the link. It was everything—"

"No it wasn't." While she was drowning, blind and lost in the blackness, he'd gotten up, and now, as she resurfaced, he was on one knee in front of her, his hands gripping hers, pulling her back. "Lis, you're all kinds of shocked right now. And Lin is too. But you're still you, and she's still your twin. You've lost the link, but you've got a thousand other things to build on. Your father's twin *died*—he never got the chance to salvage anything. You and Lin can."

"How?" Suddenly furious, she tore her hands from his. "How can we build *anything*, when I can't even see her? When, if I do, at some point she's going to try to kill me?"

All at once Cadan's eyes blazed into hers, filled with as much fury as she was. "Seriously? You're going to give up like that?"

"What choice do I have?"

"For God's sake, Lis. Think! We don't even have all the information about the trigger yet! They'll be scanning Lin's brain now. They're collecting more data every minute. There's going to be a way to block it, or reverse it, or *something*. Of all the organs in the human body, the brain is the one *most* able to repair itself—you *know* that."

"Do I?"

"Well, if you don't, you should! What did you go to science classes for? People whose *speech centers* have been destroyed have learned to talk again. The brain *repairs itself*."

But his words had stopped making sense. They fell apart, bright shreds floating on another rising tide of pain. Elissa put her hands to her head, shutting her eyes, feeling, for the first time, slow, hot tears squeeze out from under her eyelids.

Distantly, she was aware that Cadan had put his arms around her. "I'm sorry," he said, his voice coming from far away, beyond the dark sea drowning her. "I'm just bullying you. It's too soon. Just hang on, okay? It'll get better. You'll recover."

Even farther away, the door opened. The doctor, come to inspect her, to check that she wasn't—physically—hurt any worse than the tiny wound in her skull. Elissa's skin seemed to shrink. She didn't want to be touched. Not yet. Not yet.

Except it wasn't the doctor. Her father's voice spoke.

"Lissa? I thought you'd want to know. They've tracked down the terrorist group. They've been arrested. They're in custody, kept at the place they took you. It's an underground base they managed to set up in a system of caves beneath the mountain range. It was easy to secure—they're being kept there until they can be moved to one of Philomel's prisons."

Elissa managed to nod. She guessed that was a good thing. In a vague, floating bit of her mind, she wondered if Bruce had also been arrested. Or if his explanations—*it was for her own good, it was for her sake*—had convinced the IPL authorities the way they hadn't convinced her, or Ivan, or Cadan.

"I'm going to let Lin know now," her father's voice continued. "Her directions were spot on—IPL forces would never have tracked them, or at least nothing like so fast, if she hadn't been able to point out your general location on a map."

Against the stinging, heavy waves, Elissa opened her eyes. "Lin found me? But I tried—when I was there, at the place they took me—I couldn't reach her."

"She did, all the same," her father said. "She knew the instant you were taken. She screamed herself hoarse raising the alarm. Then you lost consciousness, and then you were so far away she couldn't pinpoint your location. But she could say what direction you'd been taken in." He nodded toward Cadan. "Cadan was in the shuttlebug, ready to join IPL and local forces to make sweeps of the area, when Bruce's SOS came through."

He turned back to the door. "She'll be glad, I hope, to know your abductors are to face justice, at least."

Elissa shut her eyes again. How could he, of all people, not understand that it made no difference who was to face whatever he thought of as justice? The words she'd screamed at Bruce flared once more across her brain. *Can they give her back? Can they make the link again?* Aside from that, there wasn't going to be any justice.

She was vaguely aware of her father lingering, hesitating a moment by the door, as if one of them was supposed to say something else. But she didn't speak, and nor did Cadan, and after a minute her father went away.

Shortly afterward the doctor came. He shone a light in her eyes, took a blood test, inspected her head, and told her that a therapist would come to see her later.

A therapist? Elissa had to bite down on a sudden wave of hysterical laughter. What was a therapist going to do?

Cadan had been sitting away across the room during the doctor's visit, but as the door shut behind the doctor, his eyes met Elissa's.

"It might be helpful," he said, but he couldn't suppress the wry twist to his voice.

Elissa's laughter broke out. "Oh for God's *sake*," she managed to say. "*How?* What experience can a therapist possibly have that's going to help with *this*?"

Cadan shrugged. "Yeah, I know." He looked at her, and his lips twitched. "Lis, if you don't stop laughing I'm going to start, and then it's going to look like I actually find it funny. Which I can assure you I really don't."

Elissa waved a hand, almost beyond speech. "It's fine. I promise I–" The laughter took her again and she had to stop, wiping her eyes. "I promise I won't get offended. I–" She choked on another burst of laughter. "It's really *not* funny, I know, but–"

The door hushed open, and Elissa's laughter cut off as suddenly as if someone had slapped a hand across her mouth. Her new visitor was Bruce.

Cadan was on his feet the moment Bruce stepped into the room. "I don't think we need you here."

"I didn't come to see you," Bruce said, looking straight across the room, not even glancing at Cadan. "I came to see Lissa."

Although he was looking at her, he wasn't quite meeting her eyes. She paused a moment to see if he would, but he stayed in the same position, waiting for her to speak.

"They didn't put you in prison yet, then," she said to him.

Bruce swallowed. "They might yet." He put his hand out, extending his wrist so his sleeve pulled back and she could see the steel band that had replaced his com-unit. "I'm security-shackled. If I so much as go out on the balcony, it'll set off alarms."

"Whoa," said Cadan, his voice heavy with sarcasm. "Severe sentence."

"It's not my sentence." Bruce still didn't look at him. "It's to make sure I don't escape trial. Lissa . . ."

"*What?*" She didn't even try to hold back the hostility in her voice.

Finally, Bruce met her eyes. "I'm sorry," he said. "I was as stupid as Cadan called me. I thought I was doing the right thing."

Anger licked through her. If he was going to try to *excuse* himself . . . "You really weren't."

"I know. Like I said, I was stupid."

"And what? Is that supposed to fix things?"

"No." He held her gaze, although it looked like an effort. "I know I can't fix what—what I've done to you."

"And Lin."

"And Lin. I'm just . . . God, I'm so sorry, Lissa. They—the group—they approached me a week or so after we arrived on Philomel. They said they wanted to learn from SFI's mistakes, they wanted to restore Sekoia. I did ask some questions, but not enough. I—the thought of doing something, *anything* . . ."

He looked miserable, every scrap of arrogance—or even confidence—as absent as if it had been beaten out of him. She'd have felt pity if it hadn't been for the image in her mind of how Lin had looked. Lin, who hadn't done anything to deserve it. Lin, who'd just been trying to learn how to live in a world she didn't understand.

"Was it really for my sake?" she asked him, her voice cold.

For a moment Bruce's eyes dropped, then he forced them back up to hers. "No. I mean, hearing what you said, earlier—that was like the catalyst. But I"—he swallowed—"I was looking for a reason to do it. I . . ." He spread his hands, a helpless gesture. "They said they were going to restore Sekoia. Said they were going to restore our space force."

"At what freaking cost?" Cadan interjected. "For God's *sake*, Bruce, how SFI powered the hyperdrives isn't a secret anymore. You must have known what they were planning—how they were going to restore it."

For the first time Bruce looked at him. His shoulders were slumped, a gesture as helpless as the way he'd spread his hands. "I thought of them like clones. The Spares. They *said* they were like clones. That's how people keep talking about them." He swallowed. "It's . . . God, Lissa, look. We had *lives* on Sekoia, and all of a sudden they're over. Dad's career, mine, everything Ma cared about. We can't even stay on our own planet. And it's because of these . . . these *Spares*, that we didn't even know existed. And then we're being told *we're* not the victims, *they* are. They're getting priority—safe houses, expedited evacuation, freaking *compensation*."

Anger flamed up once more behind Elissa's eyes. "You think *you're* more of a victim than they are? Because you lost *your career?*"

"Lissa, for God's sake, I'm trying to *explain*. That's not just how Ma and I thought—it's how everyone's been thinking. We had a whole *world*, and then it got taken away from us in order to protect these . . . products of abnormal births, creatures we didn't even know existed, that people were saying shouldn't have been *allowed* to exist. And then we're being told we're supposed to feel sorry for them, that we *owe* them something. It was like—I mean, yeah, human rights and everything, they're important, we all know that. But this was like human rights gone mad."

"*Human rights gone mad?* Are you even *listening* to yourself?"

"I'm *explaining* to you, Lissa! We *weren't thinking of them* as human. None of us. We were thinking of them as . . . things . . . creatures . . . that were just kind of human shaped."

"So you're *not* sorry! You're sorry for what it did to me—your nice clean *all-human* sister. You don't care what it did to Lin!"

"I do care." His eyes came back to hers.

"*Why?* Why would you, if you think all she is is"—she bit out the words with furious emphasis—"'*kind of human shaped*'?"

"I don't think that anymore. I—Lis, I know she's human. I know."

"*How?*"

"She looks like you," said Bruce, miserable. "When she came to fetch us, with Cadan and the others, when I saw her . . . She looks just like you."

"Yeah, you keep saying. Like a *clone*."

"No. I don't mean just . . . just physically. Just her features. I . . ." He swallowed again. "Her eyes. The way she *looked*. It's your expression, Lis. It's the way you looked when you were younger, when someone hurt your feelings, when you wanted to cry but you were determined not to." His mouth twisted a little. "I'm your mean big brother, after all—that's the sort of expression I recognize."

He stopped talking, folding his arms across himself, his shoulders hunching.

Elissa looked at him. What he'd done to her and Lin— it was worse than a betrayal, it was so beyond horrific she didn't know if she'd ever be able to forgive him. But seeing him like this, knowing that he, too, was feeling the impact of what he'd done, knowing that he understood how bad it was . . . She might not be able to forgive him, but at least she no longer hated him.

"Bit late." There was no forgiveness in Cadan's voice.

"I know," said Bruce. "Lissa, look, if I could do something to fix it, I would."

You can't. She was going to say it, but something caught her back. He couldn't fix what he'd done to her and Lin. But there were hundreds of Spares. There wasn't anything Bruce could do to help her and Lin, but was there anything he could do to help the others?

It was just the germ of an idea in her head. Nothing fully formed, nothing she could say out loud. Not yet. But . . .

Days ago, just after landing on Sekoia, she'd thought: *Calling them clones isn't just semantics! If everyone keeps calling them clones then everyone keeps seeing them as nonhuman . . . It does matter. It matters what you call them.*

She'd been right. Like so many people, Bruce had called the Spares "clones." He'd seen them as nonhuman. He, like so many others, had been willing to use them—despite IPL declaring it illegal, despite being told that the procedures caused pain.

Because he never met any.

It was like tiny lights snapping on, one after another, all

over her brain. Connection after connection being made, things falling into place, thoughts making sense.

IPL did it wrong. They were trying to protect the Spares, but by keeping them away from ordinary citizens, they made them even more alien than they would have been. Those people on the rescue flyer, back on Sekoia—they were scared of Lin, and angry that she was allowed to talk to them like a normal person. But if they'd gotten a chance to know her . . . Like I have, and Cadan, and Felicia and Ivan, and like how Cadan's parents got to know the Spares at the safe house, and how Sofia and Ady got to know their twins, even though there was no link to help them . . .

And now Bruce. Bruce had changed his mind. Not because of big ethical considerations, like those that Markus or Commander Dacre had. And not even because he'd had a chance to get to know Lin. Just because he'd looked at her and seen, in her face, emotions—human emotions—that he recognized.

If other people could do the same, those other people who still see Spares as nothing more than full-body clones . . .

Her mind returned to the people on the rescue flyer. *I couldn't persuade them to see her differently. But then I couldn't persuade Bruce, either—he saw me as too close, too influenced by her. But if they'd been able to talk to someone like them, someone who'd thought the same thing as they had but who had changed his mind . . .*

"Lissa?" said Cadan. "What is it?"

She looked up, frowning. What good would it do, even if Bruce could persuade people? How was he ever going to talk to all the people who needed persuading? Then, as the bleakness descended over her once more: *What do I even care? It's too late for me and Lin. Let the other twins worry about their Spares. Let them find solutions. I'm done with trying to save everybody.*

"Lissa?"

Oh but *hell*, that wasn't okay. It was exactly what she'd told Lin wasn't okay. *If you're human, you have to care about other humans.* It wasn't about whether it was fun, or fair, or whether it hurt you so much you thought you were going to die of it. It was just that you *had* to.

She opened her mouth, ready to try to explain an idea that wasn't even a proper idea yet, that she wasn't even sure was *possible*, and that Bruce might refuse to be involved with even if it *was* possible—

Then the door sprang open, and Elissa's mother rushed in, shrieking.

"That monster!" she was screaming. "That monster hurt your father!"

Lin, was Elissa's first thought. And then, *Dad? Dad's hurt?*

Bruce had swung around as his mother entered. "What happened? Ma, what's going on?"

Mrs. Ivory threw a distraught, furious look at Elissa. "That Spare—that Spare everyone keeps treating as if it matters more than anyone else—it attacked Edward! It attacked *your father!*"

Elissa was on her feet, cold with horror. *I'm the trigger. If I'm not there, she's supposed to stay safe, she's not supposed to go psycho. If she's hurt him, what will it do to her?*

At least her mother had said *hurt,* not *killed.* Then, a weird undercurrent of thought: *The link has gone, but still, a crisis happens and I'm not terrified for my dad, who I've lived with my whole life, but for Lin. The link wasn't all we had. I should have told her that*—

"Hurt how?" Cadan was saying. "Mrs. Ivory, how did Lin hurt him?"

Laine Ivory turned on him. "He's unconscious! Is that hurt

enough for you? He'd gone to see it–I told him not to and he didn't pay any attention. I told him not to go with it in the flyer, and he didn't pay any attention then, either! They let him through security, said it wasn't a risk, left him–*again!*–in the presence of that psycho, and ten minutes later he's lying on the floor, knocked out, scarcely breathing, and it's gone!"

"Gone?"

"Gone where?"

Cadan and Elissa both spoke at the same time.

Mrs. Ivory flung them a furious look. "Do you think I care? It attacked my husband! I don't know where it went after that!" She drew a breath, her eyes boring into Elissa. "It's a monster. I told you. I said so. Bruce is facing *trial* because he helped you get free of it, and still you and your father won't believe me!"

"She's *not* a monster–"

"My God, Elissa, why won't you *see*–"

"–and if she *is*," said Elissa, speaking louder, "it's because you've made her one."

Her mother gaped at her, even more fury rising into her face. "Me? You're blaming me for that–that psychotic aberration?"

"Not just you. Everyone like you. Everyone who treats Spares like they're not human." She hadn't known what she was going to say until she spoke, but it came clear to her now as she said it. "If you treat them like they're not human, they won't be human. They have to be taught. They have to learn. Back on Sekoia, people treated Lin like she wasn't human, and she stopped trying to *be* human. Bruce treated her like a monster–like an alien parasite I had to be freed from–and now she's *behaving* like a monster."

Her mother opened her mouth, began to say something,

and somewhere in the background Cadan said, *"Lissa,"* but Elissa kept speaking, speaking across her, across both of them, refusing to listen. "So yes, it's your fault. Yours, and Bruce's, and the people in the facilities, and the people back on Sekoia, and the terrorist groups trying to hurt Spares or kill them or use them. And IPL's fault, because they didn't see that what they were doing was making things worse instead of helping. You're trying to turn Lin into a monster, but I'm not going to let you. She's going to stay human, and she's going to stay my sister, and—"

"Lissa."

"What?"

"She's left the spaceport," said Cadan. "That's where she's gone. She's taken the shuttlebug. She's left the spaceport."

"She's . . ." Elissa stared at him, trying to clear her head. "How do you know?"

Cadan tipped his wrist toward her. On his com-unit, a light was flashing red. "I'm the only authorized pilot. If someone else takes it, I get told."

"But how do you know it's Lin? There's a planet full of other people—"

Underneath the concern, the tight-lipped tension, in Cadan's face, there was a trace of exasperated amusement. "Who but Lin could override the security that fast? Damn that girl, she's always taking my stuff."

"But what's she doing? What's the point of—"

Elissa stopped. Her father had gone to talk to Lin. Had gone to tell her that Elissa's abductors had been arrested, that they were being held in the place they'd taken Elissa. Lin hadn't known the exact place, but she had known the general location. And with a shuttlebug, she'd be able to make sweeps of the area, narrow it down to a specific place. Find the people who'd taken away the most important thing in her life.

Elissa remembered Lin's face, the last time she saw it, bleak with loss. *At least you got what you wanted,* she'd said, and Elissa, numb with shock and pain, hadn't been able to tell her how wrong she was.

She thinks this is what I wanted. She thinks it was nothing but the link that bound us. She thinks I don't care anymore. She thinks she has nothing left to lose.

Elissa became aware that even that slight trace of amusement had gone from Cadan's face. He was watching her, all tension, watching her face change as thought after thought went through her, shock after shock.

"She's gone to kill them," she said to him. "She's lost everything, and it's their fault. She's gone to kill them."

Horror swept her again, and she had to put out a hand to steady herself against the wall. "Oh God, Cadan, if she succeeds, if she kills those people—not in self-defense, not in a fight, but like this, *on purpose* . . . I don't know if she can recover. Doing something like that—it might trigger the thing in her mind, it might make her go completely psycho. And even if it doesn't . . . Cadan, I don't think she'll be able to come back from"—she had to swallow before she could say the word—"from murder."

Somewhere in the periphery of her awareness, where stuff happened that didn't matter, her mother's voice rose, saying more things about monsters and *no one listens to me,* but Elissa paid no attention. She watched the realization flood into Cadan's face, watched his expression change.

"I don't think she'll be given the chance," he said, and his voice was grim.

"What?"

"Mass murder? Lissa, whatever the circumstances, whatever the excuse, no authority is going to let her go free if she does that. She'll be in high-security imprisonment the rest of her life."

"But it's not her fault! Losing the link—she's not in her right mind!"

"Then it'll be somewhere for the criminally insane. Either way, Lis—"

Elissa wasn't listening. She couldn't think beyond the idea of Lin, shut away, having to face what she'd done without the link, without even Elissa's physical presence, without anything to pull her back to sanity.

I lost the link today. I thought—we both thought—it meant I'd lost her, too. I haven't. Not yet. But this—if she kills those people, that's when I'll have lost her.

She looked at Cadan. "Help me. You have to help me stop her."

"God, Lis, I don't know *how*. If we tell security where she's gone—an electrokinetic Spare planning on murdering a base full of people? They won't waste time trying to stop her—they'll kill her."

"Then we don't tell them. We go after her ourselves. Cadan, *please*. You have the *Phoenix*—"

"Lis, it's not like I'm trying *not* to help! Just let me think. I can't get the *Phoenix* out of the spaceport without fifty people asking me what I'm doing."

"Other flyers—"

"I'm not authorized. And *I'm* not electrokinetic—I can't break into them without setting off a hundred alarms."

"Oh God, Cadan, you can fly *anything*. There must be

something that'll get us there. I can't—I can't just—"

His head came up, and suddenly his eyes were blazing, relief and hope lighting his whole face. "My skybike."

"Your *skybike?*"

"It's still in the *Phoenix*'s cargo hold."

Elissa stared at him. "But it's a *bike*. Lin took the *shuttlebug*. How can you ever catch up—"

Cadan was already across the room, opening the door. "Your sister learns phenomenally fast, I know, but she's still a beginner. She can fly the shuttlebug, yeah, but no way can she get its best speeds out of it. Whereas the bike"—he grinned at her—"I've been riding it since I was fourteen. Trust me, we'll catch her."

As if the blaze in his face had reached Elissa, she was suddenly warm, her skin buzzing with relief and hope. "You can take me on it?"

"To stop Lin? Like I'd dare to leave you behind?"

Elissa was halfway through the door when her mother caught her arm, jerked her back. "Elissa, you're *not to do this!* You said yourself, she's dangerous, she's setting out to *murder* these people. Do you realize how much danger you're putting yourself in?"

Elissa dragged her arm away, not looking back. Her mother caught it again. "Lissa, *stop* this. I'm going to call security. They can go after her."

That did make Elissa look at her mother. Mrs. Ivory's face was set rigid, her mouth a lipless line.

"You're *not,*" said Elissa. "You heard what Cadan said—they'll kill her."

"Better that than she kills you!"

She's not going to kill me! The words flashed to Elissa's

lips, but this time she couldn't say them.

"No," she said instead. "It's not better, and you're not to let it happen." But now she wasn't talking to her mother. Her gaze lifted, went across the room, and met Bruce's eyes. "You wanted to fix things?" she said. "Don't let her call anyone."

Bruce came forward, unwillingness in every line of his body. "She's my *mother*. You're not expecting me to–God, physically *restrain* her?"

"I don't care what you do," said Elissa, exasperated. "Just don't let her screw this up. *Talk* to her. *Explain*. Tell her what you told me. Tell her about Lin. Be persuasive, for God's sake. She'll listen to *you*. *Everyone* listens to you–"

She broke off, the words sounding and resounding in her head.

Everyone listens to Bruce. And why not? He was tall, good-looking, charismatic. He'd been popular at school, and later at the SFI academy. People liked him. People listened to him, trusted him, believed him.

She looked straight into his eyes. "If we don't come back–"

"God, *Lissa*–"

"*Lissa*, will you *listen* to yourself?" Her mother's voice was shrill. "You stop this *right now*, or I'm calling security!"

"*Bruce*," said Elissa, loudly. "Listen to me. *Listen*. If we don't come back, if something goes wrong, you have to fix this. You're going to go on trial. You're going to be *news*. All across this side of the star system, people are going to be following the story. You have to use that–you have to tell people what happened, how you thought one thing, then you changed your mind. You have to persuade people–*all* the people–people on Philomel and back on Sekoia and *everyone*–you have to persuade them that Spares are human."

For the first time it wasn't just unhappiness in Bruce's face, but anguish. "Lissa, how do you expect me to do that? If you don't come back—if she kills you and Cay—"

"If she does," said Elissa, knowing it was cruel, saying it anyway, "it'll be you who helped her. It'll be on your shoulders too. It'll be your job to make it right. You can't fix things for me anymore. But you can make sure this doesn't happen to other Sparcs."

"Lissa," said Cadan from the corridor, "if we don't go now, we'll never catch her."

"Coming." Elissa stepped out of the room, her eyes not leaving Bruce's. "It's on you," she said. "You have to fix this for me."

The door slid shut between them.

She had one frozen instant where everything seemed to stand still, where just one stream of thought looped over and over in her head. *He has to do it. He has to. Even if it's too late for me and Lin, this is the chance we've needed, the chance to make people see Spares differently.*

Then urgency fired her, adrenaline shooting like fireworks into every nerve and muscle, and she was racing down the corridor, running as fast as she could but still aware that Cadan was pacing his stride to hers, racing toward the spaceport bay where the *Phoenix* waited.

The door of the cargo bay swung up slowly, slowly, metal grating on metal. Cadan ducked under it the moment there was space enough for him to do so. Elissa scrambled after him into the hold just as the lights auto-blinked awake.

The skybike was packed in solidfoam, strapped against one of the walls of the hold. Cadan was unclicking the catches before Elissa reached him. He nodded toward another solidfoam crate next to the bike. "Gear's in there. There's two helmets and jackets. Start getting yours on."

Elissa fumbled at the catches, pulling the straps loose, lifting the top off the solidfoam crate. She was zipping up one of the jackets—close fitting, dark blue, with the rigid feel at elbows, shoulders, and collar that meant it was reinforced against impact—when she heard the skybike roar to life behind her.

It was a sleek, silver thing, like a small-scale, slimmed-down flyer, most of its bulk in the tail fin and wings that stood up behind the tar-black seat. The seat not only looked as if it were made of soft black tar, it felt like it as well. It, as well as the handlebars, footrests, and handgrips, was made of a super-safety material, so high-friction that it seemed to cling to the skin when you touched it.

Cadan stood with his legs braced astride the bike, one hand on the handlebars, flipping switches, checking the fuel gauge. After a moment he killed the engine, holding out his free hand for a jacket. Elissa passed it to him, then felt up under her chin, finding the studs to fasten the collar closely around her neck. Her fingers were suddenly shaky. She'd never gone on a skybike before. Unlike most of the vehicles used in Sekoia's cities, they were built to be used independently of the monorails—superfast, daredevil boys' toys. Elissa's parents had never let Bruce have one, and hadn't even let him ride on Cadan's until he was seventeen. And Cadan had been right, Elissa's mother would never have let her on one.

Cadan's been riding for years. He's never crashed the thing. And I've done stuff much more dangerous than this. And I have to, anyway. But it didn't make her hands any less shaky, didn't dispel the icy flutterings in her stomach.

Cadan reached out to take one of the helmets from her, then tipped it up and pulled a pair of black gloves out. "There'll be gloves in yours, too. Make sure you strap them tight around your wrists. And Lis, fasten your hair back first."

She'd left her hair loose after the doctor's visit. Now she delved through her pockets until she found a hair tie, then dragged her hair back into the tightest ponytail she could manage, feeling it pull painfully at the little wound in her scalp. She drew the gloves on, working her fingers into the ends, strapping the cuffs tightly around her wrists, then picked up the helmet.

"Lissa."

She looked up, helmet in her hands. Cadan was watching her.

"What?"

A tiny smile came and went across his face. "That's all."

"Just 'Lissa'?"

He tipped the helmet, pulled it down over his head. His eyes looked out from beneath the open visor, very steady, very blue. "Yeah."

That was all, but for a moment she wasn't cold anymore, and as she pulled her own helmet on her hands didn't shake.

Cadan moved both hands to the handlebars, steadying the bike between his legs. He nodded down toward a footrest behind him on the side of the bike. "Step on that, Lis. I'll keep the bike steady. Hold on to my shoulder. There's space for you to swing your leg over the bike in front of the tail."

Only just, Elissa thought, all shaky with nerves again as she stepped onto the footrest, felt the bike dip toward her, saw Cadan shift his grip as he adjusted for her weight. Her fingers dug into the shoulder of Cadan's jacket as she got her

balance and slid her leg over between his back and the steep
slope of the tail fin.

Then she was sitting, snug behind him, feeling the seat grip
her, hold her steady, the footrests clinging to her feet.

"All right?" said Cadan over his shoulder.

"Yes."

"Visor down, then. And don't hold on to me, okay?
There're handgrips behind you."

Elissa's stomach fluttered again as she reached back. She'd
thought she'd be holding onto Cadan's waist, and it felt all
wrong to have to put her arms behind her.

He must have noticed her expression. "It's much more
secure, trust me," he said, and snapped his own visor down.
His face blurred behind it.

Then he turned his head away, and, again with a roar, the
skybike sprang to life. Elissa felt the vibration run through her
feet, her thighs, the inside of her calves where they pressed
against the bike, her hands where they tightened around the
handgrips.

They eased forward a few feet, so slowly the bike wobbled,
seeming to lose its balance, sending Elissa's hands closing
in a spasm of panic on the grips, then faster, smoother, the
engine noise rising around her. Cadan's hand moved on the
throttle, the bike seemed to kick beneath them, and all at
once they'd screamed out of the cargo hold, through the gray
blur of the spaceport bay, out into the thin gray twilight of
the mountains.

The spaceport—buildings, landing pads, plateaus—fell away
beneath Elissa. There was nothing but the rush of icy air, a
wheeling of gray sky, dark ridges of trees, a far-off scatter of
black shapes of birds.

Her head spun. Her stomach swooped. It was like falling *up*, feeling as if gravity had been reversed, feeling as if all control over her own body had been taken away.

Her hands and knees tightened desperately on the bike. Inside her shoes, her toes curled as if they were trying to curl around the footrests. The wind shrieked past them, and she hunched down behind Cadan, all at once convinced that, friction grips or not, she was going to be torn out of her seat.

How far is it? Last time she'd made this journey she'd been drugged unconscious. *I can't do it—I'll freeze—or fall.*

A side gust of wind buffeted suddenly against them. The bike lurched, and hot liquid terror shot through Elissa's wrists and belly. *We'll crash, we'll crash—he can't keep control of the bike up this high!*

They didn't crash. Cadan pulled the bike back under control, and they tore through the cold, empty air, far above the forested valley, far above the bare rock of the heights.

Until, all at once, far ahead of them, Elissa saw something moving, gray against gray. A glinting speck that became a minuscule arrow, that became, as Cadan dragged the throttle back and they tore, screaming faster and faster through the air, the far-off shape of the shuttlebug.

TWENTY-THREE

CADAN HAD been right. Lin might be able to fly the shuttlebug, but she didn't fly it well. While Cadan circled, descending, Elissa watched, throat tight, as below them the shuttlebug lurched and bounced, banging down onto the ground, first one side, then another, showering sparks as metal screeched against rock.

But, poor style or not, Lin did reach the ground first. Cadan was still maneuvering the skybike in its downward spiral when Elissa saw the door of the shuttlebug spring open and the figure of her sister jump down. She must have seen the bike in her viewscreens, must be able to hear its engines now, but she didn't so much as look up. She ran, cutting a line across to where skylights rose, smoothly gleaming, above the rocks. They must have been kept shuttered and camouflaged before, but now their glass surfaces gleamed, reflecting the sky, betraying the location of the place the terrorists had set up as their base, the place where they were now imprisoned.

We still have time. We have time. She hasn't done anything yet—

Even as Elissa noticed it, she saw her sister reach the nearest skylight. Lin knelt at its edge and leaned forward to spread both hands on the curve of the glass. The skybike's circling swept Elissa out of the line of sight, and she whipped her head around, trying to see past the bike's tail that was blocking her view.

Still have time. We still have time. We're nearly down. I can stop her.

But when they circled back around, farther down, suddenly much closer, there was smoke rising from the edges of the skylight.

Panic swept Elissa's hands from her death hold on the handgrips. She thumped frantically on Cadan's back. "Get us down! Get us down now! Look what she's doing!"

He couldn't hear her—even in her panic she knew that—but he couldn't ignore the thumping on his back. The bike dipped sharply, dropping from its careful circling, a hawk stooping suddenly on prey, and they plunged, in a scream of wind and shrieking engines, so fast that Elissa's stomach lurched into her throat.

They landed, as the shuttlebug had, in a spray of sparks and dust and flying broken rock, slewing sideways, Cadan's booted foot coming out to help steady them, leaving a long streak of black along the ground.

He swung around as Elissa began to scramble off the bike. "Careful of the engine!" he yelled at her, just as her leg skimmed too close to it and she felt the slash of heat even through her clothes. She snatched her foot back, making a clumsy half fall, half jump off the bike, landing staggering in the burned-smelling dust next to it.

She turned and ran, hearing the engine die behind her, that burned smell in her nose, her ears buzzing in a way that made her half-deaf.

There was more smoke rising now, enough to obscure where her sister knelt, and a flicker of sparks jumping, here and there, from the metal into which the skylight was set. Sparks that were nothing to do with the landings of either the shuttlebug or the skybike.

"Lin!" Elissa shrieked. Her voice came muted through the buzzing in her ears. "Lin! *Lin!* Stop!"

Smoke swirled. Lin rose from it like a demon from a horror movie. Her eyes were bloodshot, not just the skin around them but the whites themselves, and there was a smear of blood streaked from under her nose across her cheek. *Oh God, look what she's done to herself. The effort of knocking my dad out, and the security guards, then breaking through the electronics of the shuttlebug. And now . . .*

Lin could explode ships' engines. And she could set buildings on fire. She'd done it before, twice that Elissa knew of, forcing the electrical currents of the building to run higher and higher, overloading the circuits, jumping the breakers and exploding into flame.

She'd done it in the facility in order to escape, and in Elissa's house to help *Elissa* escape. She hadn't cared if she hurt people in the process, but at least she hadn't *intended* it. But now . . .

The people in there—they're imprisoned. They have no way out.

If Lin burned this down, she was going to burn the occupants as well.

"Lin, *no.*" Elissa took a few quick strides toward where Lin stood.

Sparks leaped in front of her, hissed out on the rock.

Sparks, and tiny tongues of flame. Their heat reached Elissa, stung against the already-scorched patch on her leg. She stopped dead.

"*Lin.*"

"You shouldn't have come," said her sister.

Elissa's eyes stung with smoke and dust. "I *had* to come. Lin, look, I know what you're doing, I get why, but you can't. You can't just kill people."

"These people? Oh, I so can." Lin's voice spat like the flames.

"*No.* Lin, I keep *telling* you—"

"*That's over.*" Even through the smoke, Elissa could see Lin's hands clench, see every muscle in her face stiffen. "I'm done, Lissa. 'It's not right,' and 'it's not human,' and 'you can't,' and you being angry with me—none of that matters anymore. It's all done. It's all over. I don't care."

"You don't have to care." Cadan's voice came from behind Elissa. "You just have to stop."

Elissa didn't turn to look at him, but Lin looked, and her eyes narrowed. "You even *try* to use that whip and I'll burn it from end to end. And you, maybe."

"You'd hurt *Cadan*?" The horror Elissa heard in her own voice was real, but at the same time she was thinking, *She doesn't mean that. She can't mean it—not Cadan. If I can just make her think clearly, see what she's doing, shake her out of this insane state she's gotten into—*

Pain and fury flashed over Lin's face. "No, I won't hurt freaking precious *Cadan*. Only if he tries to stop me. Are you happy now?"

"*Happy?*" Elissa's voice rose. "When you're going to burn a base full of people? No I'm not *happy*! Lin . . . Lin, please listen to me. You can't really be planning on doing this."

Lin's face twisted. "Yeah, I know, I know," she said. "I do this and you won't love me anymore. It's a bit late for that threat now."

Elissa stared at her, blank. "What?"

"That threat." Lin's face twisted again, impatient, furious, despairing. "It's too late to make me behave by saying you won't love me anymore. Isn't it?"

"I *never* tried to use that as a threat," Elissa said, the unfairness of what Lin was saying for a moment overriding everything else. "I *never* used it. And, anyway, for God's sake, no, it's not *too late!*"

Lin slammed her foot onto the skylight, a sudden violent movement that made Elissa jump. More sparks leaped from the metal, and the smoke billowed up around her. "That's not true! The link's gone! The link's gone and you're glad!"

"I'm *not* glad."

"You are! You *are*! You wanted me out of your head, and now I am! If you're saying you're not glad then you're lying!" She broke off, scrubbed a hand across her eyes. "I don't even know why you're here, why you've bothered. We don't have anything anymore, Lissa." The leaping, fiery fury had gone from her voice. It was flat, as gray as the smoke.

And for the first time since catching up with her, Elissa was afraid. Lin hadn't come here because she'd gone psycho. She hadn't even lost her temper. She was just . . . *She doesn't think she has anything else to try to be human for. She doesn't think she has anything left.* For the first time the realization came, cold, clear, inescapable. *I'm going to lose her. This is it—I could lose her. Here, today. Now.*

"We'll always have something," she said, but she could hear the despair in her own voice now. It didn't sound convincing to her; it was never going to convince Lin.

But at least it sparked a question. "What?" said Lin, staring at her through the smoke, her voice still flat, her face empty.

"We're twins," Elissa said.

"No, we're not. Not without the link."

Elissa swallowed. It was difficult to argue with that. Twins, doubles—it had always been the link that made them that. They might still look alike, but without the link they were just . . .

"Okay," she said. "Then we're sisters. We're still sisters."

Lin stared at her, gray-faced in the smoke. "How are we?"

"Lin, for God's *sake* . . ."

"Sisters grow up together. Sisters share . . . *things*. Parents. Lives. We aren't twins anymore—we aren't sisters, either. Not real sisters." Her face went even blanker, as if in saying the words she was cutting herself off from everything Elissa had thought they had, as if she was *choosing* to let her humanness fall away to burn and shrivel and disappear.

And as Elissa heard it, those words—*not real sisters*—anger flamed through her, so bright she could feel it burn behind her eyes, so hot that for a second it stopped her breath in her lungs.

"Not real sisters?" she said, and as her breath rushed back, burning in her throat, the heat of the flames flared through her voice. She threw up a hand. "What do you call this? *Look*, my hand's the same shape as yours. Our hair grows the same way. We walk in the same *rhythm*. We *feel the cold* the same. I grew up with *Bruce*. I knew *Bruce* my whole life. And if I tried for *a million years*, I'd never be as much like him as I'm like you!"

She stopped, chest burning, eyes burning, furious powerless

tears rising within her. "I've messed things up over and over. I was angry, and frustrated, and I did it wrong, and then I did it wrong *again*, and I— But God, look, Lin, if you do this, it just makes everything we did *right*, all the effort we made, mean nothing—"

Lin's eyes held hers, but they were too far away, too blurred by the rising smoke, for Elissa to see their expression. "So that is the bribe, then?" she said. "You're my sister *now*. You love me *now*. But if I do this, you won't love me anymore?"

This, she called it. *This*, as if it were something small. But it wasn't. Lin was planning on trapping at least four—and probably more—people here. Planning on burning them to death.

For the first time Elissa thought beyond the initial what-ifs: the *what will it do to Lin?* the *what will the authorities do to her?* For the first time she thought, *If Lin does this, if Lin kills these people, what will it do to me? What will it make me feel about her? And what will it make me* not *feel? Is she right? If she does it, if she becomes a murderer, will she stop feeling like my sister, my twin? Will I not love her anymore?*

Something like lightning cracked up from the metal around Lin, a blue-white flash.

And in Elissa's brain, the answer came as bright, as clear. She didn't know, now, whether Lin had gone too far to hear her—or to believe her if she did hear. It might not make any difference, whatever she said.

All the same, she had to say it. Whatever Lin did now, she had to know the truth of what was left to them.

"See?" said Lin, distant in the smoke. "It only worked when we had the link. When you loved me 'cause you had to."

"No," said Elissa. "You're wrong."

"I'm not wrong."

"You are. I came here to stop you killing these people. I want you to stop. But whether you stop or not, I'll still love you."

"You won't!" Lin shouted the words. "You won't, you won't, you know you won't!"

"I will."

The smell of burning metal rose, and somewhere below the ground close to Elissa's feet she heard a bang like a small explosion. Her mind went to the people trapped down there. She imagined the fire beginning, saw it sweeping through the base, sucking all the oxygen from the air, making them die of suffocation before—*oh God please before*—the flames reached them. She imagined looking at Lin afterward, knowing she'd done that.

She looked at Lin now, her face a pale blur in the smoke, her hands clenched, her electrokinetic power making the sparks leap and spit. Hurting and bleeding and willing to kill.

"I'll love you forever," said Elissa. "If you *don't* do this, I'll love you. If you *do* do it, I'll still love you. I'll just—" A sudden sob caught her by the throat. "You're so *stupid*! They'll send you to prison, and then I'll have to *miss* you forever."

"It's not true!" Lin's voice rose.

"It is."

"You're lying."

"I'm not. I'm not lying."

"You are! You're lying, you're *lying*, you're *lying*!" Her voice went even higher, so high it broke.

The lightning leaped again, a circle of it this time, making a sharp crack in the air.

"Lissa," said Cadan, urgently behind her. "Get back. She'll hurt you."

Elissa stayed still. The lightning flash had shown her Lin's face in blue-white clarity. Lin's chin was shaking, and her eyes were flooded with tears.

"Lin," she said, gently. "I don't lie to you. I never did. You know that."

The lightning didn't leap again. The sparks died. The smoke cleared. Lin stood on a skylight all hazed with soot and crazed with heat at its edges, with blood smeared under her nose and burst blood vessels all around her eyes. She was shaking all over now, her arms wrapped tightly across herself, her fingers white.

"*Lying,*" she said again, but her voice was shaking too, and all the conviction had gone from it.

"You know I'm not."

The tears in Lin's eyes spilled over. They poured down her face, making pale tracks through dirt and blood.

"I–" she said, before the tears took her voice and left her mute, swallowing, struggling to speak. "I wanted to kill them. I did. I– everything had gone and I–there was nothing else and I–"

Elissa took the few steps between them, reached her sister. Under her hands, Lin's arms were cold, as if all her body heat had gone into the smoke and the fire.

"It was their fault," said Lin. "*Their fault.* I couldn't think past making them hurt too." She looked down at her hands, and a shudder went through her. "I was going to burn them. Lis, I was going to burn them. If you hadn't stopped me–" She shuddered again, looking at her hands as if she didn't recognize them. "I don't *want* to be a monster. I don't, Lissa, I—"

"You're not a monster."

"But I—I wanted to—I was going to—"

"I know. But you didn't. And you're not a monster. It's okay. It's okay."

Lin's hands came up to grip Elissa's. "But the *link's gone.*" Tears choked her voice. "I don't know how to be human without it. Without you. All this time, I only knew how to behave because of you. But now—Lissa, without it, what am I? What might I do?"

Her hands were still cold, but where they touched Elissa's they'd warmed a little, taking blood heat from Elissa's body.

"You still have me," Elissa said. "The link's gone, but I'm still here."

"But—that thing in my brain—when it goes off, when it—"

"That's not you, that's something that SFI *did* to you. There'll be a way to fix it. There *will.* The brain *repairs* itself. That's what it *does.*"

"But if I hurt you . . . Lissa, if I hurt you . . ."

"We won't let you. They're working on fixing it, but until they do—Lin, you didn't give them any *time.* There'll be a way of keeping you from hurting me—of keeping any of the Spares from hurting people."

"Okay." Lin's voice was still wobbly. Her sore-looking, bloodshot gaze clung to Elissa's. "But, Lissa . . ." She swallowed, started again. "Lissa, the link's gone. It's not just being human. It's . . . all my life, that's the thing that connected me to you. You said we still had something, that we hadn't lost everything. You *said.* But—but—without it, *what* do we have? What are we going to do?"

Elissa's hands tightened on her twin's, feeling their returning warmth. She looked down at them, at their shape, identical to her own, knowing that Lin's fear, too, was like her own—not because they were sharing it through a link, but because she knew Lin, knew her sister, knew what made her afraid, or happy, or angry.

"I don't know yet," she said. "But we'll work it out."

TWENTY-FOUR

THE SKY could have been that of any planet.

From where Elissa sat, she could see neither forest nor mountain nor desert. Just the sky, stretching up and away forever, blue darkening to purple as, somewhere behind her, the sun slid toward the edge of the world.

There were plenty of other places she could have waited during this hour, but over the last three months this little room, furnished with almost nothing but its window, had become the place that drew her every time she came.

Against the indigo sky, a speck of light appeared. For a moment it could have been anything—a first star appearing above the Philomelen mountains, a firefly hovering above an ancient forest on Sanctuary, a raindrop lit by the blaze of a sunset on Syris II.

It was none of those things, and the sky Elissa was watching belonged to none of the places whose images had moved briefly through her memory. She stood, going to the window to see the descending spark more clearly. It was a spaceship, returning to Sekoia. To a planet renewed.

The ship hurtled toward her, resolving itself from a spark to a flare, a fiery bird of prey, diving in the light of the setting sun toward Central Canyon City, toward the spaceport plateau that Elissa's window looked out on.

A scant distance above the roofs of the spaceport buildings, the ship—one of Sekoia's smaller spacecraft—pulled out of its dive, looping briefly upward before, rockets flaring, it began to descend again, so controlled that it seemed to float for a moment above the landing pad before it settled to the ground, dust boiling up around it.

Elissa grinned—*nice landing*—and wasn't surprised when, a few minutes later, the door at the base of the ship opened, and even at this distance, she recognized her brother in the familiar figure of the exiting pilot.

The distance was too great for her to see his face, but the buoyancy with which he jumped to the ground made her pretty sure that he, too, was grinning.

Bruce had faced trial on Philomel, but by the time he did there'd been a million factors the court had been forced to consider—all of them more important than sentencing him according to the usual laws. Those factors had expedited his trial, but by the time it came, a month after the crime he was being tried for, he was already one of the public faces of the recently convened Sekoia Recovery Group.

Even Elissa, who'd guilt-tripped him into that first press interview out of desperation and sudden instinctive conviction, hadn't anticipated its results.

Bruce, tall, good-looking, speaking from the shattered background of a glittering career, talking, with genuine misery in his eyes, about how he'd realized, too late, what he'd done to his sister—*both* his sisters—because he hadn't been able to see Spares as human, had caught the consciousness—and con-science—of Sekoia's scattered, fractured population.

That first interview had sparked an instant clamor of demands from Sekoian citizens to actually see the Spares—not in distant shots of shell-shocked victims being led out of facilities, but as real people. And *that* had led to Elissa and Lin—plus a bunch of other twins and the *Phoenix* crew and Cadan's parents and what felt like half the psychologists on Philomel—being summoned to a whole flurry of behind-the-scenes discussion in order to find the Spares who had acclimatized the quickest, who would be able to come across in interviews as the most "normal."

In the end, Jay was one of those chosen. From a room on Philomel, and with Samuel sitting next to him, he'd handled the initial five-minute interview a whole lot better than Elissa would have thought. He and a handful of other Spares had done so well, in fact, that the demand to see them had turned into demands for them to return to Sekoia, to return home.

And as public opinion changed, as Sekoia's attitude toward Spares turned from one of suspicion, revulsion, and fear to one of sympathetic interest, there was less unrest, fewer riots. Sekoian citizens began to step forward to offer volunteer policing, transport, donations of previously hoarded food. IPL forces revoked the curfews and dialed back on the rationing.

Not *everyone* on Sekoia had exactly been converted to acceptance both of Spares and of the continued governance by IPL forces. IPL still got reports of terrorist activity, of the existence of "covert groups," and the apartments where

Spares and twins lived were still given a certain amount of protection as standard. But those first interviews, with Bruce and Jay and other Spares, marked the point at which the tide of public opinion had made its initial, most significant, change of course.

One more key thing had helped with both that and with Sekoia's recovery.

Elissa watched now as Bruce turned to hold out a hand to the girl climbing out after him—and then to the next, identical, figure.

Even the colorless spaceport lights couldn't wash out the flame of color from the second girl's hair. It was El—Ella, now. Like Jay, who now called himself Jason, she'd chosen to turn the code name she'd had as a captive Spare into a real name.

And she, as well as a hundred other Spares and their twins, had volunteered to work with Sekoia's reformed space force, working out ways to power the ships' hyperdrives without endangering themselves.

Bruce, Sofia, and Ella had just returned from their third flight—and, judging from the triumphant spring to Bruce's movements, their third successful attempt at achieving hyperspeed. None of the Spares was using the sockets SFI had drilled into their skulls—volunteer scientists, most of them from non-SFI-affiliated institutions, had developed what they were calling a noninvasive interface, which Spares had only to touch with one hand, leaving the other free to maintain contact with their twin.

It only worked with those twins who were linked, of course. Which was yet another miracle. Sofia and Ella had returned to Sekoia with no telepathic connection, but then, as they spent more time together, the link that must once have existed had slowly begun to re-establish itself. They had nothing like the link Elissa and Lin had once had, or that of Jay—Jason—and Samuel. But it was enough to power a hyper-drive.

It was enough, too, to keep Sofia safe from what had happened to Ady. The weekly brain scans that were now routine for every Spare showed that as the link between Ella and Sofia strengthened, the abnormal activity in Ella's brain had begun to diminish.

She wasn't the only one either. Across Sekoia, Spares and their twins were demonstrating what Cadan had once said to Elissa, what she had repeated to Lin, that the brain repairs itself.

The repair—the dwindling of the abnormal activity—happened fastest with those who had never lost their tele-pathic connection, but it also happened with those whose link was slowly being re-established, and even with those who still had no link at all.

For a while there'd been a whole bunch of different theo-ries as to why. When Elissa talked to her dad, on a long-distance call from Philomel, he'd shared his theory that the trip switch naturally degraded, that no matter how deeply an unnatural pathology was imposed on the brain, it would eventually reject it of its own accord.

"Have you said that to Mother?" she'd asked, then imme-diately regretted it when her father gave a breath of a pause before shaking his head. "Your mother doesn't talk about Spares," he'd said, and Elissa hadn't asked any more.

She'd let Lin take over the conversation instead, telling Mr. Ivory about the life skills classes she and the other Spares were being given. She was proving excellent at computer use—*of course*—and ridiculously, *unreasonably* hopeless at food preparation and hygiene.

Elissa had sat quiet, watching the play of emotion on her sister's face, noticing her father doing the same.

Eventually the scientists and doctors had come down on the side of one particular theory: the idea that, while contact with a twin *did* set off the process that led to psychosis, over time—and if that psychosis could be prevented from being fully triggered—the humanizing effect of the same contact worked to eventually counteract the time bomb built into the Spare's brain.

Elissa still remembered Lin saying, through tears and despair, *I don't know how to be human without it. Without you,* and herself answering, *You still have me. The link's gone, but I'm still here.*

And now, across the whole of their world, Spares and their twins were demonstrating that although a telepathic connection with their twin was the best safeguard against the time bombs, even a normal sibling relationship would, in time, have a similar effect.

Only the Spares—like Cassie, who'd once named herself Cassiopeia—who still had no contact with their twins showed any trace of the abnormal activity that indicated potential psychosis. The authorities were continuing to monitor them, although not anything like as invasively as they'd had to do back on Philomel, during the horrible aftermath of the first attacks.

During that first month of scans and tests and one discarded hypothesis after another, the scientists had discovered that there was a measurable chemical change in the body as switch after switch tripped to bring the Spare closer to the final descent into psychosis. They'd devised bracelets that, locked onto each Spare's wrist, would measure the chemical levels, alerting security and medical staff the moment the likelihood of an attack increased.

To start with they'd only been able to prevent attacks, but as they refined the bracelets, they'd been able to track and predict the fugue states, too. And the latest version of the bracelets could not only predict the final state of psychosis with a safe ten-minute margin, it could inject an instant, precisely measured dose of an antipsychotic drug, enough to prevent the state from occurring at all.

Out on the spaceport plateau, Bruce turned toward the central buildings. Something about his posture, as he swung behind Ella to walk beside Sofia, his body a little angled toward hers, snagged Elissa's attention. *Sofia? Really?* For a moment, a smile tugged at her lips.

Being able to fly again had done a lot to restore Bruce to the familiar, confident brother she remembered. But the guilt, the tortured conscience, although a useful part of his persona in his role as one of SRG's spokespeople, were real as well. Elissa and Lin were not the only ones who'd left Philomel with scars.

But as Elissa thought that, swiftly on the heels of her pleasure at noticing Bruce's happiness, a flood rose to drown her, grief and pain and deep, cold fury. *Compared to our scars, Bruce's are nothing! He doesn't deserve to coast into a role as planetary hero, a new career, a relationship with a cute blond girlfriend.*

As the links between Spares and twins repaired themselves, as brain scans revealed the disappearance of the abnormal activity indicating the presence of SFI's time bombs, more and more Spares had been freed from the necessity of wearing the bracelets.

Ella didn't have to wear hers anymore, nor Jason, nor three-quarters of the other Spares in the residential block where Elissa and Lin lived.

But Lin still did.

The unfairness of it boiled up in Elissa's throat. Not only did she and Lin no longer have their link—*the link that's repairing itself for so many other people*—Lin was still being treated as if she were dangerous.

The abnormal activity in Lin's brain had been gone the moment she, Elissa, and Cadan returned from the terrorist base Lin had intended to burn. The scientists and doctors who'd examined her had been convinced their equipment had stopped working, had brought in a whole new set from halfway across the continent. Which had shown exactly the same thing.

During those minutes where Elissa and Lin had faced each other, something had reset itself in Lin's brain. Just as Elissa's brain no longer showed any trace of the telepathic link, Lin's brain no longer showed any trace of the time bomb SFI had built into it. Not because it had been removed, and not because it had slowly diminished, but because Lin's own brain had—somehow—rejected it by itself.

Privately, a belief shared only with Lin and Cadan, Elissa was sure she knew the moment it had happened. She remembered how Lin's voice had changed, remembered the tears that had suddenly flooded her eyes. *It happened when she knew I loved her, when she was convinced—finally, forever—that I'd always love her, whatever she did.*

She was sure, too, that from that point Lin would have

been safe without the bracelet. That, of all the Spares, she was the one who had never needed it at all. But the authorities had felt a whole lot more cautious about it. Partly because it hadn't followed the pattern established by the other Spares, partly because so far Lin was the Spare with the most powerful—the most frightening—electrokinetic power.

Elissa had known their reasoning was fair. She still knew it, really. But . . .

It's been three months. Three months of having to come to the spaceport hospital, assessment after assessment, and every time they say they're not willing to take it off, say she needs to keep wearing it for a bit longer. Treating her like she's dangerous, keeping her shackled like a criminal, when everyone else, everyone whose time bombs disappeared later, gets their bracelets taken off, gets told they can just go, be normal.

It was the last visible sign that someone was a Spare, that silver gleam on their right wrist. You couldn't tell otherwise. *And I don't want people to be able to tell. I want them to see her as no different from me.*

Elissa screwed her eyes shut, closing out the sight of the returning heroes, trying to focus on other—entirely positive—things.

Cadan.

Cadan was out on a test flight too, but he was due back any time now. And he and Elissa had a date planned for this evening. The first couple of months after their return to Sekoia had been nearly as crazy as the weeks before, and they'd only been able to snatch time here and there, in between consultations with the SRG and extensive brain scans (Elissa) and rescue flights back and forth across the continent (Cadan) and the therapy that Elissa had furiously resisted but that she'd found—eventually—kind of helpful.

His parents had remained silently cautious about their relationship. But, as the weeks went by—and as Cadan's older sister distracted them by announcing that she and her husband were expecting their first child—Elissa thought they were easing toward a bit more of an acceptance.

And—honestly, now—she didn't even really care. Cadan took every scrap of time he had to be with her, he lost track of half of what he was saying when she came into a room—Ivan and Bruce both got a *lot* of amusement out of that—and this evening they were going out on their first real date, to the recently reopened Starlit Park.

He was going to pick her up from the apartment she and Lin shared with Felicia's family, and they were going for dinner—actual, real, grown-up dinner—at the first restaurant to reopen at the park. Elissa had a new dress, borrowed from Sofia, that Sofia and Ella and Lin all agreed was going to make him forget practically *everything* he was saying.

The sound of soft footsteps in the corridor outside brought Elissa's attention back to the present. She swung around from the window, trying not to betray any tension. The scans made them both anxious—the time when they'd only been allowed to talk through a screen wasn't that long ago—but it wasn't fair to make Lin deal with Elissa's nerves as well as her own. Especially when it was Lin, not Elissa, who had to submit to the regular hour-long assessment.

The door slid open. Lin came in. Her hair, cut short now, had mostly returned to its natural shade, and it clung, dark brown, in soft curls around her face. The black pants and low-cut flame-colored T-shirt she was wearing showed off curves she hadn't had three months ago, and she'd taken to outlining her eyes in dramatic streaks of black. But Elissa was used to that now, and her gaze went immediately past clothes and hair and eyeliner to her twin's right wrist.

The bracelet was still there.

"Oh Lin, it's okay," Elissa said instantly. "It's a precaution, that's all, you know that. It's their job to be supercautious, even when they *completely* don't need to be."

Lin came farther into the room, letting the door slide shut behind her. She hadn't spoken.

"It's okay," said Elissa again. "Lin, you *know* it's just a precaution."

Lin grinned, wide and bright, her seeing-the-stars smile. "Yeah," she said, "I know." She turned her wrist over and used the fingers of her left hand to twist something on it. The bracelet dropped open, fell into Lin's palm.

Lin lifted it up, her smile lighting her whole face, her eyes bright.

Elissa stared, at her twin's face, at the bracelet lying open on her hand. "They— *Seriously*, they unlocked it? They're comfortable with declaring you safe?"

"Yeah."

"But then why are you *wearing* it? You came in here and I thought—"

Lin slid her wrist back into the bracelet, pushed its sides up until it clicked and locked. "It's just a precaution. It still works even though it's unlocked—I asked."

"But if they've *unlocked* it, if they're saying you don't need to wear it anymore . . ."

Lin came across to the window. For a moment the flood-lights from outside rinsed all color from her face, making her look as pale, as vulnerable, as the runaway Spare she'd been months ago. She looked at Elissa. "It's my precaution, not theirs. I don't want to risk it. I don't want to risk hurting anyone."

"Lin, you're not *going* to hurt anyone."

Lin shrugged. "I might, though. I . . ." Her eyes went to the spaceport outside, rose to the sweep of darkening sky. "I'm not a monster, I know that. But I am dangerous. I can hurt people. I could have hurt you. They're sure I'm safe now, but . . ." She shrugged again. "I don't want to risk it, that's all."

Outside, another ship was coming in to land. For a second, its shadow passed by the window, drifted, like smoke, over Lin's face. Elissa put her hand out, felt her sister's fingers clasp it.

She understood what Lin was doing. It made sense, and it spoke of an aspect to Lin's character that, some months ago, hadn't existed. *That's good. I should be glad—I am glad.*

Just as she'd promised, during those horrible moments three months ago, the loss of the link hadn't meant the loss of everything. She and Lin were still sisters, still twins. As Sekoia recovered, they'd begun to think again about college, and there wasn't any question but that they'd go to the same one.

But . . .

But it's not fair. The link is remaking itself for everyone else. For people who never remembered losing it, for people who didn't care that it had died. While ours . . .

For her and Lin, despite what Cadan had said, despite what Elissa, from reading up on brain damage, knew to be true, her brain wasn't repairing itself. She and Lin no longer shared thoughts. When Lin entered a room, Elissa didn't immediately, instinctively know it was her twin.

Every time Elissa spoke to her father, she was reminded of

exactly how much she and Lin *hadn't* lost. They still had each other, they could still share a room, still talk, still reach out for comfort. Elissa *wasn't* crippled, left like half a person, the way her father had been.

But, still, every day she felt the loss of the link, the link she'd taken for granted, resented, feared. The link whose importance she hadn't fully understood—until it was gone for good.

"It's Cadan," said Lin, putting her hand up against the window in order to cut out reflections and see better. "Look, he's back, and you're not even a bit dressed up."

Elissa leaned forward to peer through the window next to her. Cadan had jumped down from the ship, and the twins— two boys Elissa knew only slightly—were climbing out. They moved toward the main building, the angle of their heads indicating animated conversation.

Elissa spread her fingers on the glass, watching him, the bleak thoughts receding, warmth tingling in her fingers and toes. His flight must have gone well too. He'd be making his way to the pilots' quarters now, showering and shaving, get- ting ready for their night out. Dinner, and then . . .

She'd been doing her research. As well as its restaurants, the Starlit Park had a whole ton of places that might have been designed for dating couples to be alone. Cadan was fly- ing again tomorrow, so he had a curfew, and Felicia's family wouldn't like it if Elissa was *too* late back, but there was still going to be plenty of time between the end of dinner and when they'd have to leave.

The warmth spread, tightening in her chest, tingling all the way through to her fingertips.

Even with all the crazy-busyness of the last few months,

they had gotten a whole lot more time alone than they'd managed before, on the *Phoenix* and on Sekoia. She remembered how she'd thought, back then, that he didn't need to worry about pushing her into stuff she wasn't ready for so much as getting the time to do stuff she *was* ready for. Now . . . her skin burned, a trail of sparks marking the path his hands had made on her body the last time they'd been alone . . . that wasn't really a problem anymore.

"Not even a bit dressed up," said Lin, with emphasis.

Elissa laughed, flushing, pushing herself away from the window. "Okay, let's go. Are you still hanging out at the apartment tonight?"

By the time they'd left the spaceport, taking one of the elevators that dropped down the cliff at the side of the plateau, and hopped out onto a slidewalk that would get them back to Felicia's family's apartment, Elissa had managed to cool her cheeks and had pushed thoughts of Cadan away too, to be taken out later.

The slidewalk curved away from the cliff side, taking them out into the last warm rays of the setting sun, then spiraled down through the lengthening shadows of early evening. Elissa, as she always had, directed her gaze forward or up, knowing that if she looked down, her stomach would swoop with vertigo. Lin, as *she* always did, peered happily down through the spaghetti tangle of slidewalks and monorails. Lin wasn't just not afraid of heights, she actively liked them.

That's another reason why she'll be the pilot, not me. With no link, she and Lin weren't going to be able to power hyperdrives, but at least Lin would be able to keep on with her pilot training. At least, one day, she'd be able to take her own ship into space.

In the meantime, she could get a skybike license. We've easily got enough left of our compensation money to buy her a skybike.

The memory came back to her, of that terrifying, headlong swoop into Philomel's sky, of the lurch in her stomach, the freezing wind battering at her body. She remembered Cadan saying, . . . *Don't hold on to me, okay? There're handgrips behind you. It's much more secure, trust me.*

Lin would love that. She'd love the speed, the height, the control. . . .

"Could I get a skybike?" said Lin.

Elissa's feet stuttered as if the smooth slidewalk had suddenly become a tripping hazard. "A skybike?"

It doesn't mean anything. This has happened before—you thought it meant something and it didn't, it was just a coincidence, it was nothing.

She looked up, scanned the rails around them, the sky above. "I— Did you just see one or something?"

Lin shook her head. "No. I was thinking about Cadan's." She frowned. "I don't know why, though. I—I suddenly thought I remembered him saying that if you rode behind him you shouldn't hold on to his waist. But"—she hesitated, looking confused—"you only rode on it that one time, to come find me, didn't you? And *I've* never been on it, he's never told me anything about it, so I *can't* be remembering that."

Elissa stopped breathing. One moment she'd been peripherally aware of all the things around them: the slidewalk under their feet, the clank and rattle of the monorail above their heads, the smell of rocket fuel gusting past on the hot breath of evening. The next moment she lost awareness of it all. There was nothing, nothing except what Lin had just said.

"That's what you were remembering? Him saying that?"

Lin was still frowning. "Yeah. He said, 'There're handgrips behind you.' And 'It's much more secure, trust me.' Did you ride on it before, Lissa? When you were living with your parents? Because I can remember him saying that, but it doesn't make sense. . . ."

Elissa's breath came back in a rush. She looked at her sister, looked as Lin's face changed, as Elissa's silence got through to her, as sudden anxiety swept over her expression.

"Lis? What? What is it?"

"I only rode on it that one time. After the link had gone, to find you."

"Oh. Oh. But then . . ."

"And he did say that," said Elissa, the words louder than her heart thudding in her ears, words to sweep away pain and bleakness, to lift her so high out of the abyss she'd never be in danger of going back. "The memory of him saying it, that came into your head just now? It came into your head because it was in mine."

Lin's face froze, the pupils of her eyes so wide they swallowed up the color. "You—" she said, then her voice froze too.

Around them and above them the slidewalks clattered, metal on metal squeaked, beetle-cars rose, humming, or descended to clank onto the monorails. All over the city, lights began to blink awake, amber and silver and no color at all. There was the scent of hot metal in the air, and the lingering, dusty warmth of a long summer day, and a sudden gust of perfume from the woman traveling on a slidewalk that ran parallel to theirs.

Three months ago Sekoia had seemed a world shattered,

unraveled. Now it was a world renewed—a world weaving itself back to wholeness.

Now, their link, the link that had brought them together, that had given Elissa pain and happiness and fear and hope, a whole confusion of good and bad that she might never make sense of, the link that had seemed as unraveled as her world . . . it, too, was . . .

"It's getting repaired." Lin's voice was no more than a breath. If Elissa hadn't heard the words in her mind as well as her ears, she might not have picked them up at all.

"Yes."

"Not just the link. I mean . . ." Lin gestured from herself to Elissa. "I mean, this. Us." Uncertainty wavered at the edge of her voice. "Don't you think?"

Elissa reached out, taking Lin's hand, feeling the nervous flutter of her twin's fingers relax into stillness. "Yes."

The slidewalk turned a corner, bringing them into the full blaze of the sun as it dipped below the curve of the world. Light broke over them, so bright that for an instant it wasn't like a sunset, but like a sunrise.

"Our world's becoming whole," she said. "And our link. And us."